Magical Girl Blues

Novels by Russell Isler

Magical Girl Blues

The Clandestine
Book 2

Russell Isler

BOTTLED
MONSTER
PRESS

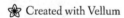

For Mom and Dad.
Thanks for all the love and support over the years. Miss you.

For everyone who ever suffered loss, and didn't get magical
powers out of the deal.

Prologue

There was no warning.

A surge of panic the girl couldn't place jolted her from her daydreams. She'd drifted, warmed by the summer sun, while picking imagined shapes out of the drifting clouds. "Pumpernickel?" She shifted on the park bench, scanned the park about her, but found no sign of the elderly Jack Russell terrier. "Baby, where'd you go?" Despite her worry, she suspected the little dog was up to his old tricks.

A flurry of distant barks confirmed that Pumpernickel had slipped away to indulge in his favorite pastime: squirrel harassment. She loved that dog to bits, but even at his age he could be a handful.

It had been, up to that moment, a picture-perfect day in Porter Valley. That morning, she'd set out to sample the new coffee shop on Main. All too soon, Pumpernickel's nose had led them on a long detour through Riverside Park. With the sun on her face and a strong breeze from the Pacific in her hair, they'd wandered on to Porter Canyon and its many hiking trails.

And why not? In little more than a week, summer break would be over. She'd be a senior, and there'd be all those decisions about college, and the endless tests, to worry about. Best to enjoy her freedom while she had it.

Pumpernickel had yapped and chased after the other hikers as the trail took them ever deeper into Porter Canyon. Beside them, a wide creek chuckled its way down from the Eel River.

At last, the Jack Russell had stumbled to a halt, planted his furry butt on the gravel and gazed up at his owner with those wide, soulful eyes. She'd carried him, "just for a bit," down the last stretch of trail.

Ahead, a helpful sign dubbed the area as "Trail's End." Here, the path split into a T-intersection. Both options doubled back to the mouth of the canyon via differing routes. A pair of benches marked the actual end of the trail. The stream flowed on, into a jumble of immense boulders. Above it all loomed the sheer, bare-faced rock of the canyon wall.

While the path was well-maintained by the city, her feet were still sore. She hadn't planned for a day of hiking, so she hadn't worn the proper shoes or brought the little pack full of energy bars, water, and a first aid kit. She'd rested on one of the benches, eyes on the clouds and her thoughts a million miles away, until Pumpernickel's absence had roused her.

Beyond Trail's End, the forest came right down to the creek's edge. A trail of familiar paw prints tailed through the mud beside the stream. "Damn it." The girl hopped over the trail's boundary chain and picked her way around the first of the massive boulders. In no time at all, the path, and the other hikers she shared the canyon with, were lost from view.

Another flurry of barks lent new urgency to her pace. Being the ripe old age of twelve, the Jack Russell would conk out before long. If she didn't find him soon, he'd plunk himself under a bush for a dog-nap. Half deaf, he'd sleep through her calls. She'd waste the rest of the day looking for his doggy butt. It wouldn't be the first time.

She picked her way through the last of the bramble and, at last, caught sight of her wayward dog. Hands on her hips, she couldn't help but laugh at the predicament he'd gotten himself into. "Aw, Pumpy. How the heck did you manage that?"

Pumpernickel had marooned himself atop a wide slab of rock in the middle of the stream. The Jack Russell had never been one to avoid water, unless it came in the form of a bath, and was now soaking wet. He danced back and forth atop his platform with his nose in the air. Pumpernickel unleashed another flurry of barks mixed with a howl or two as he strained to continue his pursuit. However, his leash had snagged on something in the water and ran taut from his collar over the edge of the rock.

Above Pumpernickel loomed the sheer granite bulwark of the canyon's end. The surface was dotted with patches of gray-green lichen and thick mats of moss. The creek, where it reached the canyon wall, vanished into the mouth of a grotto or cave, with no more than a distant roar to mark its passage. A tangled webwork of cracks and fissures spread from the declivity. This arc of radiating crevices made it appear as if the cavern had been fired into the stone by God's own shotgun.

The longer she stared at that subterranean gap, the more she gave thanks that Pumpy's leash had gotten caught up. Otherwise, no doubt, the little idiot would have been swept away while swimming to his current perch.

3

The villain of the tiny drama—The Squirrel—well satisfied with the mischief it had caused, had a fine view of the show. High above her, and certainly out of the Jack Russell's reach, the rodent was seated upon a spur of rock jutting from the rock wall. Fluffy tail wrapped about its feet, the squirrel chittered merrily at dog and girl alike.

The girl flipped a middle finger toward the furry little bastard while she considered the situation. As long as the squirrel was in view, Pumpernickel would ignore her entirely. She'd have to go to him, dang it.

Her breath caught in her chest as frigid water poured into her shoes. Though it was late summer, the water still held the chill of the snowpack that had birthed it. Even with the noonday sun bearing down on her, the water was uncomfortably cold.

The stream's depth, too, was a surprise. It had seemed shallow enough from the bank, but in midstream, as she approached the slab of stone, it rose to her thighs. Each foot had to be placed with care. The current's unrelenting pressure would sweep her from her feet at the first misstep.

Freeing Pumpernickel's leash from the submerged branch left her arms soaked and her teeth chattering. "C'mon, you adorable pain in my you-know-what. Time to go." She looped the leash around her wrist.

Pumpernickel spared her a brief, wall-eyed glance before he hurled another torrent of canine invective at his frenemy above.

The girl sloshed a knee up onto the stone, then levered herself out of the water. Before Pumpernickel realized playtime was over, she scooped him up. "Gotcha!"

Pumpernickel, still wet from the swim to the rock, soaked her thin blouse to her skin. He squirmed around in her grip and licked her face.

"Yeah, yeah. Love you too," she gasped between swipes of tongue. "You do know that we're both getting baths when we get home, right?"

Pumpernickel's answer was, as always, more doggy kisses.

With a laugh, the girl readied herself for the jump to the next rock. Her foot shifted for a better angle, and her weight shifted with it.

The stone underfoot shifted with her.

Tilting like a funhouse attraction, the slab dumped both girl and dog into the rush of the stream. A single, startled gasp was all she managed before both were swept into the fissure at the base of the canyon wall.

In the darkness beneath the water, there was no way to judge how far she'd fallen or how deep she'd plunged. Without light, spun by the current, she couldn't find up from down.

Her lungs burned. She kicked and pulled at the water, picked a direction, praying she'd chosen right. Just as panic had convinced her that she'd been swimming deeper, she broke into chill air.

I've lost Pumpy! The voice of her panic drowned out the thunder of falling water. The cavern walls, invisible in the darkness, threw an echo of the underground waterfall back at her from every direction.

Fingers and toes numbed by the cold, she tread in place and strained for any scrap of illumination. Her eyes, at last, began to acclimate to the pitiful spill of light from above. She spat water with a curse at what it revealed. Even if she could climb that slick stone, she'd be fighting a waterfall every inch of the way.

Nor could she swim to freedom. There was no telling how deep this pool went, and no current pulled at her. Wherever the water went from here, it wasn't in a hurry to get there.

Frantic, sputtering barks echoed from the stone. "Pumpy!" She paddled in a wide circle, making her best effort to track Pumpernickel's cries until her kicking feet found solid ground.

The girl clambered from the water onto a steep incline. The spill of shattered rock and gravel made for a poor beach, not that she was in a position to complain. Grateful to be out of the water at last, she flopped onto her back, focusing on drawing the next breath, and the one after that. A clatter of stone, the patter of tiny paws on gravel making their way to her. A moment later, a slimy tongue lapped at her chin. She clutched Pumpernickel to her chest and sobbed into his fur. "Thank God, you're safe."

Safe? Yeah, right. At least they could keep each other warm, if only for a while. She snuggled the terrier close and lurched to her feet, then fumbled at her back pocket for her phone. She flipped the screen open with her thumb and found the screen dark. No amount of whacking or shaking would convince the shorted battery to revive. No calling for a rescue, then. Or even a light. She and Pumpernickel were on their own.

With a resigned sigh, the girl squinted into the darkness. Her eyes, all too slowly, adjusted to the thin light from above. Three of the cavern walls descended from the fissure above into the water's depths. Beyond the rough beach of scree she stood upon, the stone receded into darkness. A passage? A tunnel into the mountain? Maybe it led to the surface!

She took a step, then paused. Her eyes had fooled her. What she'd taken for a tunnel was no more than a darker patch of stone. The ore, whatever it was, wound in a great spiral across the wall of the cavern. Around that curve of dark stone, the granite was fractured and split in a microcosm of the cavern entrance above.

The girl kicked at the loose scree upon which she stood. *Now what do we do?*

In her arms, Pumpernickel twisted, then bared his teeth. A growl rumbled his narrow chest. She froze. "What is it, boy?" she whispered. "Smell something?" Hope and fear spiraled through her. *What lives in caves, huh? Badgers? Wolves?* She swallowed the lump in her throat. *Bears?*

Then again, if there was something in the dark with them, that meant there was a way out! A better exit than holding her breath until the subterranean river spat them out somewhere in the Pacific Ocean.

Again, Pumpernickel gave his fiercest growl. She held the terrier close and whispered, "Don't worry, baby. I'll keep you safe."

The crack of breaking stone silenced them both. A portion of the ore embedded in the wall shifted. Was this how a cave-in started? The girl took one step, then another, away from the movement, bracing herself for a dive into the chill water. Drowning had to be better than being crushed, right?

The still air shifted. A whiff of the scent that had set off Pumpernickel brushed the girl's nose. Musty and dry, for all the cavern's moisture, the air was suddenly redolent of old paper and faded spice. She fought down a sneeze.

Pumpernickel gave a mighty twist and sprang from the cradle of her arms. He planted all four of his feet wide and addressed the darkness with a single, firm bark. Along the ridge of his spine, the fur rose as he pressed his ears flat against his tiny skull.

"You tell 'em," the girl said, and added, "Shoo!" for good measure. She forgot, for the moment, the cavern's imminent collapse. She hoped the sound of a human voice would scare off the badger, or whatever it was she had smelled.

Did Humboldt County have bears? The girl couldn't remember for sure, but the answer was probably "yes."

Pumpernickel's tail dropped, tucked between his legs. The tiny dog began to shiver. He slipped behind her legs, spine curved in a hunch, his head low. A thin whine slipped out of him. She knelt, intent on scooping her dog into her arms, but halted as a new sound slid from the darkness.

"*A-ba...?*"

The voice had been so faint that the girl believed, at first, that she might have imagined it. But no, there was more.

"*Menašè... ùdi?*" Movement followed the words. The dark spiral in the rock heaved, began to wrench itself free. As more and more prized itself from the stone, it became clear to the girl that whatever it was, it was much, much bigger than a bear.

A shadow within a shadow, the thing's surface drank up the wan light and gave nothing back. Even so, the creature's silhouette offered a handful of details. Long, grasping claws. Row after row of jagged spikes. Razor teeth. Twin points of light sprang into existence with a flicker. *That was a blink*, the girl realized, *those are its eyes*.

The rush of the waterfall behind her fell away, drowned beneath the roar of her pulse.

As the creature lurched from the stone cavity where it had lain for time untold, there was a splintering *crack*. Part of its long body tore away in a shower of dust. The girl now saw that the massive form wasn't... whole. Slivers of dark material shivered from its sides even as it dragged itself across the ground. In rising from its long rest, it had broken itself. The panic that had captured her thoughts receded. She might not fall beneath those claws after all. Long before it could make its way to her, it would crumble to powder.

When she attempted another step, she found her foot rooted in place. Fresh panic, raw and red, boiled in her veins. The paralysis that seized her foot seared its way up her leg until it had claimed all of her. From head to toe she found herself locked in a prison of iron, alien will.

Pumpernickel whimpered and pulled away from her leg.

Her lungs, frozen in exhale, burned with their need to draw breath. Her eyes stung with the need to blink. Unable to so much as turn her head, to avert her gaze, she had no choice but to watch as the creature made its laborious way across the final few feet. She prayed that the paralysis of her lungs would grant her the mercy of unconsciousness before those jagged claws bit into her flesh.

She expected pain. She expected to see her bones crack in the vise of those dark teeth.

Even as it reached out a clawed hand, entropy at last claimed that crumbling body. The entire dark mass collapsed into a cloud of swirling black dust.

The force that kept her frozen, pinned in place, wavered not one iota.

The billow of powder spun about her, propelled on a wind she couldn't feel. There was a pinprick of pain, then another, and another, as the dark material passed through the pores of her skin, through the membranes of eyes and nose, and into her gaping mouth.

The paralysis that held her captive now silenced her

screams as every inch of her body burned from the intrusion. As the final ebon particles soaked themselves into her flesh, there came a great roaring in her ears: a mighty wind, or the crashing of waves upon a storm-racked shore. What little light that reached her eyes guttered out. The burn of alien matter writhing within her flesh fell away. All sense of her physical body became distant, indistinct. At last, all that remained was the fluttering beat within the cage of her ribs.

Ice and fire coiled about the center of her being, invaded her with frozen flame until there was no space left for both her and the intruder. There, in the secret core of her self, something tore.

She was spun, tossed on a tempest of silence. At the apex of that dizzying spiral, to her surprise, sight returned. As if from a great distance, an immense height, she viewed her own reflection. Only it wasn't a reflection at all.

It was her.

Her body, no longer her own.

Buffeted by that impossible wind, the girl observed as the creature wearing her flesh knelt. Offered the cowering Pumpernickel a hand. The tiny dog sniffed once, then allowed himself to be scratched behind his ears. The girl watched as the arms that were once hers lifted her dog, cuddled it close. Witnessed as her stolen lips peeled back from jagged teeth of dark metal. Laughter, utterly unlike her own, echoed from the cavern walls.

Darkness claimed her.

* * *

A surge of panic she couldn't place jolted her from her daydreams. The girl raised a hand to block the glare of the afternoon sun.

Wait...

The sun might have been warm on her skin, but the breeze was not. She shivered and looked down at herself. Head to toe, she was soaked through. Dripping wet.

She found herself at the edge of a gurgling, rushing stream. The water swirled about a jumble of huge boulders. Just beyond that, the stream poured into the mouth of a small cave at the base of the canyon wall.

"Hold up." She combed at her sodden hair with her fingers, brushed it from her face, out of her eyes. "Didn't I... fall in?"

There had been an underground pool. A cavern. How could she possibly have climbed out?

Panic sizzled through her as she remembered the dark rock of the cavern... and what it had held. "No!"

Before hysteria could overrun her and spur her into headlong flight, a shadow slipped into her thoughts. Where it passed, it stole away every thought, every memory of the fall and what had transpired below.

A sharp yip drew her attention outward. "Pumpernickel! There you are, naughty boy!" She swept her dog into her arms, wrinkling her nose as she found him every bit as soaked as she. "You know this means bath time for both of us, right?" She laughed as he answered in the only way he knew, with doggy kisses.

Together, the girl and her dog began the long walk home.

Chapter One

There was no warning.

Pebbles of glass traced lines of fire across Xenia's cheek as the shriek of tortured metal filled her ears. Everything spun in a drunken arc, only to slam to a sudden, terrible, halt. The *crunk* of metal striking metal hurled Xenia out of the darkness.

Her heart thundered against her breastbone. The nightmare that had jolted her awake was shading over into confusion. Cool air burned across the raw, bruised flesh of her throat as she fought to draw breath.

Her eyes, gummy with sleep, were slow to open. *Where am I?* The night before eluded her. Her thoughts scattered, reluctant to organize. A sour, plastic flavor clung to a tongue gone dry.

Too-bright light stabbed in when at last Xenia managed to crack an eyelid. Pain flashed through her arm, drawing a gasp when she tried to rub her face. Her eyes watered from the discomfort, and she was at last able to pry her lids open.

Her left arm, palm to elbow, was wrapped in a blue cast.

When she reached for it with her other hand, an unpleasant tug stopped the movement short. Xenia found a tube, secured with a square of clear tape, running from the back of her hand and over the rail that framed the bed in which she lay. She followed the path of the IV line. Her head was too heavy. Off balance.

If she was careful, Xenia could lift her left arm without pain. Her probing fingers found a thick pad of gauze above her left ear, held in place by a halo of bandages. Prodding the wrap proved to be unwise and rewarded her with another spike of pain.

"What the hell—" Her voice was a croak. The very act of speaking was uncomfortable, as if she'd gargled with broken glass.

Xenia rubbed at her eyes, blinked until she could focus beyond her fingers. It came as little surprise that she was in a hospital. If the railed bed and IV hadn't been clue enough, the collection of blinking, humming devices arrayed about her left no doubt. Not to mention the scent of antiseptic in the air, and the distant whiff of vomit. She'd never been in a hospital room before, not even to visit. She had, however, seen plenty of them on the medical dramas her mom loved and knew one when she saw it.

Try as she might, Xenia just could not get her brain to cough up an explanation. Why was she here? Where were Mom and Dad, for that matter? One of them should have been here. They'd know what was going on. Dad would have all the answers.

A kaleidoscope spray of light twisted the border of her vision. Xenia rubbed her eyes, carefully. Weird vision after a head injury? Not a good sign. Mom would know.

Movement drew Xenia's eye. There, perched atop the counter was—*Oh, thank God!*—her best friend in the entire world, Bethany Brooks. Relief crushed her mounting panic. If Bethany was here, then Mom and Dad were close. They must have stepped out for a restroom break or, knowing Dad, a cup of coffee.

Bethany's eyes flitted to Xenia. Finding Xenia awake, her face lit up with joy and relief. She kicked herself from her counter seat. Graceful as ever, she seemed to float around the cluster of medical machines.

Confusion wrinkled Xenia's brow. Why was Bethany wearing all her best stuff? Surely a simple hospital visit didn't call for the dark, gothic-style dress, or the corset with its crisscross of purple satin ribbons, or the thigh-high leather boots. Bethany was even in her full war paint: purple lipstick to match the ribbons, and heavy, winged eyeliner.

How bad was I hurt? Xenia wondered. She'd only seen her friend wear that outfit, the one she'd bought on a family trip to Japan, once before. That was—

Pain twisted through Xenia's skull in place of memory.

"Thank the Lord!"

The exclamation drew another wince. An older woman, one Xenia didn't recognize, stepped into the room. She was clad in a loose, deep maroon turtleneck sweater and matching—was that *velvet?*—trousers. Each arm was adorned with enough bangles and bracelets to outweigh the cast on Xenia's arm. Loop after loop of shells and lacquered beads hung about her neck. The woman's gray hair was short and might have been stylish, if her locks hadn't been plastered to her scalp with sweat. The dark shadows beneath her eyes suggested that she hadn't slept recently, or well.

"I cannae believe you're awake at last, lassie," the woman said, a hint of brogue in her words. She set a steaming cup on a table as she rushed to Xenia's side. "How are you feeling? Any pain?" Worry creased the woman's face, deepened the lines that already graced her features. "I've been worried half to death..." The woman reached out as if to pat Xenia's head. She paused, then, taking care with the IV line, took her hand instead. Hazel eyes peered into Xenia's, searching, waiting.

Those eyes, so much like Dad's. So much like her own.

"Umm..."

"Elspeth, dearie," offered the woman. "Your great-aunt, on your father's side..." Her voice caught as she spoke.

"Elspeth," Xenia murmured. A rush of holiday images spurred the woman into familiarity. There had been an extravagant Christmas tree, so tall she had to stand on tip-toe to see the star. The warm aroma of cinnamon, nutmeg, and fresh-baked cookies. Elspeth, only a little younger, beamed down at Xenia over an armload of presents. How old had she been? Five, maybe. Or six.

Bemused, Xenia realized that she must be pretty messed up. If a great-aunt she hadn't seen in almost a decade...

Oh God, no.

She turned. Struggled to sit, heedless of the pain. Desperate, she searched the hospital room for any sign of her parents. Any clue that they'd been there. That they really had only stepped out...

Nothing. Xenia could find no hint of their presence.

"Ah, lassie." Elspeth sagged against the bedside rail.

"No!" Xenia knew that nothing, *nothing*, could have kept her parents from her side. Not if she was in the hospital. Dad, especially, should have been hovering like a mother hen, just as he'd done when she'd come down with that flu. Even when he'd caught it from her, he'd pulled his favorite chair to her bedside. There, wrapped in his own blanket cocoon, he'd watched over her while Mom brought them both soup and crackers. If they weren't here...

The grief, the sympathy in Elspeth's hazel eyes confirmed Xenia's worst fears. "There was a terrible, terrible accident, I'm afraid." She mopped her eyes with a tissue.

Xenia stared at Elspeth, this stranger she hardly knew. "Who..." The well of sympathy in her eyes, the gentle squeeze of her great-aunt's hand on her own were an answer of their own. The answer she didn't want. *Not both of them!* Xenia struggled, her chest tight—she couldn't breathe. Each beat of her heart tore the wound deeper. *This can't be real.*

The cast on her arm, the pain in her skull—those were all too real.

Little wonder Bethany was dressed in her funeral finest. "Bethany!" The surge of relief at the thought of her friend flickered as Xenia found her absent. Where had Bethany gone? She was just here...

"Oh, lassie. I can hardly bear to tell ye," Elspeth's voice quavered. "Your friend was beside you in the car. You're the only one..."

Xenia snatched her hand away. "No. *No!*" An echo of the dream, the nightmare that had spurred her to consciousness, swam through her head. The *crunk* of impact. The sickening lurch. The sting of flying glass. Xenia snatched at the bed rails, ignored the flare of pain from her arm, as she fought to pull herself upright. She had to go. She had to find—

"Xenia!" Elspeth's hands caught her shoulders. Gently, she eased the injured girl down. "What can I say," she murmured, "but how sorry I am."

Xenia fought against her great-aunt's hands. Fought the inexorable truth. She lost the struggle, and Elspeth's arm slipped about her. Xenia grasped for the embrace she'd rejected a moment ago, buried her face in her great-aunt's shoulder. A great, racking sob tore its way free of her chest. Xenia clung to the only lifeline left to her as the world collapsed.

Chapter Two

There was no warning.

Bethany Brooks winked at her best friend in the world, Xenia Findlay. "You ready, Zee?"

Xenia reached across the back seat of her parent's Toyota to bump knuckles with Bethany. "Born ready, Beebs!" She aimed a glare between her parents to the traffic light that impeded their progress toward what promised to be the best night of their lives. "Assuming we ever get there," she added.

"We're making good time, sweetie," Mrs. Findlay said as she ground the older car into gear. "You're not going to miss—"

A force larger than the world snatched Bethany up and hurled her down again. Pulled in three directions at once, there was no time to draw breath, much less scream. Searing pain, more than she could possibly bear, drove all thought from her.

Then, nothing.

Then... something?

Bethany blinked, confused, at the dull gray that filled

her sight. The pain, already a distant memory, was gone. As was the panic that had come with it. To be honest, she was a little worried about how calm she was.

Now that she was thinking about it, calm was the *only* thing she felt. Fear and pain were absent, as was every other sensation. Even the ones she'd long since taken for granted. The tension of her hair bands, the constriction of her corset, even the tug of gravity. All gone.

Bethany lifted her hand. She was gratified to see it rise between her and the gray. She still wore the lacy, fingerless gloves she'd donned for the evening's event. Only, she could see the gray surface right through both glove and hand.

"Ah, beans." She'd seen more than enough spooky movies to know what that meant. At least she could still hear, and she still had a voice. Even if it was a hollow, distant echo of itself.

Disappointment, and more than a little anger, bubbled up. *It's not fair! That's all? I didn't even get to see the concert!* Not to mention, Todd Messerschmidt had finally asked her to the winter formal. Sure, it wasn't her first dance, just the first one with a guy she was into.

Bethany took her frustration out on the featureless gray void. There wasn't the faintest hint of contact as her hand vanished beneath the surface. No sensation whatsoever.

What she did receive was a bit of perspective. The gray void wasn't a void at all. A step back, and the "void" was revealed as a scratched and well-used sheet of steel. There was a pull handle on one side and, as she backed away, Bethany saw that the door, or hatch, was repeated across the entire wall before her.

"A morgue. Should've guessed." Bethany shook her head.

Why here, though? How long had she been out? What

had happened to her—*okay, be honest with yourself, Brooks* —her soul between her death and reawakening?

Scratch that, why was she here at all? And awake to ask the question?

Her mama was a churchgoing, God-fearing woman, and her dad had mostly deferred to his wife on matters spiritual. All throughout Bethany's childhood, Mama had done her level best to instill in her daughter the same values she cherished.

Bethany had done her best to heed Mama's teachings. She'd gone to church every Sunday for the first twelve years of her life. Then, she'd grown independent, developed her own take. On life, and the afterlife. Despite her love of creepy, supernatural movies, Bethany had come to believe that you lived until you died, and that was that. Lights out, baby.

Only, her lights were still on. Bethany glared at her semi-transparent hand. Okay. Mostly on.

A quiet snuffle, followed by a muffled sob, pulled Bethany from the contemplation of her state of being.

"Mama?" Bethany found her mother and father beside a waist-high table. A shrouded form lay before them. A man in blue scrubs who Bethany didn't recognize stood between her and the body's head.

She spared little more than a glance at the corpse. Intellectually, she knew it was hers. Perhaps she should have felt something for the familiar silhouette. Some sense of loss, perhaps. Only, she didn't. It wasn't *her*. Not anymore. Right now, her sole concern was for her parents.

Her father stood with his arms about her mother. He'd placed himself half between his wife and the shrouded form, as if to shield her from the inevitable. Mama had one of her little lace hankies pressed to her eyes. Her shoulders trembled, and she buried her face against her husband's shoulder.

Bethany was shocked by her father's haggard appearance. His eyes were hooded, their familiar, joyful light absent. Fresh, deep grooves framed lips compressed to a bloodless line. In the time since she'd last seen him, her father had aged a decade.

He pulled Mama close. Took a deep breath. Nodded to the man in scrubs.

The orderly returned the nod. His movements were gentle, precise, as he lifted the sheet to reveal the face waiting beneath.

Bethany's father staggered back, his face stricken. He turned, putting more of himself between his wife and the terrible truth on the slab. It took him three racking breaths before he could speak, his voice a rasp. "Yes, that's her." Tears poured unchecked from his eyes.

The only time Bethany had ever seen her father cry was when Papa Brooks, her grandfather, had passed away.

As the orderly replaced the sheet, Bethany's mother drew in a huge, wet sniff and pulled herself from the cradle of her husband's embrace. Her eyes, usually so luminous and wide, so full of love, were raw, puffy, and red-rimmed.

The heartbreak Bethany felt at seeing her parents in pain was a welcome surprise. She'd half-believed that, without a body, pain such as this would have been behind her. Empathy, it seemed, and love, were more of the soul than of the body.

"Mama," Bethany said. "I'm here. Mama?" She raised her hand to catch her father's eye. "Dad?"

Neither her parents nor the orderly looked to her. There was no sign they'd heard her at all. Her parents clung to each other as they wept for what had been taken from them.

Bethany's mother twitched away from her husband. She stumbled to the table, one hand raised. Her fingers hovered above the layer of cloth between her and her only child. "Beloved…" What little strength she had left fled her, and she swayed on her feet.

"Tessa!" Bethany's father rushed to catch her, as did the orderly—and Bethany. The two men caught her mother's arms, while Bethany passed clean through all three of them.

"No," gasped Bethany. Her father gathered Mama in his arms, supported her until she whispered that she could stand on her own. Bethany stared at, and through, her useless hands. What good was this illusion of a body if she couldn't comfort Mama? Why was she here at all, if her voice went unheard?

"We should go, Tessa," Bethany's father murmured into the braid of his wife's hair. When she nodded, he slipped his arm about her waist and guided her away from the shrouded form on the table. They made their slow, halting way toward the morgue exit, passing through their unseen daughter as they went.

Bethany, in shock at these unwelcome revelations, trailed her parents into the clutter and clash of the hospital.

She might not be able to speak to them or touch them, but she'd find a way, Bethany vowed. She would get through to them, reach them. Comfort them. Somehow.

The Brooks trio, two living and one not, were halfway across the hospital lobby when Bethany realized she was now floating instead of walking. "Well," she said to her parents' backs, "it's official. I'm a ghost." Well, she'd already known that to be the case. It just hadn't sunk in all the way.

Bethany paused, two feet above the institutional

linoleum, as a voice cried, "Xenia Findlay!" There, past the clustered people waiting for their own stories to resolve in joy or tragedy, an older woman was leaning so far over the faux marble of the info desk that she was at risk of tumbling into the poor orderly's lap. "You must tell me where she is, lad!" Grief and worry chased each other across the woman's face. In between demands, she mopped at her eyes with an eye-searing paisley silk handkerchief.

Zee was in the car, and her parents! How could I forget that? Okay, she'd been preoccupied with her own death. And her parents' grief. Still, no excuse. If Xenia was here... would she be alive, or would she be floating just like Bethany?

As much as she would might have welcomed the companionship, Bethany hoped against hope that Xenia had survived the crash.

"Mama, Dad? I'll catch up at home. Promise," she called after her parents. A thought sent her across the lobby toward the door the older woman had vanished through. The bright colors of her kaftan made for an easy target in the busy hospital corridors. A wave of relief crashed through Bethany as the woman turned, not toward the morgue but to the ICU.

Xenia was alive!

Chapter Three

D ays dragged into weeks as Xenia endured the ministrations of the hospital staff.

Her doctor informed her that, due to the blow to her head, she had been unconscious, in a coma, for over a month. The extended inactivity had rendered her too weak to stand and unable to walk without a nurse's assistance. Physical therapy became the order of the day. With the loss of her parents and of Bethany raw in her mind, in her heart, Xenia was unable to muster much energy for the task. Still, she did what the overly spunky trainer told her. Before long, she could wobble as far as the restroom.

In the aftermath of a particularly grueling session, the trainer pulled Great-Aunt Elspeth aside. "She's young," the woman said, face beaming with pride at Xenia's progress. "She'll be up and about in no time at all. It won't be long before she can go home."

An empty home, Xenia had thought to herself, but only to herself.

She'd be wearing the cast for a while. Both bones in her

forearm had shattered in the crash. A fragment had poked through her skin. The surgeon had inserted a metal pin to hold it all in place so she could heal. Her doctor was confident that she'd regain full use of the arm, in time. Xenia didn't care one way or the other.

As news of her awakening spread, there came a small procession of well-wishers and sympathetic faces. An assortment of her parents' friends, a neighbor or two, and a scant handful of Xenia's classmates who, on a good day, might have been considered distant friends all marched through the space beside her hospital bed.

"You poor thing," and "How terrible," and "We're praying for you," were repeated until the words lost their meaning. "So sorry for your loss," stood out in particular each time it was uttered. *My loss?* She hadn't *lost* her parents. She hadn't misplaced her sister in all but blood like a set of house keys. They had been taken from her. Stolen from her. Torn from her life by the thoughtless action of a drunkard.

Xenia nodded. Mumbled whatever words were required to send a particular visitor on their way. The other words, the ones rising from her resentment, her pain—those she bit back. She shoved them down as far as they would go, no matter how much she longed to fling them at the unwanted sympathizers, at the kind but condescending hospital staff, at the stranger ever at her bedside.

Thanks to the coma, Xenia had missed her parents' funeral. Bethany's as well. With no way to know when, or even if, Xenia would awaken, the Brooks had buried their daughter. Great-Aunt Elspeth had handled the arrangements for her nephew and his wife. She'd brought photos of both ceremonies for Xenia, in the hopes they might grant some sense of closure. What's more, Elspeth had saved the

Findlays' wedding rings, and her mother's gold necklace at the last moment. She had been determined that Xenia would have something, some token of her parents, to remember them by.

Xenia had shoved the photos away, refusing to look at any of them, ignoring the hurt in the older woman's eyes. Her parents' rings and her mother's necklace she had balled up in her fist, and held them close to her heart every night in the false darkness of the hospital room while she tried not to fall asleep.

The holidays came and went without fanfare.

The Findlays had named Elspeth as their daughter's guardian, should the worst come to pass. As it had.

Great-Aunt Elspeth. A relative that Xenia had met only once before. Related by blood she might be, her closest living relative, yet the woman was little more than a stranger, but one she now had no choice but to live with. In Porter Valley, a town she'd never heard of, hundreds of miles from everyone and everything she had ever known.

The Brooks had come to visit Xenia only once, on the day she'd been discharged. There had been so many sleepover nights at their house, so much time under their supervision as a child, while playing with Bethany, that Martin and Tessa Brooks were as close to a second pair of parents as one could have. Xenia given it her best effort, to little success, not to resent them for their absence. Or for holding Bethany's funeral without her.

As soon as the nurse had wheeled Xenia to the edge of the hospital lobby, the Brooks had said their goodbyes and vanished into the depths of the parking garage. Even though she couldn't recall a single word either of them had uttered, the look Bethany's mother aimed over her shoulder spoke volumes. Yet she couldn't blame them. After all, if it hadn't been for Xenia, their daughter wouldn't have been in the car. Bethany would still be alive.

Xenia helped her new guardian pack the shattered remains of her old life in preparation for the move up north. Beneath the numbing blanket of her grief, anger began to slither into Xenia's heart. The outrage wasn't for her great-aunt or Bethany's parents. They didn't deserve it. She could have easily hated the other driver, the drunk who'd destroyed her world, but he was dead. Killed in the same collision he'd caused. No surface remained for her hatred to adhere to.

With no external subject, her rage turned inward. Toward the only target remaining. Just as Mrs. Brooks' unspoken recrimination had suggested, if it hadn't been for Xenia, if she hadn't insisted upon that night's event, none of this would have happened.

"There it is, lassie! Home sweet home," Elspeth beamed across the width of the ancient station wagon as she hauled on the steering wheel. The boat of a car lurched to a halt beside the curb. Elspeth plucked the maroon beret, which she donned each time she clambered behind the wheel, from her head and tucked it behind the visor. She made no attempt to conceal the excitement and anticipation glowing in her face.

A long moment later, Xenia lifted her head from the nest of her arms. The skin of her cheek, sticky with half-dried tears, peeled away from her cast. Her neck was stiff. Her shoulder ached from unwieldy weight of the fiberglass wrapped about her forearm. When they'd departed that morning, well before dawn, she'd slumped into the passenger seat and curled up against the door. There she had remained for most of the six-hundred-and-fifty-mile drive from her former home in Los Angeles to her new home in Porter Valley. The entire time, she'd stared out the window, seeing none of the varied California terrain flying by.

Great-Aunt Elspeth had done her level best to engage Xenia's interest, if not with her then with the ever-changing vista and the history behind it. Xenia hadn't meant to ignore her, not really. She just hadn't been all the way present for any of it. Instead, what little she remembered of the crash had played on a loop in her head. The last words she'd spoken to her father and mother had been a complaint. The jolt of impact. Then there was that moment, just after she'd come awake, when she thought she'd seen Bethany safe and sound. Wishful thinking, of course. A comforting lie conjured by her broken brain. Round and round her thoughts had spun, a carousel of self-recrimination.

Xenia dragged her free hand across her face and raised her eyes to what was apparently her new home.

The picturesque Victorian-style house was set behind a tidy little garden, which itself was bordered by a white picket fence. The Victorian's blue siding and the white "gingerbread" trim were clean and well maintained, with no sagging boards or missing shingles to mar their appearance. An abundance of well-trimmed shrubs and flowers in a rainbow of hues filled the garden. A quaint little gate, complete with vine-wrapped trellis arch, occupied the fence front and center. Stained glass hung in a simple wooden frame above the porch, the house number sketched out in the floral pattern. The porch light, bright in the growing dusk, shone through the stained glass and sent rays of glorious color out into the night.

Elspeth's home shared its side of the street with only one other house of the same vintage. The opposite side of Bluff Street, in contrast, held a row of single story, ranch-style houses.

Xenia tugged on the chrome handle until the car reluctantly disgorged her onto the sidewalk. The ancient suspension creaked as Elspeth clambered to her feet. The two of them swung their doors shut in the same instant. The combined *thud* launched a cloud of cawing, squawking birds from the branches of a craggy oak growing beside the old Victorian. The flock swirled about the tree, jeering at the humans that had startled them from their roost, until they at last departed en masse in search of a quieter perch.

One bird, less flighty than its companions, remained. The crow, or raven—Xenia didn't know if there was a difference—had taken the highest branch all for itself. It cawed once, as if it had been waiting just for her. The bird ruffled its feathers into a scruffy mess, then shook them back into place. That accomplished, it stepped into open air, spread its wings, and flapped off into the dark.

"That'll be your room there, dearie," Elspeth called. She pointed at the cylindrical turret, with its conical roof and slate shingles, built into one corner of the house. "Those windows have the most delightful view of the sunset. You'll even have your own bathroom, shower and all!"

Xenia stared at the arc of second-floor windows, following the line of the wall up to the shingled cone of the roof, to the rustic wind vane at its peak. *Your own shower might be nice*, a tiny voice in the back of her head offered. Xenia ignored it.

"Miss Findlay!" The *thump* of a basketball accompanied the shout. "You're back!"

"Lad, I've asked you time and again." Elspeth turned to the newcomer. "Elspeth, if you please."

A boy close to Xenia's age crossed the street to stand beside Elspeth. More than a little lanky, he was built like a number 2 pencil and towered over the both of them. Bright brown eyes darted from Elspeth to Xenia and then back. A worn basketball was tucked under one arm. Dark hair, nearly black, stuck out every which way. When he brushed it back with his free hand, it immediately sprang up, undaunted. A grin split his face from ear to ear as he said, "Yes, Miss Findlay." He released the basketball, allowing it to bounce once before catching it again in the crook of his arm.

Elspeth planted a fist on each hip and let out a theatrical sigh. "Xenia, this rapscallion is Sal. He likes to sneak around and steal as many of my pastries as he can." The warmth of her grin stole any gravity from her accusation. "Lad, this is my great-niece Xenia. She'll be staying with me from now on." Her tone was light, but her smile flickered as she spoke.

Sal ducked his head. "Salvatore," he said. "Sal Serrano." His free hand waved beside his head in something between a wave and a salute. He met Xenia's eyes for a moment and then looked down. "PV ain't that bad," he said, though his smile was hesitant, "even if it's a billion miles from anywhere." He met her gaze again and then looked away. "I —my family I mean—we moved up from Phoenix last year, so I know how it can be. Being the new kid in town, I mean."

Xenia forced her head to move. Down. Up. The tiniest nod, to acknowledge his words.

"*Saallll!*" The front door of the house behind Sal slammed open as a pint-sized tornado blew itself into the front yard. The girl, six or seven years old, stumbled to a halt in the center of the lawn, arms windmilling for balance. No sooner had she spotted the three of them than she put her head down and barreled to the very edge of the sidewalk by the base of a portable basketball net. Her head swung first left, then right as she made a big production about looking both ways. Her headlong run carried her past Sal and Elspeth, around the station wagon and up onto the sidewalk. Her blue dress swirled about her legs as she came to a halt directly in front of Xenia. The girl craned her head way back and examined Xenia with wide, dark eyes identical to Sal's. "Hullo," she said and then dropped her head, suddenly shy. The sweep of her hair hid her face as she dug a toe into the sidewalk. One gleaming eye peeked through a gap in her tresses.

Xenia was unable to stop the tiny smile that crept, unasked for, across her lips.

When the girl saw that her shy act had hit its target, she threw her head back and let out a joyous cackle. She swung her arms in wide arcs as she bounced on her heels.

"Bug, this is our new neighbor, Xenia," Sal said. The bounce of his basketball punctuated every other step as he came around to his sister's side. "She's Miss Findlay's niece." He patted the head bobbing next to him. "This is my sis, Marisol. Everyone just calls her Bug, 'cause—"

"*Mariquitas!* Ladybugs!" The girl seized the hem of her skirt and held it out for Xenia's inspection. A party of red and yellow ladybugs danced across the blue fabric. Marisol dropped her skirt and tilted her head. One chubby finger pointed out the row of hair clips, each with its own bright, plastic insect. "Ladybugs!" She thrust her arm out. There, a cartoon ladybug posed atop the back of her hand. The dye of the temporary tattoo was cracked and had begun to peel.

"Ladybug!" she cried. With her show-and-tell complete, she clasped her hands before her and gazed up at Xenia. Expectant.

Xenia blinked. "Um." As she did her best to drag a coherent through from the morass of her grief, Sal caught her eye. He gave her an exaggerated nod, pointed to his sister, then popped a thumbs-up. "They're... nice," Xenia said, though she'd never really cared for insects. Too many legs. "Very cool," she added for good measure.

This seemed to satisfy Bug. "Thanks! Bye!" She turned to her brother and seized his free hand with both of hers. She leaned her minuscule weight into the task of dragging Sal into motion. "Mama said get you it's dinner time!"

Sal grinned and allowed Bug to "force" him home. Over his shoulder, he called, "Later! See you at school?"

Xenia's mouth dropped open. With all that had gone on since the accident, her physical therapy, the packing, the move, she had just... forgotten about school. "I think so?" She turned to Elspeth, who nodded. "Yeah, I guess so."

Why was Aunt Elspeth looking at her like that? Smug didn't even begin to describe the expression on the woman's face.

"Cool." Sal, his free hand still captured by Bug, dropped the basketball from under his arm to offer up an easy wave. The ball bounced once before he, in a single motion, scooped it up and lofted it ahead of him. With no more than a *swish* of net, the ball dropped through the hoop across the street. With the same ease of motion he'd used to lob the ball, Sal caught the rebound and settled into a steady dribble. Before he vanished through his front door, he paused, his eye darting back to see if Xenia had seen the shot.

Only once the Serranos' front door was closed did she

realize that the move had been for her benefit. She'd just arrived, he didn't know her, so why bother to show off? Xenia looked at her great-aunt, who hadn't moved an inch the entire time. Elspeth was looking *right* at her. "What?"

"Nothing, dearie. Not a thing." Elspeth winked and then made her way to the station wagon's rear hatch. With a grunt, she flung it open and took hold of one of the boxes filling the compartment. "The sooner we get this lot inside, the sooner I can get a kettle on." Burden in hand, she aimed her chin at one that Xenia, with her cast, could lift.

With a final look at the Serrano residence, Xenia levered the cardboard box onto her good arm and followed her great-aunt into what was apparently to be her new home.

* * *

"...and he says to us, just as cool as a cucumber, 'Please call me Mick!'"

Elspeth barked in merriment as she dragged the back of her hand across her forehead. She'd left for Los Angeles the instant she'd learned of the accident. There had been no time to prepare the house for its new resident. As soon as the car had been unpacked, Elspeth had charged upstairs to prepare what had been a guest room for Xenia. While they worked, she'd spun a series of tales for her great-niece. Tales that Xenia hardly heard a word of.

A table, and its chairs, were shifted across the hall into a room Elspeth used as a library, with a bookshelf for every wall. Each shelf groaned beneath a cargo of books in every size and vintage. Despite herself, Xenia peeked at a shelf and found the spines graced with names like: Butler, Cherryh, Heinlein, Herbert, Norton, and Le Guin. She didn't recognize a single author. Before the accident, she'd been an avid reader of the *Armored Princess* series, but in all honesty she'd preferred her fantasy tales projected on the big screen.

Elspeth showed her the linen closet and, burdened with fresh sheets and a heavy quilt, they set about making up the massive four-poster bed. Elspeth tossed one end of a sheet to Xenia. "Ah, lassie. I wish you could have seen the *look* on Sister Josephine's face when that taxi cab started right up! Hadn't I just said that we wouldn't need the keys?"

Xenia nodded, only half listening. Together, they worked the bedcovers into place around the king-sized monster of a bed, which was twin to the one in Elspeth's master bedroom. She wondered, for a moment, how anyone could have maneuvered it up the staircase, much less through the bedroom's narrow door.

The room's other furnishings included a small desk with its matching chair, a chest of drawers, and a battered old steamer trunk. At the front of the room was the arc of windows Xenia had seen from outside. The casement windows would, once the sun rose, no doubt flood the room with light. The space below them was piled high with cushions. The perfect space in which to lounge with a book. Bethany would have adored it all.

Just like that, Xenia's mood, which had been buoyed by the encounter with Bug, crashed through the floor. She turned from the bed and her great-aunt to hide the fresh spill of tears. One hand rose, of its own accord, to the arc of her mother's necklace beneath her shirt. She'd come across the keepsake while packing and hadn't taken it off since. She'd briefly considered threading her parent's wedding rings onto the chain, but had instead stashed them in a shoebox with the handful of mementos she couldn't bear to part with, but couldn't bring herself to look at.

"'Mademoiselles,' he says, in French because he'd taken us for locals, you see. Which, you have to know, sounded hi-lar-ious in that Dartford voice of his. 'I simply must be at the Palais des Sports in *dix minutes* if we don't want a riot on our hands.' What could I do but aim our purloined cab down the Rue du Bac and stomp that pedal right to the floor? This, of course, sends Sister Josephine, who at the time had been trying to clamber into the front seat beside me, tumbling arse over teakettle into the lap of the man himself." Elspeth tucked a final corner of the sheet beneath the heavy mattress and dusted off her hands. "Now, here I am, driving like a madwoman, and I chance to look at the rearview. What do my eyes behold? The sister's gone and torn the habit from her head. She and he are snogging away, bold as brass, right there in the back seat!"

Elspeth paused to draw breath. "Ahh, lassie, listen to me prattle on. You have to be knackered from the drive."

"I don't mind," Xenia lied, "but if it's okay, I think I will go to bed." She turned, nodded at the freshly made bed between them. "I can finish unpacking in the morning." Xenia returned her attention to the windows, and the dark-ness beyond. Her great-aunt, reflected in the glass, pinched the bridge of her nose and turned her gaze to the ceiling. *I'm just in the way*, Xenia thought. *The last thing Elspeth needs is me crashing into her life. Taking up space in her home.*

Xenia slipped a finger beneath her cast and pushed into the flesh of her injured arm until her efforts were rewarded by a fresh spike of pain.

"Of course, lassie, of course. You get your rest. Lord knows you need it after all you've been through." Elspeth took a final look about the room. "I'll leave a sandwich in the fridge for you, should you get peckish. You've got your headache pills?" Elspeth crossed over to stand behind Xenia and then wrapped her arms about the girl's shoulders. She squeezed once. "I am a hugger, dearie. Best be getting used to the notion." A pat upon the crown of Xenia's head, and then the door clicked shut in Elspeth's wake.

Xenia stared out into the night. She didn't see the house across the street. Or the glow of the town center in the distance. A relentless parade of memories obscured them all. Mrs. Brooks' reproachful glance. Her mother's sigh of exasperation when she had at last given in to Xenia's begged request. Xenia's own whining, final words to her parents.

She slipped her finger into her cast one more time and dug in until the pain from the half-healed bone drowned out the one in her heart.

Chapter Four

Bethany entered the kitchen via the most convenient route, which was through the wall. Since she'd woken up dead, the whole "floating and going through solid things" thing had become second nature. Not that nature had much to do with her condition anymore. "How are you feeling today, Mama?"

Mama gave no sign of having heard her phantom daughter's question. She stared blankly through the kitchen window. Bethany shook her head. Being both invisible and inaudible had sucked all the fun out of being a ghost. No one, not her parents, not her neighbors, not even her mother's pastor had shown the least awareness of her presence. Well, there had been a moment, with Xenia...

No matter. Bethany wouldn't give up. She'd stay close to her mother and father. Would speak to them every day until, at last, they saw her.

Bethany didn't like to leave herself half in-half out of things, so she arranged herself with some care above her usual chair. Not as easy as it looked, when one was insubstantial. At least she would stay in place once she put herself somewhere. Being unbeholden to gravity was good like that.

A bit of her skirt ruffle stuck through the kitchen table. She shifted lower. Why did she even have clothes, anyhow? Did her wardrobe have a soul of its own? Was this a self-image thing? Ghost stories never, in her experience, described the dead as buck naked. Spirits were always clad in shrouds or, like Bethany, the clothing they had died in. Then again, if she simply must wear a single outfit for the rest of eternity, Atelier Pierrot wasn't the worst choice.

"It's garbage day, Mama," Bethany said. "Don't forget to take the cans to the curb." Even though her mother had been vigilant in reminding Bethany of her chores, now that they had fallen to her, grief had pushed them to the wayside. Bethany, distracted by her movies and, recently, Todd Messerschmidt, had needed the reminder. Now, she had nothing better to do than watch the calendar slip by.

Her mother trudged to the sink and dabbed at the few dishes from breakfast. She still wore the same, simple black blouse and skirt she'd worn the day before. Mama had cried herself to sleep, as she did most nights, sitting in the big chair by the front window. The sharp contrast between neat-and-tidy Mama from before the accident and her current, unkempt, self had kindled a persistent flame of worry within Bethany.

At the sink, Mama dragged a sponge listlessly across an already-clean plate.

"Look, Mama," Bethany paused. What could she say that she hadn't already said a thousand times? What good were words that went unheard? How long was she supposed to stay like this? Forced to bear helpless witness to her family's mourning, unable to offer an iota of support or closure?

There had been, Bethany grumped, no white light for her to enter. No guidance of any kind. No choir of angels, or devils, had appeared to usher her to the hereafter.

Was this what death was? For everyone? Unable to bear spending every hour of every day watching her mother's not-so-slow decline into depression, she had gone in search for the others. The other dead people.

After all, people died every day. All day long. All over the world. But not a single one had popped in to say, "Hi!" Nor had her search turned up a single ghost.

Bethany had begun to suspect—and frankly, the idea terrified her—that being dead meant you were cut off. No one could see or hear you.

Not even other ghosts.

If that were true, then that meant the world overflowed with the spirits of everyone who had ever lived. Each of whom was alone for all of eternity.

No, Bethany decided, that idea sucked, and she just wasn't going to think about it anymore.

"Mama, no," Bethany looked on, helpless, as her mother plucked yet another bottle of wine from the pantry. The bin under the sink overflowed with empty bottles, each of which marked another day since her parents had buried her.

As her mother filled a tumbler and took the first sip of many, Bethany floated to her side. "Mama, please. Just go outside. Go for a walk. Go shopping. Go see Pastor Jim. Anything, I'm begging you."

Bethany's mother walked through her unseen daughter and into the living room.

Of all the things death had taken from her, the ability to shed tears, to find release in a good cry, snot and all, was the one Bethany missed the most.

She settled herself on the couch beside her mother and then paused. "What was that?"

Bethany had felt something.

The sensation hadn't been all that strong. Little more than a tickle at the edge of her awareness. Then again, she hadn't felt anything at all since she'd died. This new sensation, faint as it might have been, stood in sharp contrast against the absence of all others.

She felt it again.

The "tickle" didn't match anything she could recall from her corporeal days. It correlated with none of the five senses. If Bethany had to describe it, it would be as if someone had looped a rubber band around the core of her soul and given it a tiny tug.

Intrigued, Bethany hopped into the air. She turned about, trying to narrow the angle from whence the tug had come. Could this be a new ghost power? Guidance from the Almighty? About frickin' time!

The tiny tug returned and, suddenly, it was anything but tiny. Bethany, against her will, began to slide through the air. "Yo, what the hell?" She strained against the pull, to no avail. Try as she might, she was powerless to halt her movement. "Mama! I'll be right back. Just—"

Before she could finish the thought, the pull trebled, and Bethany was yanked through the wall. She accelerated, out of control, as the pull grew ever stronger. She passed through house after house, through buses, trucks, and at least one shopping mall as the world became a blur.

* * *

The involuntary acceleration ended just as abruptly as it had begun. The world snapped into focus as her movement ceased. Bethany spun, disoriented, grateful that she no longer possessed the ability to barf.

"What the fu..." Bethany had no way to measure how long she'd fought, screaming all the way, against the irresistible force. When her headlong, unwilling flight had begun, it had been midmorning. Now, the sun was long set. Once again in sole command of her movement, she turned in a slow circle.

Below her was a quiet residential street. A row of perfectly banal ranch-style homes lay to one side, no different from those in her neighborhood. Across from them stood a quaint, blue-and-white Victorian house, similar to those she'd seen while visiting an uncle in San Francisco.

This, however, was not San Francisco. Bethany rose above the trees lining the narrow street. Other than a cluster of lights to her left, the whole area was shrouded in darkness. Definitely not San Francisco, Los Angeles, or any major metropolitan area. Wherever she was, it wasn't home. That was what mattered right now.

She rose higher.

While the night was overcast, enough of the crescent moon peeked through to outline the loom of mountains all around. A valley? Which one? Immense trees towered above the valley. Sequoias? There, at the base of one valley wall, the glimmer of water suggested a river.

Accelerating, Bethany passed over the town center and followed the wide, main street that ran through it. She wasn't much of a navigator, but she guessed, based on the moon's position, that she was going west. Ahead of her, the valley squeezed itself into a narrow chasm. Beyond that, it opened up into an even larger valley. There, beyond a final curve of hill, was a body of water stretching to the horizon.

A thin cusp of white foam rolling at the water's edge told her she'd found the Pacific.

"Okay. No clue where I am, but if that's the ocean, then home is that way," Bethany said out loud. Since no one could hear her, she'd picked up the habit of talking to herself. "Hold on, Mama. I'm coming!" A thought sent her hurtling to the south. She wasn't capable of the same speed at which she'd been involuntarily transported—yet another ghost-life mystery—but she wouldn't tire. As long as her guess was right and she wasn't actually in Europe some-where, she'd be home by nightfall tomorrow.

The instant Bethany crossed the ridgetop, she slammed into an invisible wall. The abrupt halt didn't hurt, didn't feel like anything at all. She just stopped. "No!" Even though she gave it everything she had, she was unable to push through the unseen boundary. Then, to her horror, she was yanked back along the course she'd flown.

In a handful of seconds, Bethany was again confronted with the quaint little Victorian. "Oh come on!" Bethany glared at the stars shining through the gap in the clouds. "Yo. Powers that be. You dudes want to toss a girl a hint? A *Handbook for the Recently Deceased* would be nice, but at this point I'd settle for a pamphlet." She drifted above the street while she waited for an answer.

As with every other time Bethany had entreated the heavens for guidance, the only answer was silence.

"Yeah, didn't think so." Bethany rolled her eyes.

"*Caw.*"

Bethany turned at the sound. A portly black bird was perched atop the weather vane on the Victorian's roof. "You talkin' to me?"

Just like everything else in the world, it ignored her. With a flick of its wings, the crow hunkered low on its perch, stretched its beak wide in a mighty yawn, and tucked its head beneath a wing.

"You're losing it, Brooks. Just a bird. Besides, you know your spirit guide is a red panda. That fortune teller in Venice said so." She gestured at the obvious lack of pandas, red or otherwise, available to guide her. "What a waste of ten bucks."

Bethany did an angry little circle above the street. Being dead wasn't enough. Now she had to get stuck in some rando town.

While she grumped, the lights in the second floor of the Victorian went out. A glimmer of gold within caught her eye. Intrigued, Bethany drifted closer.

At the window, the odd glow was even stronger. It was as if an unseen sun were reflecting from a pond into the room. She traced the source of the wall-dappling radiance to the massive four-poster bed in the center of the room. Despite the ire of a moment ago, the slow undulation of the golden light was calming, if not downright mesmerizing. The source of the glow shifted, then rolled over, tugging the covers up to her chin as she did so. Even through the uncanny shimmer, Bethany recognized her friend right away.

"Zee! Holy crap!" Bethany sped through the glass and came to a hover beside the bed. "What're you doing up here? Where are we?"

Xenia slept on, unaware.

"Actually, the real question is: Why are you glowing, girlfriend?" The rich light was visible even through the heavy quilt.

Bethany drifted to the window and back, the ghost version of pacing, while she considered everything she knew about ghosts. Most of her knowledge, admittedly, came from horror movies. Still, the answer was obvious. She slapped her forehead, then scowled when her hand passed through without the satisfying *whack*.

"You're slipping, Brooks! Duh, you're a ghost! And what is it that ghosts do?" she asked herself.

Bethany jabbed a finger into the air to mark her point. "They haunt!" She aimed the finger toward the glow of her sleeping friend. "It seems, my dearest Zee, that you are today's lucky contestant." Some of the jubilation slipped away as she remembered the circumstances that had brought them both to this place. She pressed on, glad at last to have guidance, however obscure. "Looks like I'll be haunting your pale ass!"

Xenia grunted in her sleep. Brow furrowed, she pushed her face into the pillow. "No," she murmured, "please." Beneath the quilt, her legs churned, as if they could carry her away from whatever night terror approached her dreams.

"Shit." Bethany pressed close. "Zee, wake up!" Back in the hospital, she'd seen Xenia scream herself awake more than once. She raised her voice. "This isn't real, okay? You're just dreaming."

Greasy sweat sprang up across Xenia's forehead. She tossed her head back and forth. The bedsheets knotted between her hands.

Bethany swung around to keep her friend's face in view. "Xenia! *Wake up!*"

A thin whine slipped from Xenia's throat. One questing hand found the pillow. Pulled it over her face. Her breathing slowed. Some of the tension bled from her shoulders, the angle of her back, as she sagged into the mattress. A moment later, she began to snore.

Relieved, Bethany rose into the air. "Poor thing." She

drifted to the windows and gazed past the trees toward her unreachable home. "I'll come home soon as I can, Mama." She was still worried about her mother's drinking but, stuck as she was, invisible as she was, dead as she was, she wouldn't be the one to help her. As much as that truth might hurt, Bethany had no choice but accept it. She had to trust that her father wouldn't be too caught up in his own grief to see how his wife was suffering.

Once she found a way to make contact with the living, Bethany vowed, she would return home and find a way to offer them the closure they needed.

Which left only one problem. How do you haunt someone who couldn't see you? She recalled the moment, back in the hospital, when they'd locked eyes. A slow smile crept across her lips. "You did see me, didn't you?" Bethany murmured. She was sure of it.

As for why it had been Xenia she'd been "assigned" to haunt, that one was obvious. Back when they'd first met, the day they'd both lost a tooth falling from the playground fort, they'd hooked their fingers together in a promise. "We did swear to be best friends for fuckin' forever, didn't we?" Taking care not to pass through, Bethany drifted onto the bed beside her sleeping friend. She laughed. "Who knew pinky swears were so powerful?"

Chapter Five

The impossible had been achieved: Xenia had convinced her mom, who had granted her permission to attend a live concert! Her very first! The event would be in Hollywood, at the House of Blues, which had required even more impassioned negotiations.

With Mom's approval secured, Dad was a cinch. He thought he kept it under wraps, but Xenia knew he prized the illusion that he was "Cool Dad." He had balked, a little, when he'd seen the ticket price, but she'd won him over in the end. Then it was Xenia's turn to balk when he announced he would chaperone the expedition.

Bethany, her BFFFF, was going too! The Brooks allowed their daughter so much more leeway than Xenia's parents did. She had no need to wheedle and cajole them into agreement. Not that Xenia was jealous. Not at all.

With her ticket secured, the two months between her victory at the negotiating table and the actual concert crawled by. Ironically, she saw a lot less of her best friend in that time. Extra chores and a guarantee of straight As had been her side of the bargain.

With mere hours to go, Xenia's mother helped her into the dress she'd altered to fit her daughter. Xenia had dismissed her usual attire (worn, comfy hoodies, torn jeans, and ratty high-tops) as unacceptable for so momentous an occasion. Her mother's assistance was also required for the unfamiliar task of painting up her face.

Xenia stared at the stranger in the mirror with open surprise. "Woah." She turned her head, amazed by the way light shimmered across her hair. Mom had applied a blend of products that had lent it new luster. She'd even tamed the flyaway strands that would otherwise have formed a scraggy halo about her shoulder-length tresses. *Where did* she *come from?* Simple as it might have been, the "little black dress" her mother had altered was nothing short of transformative.

For as long as she could remember, Xenia had shrunk from attention. When the other girls in her class had begun to wear makeup, she'd settled for ChapStick. Her social circle was tiny: Bethany and a few slumber party friends. An encounter with anyone outside of that circle, other classmates, teachers... *boys* had her hood up around her face and would render her capable of little more than a mumble.

The girl in the mirror, though. Xenia's shoulders eased from their characteristic hunch. *That Xenia doesn't mumble*, she thought. Once, she had asked Bethany how she could be so confident all the time. "Fake it till you is it," had been her reply.

Xenia was *so* going to fake it tonight.

Bethany, when her parents delivered her to the Findlay front porch, was a vision. For more than a year, ever since she'd returned from a family trip to Tokyo with a taste for anime and a whole new wardrobe, she had adopted a style she insisted was called "Lolita Goth." Tonight, she had outdone herself.

A wide, floofy skirt bloomed from her waist, layers of lace alternating with ruffled satin all the way to her knees, where leather boots wrapped in a multitude of buckles took over. A corset cinched her waist, and a double row of purple ribbon crisscrossed up to the puff of lace that bordered her neckline. A matching ribbon, looped into a wide bow, perched between the twin puffballs of her hair.

Dressing up made Xenia feel as if she was a whole new person. When Bethany did it, it just made her even more "Bethany."

"Where's the funeral?" Xenia's father asked, winking at his daughter.

"Dad!"

Bethany, unperturbed, glided to Mr. Findlay. She elevated her nose to the precise angle required to convey how serious she was. "To thine own self be true, Mr. Findlay," she sniffed. "I must always be true to my muse." A wicked grin dimpled her cheeks. "And tonight, the muse says it's time to *par-tay!*" She crooked her arms, elbows high and, despite the corset and platform boots, managed an effortless Cabbage Patch. She bopped across the porch. Without slowing, she seized both of Xenia's hands. "You ready to party, Zee?" She dragged Xenia toward the Findlay family car, Cabbage Patching the entire way.

Xenia lacked her friend's coordination, but in the spirit of the promise she'd made to the mirror, did her best to match her BFFFF's moves. "Born ready, Beebs!"

"Dear? I'm having second thoughts," Xenia's mother said as she locked the front door. "The news coverage of last night's show in San Francisco... Those performances don't seem appropriate for girls their age—"

"*Mooom!*" cried Xenia.

"*Mrs. Findlay!*" echoed Bethany, with the same wicked grin as before.

"We already bought the tickets," added Cool Dad. He graced his wife's cheek with a peck.

Mom sighed, raised her eyes to the heavens and, knowing she was outvoted, led the way to the Findlays' old Toyota.

As she steered them to the freeway, Mrs. Findlay outlined the plan for Bethany. She would drop the three of them off outside the HoB, eliminating the need for expensive Hollywood parking. While Dad was stuck shepherding the girls through their first concert experience, she would spend a leisurely evening shopping and dining. Then, when the show was over, she would swoop in and rescue the lot of them.

Traffic, as was to be expected for the 405, was a living nightmare. At the urging of two very impatient back-seat drivers, Mrs. Findlay took the next exit in the forlorn hope that surface streets would be faster.

Xenia's stomach boiled. Anxiety and anticipation wrestled in her gut. She hated crowds and the press of overly close people, but there was no way she was going to miss this show. She focused instead on the dim reflection in the window beside her. Looked to the girl she was pretending to be for her cue. That girl didn't let crowds bother her, so Xenia wouldn't let them, either. Some of the tension in her middle faded, but not all.

The row of palm trees outside her window had been stationary for way too long. Xenia leaned over to glare at the traffic light impeding their progress. "How long is this damn light?" she demanded.

"Language," her mother said, while her father stifled a laugh.

"Yeah, well." Xenia flopped against the seat back. "Traffic sucks. We always get stuck and miss everything."

"Zee." Bethany's voice took on a strange urgency.

Xenia tore her eyes from the glare of the red light and found an expression of deep concern knotting her friend's plucked brows. *Beebs never gets car sick...*

"This isn't real, okay?" Bethany leaned in close. She pressed her hand to Xenia's arm, and it felt like nothing at all. "You're just dreaming. You have to wake up!"

"What?"

The traffic light flipped to green. Mom ground the gears and pulled forward into the intersection.

The world lurched. The car seat hurled her up. The shriek of tearing metal filled the air as the girl in the window sped toward her. Pain exploded in her arm, her head, as rainbow sparks erupted across her vision.

Darkness claimed her.

* * *

Xenia sat bolt upright. Her pulse thrummed in her chest, in her ears. Her arms and legs were caught, cocooned in a tangle of sheets. She twisted, squirmed across the too-big mattress until she had won her freedom. Careful of the cast on her arm, she slid from the bed to the cold hardwood floor.

Every night since she'd emerged from the coma, the nightmare had come. No matter how much she resisted, urged herself to stay awake, eventually sleep would claim her. The nightmare would follow.

Why won't this crap leave me alone? The answer, of course, was obvious. The whole thing, the concert, inviting Bethany—all of it had been her idea. It was her fault that her mother and father were dead. Her fault that Bethany was dead. She might as well have driven the other car herself. The nightmare was no more than what she deserved.

A ripple of color, the rainbow fringe that now clung to the edges of her vision, only added insult to injury. "This crap again." Xenia drew her knees up and buried her head in her arms.

During her recovery, the cloyingly sympathetic doctor had explained that her brain had taken quite a beating. There had been a great deal of swelling, hence the coma. The traumatized tissue would need time to finish healing. While it did, she could expect a few symptoms. These rainbow colors had been the first to show. The doctor said it wasn't uncommon to see a "migraine halo" before a headache. Sure enough, in short order, the headaches had followed.

"Don't panic," he'd said. "A halo doesn't mean a migraine is guaranteed. Take your medication and, most importantly, take it easy. It is very important to avoid reinjuring your brain. You're a strong kid, you'll be fine."

Yeah, right.

A cold prickle of goosebumps down Xenia's neck brought her head up. There, by the windows, poised atop the cushions and looking for all the world as if nothing had happened, was Bethany. She still wore the frilly, corseted dress and the thigh-high leather boots she'd been wearing when she'd...

With a gasp, Xenia scooted her backside across the floor until she thumped into a bedpost. From her window seat, Bethany glanced over. Their eyes met, and Bethany's kohl-lined lids went wide. A smile bloomed, and she waved exuberantly.

Xenia squeezed her eyes as tight as she could and buried

her face in the nest of her arms. *No. The migraines and weird halos weren't enough, were they?* Actual, no-shit hallucinations were the last thing she needed. She cracked an eye. Peeked over the rim of her arm.

Sure as shit, the image of Bethany was still there. Xenia knew it must be a hallucination because the window frame was visible right through her. The phantasm's painted lips moved, shaped something that might have been "Hey," but no sound emerged.

In the air between them, streamers of light flexed and swam.

"No," hissed Xenia, "it's not real!" Eyes clenched again, she repeated the mantra. Forced herself to believe it. "I'm not seeing her. Bethany is not here." Her hand went to the comforting weight of her mother's necklace, still about her neck.

The first splinter of agony, the first stage of the inevitable migraine, jabbed the space behind Xenia's eyes. As more and more splinters joined the first, a keening whine slipped out of her.

Off balance from the throb in her head, eyes shut tight against what she didn't want to see, Xenia fell sideways. In between surges of pain, she wormed her way to the desk, where the bag of prescriptions waited. She reached for them, only to fall back as the next pulse sent white-hot streamers across the dark behind her eyelids. She gasped and pulled at the air, desperate for relief. In a handful of seconds, this migraine had become the worst one yet.

She lurched again and swept the bag of pills from the desk to her lap. She cracked an eyelid no more than a hair and, careful not to look up and see... her, found the bottle she needed. The capsule stuck in her throat as she dry-swallowed, and she coughed until it at last went down.

None of the pills they had given Xenia stopped the migraines, but sometimes they allowed her to endure until the pain passed.

She curled up on the hardwood floor, her back to the window. Counted to ten, to twenty, one hundred, one thousand, as she waited for the pill to work. Somewhere between one thousand and two, merciful sleep claimed her.

In the morning, when the light of the rising sun roused her, stiff and cold, from her floorboard bedding, the migraine was gone. Reluctantly, Xenia cracked open one eyelid. She sagged with relief. No halos, no hallucinations. No *her*. The ordeal was over.

Until tonight.

Chapter Six

Days slogged past until they, grudgingly, became weeks.

Great-Aunt Elspeth insisted that Xenia was free to recover in her own time. No need to rush back to school. It would still be there when she was ready. Xenia had taken her at her word. She whiled away her days, alternating between staring off into space and moping about the grand old Victorian house.

Elspeth had gone to great lengths to cheer her up. She prepared lavish meals. Distracted her with board games. Took her up the coast to walk among towering redwoods. All the while spinning tale after unlikely tale of her globe-trotting youth.

All of this only served to add new depths to her depression. After all, Xenia had realized, during yet another sightseeing excursion, every day Elspeth spent with her was a day that her shop on Main Street, Bits 'n' Pieces, remained closed. Each activity designed to cheer her up served only as a demonstration of the burden she was to her guardian.

At Xenia's insistence, Elspeth registered her at Porter Valley High School. She would start next week.

Bright and early Monday morning, Elspeth whipped up a breakfast fit to feed the whole school. There were eggs poached and scrambled, home-baked bread toasted in grease from thick slabs of bacon, a tall stack of waffles with fruit and jam, and a pitcher of OJ that she claimed to have squeezed herself.

Xenia's appetite had died with her family. She nibbled what she could stand and then chased the remainder about her plate with her fork. The guilt twisting in her gut soured what few morsels she had eaten. It hadn't been her intent to waste all that food. Then again, she hadn't asked Elspeth to make such an expansive meal. She mumbled an excuse and hurried off, book bag in hand, to school.

She made it no more than halfway down the block before Elspeth called her back to the garden gate.

"I haven't burdened you with all that many rules, lassie," Elspeth said, as close to upset as Xenia had yet seen her, "but I do ask that you, please, always shut the garden gate when you leave." She pushed the gate closed in demon-stration. A firm *clack* sounded as the latch engaged. "See, nothing to it." The twinkle returned to her eye as she offered up a paper bag. "I packed you a lunch, just in case your appetite does put in an appearance." There was no sign, now, of her earlier annoyance. No sign that Elspeth was upset over all the food left on the table. Only a warm smile for her great-niece.

Twenty minutes and several blocks later, Porter Valley High's massive edifice hove into view. At the entrance, a wide staircase rose to a triplet of doors ensconced in a gothic arch. The school's year of establishment, 1910, was carved into the arch. Above the entrance rose something that Xenia could only describe as an honest-to-God belfry. She supposed that, when it was built, the school used actual bells instead of the blaring, electronic chime that had echoed about the neighborhood minutes earlier. A blue-and-white banner was slung across the brick facade. Cartoon capital letters declared "Banana Slug Pride!" Xenia had stumbled over one of the sickly yellow slugs while taking out the trash the other night. What about the grotesque things one could be prideful of, she had no clue.

Her hand went to her neck. Her fingers found the chunky gold links of her mother's necklace. She'd almost left the keepsake at home, but Mom had considered it her good luck charm. Even though it had ultimately failed her, its weight offered Xenia a tiny morsel of comfort.

Okay. She could do this.

Xenia fell into step behind a trio of students and made her way up the wide staircase. Above her, lamps within the twin windows below the belfry's open top gave the appearance of glowering eyes.

She could just bail. Try this again in a million years.

Instead, she slipped through the leftmost door before it could slam shut. She was immediately shoulder-checked by a passing teen in a blue-and-white varsity jacket. No apology was offered, and she didn't have the guts to demand one. She shuffled out of the thick of traffic while she sought her bearings. Class and sports team photos were mounted on the wall beside her. Disturbingly, someone had scratched the eyes from several of the students depicted in the current year's photo.

There, the administration office. Xenia dashed through the churn of the hallway to the receptionist's desk. The gray-haired woman raised a finger as she barked into the phone clamped between her generous helping of chin and shoulder. "...no, you're out of your mind. Everyone knows Ambrose is the best long stick middle the Banana Slugs have ever had. We've got that championship on lock. No. Yes. What? Fine, talk later. What can I do for you?" she addressed Xenia at last.

Xenia mumbled her name and received a packet that contained her new class schedule. She mumbled her thanks and then ducked into the hall as the receptionist again reached for her phone.

She found shelter from the tide of student bodies between two of the locker banks lining the hallway. Xenia shuffled through the packet until she located a photocopied map of the school. She turned it this way and that but was unable to puzzle out how the faded blue lines aligned with her current location. She began to regret her too-hasty refusal of Sal's offer to give her a quick tour before class.

"Oh. Em. Gee." The snap of chewing gum punctuated each syllable. "You are totally new here, aren't you? Gracie, newb alert!"

Xenia found herself bracketed by a trio of girls, the same ones she'd followed inside. Three pairs of eyes regarded her with varying degrees of curiosity. She racked her brain for a clever response, some combination of words that would nip the "new girl" stigma in the bud. Naturally, the English language chose that moment to absent itself from her brain. "Umm."

The blonde to the right goggled openly at Xenia. "No frickin' way. Been a minute since we had any new blood up in here."

"Right?" The redhead on the left tugged her hairband.

Both turned their attention to the third, the gum-chewer who'd called out Xenia's presence. Tallest of the bunch, she blew an enormous gum-bubble and sucked it back in, all without smudging her lipstick. "New Girl, please tell me you moved here from someplace interesting. I'm talking New York, London, or Miami, even. I mean, sucks for you, coming here but whatever." A perfect, plucked eyebrow arched in expectation.

A cloud of artificial fruit scent enveloped Xenia as the girl spoke again: "We are in dire need of some class up in this bitch, know what I'm sayin'?" She gave Xenia a head-to-toe examination thorough enough that she regretted wearing her comfortable, if worn, hoodie and jeans. "Maybe not, huh?"

Xenia's cheeks burned. She dropped her eyes and wished Bethany were here. Beebs had never judged Xenia for choosing comfort over fashion, even though she had been obsessed with clothing herself. Bethany would have known how to deal with this bunch. She clenched her teeth, promising herself she wouldn't cry.

In contrast to her casual attire, each of the girls between Xenia and freedom had dressed from the expensive side of the mall. The brunette in the center, the obvious ringleader, wore a deceptively simple white T-shirt that had clearly cost her, or her parents, a small fortune. Over that was an open fringed vest, with a small hat and skin-tight leggings to complete the ensemble. Her friends were dressed in similar fashion. Coordinated, but not identical.

"Madison!" The redhead laughed and then nudged the brunette. "You're such a bitch." She turned to Xenia. "That's just Mads, okay? She thinks she's being so outrageous when all she's doing is stirring shit up. Ignore her, m'kay?" She shifted her armload of books to free up a hand, which she offered to Xenia. "I'm Courtney." She nodded at the blonde member of the trio. "That's Gracie."

Again, three pairs of eyes pinned Xenia.

Xenia, eventually, took Courtney's hand and managed something that resembled a handshake. "Xenia."

"Ooh, so exotic," crooned Madison. "I've never met a Xenia before."

Xenia fended off an impulse to crawl into her hood and vanish forever. Her shoulders inched toward her ears. Why did they have to stand so close?

"Why are you here?"

"What?" Xenia blinked.

Madison smirked, "Why Porter Valley, huh? No one, and I mean no one, moves to this dump. So how did you"— she poked Xenia in the shoulder—"wind up here?" She snapped her gum.

"I—"

"I know! Messy divorce!" Courtney's green eyes flashed with excitement.

"No, I—"

"Totes messy divorce. New Girl has all the signs." Madison had seized the idea in her teeth and was running with it. "Daddy got a little too hot 'n' heavy with his 'personal assistant'"—she made air quotes—"in his corner office, didn't he? Mommy got suspicious, hired someone to snoop up the proof and *bam!* She lawyers up. Divorce city. She takes Daddy for every penny, the house, even his precious midlife crisis 'Vette." Madison's eyes were distant as the scenario played out in her head. She snapped her fingers and then thrust one at Xenia. "Who got custody of New Girl, that's what I wanna know." Her eyes swung between her companions, in search of a juicy answer.

"Mommy," offered Courtney.

"Nu-uh." Gracie dipped a hand into her tiny purse and produced a tinier phone. Her thumbs *tick-ticked* across the keyboard as she stared at Xenia. "Dad got her, obvi."

"I like where your head's at," Madison said. "Mama wants the deets." Manicured fingers beckoned for more.

What the hell is going on? Xenia's attempt to back away brought her up against the wall. She fought down the impulse to slip a finger into her cast and push until she couldn't hear her own thoughts.

"If Mommy got all the cash, and the house, why is New Girl wearing..." Gracie's blue eyes flicked down to Xenia's ratty high-tops. "That?"

"Gracie!" Courtney's voice held a note of warning, ruined by her giggle.

Madison took the baton. "Yeah, I see it now. Poor Daddy, disgraced, fired, without a penny to his name, gets stuck with the kid so Mommy can go party in Monaco. How else is he gonna end up here when—uh-oh! Waterfall alert!" Madison's gum snapped with obvious glee.

Xenia brought a hand to her cheek. Her fingers came away wet. She was so used to the tears by now she hadn't noticed their return. She mopped at her eyes with the edge of her hood, then tried, and failed, not to drag in a huge, wet sniff.

"Enough, Madison."

The newcomer, who towered over Madison by a good two inches, snaked an arm between them to snag Xenia's sleeve.

Xenia allowed herself to be extracted as the tall girl glared daggers at Madison. Once a hall length lay between them, Xenia's rescuer broke off her stare.

"Nice meeting you, New Girl," Courtney called out. She elbowed Madison again and then ushered her friends in the opposite direction.

"Ignore 'em. They're idiots." The tall girl tossed her head to flip a long mahogany braid over her shoulder. "But

Mads is the biggest idiot of them all." She glared after the trio and then took a deep breath. Clearly, there was history between the towering teen and the terrible trio. "A little of her goes a long way, y'know?"

Xenia's eyes stung; she knew they were all red by now. She stepped back so the tall girl didn't loom over her quite as much.

"New, right?" The tall girl pointed to the class schedule and map Xenia still clutched. She held her hand out for the bundle.

Xenia passed them over. While the other girl examined the schedule, she scrubbed at her face with her sleeve.

"Wow, they're not going easy on you, are they?" The other girl tapped the paper with a clear-painted fingernail. "AP Calc? Dang. So, Mr. Druszcz's room is all the way on the other side of school." She offered Xenia a sympathetic smile and then traced a finger over the map. "You need to go up this hall, left, then left at the second hall. It's at the end, on the right." The girl's braid almost clipped Xenia as she turned to point the way.

A warbling buzz cut off any remark Xenia might have made.

"And that's the warning bell. Good luck." The tall girl shoved the bundle of papers into Xenia's hand and, with a wave, vanished around a corner.

"Hi, I'm Xenia," Xenia said to the space where the girl had been. Her chin dropped to her chest. "I'm an idiot."

She resettled her book bag on her shoulder and glared at the photocopied map. Where had the tall girl said calculus was?

Her first day, and she was already lost.

* * *

Xenia hovered in the doorway until an older teen, a senior, hip-checked her into the classroom. If the varsity jacket slung from his shoulder was any clue, he might have been the same guy who'd knocked into her when she'd first arrived.

The balding, portly man behind the big desk waved her over, asking, "New student?" Mr. Druszcz, no doubt.

Xenia nodded and handed over her papers. He selected one sheet of many and returned the rest. "Take one, then have a seat," he said, tapping the stack of calculus textbooks at the corner of his desk.

New textbook in hand, Xenia kept her eyes down as she picked her way down an aisle. The pair in the middle two seats of the back row brought her to a stumbling halt. Gracie offered up a tiny, distracted wave. Madison merely smirked.

How the heck did they *get into AP Calculus?*

All too aware of the eyes on her, Xenia retreated one row and fell more than sat in the nearest empty seat.

"Ladies and gentlemen, please join me in welcoming the latest addition to our group." The teacher smiled at his own joke. "Miss Xenia Findlay. Who, I might add, scored a five on the AP placement exam. It seems that some of you have a little competition on your hands." His eyes tracked across the classroom.

Xenia half-jumped from her seat as Mr. Druszcz slapped his hands together with a resounding *crack*. He rubbed his palms, face alight with scholastic enthusiasm. "Now, who can tell us where we left off on Friday?" He pulled a marker from the breast pocket of his checkered button-down and aimed it at the teen slouched at the corner desk by the window. "Mr. Ambrose."

Xenia breathed out a long sigh. She was out of the spotlight at last.

Mr. Druszcz's new target, the senior boy who'd bumped Xenia twice that morning, pulled his fingers through tousled blond hair. A lazy smile played over his lips as he crossed one Air Jordan over the other. He curled his arm and flexed enough to make the bicep stand at attention. "The Power Rule." He met the scattered laughter with half-lidded eyes.

"Very good, Mr. Ambrose, seems you were paying attention after all." Mr. Druszcz popped the cap from his marker, rose from his desk, and turned to the whiteboard. "Now, as you may recall from the previous chapter—"

A knock from the door set his back ramrod straight. His movements were precise, measured, yet still betrayed annoyance as he capped the marker and replaced it in his breast pocket. The muscle in his jaw twitched as he crossed to the door.

"I'm sorry for the interruption, Theo, but this can't wait."

"Fine. Ladies and gentlemen, if you would be so kind as to give Mrs. Wedgwood your attention." He swept his arm in a mock bow. "Take it away."

The woman's blocky heels clacked against the linoleum as she made her way to the front of the class. Mrs. Wedgwood was of similar age to Mr. Druszcz and wore a conservative pantsuit in a deep indigo. Heavy, turtle-framed glasses rode the arch of her forehead. Her mousey brown hair, liberally salted with gray, was pulled back into a bun so severe that it only emphasized her sizable nose all the more.

"I apologize for interrupting your lesson so soon after it's begun, however—put that phone away, Gracie Jones!" Mrs. Wedgwood's quiet voice gained the snap of a drill sergeant as she snapped at the girl.

Xenia snuck a look in time to catch the blonde slip her

phone beneath the desk. She plastered an innocent smile across her face even as her thumbs rapid-fired another text.

"Thank you." Mrs. Wedgwood's voice returned to its former amplitude. "Now, I need to know if anyone has seen Lucas Shepherd today." Her eyes tracked around the room. Murmurs flitted from seat to seat.

Since Xenia had no idea who Lucas Shepherd was, or where he might have gone, she turned her attention to her new textbook. Calc was the one subject she had actually been looking forward to. She paged through in search of the chapter concerning the Power Rule.

"This is the fifth consecutive day that Lucas has been absent," Mrs. Wedgwood went on. "What's more, he hasn't only been absent from school, his parents have no clue as to his whereabouts. They are, at this very moment, in my office. As is a member of Porter Valley's finest. Believe me when I say they are sick with worry." She paced as far as one edge of Mr. Druszcz's desk, spun on her heel, and clacked back the way she had come. "He did not return home following practice last Monday. Even though the police are involved, and I am sure they will do their best—"

One of the boys seated in front of Xenia snickered.

"The Shepherds have asked that I come to you, his friends and classmates, for help. I know some of you might believe that coming forward will make you a 'snitch,' but Lucas's parents are literally begging for help, any crumb of information you might have." Mrs. Wedgwood shook her head. "With all that has been going on, we just want a safe homecoming for Lucas, as I am sure you do as well. Should any of you have something to say that you don't feel can be said in front of your classmates..." She crossed to Mr. Druszcz and plucked the marker from his breast pocket, eliciting a scowl, and dashed a phone number onto the whiteboard. "This is a hotline provided by the school district. I assure you that anything said or texted to this number will be passed on in absolute anonymity."

Xenia tuned out the remainder as her finger traced across the page. In LA, she'd covered the Power Rule last semester. But then, math was her favorite subject, and she didn't mind the refresher. She couldn't remember if she'd packed her old notebooks for the trip north or not. She'd have to dig into the pile of boxes that waited, unopened, in her bedroom closet. For the first time since her world had ended, the gloom that clung to her heart, to her thoughts, began to lift.

A cold prickle of icy goosebumps danced their way across the back of Xenia's neck.

Ugh. Those two are staring at me, I just know it. That tall girl had been right—a little of Madison really was more than enough. Xenia snuck a look over her shoulder and found Mads and Gracie hunched over their phones, sending out hot gossip about Lucas, no doubt.

Xenia dug her fingers into the nape of her neck and tried to ease the icy tingle. If anything, it only grew stronger. She used the fringe of her hair to hide her eyes as she searched for whoever was staring.

A teen, his movements furtive, slunk into an empty seat. The same seat everyone had looked to when Mrs. Wedgwood had mentioned the missing boy, Lucas, by name.

Xenia bit her lip, stifled a snort of laughter. Everyone had been so busy working themselves up over his absence, were so caught up in their gossip, that they had all missed him sneaking into class. *Hah!*

She flipped through her notebook and worked her way through the first exercise. A *drip, drip, drip* yanked her out of the numerical reverie. A rivulet of liquid snaked over the scuffed linoleum by her foot. She tracked the water across the floor to Lucas's seat. The assumed missing boy sat ramrod straight, hands folded in his lap. His varsity jacket was soaked through and hung heavy on his shoulders. His short hair, likewise, clung to his scalp. Trickles of water skated down his pale neck. Drop after drop pattered from his leg to swell the puddle beneath him.

Why hadn't she noticed he was dripping wet? Why hadn't anyone else? How had he gotten soaked, for that matter? Did the school have a swimming pool? *Oh crap.* Xenia rocked in her seat, mortified. *No one told me I'd need a swimsuit for gym!* Maybe Aunt Elspeth could write her a note—

A stuttering triple beat of her heart brought Xenia up short. The far wall was visible right through Lucas.

Just like the other night, her broken brain was playing tricks.

The hallucination she'd mistaken for a missing student turned its head. The movement was slow, disjointed, as if the bones of his neck no longer agreed upon the order in which they should rotate. She knew it was a bad idea to legitimize this symptom of her injury, but she lacked the power to avert her eyes. The boy's lips were pale and blood-less. His skin pallid. Beneath the sweep of his sodden hair, his eyes—

Oh God, where are his eyes?

A skein of ink blackened the boy's face. A shadow cast by no light she could see. No hint of iris, no gleam of sclera graced that ebon pit where his eyes should have been.

Xenia ground her teeth. Fought to turn her head, to avert her gaze, anything. Her lungs seized as she labored to drawn breath, to speak, to cry out. The muscles of her neck and back hummed with tension as she battled the dread that had seized her. *I don't want to see this! I don't—*

Lucas's mouth fell open upon the same void that had claimed his eyes, a breach in the fabric of the world, bound within the cusp of bloodless lips. The cords of his neck stood taut as he tried to speak. No sound emerged, despite the furrow of effort that creased his brow. His cheeks tore as his mouth yawned wide. The skin of his throat rippled, and still no sound emerged. All about Lucas, the world convulsed. The ceiling tiles above, the panels of the floor, even the window glass shuddered in echo of the boy's mute agony.

Rainbow whorls of light crowded Xenia's vision as, at last, she found her voice and screamed for him.

Chapter Seven

Bethany drifted after Xenia and kept an eye out for that jerk who'd gone all horror show in class. "I swear, Zee. When I find him I'm gonna..." What? What could she even do? Punch him in the mouth? Might as well punch air.

Bethany had been as off guard as Xenia when the other ghost had dropped in. She'd been at the window, bored by the prospect of a calculus lesson she now had even less use for. Math was Xenia's thing. She'd only gone to keep Zee company... and in the hopes that if Xenia did see a ghost, it would be her. Not some rando. Then, a scuffle had broken out on the field outside. Even if her interest in the sight of athletic boys tussling had died with her body, drama would always be her kryptonite. And so she hadn't noticed that creep until Xenia screamed.

If that hadn't been bad enough, he had completely ignored her! Rude! Was there no solidarity among the dead? Distracted by Zee's entirely understandable breakdown, Bethany hadn't seen which way the ghost had gone. By the time Xenia was in the counselor's office and had regained some measure of calm, the dead boy was long gone.

"Hey, you gonna be okay?"

Sal, Xenia's new neighbor, pushed through the crowded hallway to Zee's side. Bethany smiled. Even if her bestie was a bit slow on the uptake, she was glad to see that Zee had a new friend. Finally.

Xenia dropped her eyes. Offered Sal a one-shouldered shrug.

He blew out an explosive sigh. "Well. If you do need anything..." Sal jammed his hands into his pockets.

"'Kay," Xenia continued to avoid eye contact.

Bethany threw up her hands. "Talk to him! He's head over heels already." Honestly, she was thrilled. These two nerds made a perfect couple. If only Zee would—

"Hey," Xenia mumbled, "you said you could show me around? If you still want to..."

"There we go!" Bethany pumped her fist. Xenia had gotten herself lost on the way to every class. It was tragic, really.

Sal's face lit up, eyes shining. "Yeah! But—" The warble of the school bell cut him off. "Crap. I had first lunch period. History, now." He jogged a few steps backward, then paused. "After school? I could show you around, then we could walk home? Together, I mean? Only 'cause we're neighbors..."

"Sure." Xenia raised her eyes for a moment. "S'fine."

"Cool, cool." Sal beamed at Xenia, gave her a little wave, and vanished into the press of the crowded hallway.

"Wow, Zee, he's got it bad." Bethany shook her head, laughing. "Okay, you need to break through whatever hangup keeps you from seeing me." She planted herself in

Xenia's path, only to have her friend walk clean through. "You and me, we need to have a serious talk."

* * *

PVHS's lunchroom might have been lifted right out of any high school drama. There were the usual long tables with bench seats. The crowds at those tables might not have been a "clique-y" as on TV, but there was a definite "jock/normie" separation thing going on. A glass-shielded cafeteria line, complete with a pair of hairnet-wearing lunch ladies, occupied one wall. It was nothing like the lunchroom at the school Bethany and Xenia had attended, and yet it was instantly familiar.

Bethany did a quick pass around the room while Zee searched for a place to sit. She was relieved, and frustrated, to find no sign of the creep ghost. She really wanted to give him a piece of her mind, but not if it meant scaring the bejeezus out of Zee again.

How did he do that thing with his eyes?

Wait, was that what *she* looked like? *Crap! No wonder Zee won't look at me.* Bethany craned her neck in another attempt at self-examination. As far as she could tell, she looked exactly as she had the moment she'd woken up dead. Mirrors were useless; she didn't have a reflection.

As soon as Xenia was seated, Bethany shot through the ceiling and onward. Time for another test of her limitations.

Since her involuntary relocation to Porter Valley, Bethany had been stuck here. Each time she tried to exit the valley, an invisible barrier would bring her up short. She'd made attempt after attempt that first week in town, which had given her a mental map of the "border."

She wasn't sure, but there might be a bit more leeway along the northern ridge line. Since she was mostly certain that she was here to haunt Zee, it made sense that the ghost boundary would be centered on her. This was the first day Xenia had ventured far enough from the old Victorian for Bethany to see if the borders shifted with her.

Bethany slammed to a halt in midair just below Porter Valley's near-perpetual cloud cover. This was expected; she'd long since established her vertical limit. She arrowed southward. Below her, the school gave way to a steep bluff, beyond which curled the Eel River.

"Damn it!" The same unseen force had yanked her to a halt directly above the redwoods atop the ridge line. Exactly where she'd stopped every other time.

That settles it. She was trapped in Porter Valley, not leashed to Xenia.

This had disturbing implications. What happened if Zee moved again? Would she be relocated to her new residence, or would she be stuck here? Alone.

Bethany offered the offending, invisible barrier her middle finger as she drifted back to the lunchroom and Xenia.

* * *

Xenia upended the bag lunch Aunt Elspeth had packed for her. Two turkey sandwiches (one wheat, one white), a bag of barbecue-flavored chips, bottled water, a juice box, a Granny Smith apple, and one of her great-aunt's homemade "fern cakes" tumbled onto the table before her.

At the sight of this unexpected banquet, her stomach gave a mighty rumble, its first since before the accident.

Before she realized what she was doing, she'd wolfed down an entire sandwich.

"Don't they feed you at home? Damn!"

Xenia paused, teeth buried in the second sandwich, as the blond senior from AP Calculus, Ambrose something, grinned down at her.

"C'mon. I was kidding. You do you." He crossed his arms.

Heat crept over Xenia's collarbone: part embarrassment, part something new. Something unfamiliar. She fought down her urge to sweep everything into her bag and hide in the girl's restroom. Instead, she looked him straight in the eye.

Well, the middle of his forehead. Close enough.

Xenia forced down the half-chewed mouthful. Dropped the sandwich onto the wrapper. The senior just stood there, staring. "What?" she asked.

He raised his hands in mock surrender, slung a leg over the bench seat, and sat. "Fine, fine." Concern swept the cocky grin from his face. "Are you okay? For real, I mean. You sounded... back in AP Calc. I dunno. It sounded serious. More than just a panic attack."

The heat under Xenia's collar ticked up a notch. Everyone just had to bring that up, didn't they? Each new class had already been abuzz with the tale of her little screaming fit by the time she arrived. Room after room of staring eyes. Whispers that were anything but subtle.

Like being the new girl wasn't bad enough.

Xenia wished for all the world that she could crawl up into her hoodie and just die. Instead, she looked away. Broke off a bit of crust. Nibbled. "I'm fine."

His eyes tracked across her face over a long, uncomfortable moment. Rather than pressing the issue, he leaned back and ran fingers through the tousle of his hair. "You're coming to the game on Friday, right? Can't miss it."

"What game?"

His eyebrows did a credible job of reaching his hairline. "The quarterfinal game? Hello?" He spread his arms. "Lacrosse? The Slugs"—he tapped the lapel of his varsity jacket, where three brass pins were affixed to the letter patch—"have dominated finals three years in a row. We're a lock for numero four-oh."

"Uh-huh." Xenia had only the vaguest notion how lacrosse worked. Sticks and balls. When she reached for the remainder of her sandwich, she found she'd already eaten it. She settled for the apple. "Good luck."

He laughed and thrust his hand across the table. "I'm Ev. Everard, really, but everyone," he said, stressing the first syllable with a wink, "calls me Ev."

Xenia looked at his hand, up to his face, then down to her apple.

"Bro, you down for Saturday night? Dom says there's a rager up at Clam Beach!"

Ev swung around to slap hands with the other boy. Like Ev, the newcomer wore a blue-and-white letter jacket. Only two pins graced his patch, however.

Ev stood and bumped elbows with his teammate. "You know it!" He aimed a look at Xenia. "I have the hookups. Kegs are a go."

Shit, does he expect me to go? Does that mean I'm invited? Do I even want to go? The most outrageous party she'd ever been to had been a slumber party with Bethany and two other girls from her old school. The most illicit substance present at the not-rager had been cookie dough ice cream, and the riskiest activity had been karaoke after midnight. A "real" high school party, on a beach, with alcohol, would be a whole new level for her.

If Bethany was here, she would have dragged Xenia along for the experience, invited or not. She sighed.

The other lacrosse player looked at Xenia for the first time, frowned, and then threw his arm around Ev's shoulders. "Bro, a freshman? For real? Jane'll shit a whole brick wall she sees you hitting on other girls."

Of course he's got a girlfriend. The thought popped into her head, unprompted. With the accident still fresh in her heart, she wasn't at all in the mood to think about this guy. Or anyone, really.

Why, then, was she disappointed?

Ev's teammate urged him toward the gaggle of blue-and-white-clad bodies on the far side of the lunchroom. As they drew away, the boy shot a look at Xenia and then said, loud enough to be overheard, "Hear that new girl's a screamer, though!"

Ev doubled over as he and his teammates erupted in laughter. An inferno of humiliation boiled away whatever disappointment she had felt. Her eyes burned with unshed tears as she swept the remains of her lunch into her book bag and bolted for the nearest exit.

Xenia stumbled outside. Blinded by tears and sudden sunlight, she blundered straight into another student. Strong hands caught her before she could tumble.

"Woah, what's wrong?" The tall girl, the one who'd extracted her from Madison and company, offered a gentle smile. The smile twisted into a scowl as the sound of jock hilarity reached them through the lunchroom doors. "Just ignore those jerks. You know how jocks are. Bunch of freakin' dogs. If they're not trying to hump your leg, they're peeing on it."

Despite the gloom that had closed about her, Xenia laughed. This launched a snot bubble from her tear-loosened nose. Mortified, she spun away to wipe her face.

"Maia," said the tall girl.

"What?"

"My name? I'm Maia."

"Oh. Xenia."

"Cool. How was AP Calc?" Maia pronounced it as a single word: "apcalc."

"What?" Xenia scrutinized the taller girl's face for any sign of mockery or that she was referring to the "panic attack." Not a hint of derision shone in the tall girl's eyes. "It was okay. Calc's my favorite."

"Nice." Maia's eyes tracked to Xenia's wrist. She reached out to pluck at the hoodie sleeve and flicked a finger against the fiberglass shell underneath. "What'd you do to your arm?"

Xenia looked away, across the athletic field behind the school. After a moment, she managed to mumble, "Car accident. S'why I had to move here." She dabbed at her eyes.

"Ah," said Maia. Her eyes widened. "Oh. Oh damn. I'm sorry."

"Yeah."

One of the students milling at the center of the field called out. Maia half-turned to wave. "Crap, I have to get over there." She did a little jog in place. "Track team's calling." She began to jog backward toward her friends.

Xenia, desperate to evict the gloom from her thoughts, blurted the first thing that came to mind: "Track? Doesn't that make you a jock, too?"

Maia came to a halt. Tapped her chin. "It does. But if I wanted to hump your leg, I'd ask first." Her lopsided grin vanished as she spun away, braid swinging, and loped across the grass.

Xenia blinked as Maia joined her friends in some sort of stretching exercise. The heat under her collar returned. Sizzled its way up her throat.

"You'd what?"

Chapter Eight

"Ah crap." Xenia kicked a spray of gravel ahead of her. When the final bell had warbled across Porter Valley High, she'd been so intent on putting as much distance as possible between her and the disaster of her first day that she'd forgotten about Sal.

As the guilt rushed in, she slipped a finger into her cast. The resulting flare of pain did nothing to drown out her regret. It only made her all the more miserable.

She hadn't been in the mood to head straight home and face Aunt Elspeth's bottomless pep. Instead, she'd gone the opposite way, following the curve of Redwood Boulevard, not caring where it led. "Away" was good enough.

Her aimless wandering had carried her on until she ran out of street. Just ahead, a small parking lot served one of Porter Valley's many municipal parks.

With the Eel River visible just beyond the parking lot, Riverside Park certainly lived up to its name. A pleasant walking path surrounded a wide swath of manicured grass. There was a picnic area, currently empty, located conveniently close. There were enough wooden tables and battered iron barbecues to serve an army of picnicking families.

At the center of the green space was an absolute geezer of a man, all knobby knees and gangly elbows. No more than a gossamer fringe of snowy white hair wreathed the spotted dome of his head. His eyes were fixed on the low cloud cover. A taut cord ascended from the spindle clutched in his hands to the crimson-and-mustard diamond that hung just below the lowest cloud. The paper kite looped and swooped as the old man guided it through the steady breeze from the Pacific.

Xenia fluffed her hood up around her ears. The coastal valley was much colder and blusterier than the SoCal weather she was used to. She took a seat on one of the benches by the river's edge, where the grass gave way to a jumble of rocks and brambly growth that filled the thirty feet or so to the water's edge. The Eel River, swollen with runoff from the mountains to the east, tossed the occasional spume and spray into the air as it churned along the curve of its bed.

On the far side of the river, a wall of granite, dark with moisture, rose in craggy layers to the redwoods hundreds of feet above. Lichen in shades of pale cream, wan orange, and surprising pops of red lent a painterly touch to the dark stone. Here and there, heavy mats of green moss hung from outcroppings. Trickles of water streamed from the growth to the rush below.

Xenia swore under her breath as new color bloomed. The granite gained an inner luminescence and specks of light traced the craggy edges. Today just got better and better, didn't it?

She'd been grateful that a migraine hadn't followed the morning's hallucination. Now, it was clear the universe thought she'd gotten off too easy. The migraine halo spread across her vision, and she pawed through her book bag. "Shit." She'd left her pills at home.

Idiot.

She scowled as glowing ribbons of light swirled and danced like the old man's kite above the river. *Fine*, she dared her injured brain, *do your worst.*

The stones by her feet glowed in hues she had no name for. Colors that had never graced a crayon box rose as drifting sparkles from the mats of damp moss.

Impossible ribbons and delicate streamers of light swam through the air as far as she could see. The fact that she could still see the normal world, clear as day, through the spray of light was a definite sign that she was well and truly losing it.

You need to tell Aunt Elspeth that it's getting worse. That you're having hallucinations too. Sure, if she did that, she'd have to go back to the hospital. Who knew what sort of crazy treatment she'd have to endure then?

Xenia was really, really tired of the hospital.

She slid low on the bench, set her fingers atop the curve of her mother's necklace, and rubbed the heavy links through the fabric of her shirt. The migraine, with its jagged spikes of agony, would be here any second now. "Just get it over with!" Xenia's voice slid from yell to a whimper: "Please."

"*Caw!*"

Xenia rolled her head against the bench. A crow, its silhouette a black cutout against the backdrop of illusory colors, bobbed its head at her from the far end of the seat. It stared at her with an ebony bead of an eye as it shuffled clawed feet on the wood.

"Hullo."

The crow took one step away from her, spread its tail feathers wide, and shook them together again. Xenia considered the bird's size and decided that it was probably a raven. The raven, in return, busied itself by digging its beak into the space beneath a wing.

"Sorry if I scared you," Xenia said. The bird was the only thing in her field of view free from the hallucinated riot of color. She kept her eyes trained on it while she waited for the pain to arrive. After a moment, rather than the first pangs of a migraine, her stomach sent up a demand for tribute.

Moving slowly, she reached for what little remained of lunch. In the depths of her book bag, her fingers brushed the fern cake Elspeth had packed.

Her great-aunt had spent a good chunk of the night before baking the little confections, which she'd called "a taste of home." Strawberry jam burst across her tongue as Xenia bit through the flaky shell. She made a tiny "mmm" of pleasure as she chewed.

The raven's head bobbed up. A beady eye fixed itself upon the treat in her hand.

"How rude of me," Xenia said around a mouthful of frosting and almond. A shower of crumbs pattered her jeans as she broke off a morsel. She froze as the raven's wings half-opened. Once it had assured itself she wasn't about to pounce, the bird settled. She set the offering on the bench seat between them.

The tiny round head twitched as its gaze darted from Xenia to treat, then back. She licked sugar from her fingers and waited.

The strawberry jam and almond paste proved to be too great a temptation, and the raven fluttered down to the seat. It stepped one clawed foot over the other until it was within range. The ebony line of its beak split as it canted its head to one side, then closed about the morsel. Prize secured, the raven backed to the very edge of the bench before downing it in three quick bobs of its head.

"Yeah, my great-aunt knows how to cook, doesn't she?" Xenia said as the raven strutted in a little circle. "We good?" She pretended that the next bob of the bird's head was a nod. "Cool."

Xenia allowed her head to roll onto the pillow of her hood. To her surprise, the halos had passed. The whole circus of crazy colors was gone. Even better, there was no pressure in her head. No hint of an imminent migraine. *Oh thank God.* She popped the last of the tart into her mouth and savored the absence of pain even more than the confection.

There was a *tap, tap, tap* from the far end of the bench. Xenia slid an eye toward the raven in time to see it hop closer. The beak descended. Pecked the wood bench again. *Tap, tap, tap.*

"Sorry little dude, that was the last of it. I'll bring some homemade bread next time." Elspeth loved to bake almost as much as she enjoyed puttering in her garden. Thanks to the endless font of baked goods, Xenia could feed her avian friend until it was too chubby to fly.

The raven tapped the bench again.

"Seriously, that's all I had. See?" Xenia shook crumbs from her hoodie and tried to aim as many as she could onto the bench.

The bird tilted its eye to the scattering of crumbs. The glossy feathers covering its robust form fluffed outward. It did a full-body shake to settle them into place. Then, with great deliberation, it stepped over the spray of crumbs. The raven was little more than a foot from Xenia's leg. The ebony wings spread wide, the point of its beak descended, and it pecked the bench with great deliberation. *Tap. Tap. Tap.*

Having delivered whatever cryptic message its bird brain had demanded of it, the raven burst into the air and settled into a wide, soaring arc above her.

"You're weird. You know that, right?" Xenia called up to the raven.

"*Caw.*"

* * *

"Hey, Sal." Xenia paused in front of the old Victorian's garden gate. "I'm sorry about ditching you after school. I had a lot on my mind and... I just forgot. Tomorrow, okay?"

Sal caught a rebound from the basketball hoop that dominated the end of the Serranos' driveway. He held the ball between the fingertips of both hands as he turned to her. If Xenia's earlier thoughtlessness had upset him, there was no sign of it in his wide smile. "No worries." He bounced the ball once and then inclined his head toward the hoop. "Feel like some HORSE?"

Xenia glanced over her shoulder, toward her new home. "I'm not..." She settled for raising her left arm. Tugged the sleeve back from her cast. "It's still healing. I'm supposed to take it easy." Also, she had no idea how to play HORSE.

This time, a hint of disappointment did color his grin. "All good." He nodded. Bounced his ball. The hint vanished. "When that comes off, though," One-handed, he set the ball spinning atop a finger. "No excuses. It'll be good physical therapy. You'll see."

Xenia forced a chuckle to humor him. Maybe she would

give it a go, once the cast came off. Assuming it ever did. "Okay. Maybe. No promises."

Sal smiled and returned to his obsession.

Xenia was halfway through the gate when she spotted the paisley-clad form of her guardian in the window of the upstairs library room. Xenia made a show of pushing the gate shut, and her great-aunt beamed and lifted a jaunty thumbs-up before she vanished from the window.

Her cheeks burned with embarrassment as Xenia realized Elspeth had seen her whole exchange with Sal. Each time she'd spoken with the "the boy across the road," as Elspeth called him, she'd worn the most insufferable smile. That knowing expression would be on her face all through dinner. Xenia just knew it.

Her first day at school had been bad enough without adding the curdling embarrassment of whatever Elspeth was up to.

Chapter Nine

Halfway through dinner, Xenia's restored appetite deserted her.

"How was school, dearie?" was all that was required to bring the morning's humiliation crashing back in. It must have shown on her face, because Elspeth took a long sip of her tea and added, "That bad?"

Xenia dragged a starchy riverbed through her mashed potatoes and blinked away the sting of tears as a rivulet of brown gravy followed her fork. "It was okay, I guess." There was no way she was going to talk about that horrible hallucination. Or the social fallout that had followed. Not ever.

"If it's bullies, and I knew my share when I was your age, well... you can't allow the braggarts and loudmouths to overwhelm you." Elspeth scooped up a forkful of the ground beef and carrot mix she'd called "mince" and chewed for a thoughtful moment. "I know it might be trite to say it, but high school isn't forever. A bad batch of school-mates isn't the end of the world."

"It's not that." Xenia stared into the wreckage of her

uneaten meal. The moment stretched. She shook her head and mumbled, "Never mind."

"I was just like you, when I was your age."

"You were?" Xenia took in her great-aunt. Her guardian had traded the voluminous tie-dyed kaftan and the rock crystal-and-silver bangles and necklaces that she'd worn earlier for billowy pants and a sweater so fuzzy that the air about her crackled with static. Other than the hazel eyes they shared, they were nothing alike.

"Aye. My father and brothers were, to a man, brash and bold. Prone to strutting with their chests puffed out. Not at all shy in giving voice to each thought as it arrived." Elspeth's eyes crinkled with affection. "That lot took up so much space that there was little room left in the house for a wee girl such as myself, or so it seemed at the time. If I tried to speak up, make a place for myself, one of my brothers rushed to add his tuppence worth. 'We'll take care of it,' they'd say, never allowing me the freedom to speak my mind or make my own choices."

Xenia tried to imagine the woman across from her at her own age, with the same tiny, mousey voice, the same reluctance to meet another's eyes. How could Elspeth, who spun tales of travel while hobnobbing with rock stars and celebrities every step of the way, have ever been unable to speak up for herself? No, she just couldn't see it.

"It was Granny, you see." Elspeth mopped her plate with a scrap of bread and popped it into her mouth. "She saw what that smothering embrace was doing to me and didn't care for it one bit. The woman marched up to my father and told him she was taking me off of his hands. From that moment on, she would see to my education and upbringing. When I saw how my father, who feared neither man nor beast, wilted like old lettuce under the glare of a woman twice his age and a third his weight, his own mother no less... Well, the thought popped into my head right then. If this elderly woman, God love her, could stare down a man like my father, then I wanted that strength for myself." Elspeth snorted. "Father never did forgive the old woman for backing him down. Less so once I'd gone off on my travels. He was convinced she'd put the idea in my head. Hah! Those were my own wishes, lassie, and no one else's."

Elspeth rose, plate in hand. A pang of guilt cramped Xenia's stomach when she followed her gaze to her own plate, still full.

"Sorry." A fresh crop of tears burst from her. She scrubbed at her face with both hands.

A hand, warm and gentle, rubbed her shoulder.

"There now, lassie. No need to blame yourself when I let my love for the kitchen get out of hand. Come now, let's tidy up. We'll freeze what we can, yes?"

Xenia nodded. No sooner had the last dish been dried, the last leftover packed into the freezer, than she made her excuses. There was homework to do, which wasn't entirely a lie, and she was tired.

"Good night, dearie. Sweet dreams."

Bethany elevated her nose to the precise angle required to convey how serious she was. "To thine own self be true, Mr. Findlay," she sniffed. "I must always be true to my muse." She favored Xenia with a kohl-lined wink. "You ready, Zee?"

Xenia tore her attention away from the glacier-slow traffic outside her window. High-fived her BFFFF. "Born ready! If"—she glared at the red light that now kept them from reaching the concert—"we ever get there."

Cool, salty sea air brushed her cheek. Outside the car, row after row of palm trees marched to the horizon, and beyond. The ribbed trunks beneath those swaying fronds were pregnant with heavy clusters of dates ripening in the sun. As the wind rose, it carried the sharp, arid scent of dust and sand from across the narrow channel.

The orb of the rising sun, red and swollen, shimmered upon the water. Men, their skin burnt umber from years of exposure, hurled nets from their narrow canoes.

The girl blinked, confused, as the sun's radiance flushed from the bright carmine of sunrise to an uncanny emerald.

Pebbles of glass scored lines of fire across Xenia's cheek. Metal screamed against metal. The whole of the world spun as she was snatched up into the air, then flung at the trunk of a nearby palm.

The shock of impact hurled her through darkness and up into muddled consciousness. Her eyelids fluttered as she fought to focus on the still unfamiliar space of her new bedroom. Her pulse thundered in her ears. She gasped as she fought to draw breath from air gone suddenly, impossibly dense.

Once Xenia dragged away the sheets tangled about her head, she savored that first, effortless breath of cool air. The moment of calm crashed to an end as she found the air above her alight with braids and ribbons of impossible light. Every surface of her room, even her own skin, shone with an inner radiance. "Not again."

Even worse, an all-too-familiar form sat at the foot of her bed. The hallucinatory Bethany, her expression creased with worry, waved her arms as if to catch Xenia's attention.

Although her mouth moved, no sound accompanied the rapid-fire speech.

Their eyes met. The illusionary Bethany leaned in. Worry and, oddly enough, hope shone in those dark eyes.

"Nope." Xenia'd had enough of hallucinations. Of stupid colors. All of it. She screwed her eyes shut. Leaned over. Fumbled blind at the desktop. Grabbed the pill bottle she'd placed for this exact scenario. Once she'd dry-swallowed the horse pill, she flopped onto the mattress, where she dragged the covers over her head and jammed her face into the pillow. Just because her brain wanted to play stupid games didn't mean she had to play along.

Still, she'd had two, no, three of the halos today and so the inevitable finally caught with her. Xenia whimpered as the first jagged migraine claw plunged into her brain. It became very clear, very quickly, that this migraine would be one of the bad ones. As the muscles of her jaw spasmed, she wondered if it would be bad enough to finally end her.

Fine, she thought. *At least then it'll be over.*

Chapter Ten

Xenia allowed herself a practice bounce and eyeballed the distance to the hoop. Even as the ball left her hand, she knew she'd flubbed it. How the hell did Sal make this look so easy?

Her throw sent the ball careening from the underside of the metal rim. Marisol squealed with laughter and dashed off in pursuit. She'd appointed herself Xenia's "assistant" and took entirely too much glee in chasing down her ricochets.

"Well. You actually made it to the hoop this time?" Sal offered with a sympathetic grin.

"Shut up." Xenia rubbed her hand. "Cast threw me off." Truth be told, she hardly noticed the fiberglass wrapped about her arm anymore. It was her complete lack of any skill that was the culprit here. Not that she'd admit it out loud.

Sal folded himself nearly in half as he accepted the ball from his sister. "Thanks, Bug." Even as he ruffled the girl's hair, he was already lining up his shot. He squinted an eye. Bounced the ball once. Sent it soaring through the net with no apparent effort.

"Oh come on!" Xenia threw her hands in the air.

Bug scrunched up her face in concentration. One by one she folded chubby fingers until she arrived at a tally. "Six to nothin'." She held up her fingers as proof.

Xenia stuck out her tongue and got a torrent of giggles in return.

"Here." Sal offered her the ball. "No, hold it like this." He demonstrated, and Xenia attempted to copy his posture. He tilted his head. Nudged her elbow. "Better."

Despite her discomfort at Sal's proximity, Xenia found his single-minded focus on his beloved sport a relief. Of all the new faces she'd encountered in her move to Porter Valley, Salvatore alone didn't preface each conversation with "How are you doing?" Other than a single word of sympathy the day after she'd arrived, he'd never once brought up the events that had brought her here. That alone was worth the mild humiliation of losing so many games of HORSE.

Sal's brow furrowed as he circled her. "No." His tone was suddenly brusque, all business. "Your feet should be shoulder-width apart. Dominant foot six inches ahead. Bend your knees. Too much!" He bent his own skinny legs in demonstration.

Once he was satisfied with her posture, he turned his attention to the hoop and pointed. "See those three hooks in front? They're as far apart as the ball is wide, mostly. Don't aim for the backboard. Just try to send the ball over the hooks.

Xenia raised the ball and winced. Every now and then, her arm would send out a little reminder of the injury it had suffered.

Sal hurried around to her left side. "You don't need to bend your wrist for this. Use a light touch. Just steady the ball on your throwing hand." He pantomimed the motion. "That's it." Fingers at his chin, his eyes darted over her stance. "Upper arm parallel to the ground. Now, just let the ball roll off your fingertips."

From her seat on the curb, Bug thrust out both hands in a double thumbs-up.

Xenia took a slow inhale. Lobbed the ball on the exhale.

This time, the ball's arc carried it over the rim. On its rebound from the backboard, it juddered from the inner hoop. Xenia held her breath as the ball seemed to hover in place.

Momentum spent, the ball fell through the hoop.

Marisol's hands shot into the air. "Yay!" She jumped up and down and clapped her hands above her head.

"I did it!"

"Perfect three-pointer," Sal said. "See? Easy-peasy."

"Sure." Still, Xenia couldn't deny herself the crumb of satisfaction. Not that she'd be a draft pick any time soon, but at least she'd—

"Shit." She rubbed at her forehead. Rainbow light twisted in the corners of her vision. *Of course this happens now.* She waved off Sal's hand as she lowered herself to the curb beside Bug.

"Zeenie? Whas' wrong?" The girl was instantly in front of her. She planted a hand on each of Xenia's knees as she leaned in to examine her face with wide, worried eyes. Sal loomed over the both of them, his expression twin to his sister's. In that moment, the Serrano family resemblance was unmistakable.

Xenia sighed. "It's nothing, Bug. I hit my head." She pushed down the memory before it could trigger her tears. "See?" She tilted her head and brushed her fingers through her hair to expose the scar in her scalp. "This is where they patched me up."

"Gross!" The girl's face shone with disgusted delight.

"But I'm still healing, which means sometimes I get headaches." Neither of them, she decided, needed to know about the halos, or the hallucinations.

Sal winced. "Crap. This is my fault. I shouldn't have pushed you—"

"Please. This was going to happen today no matter what I did," Xenia snapped. She paused to force a calm she didn't feel into her expression, her voice. "I'm good," she lied. "They gave me pills for this. Clears it right up."

Marisol threw her arms around Xenia and gave her forehead a careful pat-pat. "Get better!"

"Thanks, Bug."

Sal lowered his gangly frame to the curb beside them. His eyes darted to her face, then away. Clearly uneasy with all this injury talk, he plucked at his Suns T-shirt.

Despite the imminent threat of migraine agony, Xenia smiled. Either Sal had a whole closet full of his favorite team's shirts, or he wore the same one almost every day. In an attempt to steer the topic away from her, she said, "You never told me why you guys moved here."

Sal favored her with a brief look of gratitude. "Pop got a promotion. KSI." He paused to see if she recognized the name. When she shook her head, he pressed on. "They opened a whole new division up here." He pointed off in a westerly direction. "Pop's in charge of his own team of software engineers now. He hasn't said what they're working on, though." He gnawed on his thumbnail.

"It's top secret!" Pride and awe shone in Bug's eyes.

"Phoenix, right?" asked Xenia. When the Serrano siblings nodded, she added, "Long drive."

"We drove *everywhere!*" Marisol mimed turning a steering wheel back and forth.

"Yeah, we did." Sal nodded. "We road-tripped all through Utah, a bit of Idaho and down into Oregon while the movers did their thing. Dad said we all needed a break, but I think it was mostly for him. This one"—he tousled Marisol's hair—"tried to keep every bug she found. Mom was, ah, less than pleased when she found her collection in the car." He laughed.

"Cay-ter Lake was so pretty!"

"Crater, Bug. It's Crater Lake."

Bug scowled at Sal. "That's what I said!" Her eyes shone as she turned to Xenia. "Poppa says we're goin' to Dinny-land this summer!"

Xenia pinched her cheeks. "You're going to love it." Images of her last theme park visit bubbled up. She and Beebs had gone on every ride twice, even though she'd gotten sick on Space Mountain.

She shivered as icy goosebumps danced across the back of her neck.

Across the street, Bethany's illusory form lounged atop the hood of Elspeth's station wagon. Their eyes met, and the hallucination waved enthusiastically.

Xenia ducked her head and squeezed her eyes shut. *I am not seeing this! Not today. Not now!*

"Zeenie?" Bug shook her knee.

Even as she drew breath to reassure the girl, the first slivers of broken glass sliced through the space behind her eyes. Her gasp of pain drew a whimper from the girl.

"Crap. Bug, get Mom. Xenia's—"

"I'm fine!" The throb of her growing migraine lent an edge to her words that she hadn't intended. "I'm fine," she echoed with less heat. "I just need my pills." She heaved herself to her feet and stumbled as the world lurched with the movement. Had it not been for Sal's hand on her arm, she would have tumbled to the pavement. She offered a mumbled thanks even as she pulled away.

She cracked an eye and found Bethany, fraught with worry, right beside her. She flinched away and nearly lost her balance again. Xenia waved off Sal's help. Eyes averted from the intrusive hallucination, from the colors that clung to every surface, Xenia focused on placing one foot in front of the other. As she crossed the street, she knew that Sal and Marisol were staring. She could feel their eyes on her as she braced herself against the station wagon. Not only did she have to endure another stupid migraine, it had to blindside her where her friends would see. Xenia pushed off from the car and maneuvered her way, half by touch, through the garden gate.

When she achieved the front door, she chanced a look back. Marisol clung to Sal's leg, her eyes wide and upset. Sal raised his hand and gave her a tentative wave. A host of questions lurked, unasked, on his face. The illusory Bethany stood at their side, hands a-flutter as if unsure what to do with them.

Xenia grimaced. Fumbled her way inside. Stumbled up the stairs to her room, and the pills that she knew would be no help at all.

Chapter Eleven

The following week passed without further incidence of phantom lights or hallucinatory visitors. Xenia's classes settled into a routine that she hoped might carry her through what remained of the semester. For once, her luck failed to desert her. The difference between her progress in LA and Porter Valley High's curriculum actually placed her a bit ahead of Mr. Druszcz's lessons. AP Calculus remained her most looked-forward-to class of the day, even if that lacrosse jerk, Everard, had to be there. For the most part, he was content to ignore her, and she him.

Despite the absence of the migraines and their blasted "halos," her nightmares continued. The nightly visitations left her exhausted, groggy, and prone to nodding off in class.

Xenia groaned as the first glimmers of daylight bored through her eyelids. She'd only just managed to drift off and it was morning already? She ground her palms against gritty eyes as she swung her legs over the edge of the mattress. At least it was Saturday. She had a whole day to—

"Oh come on!"

Her bedroom was awash in the false color of a migraine halo. So much for her weekend. Aunt Elspeth would be at her shop until eight, which meant she would have had the house to herself all day. Now, all she had to look forward to was a massive headache. "I swear to God, if I get another one tomorrow too..."

At least, and this was a very small favor indeed, there was no sign of her hallucinatory "friend" or any other phantom visitor.

Xenia glared at the gleaming ribbons of light. Her brain was really going the extra mile to ruin her day. Cables of radiance big around as her waist made a stately progression from floor to ceiling. Others, finer than spider silk, drifted on an unfelt breeze. All throughout that forest of radiance, motes of glittering light chased one other.

Every surface, every object in her room had come alive with phosphorescence. Glimmers of emerald churned beneath the rugose surface of the oak tree outside.

When she raised her hand, opaline fire blazed beneath the surface of her skin.

Xenia flopped onto the mattress with a groan. If the light show hadn't been a concerning symptom of whatever was wrong with her brain, she might have called it beautiful. Which, of course, only made the experience all the more annoying.

"I'm off, dearie," Elspeth called from the hallway. "Don't be a layabout all day, if you please. Go outside. Have yourself an adventure. I wouldn't mind at all if you were to drop in and see the shop."

"Okay."

"I've left sandwiches in the fridge. If you're feeling up to it, what would you say to a nice pizza this evening? Luigi's has the best crust in town."

"That's fine." Xenia bit down on what she'd nearly uttered. Aunt Elspeth didn't deserve to bear the brunt of her frustration. She had nothing to do with Xenia's ruined weekend, after all. "I won't stay in bed much longer," she lied.

"Toodles!" Elspeth's clogs clattered down the hall.

Xenia followed her great-aunt's progress down the creaky staircase. Out the front door. The garden gate clattered shut, and Xenia blew out a long breath. Now it was just her... and these stupid halo things.

"Whatever." Xenia fluffed her pillow and glowered at the impossible lights. At least she'd be in bed when the migraine clobbered her.

Some time later, the *thump thump bonk-thud* of Sal working his three-point game started up. Despite her dread, Xenia grinned. He'd spend most of the day on his obsession. The only time he'd stop would be when he allowed Bug to drag him away for one of her improvised games.

Nature made its inevitable demand. Afterward, eyes clenched tight against the possibility of unwanted visitations, she tottered to the pile of cushions in the window nook. She propped her head against the window sill and cracked one eye open.

Yep, the colors were still there.

Across the street, Sal hoisted the diminutive Marisol over his head. She squealed with glee as she dunked the ball. Just like her own hands, both Serranos glowed with an inner, opaline fire. Beautiful as the effect might be, the sight of her friends wreathed in flame was disconcerting. She turned her eyes to the sky above where, for once, blue had broken through the omnipresent cloud cover.

Ensconced in the cushioned nook, she dozed. The

comforting *thump* of Sal's basketball and Bug's laughter filled her ears.

She started awake as a gust of wind sent a shower of twigs and leaves pattering against the glass by her head. She drifted to her feet, unwilling to rouse herself from her reverie. Intent on her bed and the invitation of her pillows, she paused as another gust rattled the walls.

As if carried on that gust, a new band of radiance surged through her bedroom wall. The uncanny luminance rose and fell with the breeze; it was as if she could see the wind itself. The motion was mesmerizing, captivating. She knew she shouldn't allow her hallucinations such validation, but she was just so tired of fighting. At least it wasn't a nightmare.

Bed forgotten, Xenia returned to the window as the not-quite-blue light flowed over the treetops outside and poured itself down Bluff Street. The ancient oak tree beside the house moaned in the breeze.

A slip of wind-light, no more than a hand's breadth, flowed through the glass beside her. She leaned away and then chided herself. She batted the light away as another gust sent it toward her face.

The ribbon curled about her fingers, its illusory surface cold to the touch. Glowing wisps trailed her hand as she yanked it back.

Xenia flexed her fingers and stared at the current of light. Then, she turned to the streamers of light that filled her room and swung her arm in a slow arc. The ambient drifts of light slid away from her arm, flowed about it like water around a rock.

The wind came scudding once more down Bluff Street, and the same not-blue slipped through the glass. Xenia peered at the current as it flowed by. She had to congratulate her brain, damaged as it might be, for the layers of texture revealed within. Before the glowing mass could slip away, she reached for it.

Just as before, the surface was cold against the pad of her fingers. But this time, when she drew her hand back, a fragment came away with it. The thread, gossamer fine, wrapped itself about her index finger. The icy tingle became the sting of a frigid nettle.

Panic surged with the unexpected pain. Xenia flicked her hand to dislodge the scrap of light. "Get off!"

As the impossible fragment flew from her finger, it vanished like a droplet of water on a hot skillet.

Cold air surged across Xenia's face and swirled her hair about her head. Every magazine, every loose note and homework page on her desk flew into the air. A plastic tumbler sent its cargo of pens and pencils rolling across the desktop to clatter on the hardwood floor.

Xenia stared at the sudden mess. Combed fingers through the tangle of her hair. *What. The. Hell.*

On one hand, she knew for a fact that she'd had hallucinations. All these lights, the horror show of her first day at school, and Bethany. None of those could possibly have been real.

She rubbed her thumb across the residual sting in her fingertips. Stared at her desk. When she turned to the view beyond her windows, the sight of another glowing gust flowing over the treetops sped her heart into double time.

There was a screech from the roof as the wind vane spun in the wind. The walls rattled even as the current of wind light passed into Xenia's bedroom. Despite the nervous sweat springing up on her forehead, she held her ground.

On impulse, she cupped her hand through the current.

It burned as if she'd plunged her hand into an ice bath. A softball-sized mass of radiance came away in her grasp. Xenia gritted her teeth against the iced-electricity sizzle on her skin as she examined her catch. All throughout the mass, flecks and threads of light, each a variation of the overall hue, danced and swirled. She rotated the glob and found threads of light, looking for all the world like a glowing cheese-pull, trailing from her hand to the current she'd pulled it from.

She jumped as another gust, the fiercest yet, slammed into the old Victorian. The wind-light surged, and the delicate threads trailing from her hand swelled as they fed more of the impossible radiance into the mass she held. The softball became a grapefruit, then a basketball that enveloped her hand. She gasped as a dry ice burn sizzled into her skin.

The blob of light popped.

A wall of wind slammed Xenia across the room. Jagged, actinic fireworks exploded across her vision. The colors painting the air, both real and imagined, inverted for one stuttering heartbeat.

Xenia caromed from the corner post of her bed. Somehow, she kept her feet and staggered across the room as darkness crowded the edges of her vision. Acid fingers clawed at the inner curve of her skull. Her spine arched as the long muscles of her back spasmed. The room tilted, spun. Only the mass of cushions in the window nook saved her head from impacting the hardwood floor.

Bethany, her face twisted with panic, mouthing frantic, silent words, filled her vision. The hallucination grasped at Xenia's arms in a useless attempt to lift her. With a last, terrified look for her stricken friend, she flew straight through the wall.

Darkness dragged Xenia down within its embrace.

* * *

"Thank the Lord, she's coming around. Xenia, dearie, can you hear me?"

The drumbeat throb that filled Xenia's head differed from her usual headache. In contrast to the migraine's jagged glass and fire, her whole brain seemed to pulse against the curve of her skull. This was in no way an improvement.

Scared of what illusions might be waiting for her, she hesitated to open her eyes. When she finally cracked a lid, nothing but Aunt Elspeth's worried face was visible. The most vibrant thing in her view was her guardian's Roma-inspired dress. The floating lights and... *her*... were gone. *Oh thank God.*

Elspeth was perched on the very edge of the desk chair, which she'd dragged over to the bed. "How are you feeling?" She placed her hand on Xenia's brow for a moment.

Xenia worked her tongue around a mouth gone desert dry. "I'm... okay. I think. Ow." She winced as the throb in her skull almost made a liar out of her. She tried to sit, then abandoned the effort as the drumbeat in her skull redoubled its pace. "Head hurts."

"Oh Lord, that's not a good sign," Elspeth's brows furrowed. "Did you hit it when you fell?" Her gentle hands felt through Xenia's hair.

"No. I don't think so," Xenia said. The rasp of her voice mellowed as she spoke.

"Lad, would ye be so kind as to fetch us some ice?" In her day-to-day speech, Elspeth's brogue was little more than a hint. Now, with her concern for Xenia burning on her face, it was out in force. "Hall closet for the bag, ice in the icebox."

"Yes, Miss Findlay!" Sal, who Xenia hadn't noticed until that moment, thundered off at full gallop. Before she could wonder why he was here, he'd returned. An old-fashioned ice bag, its bladder gravid with ice and beaded with condensation, hung from one hand. In the other was a towel.

"Laddie, you're a peach," Elspeth said as she draped the towel across Xenia's forehead.

Xenia sighed as blessed relief spread from the cool contact. A fragment of the tension that had burrowed into her slipped away.

Sal, eyes wide with concern, resumed his hover in the doorway. Xenia experienced a moment of panic as she realized she was still in her PJs. Even though her quilt was up to her chin, she shrank beneath the covers.

Elspeth patted her shoulder. "You and I owe the lad a great deal of thanks. If he hadn't called me at the shop, who knows how long you would have lain there?" She waved at the spot where Xenia had collapsed.

"I saw it when you... I mean, through the window?" Sal's hands fluttered about each other, birds unsure of a safe roost. His eyes flicked from Xenia to Elspeth. "I wasn't spying. I mean, I just saw her"—his gaze went back to Xenia—"you, in the window. Bug asked if maybe you would come out so she could show you her new stuffed ladybug." His hand sketched out a wave, an echo of his attempt to catch Xenia's attention. "Then you just... fell down. Bent over all weird. It looked bad. Really bad. So I called Miss Findlay."

"I was ready to whisk you off to the ER, lassie." Elspeth took Xenia's wrist in her hands. "Your pulse was strong, and your breathing. I couldn't find an obvious injury, so when you started to snore..." Her smile was faint. "Well, here you are."

Another surge of embarrassment. "I'm sorry. I didn't mean to cause problems. Make you close the shop—"

Elspeth patted her arm. "Psh. The world can do without gewgaws for one day. You are my top priority, lassie." Elspeth blinked away some of the moisture rimming her eyes. "I think Xenia's out of danger, lad. Thank you for all the help."

Sal shifted his weight from foot to foot and plucked at the faded, flaming basketball on his shirt. "Uh, right. Anytime." He blinked. "I should go. Mom's got to be wondering what's up. She always has chores for me..." He took a step into the hall. "See you on Monday?"

"Sure," Xenia said. Then, on impulse, "See you out front." They'd begun to walk to school together, at least on days when Sal made it out in time. He was not the promptest of individuals.

A grin bloomed across his face. "Cool. Bye, Miss Find-lay." As soon as the thunder of his footsteps passed the front door, the *thud* of his basketball joined them.

"Lord, that boy has a one-track mind and it leads right to a hoop," said Elspeth, a wry crinkle in the corner of her eye. Her expression sobered as she faced Xenia. "Lassie, I hate to level accusations at you while you're still in bed, recovering..." She took a deep breath. "You haven't been mucking about in the sitting room cabinet, have you?" There was no anger in the woman's face, only concern.

"What?" The question had come out of nowhere. What did a cabinet have to do with her condition? *Oh, right.*

The morning after Xenia's arrival, her great-aunt had given her a tour of her new home. Elspeth had been overflowing with excitement as she shared her pride and joy. Xenia had given the tour little attention; her mind had been miles away in Los Angeles, stuck on all she'd left behind.

Elspeth, she semi-remembered, had asked her to stay clear of the towering wooden cabinet that graced one wall of the sitting room. Xenia had nodded her acceptance and hadn't spent a single thought on it since. "No, I've never touched it."

"I have a good reason behind each of my rules, however few they might be. I am well aware the first thing a teenager does when someone declares a thing to be off limits is to stick their nose straight in first chance they get." Elspeth's lip quirked.

"What? No—"

"This old lady has been around the block more than once." Elspeth rubbed the side of her nose and coughed. "Much more, truth be told. Tempting as that old cabinet might be, there are no great secrets I've hidden within." Elspeth blinked and looked away for a moment. "Keepsakes, for the most part. Memorabilia of a misspent youth. And... there might be one or two substances of a recreational nature. It's not that I partake all that often, mind. Leftovers, for the most part. Nothing I want sitting around with children in the house." She held up a hand to forestall Xenia's protest. "I know you've had a rough time of it, much rougher than anyone deserves. These things might sound like just the ticket to send your woes packing..."

What on earth was Aunt Elspeth talking about? Substances? Wait. *Drugs?* Aunt Elspeth did drugs? When? Xenia's head spun, and not from the headache. "I don't... do any of that stuff. I've never even had a beer." Back in LA, she'd known a few—okay, a lot of people—who smoked pot and took other things. She'd never seen the appeal of the foul-smelling stuff. Her eyes watered just thinking about it.

"Ah, lassie, I'm sorry." Elspeth pulled Xenia into a sideways hug. "I'm not casting aspersions on your character. I just wanted to assure myself that you were safe... and that I wasn't a horrible guardian who'd allowed the girl she was responsible for to tumble down the rabbit's hole." Tears swelled in her eyes, then spilled over. "When I got that phone call from Salvatore... When I saw you there on the floor..." She swallowed hard. "I thought I'd already lost you. Failed you, and your parents. How could I face myself? Your father was a fine lad, and I loved him dearly. Your mother as well, although I admit I didn't know her as well as I would have liked."

Xenia dabbed at her own leaking eyes with the towel on her head. "I'm not going anywhere, Aunt Elspeth." She snaked an arm around to return the hug. "I just got here. I'm just getting to know you."

"Ah, lassie—"

The gurgling snarl from Xenia's midsection drowned out whatever she'd been about to say. Both of them stared at the quilt covering the growl's source.

"A bit peckish, are we?" Elspeth glanced to the window, where the day's light was fading. "It's nearly dinner, and I believe someone slept clean through lunch."

"Breakfast too," Xenia added after another hungry growl from her stomach.

"Well!" Elspeth slapped her hands together and gave them a rub. "I'll fetch that sandwich for you, lassie. After, if you're in the mood, I'll give old Luigi a call. Do you believe you're up for a proper pizza pie?"

"Can we get mushrooms on half?"

"Consider it done! Back in a tick." Elspeth strode from the room in a swirl of flower-patterned fabric.

Xenia shifted the ice pack on her head as she sank into the pillows. *How much of that was real?* Passing out, that had been real enough. But the lights? The wind... stuff?

That had to have been her imagination, her injury at work. Right? She rolled her head toward her desk.

Everything, her homework, her notes, was how she'd left it the night before. All of her pencils and pens were in the tumbler where they belonged. The few magazines she had were piled at one corner.

Right. It had been all in her head.

Fantastic. She was completely bonkers. Just what she needed. Xenia knew that she had to tell Elspeth. Inform her that the head injury wasn't healing right. That the headaches were getting worse.

Her hand drifted to her neck. She looped her mother's necklace around her finger and rubbed the precious metal with her thumb.

Telling Elspeth meant she'd have to go back to the hospital. There'd be more tests. More needles. Hell, if it was as bad as she suspected, they'd make her stay. Lock her in one of those padded rooms.

"I know, Mom," she whispered to the necklace. "I have to say something." Xenia tucked the necklace beneath her pajama top as Elspeth's jaunty whistle echoed up the stairwell.

If it happens again, Xenia told herself, *then I'll tell Aunt Elspeth*. All of it, even the horrid thing she'd seen her first day in school. After all, her great-aunt didn't need more bad news piled onto her plate. Running her own store on Main Street was trouble enough without Xenia's mental issues.

She forced a smile as Elspeth wafted in, tray in hand.

Chapter Twelve

B ethany hurled herself through the front wall of Xenia's bedroom in a storm of frustration.

"Useless, useless, frickin' useless!" Bethany howled her ire at the evening sky.

The day's ordeal—Xenia's seizure, the agonizing wait until she'd at last awakened—had Bethany at her wits' end. Being a ghost meant she was unable to so much as call for help as her best friend lay, possibly dying, sprawled on the floor.

Xenia's seizure had been so sudden, so unexpected that Bethany was half-convinced it would finish what the accident started. If Xenia had died, would she have passed on to the great whatever, just as her parents had? The idea that Bethany would be stranded here, alone, for all of eternity, was worse than the worry for her friend's safety.

It's not that she wanted Xenia trapped in this non-life too. Hell no! It was just... the more time she spent in this one-sided solitude, the harder it became to maintain anything like a positive outlook. Being a fly on the wall while Xenia moved on, met new friends, and found her way, was not what anyone would call a fulfilling afterlife.

Bethany glared at the blanket of stars above and spat her rage at that uncaring sky. "Is this a punishment? Is this what Hell is?" The stars, which had become her surrogate for the uncaring force that trapped her here, said nothing. "What could I have possibly done to deserve this? Skipped my homework? Snuck a beer? *Fuck you!*" Incorporeality had even stolen the catharsis of a good scream. She couldn't even cry over her predicament.

At least Xenia was awake and well enough to wolf down a seriously impressive amount of pizza. In desperate need of a distraction, Bethany flung herself into the air. Maybe the single-screen theater on Main would have something new—

"You!" Bethany reversed course. "The hell are you doing here, you creep!" She slammed to a halt a foot above the sidewalk and glared at the only other ghost she'd yet seen. "I've been looking for your ass, dude. Scaring Xenia in front of everyone like that was a dick move. And now you have the balls to come here?"

The other ghost only stared at her from the creepy shadow where his eyes should have been. How he'd managed the *Grudge* look, while Bethany was unable to so much as change her outfit, was a mystery. *Maybe we're not the same kind of ghost?*

The dead boy's shoulders shook as he twisted away from her. His feet, she couldn't help but notice, were flat to the pavement, as if gravity still held him in its grasp. Only when she joined him on the ground did she notice he was taller than her. His head drooped, and he aimed that shadowed stare at his feet.

"Hey, I'm sorry. It's just... she's my best friend,"

Bethany said. "Lucas... you are Lucas, right? The one that teacher was worried about?"

His nod, when it came, was the barest inclination of his bowed head. His lips trembled, but he didn't speak.

She waved at herself. "I'm Bethany. I'd say 'nice to meet you,' but, y'know what with being dead and all..."

Lucas' face twisted into a mask of anguish.

So much for post-mortem humor. "So you're stuck here too, eh? I thought it was just me."

Lucas raised his head and fixed his attention on the old Victorian's second floor. When he opened his mouth, it revealed the same shadow that obscured his eyes. His lips moved but made no sound. He pawed at the air, fingers writhing in frustration. Again, he lowered his head.

She bent to make eye contact with the other ghost. "Serious question. Are you haunting my friend? Was that you in her room this morning? Did you poltergeist her? Knock her desk around? Did you give her that seizure?" She hadn't seen him in Xenia's room, but considering how little she understood of this ghost stuff, that didn't mean much.

His void gaze snapped to hers. Confusion twisted his face. The emotion was so vivid, so raw, that Bethany almost regretted the line of questioning. She pressed on.

"Why are you here, Lucas? Why Xenia?"

At the sound of her friend's name, Lucas again gazed toward the old Victorian. Again tried to speak, to shape words with a mouth that had lost the knack of it. He groped at the air as if he could wrest meaning from the night itself. Tremors racked his translucent form as his shoulders sagged in a dejected slump.

Bethany turned and followed his gaze to the eerie, beautiful glow of Xenia's aura visible through her bedroom window. "You see it too? Her glow?"

The boy's nod was nearly lost in the tremble of his body.

"How'd you die? If you don't mind me asking." Bethany indicated herself. "Car accident for me. Quick. I hardly felt a thing," she offered, in the spirit of sharing.

Lucas stumbled away and fell to his knees. He threw his head back, void mouth wide, and howled in silent despair. For the first time, Bethany noticed the scarlet crusting the spectral varsity jacket he wore.

Bethany fell back a step. "Oh, no." She'd assumed that, like her, there'd been an accident. Or, more likely, something that involved drinking and the phrase "hold my beer."

"Lucas, were..." She hesitated to say the word, as if speaking it aloud would make it real. "Were you murdered?"

Lucas cupped his face in pale hands. Nodded.

"I'm so sorry." Bethany knelt beside him and wished with all her heart that the simple comfort of an embrace hadn't been denied them both.

"Do you know who did it?" Silly question, perhaps. But she had to ask.

Lucas nodded, hesitated, shrugged once, then shook his head. His face rose from the cradle of his hands and, again, he turned his gaze toward Xenia's bedroom window.

"Okay, yeah, I get it. She glows. But—" Bethany stopped, thoughts whirling. "I thought that I could see it because I'd been assigned to haunt her."

Lucas tore his empty eyes from the old Victorian to favor her with a look of pure bewilderment.

"What? I don't know! Did you get instructions when you died? Sorry! Sorry," she added as his face twisted again. "Look, dude. Zee's been through a lot. Her folks died in the same accident that got me. Unlike us, they were lucky and went on to heaven or whatever." At least Bethany hoped they had. She'd seen no sign of Mr. and Mrs. Findlay after the accident. "We're dead. We're stuck here and it sucks. But we have all the time in the world to wait while she heals, gets her head straight. When she's ready, assuming she can see us then, you can ask for help. Until then, please leave my friend the fuck alone."

Lucas staggered to his feet, hands balled into useless fists. He took a step away from her. She was shocked to see him stumble at the curb. Dead as he was, ghost that he was, Lucas should have been free of the confines of matter and gravity. Why didn't he just float like she did?

The ghost boy staggered into the street and flung his arms wide, as if to encompass all of Porter Valley. His empty gaze darted this way and that. He pointed up the street, then ahead of him. His pale finger marked angle after angle of a compass only he could perceive. He sagged like a puppet cut from its strings. The sudden fit had ended as abruptly as it had begun. Her turned, the movement halting and unsure, to face Bethany.

What had that lady—Mrs. Wedgwood?—said to Zee's class? She chased the thought, racked her memory of the moments before Lucas first appeared. *With all that's been going on, we just want a safe homecoming for Lucas—*

Bethany's eyes flew wide. "Holy shit! You're not the only one, are you? The person who murdered you... They've killed others?"

Relief crashed across Lucas's face. He nodded. The fingers of both hands knotted in a gesture she couldn't interpret. He stared at his fingers, brow lowered above the shadow of his eyes. His hands dropped. The void of his gaze bored into her.

"It's not going to end with you, is it?"

Lucas shook his head.

Horror blindsided her. Bethany spun toward the old Victorian. "No!"

Elspeth Findlay had brought Xenia into her home believing that it would be a refuge from the trauma that had upended the girl's life. A safe place in which to raise the great-niece who was now her responsibility.

Instead, she'd brought Xenia to the heart of danger. The hunting ground of a serial killer only the dead knew of.

The decision was no decision at all. "Okay. Here's what we're going to do. You"—Bethany aimed a finger at the other ghost—"are not going to bother Xenia again. Got it?" She charged on before he could object. "In return, I'm going to help. You and everyone else who got killed."

Lucas stared at her.

"Yeah, yeah, I'm as dead as you are. No one can see us. Blah, blah. Here's the thing, Xenia can see me! Us. Sometimes. You and me, we're going to find the others." Bethany paused. If Lucas's speech impediment was related to the manner of his death, the others might be similarly afflicted.

Which meant her plan to press them for details about their deaths just got a lot more difficult.

"We'll get the facts from all of the other victims. Put a name and a face to your killer." *Bethany Brooks, Ghost Detective!* Despite the gravity of the situation, she rather liked the sound of that. "Once Xenia's ready to handle the truth, when we have the whole story... That's when I'll tell her. Zee trusts me." *At least, she used to.* Lucas, she decided, didn't need to know that her best friend in the world was bound and determined to ignore her entirely. One problem at a time.

The expression creeping across his face suggested that she, in his opinion, had gone totally bonkers.

Fair. She probably had.

Bethany held out her hand. "Come on, show me the scene of the crime." *Chill with the detective lingo, girl.* "If you can remember it, I mean. I know dying is traumatic—"

Naked dread shone in Lucas' face. A paroxysm of terror rattled his narrow shoulders. Clearly, the memory was harrowing. Bethany's phantom heart went out to the boy, truly it did. But she had a purpose now, one so much more concrete than merely "haunting" her best friend.

"It'll be okay, I promise. After all, we're dead. The worst has already happened."

Lucas gave the old Victorian a long, desperate look. His shoulders heaved in a great sigh, and then he nodded his assent. He turned away and began to plod down the very center of the street. His gait was no more than a shuffle, as if all the weight of the world lay upon his shoulders.

Puzzled, Bethany drifted to his side. "Can't you float? It'd be quicker."

Lucas kept his gaze fixed on the road ahead. Limped on without answering.

"Oh." Perhaps, Bethany thought, his death had stolen more than his voice. She fell into step beside the poor, damaged soul.

Side by side, the two dead teenagers made their way through the sleeping town, toward the place where Lucas had been murdered.

* * *

She'd been certain the creepy old house would be the place. Situated on a prominence overlooking Riverside Park, the decrepit mansion, with its boarded windows, clinging vines, and general air of abandonment, would have been the perfect venue for a murder mystery.

Lucas hadn't so much as paused as he led her past it.

She gave the emblem wrought into the gate a final, lingering glance. There had been another letter in the monogram beside the ornate "S," but vandals had long since marred it beyond legibility. *Get serious, Brooks, this isn't one of your movies.* Still, she promised herself, when all of this was over she and Zee would explore the old mansion.

When the ghost boy exited the well-lit avenues of Porter Valley and continued along one of the many hiking paths, Bethany excused herself and sent herself into the air with a mind to get her bearings.

From her bird's-eye view, she traced their path. From Riverside Park, past Main, all the way to the Xenia's house on Bluff Street. Below her, Lucas' shamble looked as it would lead away from the Eel River and into a narrow declivity. A bright little creek, an offshoot of the river, burbled alongside the trail Lucas now followed. As he ventured further into the gap, it fell away to either side, becoming a proper canyon. From her altitude, it looked for all the world as if a giant had gouged a trench into the floor of Porter Valley with a massive trowel. Fortified with a general sense of their location, she rejoined Lucas.

Their journey had carried them well past midnight into the wee hours of the morning by the time Lucas finally came to a stumbled halt. He lifted a shaking hand to point.

"We're here?"

He gave her a tiny nod. She was surprised to find that, while she was airborne, the shadows that obscured his face had cleared. Now, he regarded her with a pair of ordinary, if melancholy, brown eyes.

Actually, now that she was actually paying attention,

she realized that much of his bleached appearance had changed. The bright blue and white of his jacket glowed in the light of the moon, and his skin had lost the pallor of death. He'd even lost most of the spectral transparency they shared. She could hardly see the trees through him at all.

Just ahead, the trail ended in a T-intersection. A pair of wooden benches had been installed beside the chuckling creek, just where a weary hiker would want to rest aching feet. Beyond the low chain that marked the trail's end, the stream flowed on, gurgling merrily about a cluster of massive boulders left, no doubt, by the passage of some ancient glacier.

As Bethany made to approach the nearest of the giant stones, Lucas thrust his arm across her path. She didn't want to be rude, didn't like the idea of just passing through the way the living had passed through her, so she stopped.

Lucas shook his head. The gesture was emphatic, nearly violent. His eyes, bright in the moonlight, were haunted.

"You don't want me to see."

He opened his mouth and, when his voice failed him yet again, settled for another shake of his head.

"It's okay. There's nothing to be afraid of. You don't have to..." Bethany trailed off. The fear in his eyes wasn't for him, she realized, it was for her. "Don't worry. I'll be fine. I can handle it, I'm dead too. Remember?" She chose not to share her love for gory slasher movies, which she assumed would inure her to whatever crime scene they were about to view. She held out her hand. They might not be able to touch, but it was the thought, she hoped, that counted.

Something close to a smile, vanishingly brief, flitted across Lucas's lips. He placed his hand in hers. For an instant, the barest fraction of a second, there was a brush of contact. A gossamer caress upon the palm of her hand. A hint of warmth, no more.

Then it was gone.

Before she could speak, before she could ask if he'd felt it, Lucas stepped across trail's boundary. As his foot made contact with the ground, he flickered and vanished. A moment later, he reappeared, just to the left of where he'd been. He'd lost the forlorn, hollow expression he'd worn since she'd first laid eyes on him. Now, he appeared to not have a care in the world. His face was alight with surprise and wonder. He was even brighter, somehow. As if a single ray of the noonday sun had found him here in the dark of the canyon.

Lucas laughed and shouted, "Wait!" Without so much as a look to see if Bethany had followed, he jogged down a narrow track beaten into the brush beside the stream.

"Crap." Bethany, taken off guard by the sudden change, hurried in pursuit. She caught up with him at the very end of the canyon. Here, the burbling waters of the stream vanished into a hole at the base of the towering stone wall. She eyeballed the shattered rock, the extensive cracks and fissures that radiated from the cavern entrance, and hoped that Lucas hadn't fallen in there.

To her guilty relief, he took a sharp detour between the trees and the crag of the canyon wall. Bethany gasped in delight as they broke through the tree line into a wide, open meadow. Here and there wildflowers, vibrant even in moonlight, rose above the knee-high grass.

"You were right. This is amazing!" Lucas said, his voice filled with awe. He spun in a circle, eyes wide as if drinking in the view for the first time.

"Lucas, who are you talking to?" Bethany floated into his line of sight. When he failed to react, she waved a hand before his eyes. This, too, received no response. Instead, Lucas laughed and ran through her into glade.

When she caught up, Lucas held his arm before him, fingers canted as if to interweave with another's. The fabric of his sleeve rippled under the touch of an unseen hand.

Understanding dawned. She knew what was happening, now.

By returning here, the site of his murder, Lucas would now relive the events of his death. This was what he'd hoped to spare her.

Bethany wondered, just for a moment, if she, too would be forced through the same ordeal, should she return to that intersection in Los Angeles.

"I can do this," she muttered. "I can do this for him. I need to do this." She assumed that, when the time came, it would happen fast. A gunshot. Or a knife. Lucas had been sturdy, athletic. In a straight-up fight, he'd have stood a decent chance. *Eyes peeled for clues, Ghost Detective!* She would be the witness that Lucas, and the others she had yet to meet, required.

Lucas laughed again. He turned, suddenly bashful. Blushed. "You think so?" The memory of his companion's hand on his pulled him close. The folds of his jacket ruffled, one half of a hug. "I... I think you're cool too." He snorted. "That sounded lame. Seriously, I really like you." His arms rose to embrace the air.

"Say their name, Lucas," urged Bethany. "Give me something to work with." As embarrassing as it might be to watch such an intimate moment, it might be the only opportunity for him to use the voice that had been stolen from him.

She couldn't bear the thought that she might have to ask him to relive this again. If he didn't name his companion, his killer, right now, learning their identity would be next to impossible. Without knowing if Lucas had been straight or gay, or bi, his date might have been anyone. Well, anyone at Porter Valley High, she thought.

Teenage Serial Killer would make one hell of a documentary, once she and Zee cracked the case. Assuming her friend managed to process her trauma and finally admitted that she could see ghosts, that is.

Lucas, eyes half closed, lips pursed, leaned into his companion. The kiss ended before it could begin as he flung up an arm. The fabric of his sleeve burst open on a gout of crimson. "Oh God, no!" Terror turned the boy's voice into a hoarse croak, made a mockery of the budding desire that had filled it only a heartbeat earlier.

Bethany was determined not to miss a single detail. She pushed as close as she dared. The angle of the wound... Had the attack come from Lucas's date, or from a newcomer? She couldn't tell.

White shone all around his eyes as Lucas stumbled away. His gaze seemed as if it tracked a falling object. His date's body? Had they been struck from his arms by that first, bloody blow? Who else was missing?

Lucas tripped over his own feet and went down hard in the tall grass. He surged upright. Hurled himself across the glade. Ran, desperately, for the unlikely shelter of the tree line.

He never made it.

Bethany, in her mental preparation for what she knew must occur, had assumed she'd see the crimson bloom of a gunshot. The narrow track of a stab wound.

The blow, when it came, was so much worse than anything she'd seen in her beloved horror movies.

The fabric of his jeans, and the calves beneath were laid

open to the bone in a single strike. Lucas tumbled headlong to ground. He shrieked, his voice cracking. He scrabbled at the damp soil, desperate for purchase. Fear sweat plastered his short hair to his scalp. He managed to drag himself only a handful of feet farther. His blood left a trail of scarlet in his wake.

"Lucas, stop!" Bethany fell beside the tormented boy and waved for his attention. "It's enough! You don't have to go through this again. I don't need to see it. Please stop!" He'd already died once. There was no need for him to suffer all over again, just to indulge her detective fantasy.

Oblivious to her cry, trapped within his terminal moments, Lucas screamed himself hoarse as the fabric of his jacket bunched in an unseen hand. He rose, suspended from that grasp, until his feet dangled above the grass. He kicked at his assailant and only succeeded in dislodging his shoe.

The killer, Bethany noted, unable to tear her eyes away, *must be enormous.*

Lucas, weak from blood loss, batted at the arm holding him aloft. His movements had already grown sluggish. Sobbing, he begged for his life.

His scream rose to an anguished mewl as his belly bloomed scarlet. A gutter of red incised itself from navel to sternum. His head lolled on a neck gone slack. He sagged as his hands lost their grip upon his killer's arm. The coil of his intestines, dark with blood and worse, boiled to the ground below.

The invisible grip released him, and Lucas collapsed in a heap beside his insides. His eyes, so bright with joy and hope a moment ago, were dull marbles in their sockets.

Lucas was dead. Again.

At least now, she thought, it was over.

It wasn't over.

Fear, bright and hot, unlike any emotion she'd felt since her death seized her, rooting her in place as the memory played on. *I don't understand. He's dead. What more could there be?*

The unseen killer heaved Lucas onto his back. The flesh above his breastbone dimpled, then tore. Bone gleamed yellow-white in the light of that remembered sun before it shattered under an immense blow. The wings of his rib cage, gripped by the same force, splayed wide. The hideous wet *crack* was like nothing Bethany had ever heard.

I don't want to see this anymore. Make it stop. Please make it stop! Pinioned by dread, captured by her promise to help, Bethany was helpless to look away. She would witness the entirety of Lucas's death, whether she wanted to or not.

A gob of flesh rose from the ruin of the boy's chest. *Is that his heart?* Bit by bit, bite by bite, the vital organ disappeared from view as the killer devoured it.

But Lucas is dead? How can he remember this? She could remember everything right to the exact moment of her death, but after? Bethany recalled nothing at all until she'd come to in the morgue.

The killer, whoever... or whatever it was, continued to fish morsel after obscene morsel from the basket of the dead boy's innards. Each was consumed, just as his heart had been. His eyes, she noted as dispassionately as she could manage, were extracted with great care before they, too, were devoured.

A new dread wormed its way into her thoughts. *What if it didn't just eat his organs, his flesh. It ate* him. *Or parts of him, parts of his soul. That's why he remembers this. No wonder this is all burned into his memory.* The concept that the soul was real had come as a bit of a shock to her. This proof that the essence of a human being might be not be as inviolate as her Mama's beloved scripture had promised, that it was vulnerable to such predation... This was a violation beyond than anything so tritc as murder.

Was she still vulnerable? Or did the killer require a fresh kill? Must they eat the flesh to partake of the soul it craved? Bethany had no way to know, and no desire to test the thought.

After far, far too long, the foul banquet came to an end. Lucas was seized by the ankle. Dragged back along the path he had fled.

Toward the rift in the canyon wall. Where the creek's waters vanished into darkness.

"No wonder your body hasn't been found," Bethany said with forced calm. If the killer had thrown him into that cavern, it was unlikely he would ever be.

At the edge of the meadow, his body crossed some unseen spiritual marker. Lucas vanished.

"Lucas?" Bethany rose above the clearing. Below her, the grass once again stood tall. No mark remained of the events that had transpired out of the boy's memory. "Lucas!" Bethany was unable to keep an edge of hysteria from her voice. "It's over, okay? You don't have to come here, ever again!"

The only answer she received was the whisper of the wind through the trees, the burble of the creek making its merry way into its terminal fissure. Of Lucas, she could find no sign whatsoever.

He was gone.

Chapter Thirteen

Xenia settled in beside her book bag on her usual bench. Most mornings, she and Sal walked to school together. But now that the basketball team was back in session, she was on her own for the walk home. Which, in all honesty, was fine with her. More often than not she'd while away the afternoon, just watching the water go by.

She hadn't caught on to it. Not at first. Now, however, it was obvious even to her that the lanky teen was hoping that they would be "more than friends."

Xenia wasn't sure how to feel about that. It was nice to have a friend, someone to talk to, again. And she was grateful, absolutely, for his help when she'd had that seizure. But dating? That was a lot to process. If Bethany were here, Xenia knew, her hints would be not-at-all-subtle that Xenia should go for it.

Honestly, she wasn't ready. The accident was still fresh, still raw, in her heart. Also, she just didn't see him that way. Or anyone, really. She needed a friend right now, not a date.

"Pumpkin, you're just a late bloomer," her father had

told her, not long before the accident. She'd been in a mood, having just found out that Bethany had a date for the winter formal. Xenia had made big plans for a girls' night sleep-over. Since she had no interest in the event, she'd assumed that her BFFFF wouldn't either. "There is no shame in being yourself," Dad had gone on, scooping out two bowls of emotional support ice cream. "Proceed at your own pace and don't let what others think, or want, push you into something you're not ready for." Now, when she needed him more than ever, he was gone. Everyone she needed was gone. She had no idea what the hell her "pace" was.

"Bah." Xenia kicked a pebble and watched it skitter into the rocks by the river's edge. Stared at the clouds that caught like cotton balls in the trees high above the river. Ignored the shouts of the children playing in the park behind her. Ignored, as well, the all-too-familiar sting of tears.

Her midsection bumped that train of thought from its inevitable, gloomy, track with another earthquaking growl. Ever since her "fainting spell," her appetite had been off the charts. Elspeth, of course, had been pleased as punch. Now her cooking would receive the attention it warranted.

Xenia rooted about in her book bag for something to snack on.

"That's pretty."

A boy of about ten, a picnic party escapee no doubt, stood on the gravel path before her. His open, round face was framed by a mass of black, shoulder-length hair. His eyes, as dark as his hair, crinkled with mischief. He wore a simple black T-shirt, torn black jeans, and black-and-white high-top sneakers. The breeze blew strands of his hair across his wide smile, and he tried, and failed, to push it back behind his ears.

"What?" asked Xenia. The boy pointed. She followed the line of his finger to the open neck of her hoodie. There, her mother's necklace gleamed in the wan sunlight. She brushed a finger along the chain before slipping it out of sight beneath her shirt. "Thanks. It was my mother's. She never took it off. So, now I won't either."

The boy nodded, expression sober, as if he understood completely.

Xenia twisted to search for any sign of the kid's parents. A multi-family affair, consisting of a handful of adults and three times as many children, overflowed the picnic area. The flock of kids, all the same age as the boy or younger, milled about the trio of grown-ups laboring to inflate a bounce house.

The kite flyer, who had been in the park every time Xenia had come by, and who so far had never flown the same kite twice, scowled at the shrieking horde of rug rats. He shook his head and began to wind in the cord of his box kite.

"You going to get in trouble, wandering away like this?"

An impish grin split the boy's face ear-to-ear . He clambered onto the bench beside her. "Probably!" He plunked his butt onto the wood and then fussed with his T-shirt for a moment. Assured that his belly button wasn't showing, he added, "Father says I am a natural-born troublemaker." His eyes, without a hint of shame, locked on to the food in Xenia's hand.

"I bet." Despite her dour mood, she found the kid's grin endearing. Another glance at the party confirmed his absence had yet to cause a panic. Two men at the barbecue high-fived as their efforts produced a tall column of greasy flame. She glanced at the snack she'd rescued from her book bag. "Tell you what, I'll split this with you. It's a fern cake.

My great-aunt makes a ton of them and, honestly, they're addictive as heck."

The boy, eyes saucer wide, nodded.

Xenia laid her thumbs along the fern pattern in the icing and did her best to break the tart into equal halves. The flaky crust was just up to the task of preventing a cascade of raspberry jam and frosting from spilling over her hands. She deposited one gooey half in the boy's cupped hands and licked jam from her fingers.

The boy crammed the entire bit into his mouth in one go. Cheeks puffed like a chipmunk's, he beamed at her. "I wuff theeth things," the boy declared in a spray of moist crumbs.

"Told ya," Xenia said between bites of her half.

The boy licked frosting from the palm of his hand, then let fly with a belch that would have been impressive from a grown man. Satisfied, he sagged against the bench. His eyes flicked her way. "You should be careful with that."

Xenia tugged the sleeve of her hoodie over her cast. "Yeah. It's still painful if I try to lift something too heavy. I have a doctor visit Thursday. If I'm lucky, it'll be off in a couple weeks." She wiggled her fingers. "We'll see."

"No," said the boy. He raised a sticky finger, aimed it at her collar. "I meant that. Something special like that, I'd be super careful not to lose it." He caught her eye and held it long enough to be awkward.

Xenia looked away. "I know." Her fingers drifted to her shirt and pressed the precious metal into the skin over her collarbone.

"Do you?"

Before Xenia could think of a reply, the boy launched himself from the bench. Without so much as a wave, he raced toward the picnic. One of the women caught him by the arm. He submitted to having his face dabbed at, fidgeting all the while. She spoke to him, and the boy laughed in reply. The woman stood, her hand tight about his arm, and called to the other adults at the picnic. A wave of shrugs and head shakes circled the table. The boy tugged free and, as the woman shook her head, ran to the fully inflated bounce house. His shriek of laughter was audible across the entire park as he launched himself into the buoyant fray.

Xenia turned back to the river. She glared at the stone wall on the far side, dared the granite to show even a hint of that false, inner light, defied the air to come alive with rainbow streamers.

Nothing. Not even a glimmer.

Satisfied, Xenia slung her bag over her shoulder and made for home.

* * *

"Zeenie? You seen Sal?"

Xenia paused, hand on the garden gate. Marisol stood at the very edge of the sidewalk across the street, Sal's battered basketball clutched to her chest. "What? Not since this morning. Isn't he back from practice?" She'd taken a circuitous route, much longer than her usual. Sal should have beaten her home. Even though he'd spent the afternoon at practice, he should be in his driveway, shooting hoops by now.

Bug eschewed her usual caution and, to Xenia's dismay, ran straight across the street without looking. She stumbled to a halt in front of Xenia, where she continued to vibrate with fraught energy. Wide brown eyes begged Xenia to produce her brother.

Overhead, the streetlight flickered to life.

"Halloooo!" Elspeth's call drifted from the end of the block. When the two girls turned her way, she gave a cheerful wave.

If Aunt Elspeth had already closed Bits 'n' Pieces for the day, then it was even later than Xenia had thought. She scooped the ball from Marisol and took her by the hand. With more care than the girl had shown, they crossed the street and hurried to meet Elspeth.

"Did you see Sal back there? He wasn't hanging out on Main with the basketball team, was he?" Xenia nodded to the girl beside her. "Bug says he hasn't come home. He's should be back by now."

Elspeth's eyebrows rose. "That does seem a bit out of character for the lad, doesn't it?" She'd known Sal much longer than Xenia and had to be familiar with his habits. "He made it to class, didn't he?"

"Yeah, we walked in together..."

For once, the knowing expression was absent from Elspeth's face. The two of them looked to Marisol, at a loss for words. Bug's face scrunched in misery. A fountain of tears followed. She yanked the basketball from Xenia and threw herself headlong toward home. "Sal! Saaaaalll! *Mama!*" The girl vanished through the wide-open front door of the Serrano home, wailing every step of the way.

Elspeth squeezed Xenia's shoulder. "The lad has himself a cell phone, I'm sure?"

"Yeah," Xenia answered. Sal had given her his number the day after she'd moved in, although she'd never called. Her phone had been lost in the crash. Acquiring a replacement hadn't been all that high on her list of priorities.

"Let us go be good neighbors, lassie." Elspeth's hand on her shoulder ushered her, gently, in Marisol's wake.

* * *

Later, much later, Xenia lay in bed. Her dread over her usual nightmares was absent. There was no space for it now, thanks to the fresh, new anxiety that seethed within her.

She and Elspeth had spent the evening with the Serranos. Xenia had done her best to distract a frantic Marisol, attempted to coax her into sharing her favorite games, her favorite toys. All to limited success. Elspeth, meanwhile, had assisted the adult Serranos in calling every number they could think of in a desperate search for their son.

Xenia had been sure, so sure, that any moment, Sal would come barreling through the front door, full of apologies and embarrassed over all the trouble he'd caused. She'd been able to picture the sheepish grin on his face so clearly.

She'd been wrong. Sal hadn't come home.

Xenia had begun, at long last, to drift off when the slam of car doors jolted her awake. She padded to the window just as a pair of uniformed policemen knocked on the Serranos' door. A cruiser, its light bar painting the night in alternating shades of crimson and cobalt, was parked across the end of their driveway.

A haggard Marcelo Serrano, Sal and Bug's father, appeared in the doorway. He dragged a hand across his face before inviting the officers inside.

Xenia went to her desk and rolled the chair to the window. There she sat, wrapped in a quilt, in vigil for her friend's safe return. Only when slumber crept in like a sneak thief did she finally sleep.

Her dreams, when they came, were less of shattering glass and twisting metal than they were of rich barley fields and wide groves of date palms that grew under a distant, ancient sun.

Chapter Fourteen

Xenia winced as the speaker mounted in the ceiling crackled to life and the squeal of feedback set her molars aching. A moment later, the hellish noise resolved into the voice of the vice principal, Mrs. Wedgwood.

"...assembly will begin in ten minutes. Attendance for all grades is mandatory. Students, please begin to make your way to the auditorium. That will be all." A crackle of static punctuated the end of her statement.

Mr. Druszcz turned his eyes to the heavens above and muttered in a language Xenia didn't recognize. "You heard your vice principal, ladies and gentlemen." He capped his marker and thrust it into his breast pocket. "Out with you." He made little shooing motions with his hands.

As Xenia packed her textbooks, Madison and Gracie wasted no time in their dash to beat the mad scramble. Ev sauntered from his usual seat by the window and shot Mr. Druszcz a lazy salute as he exited the classroom.

Once she was reasonably certain she'd avoided the

worst of the hallway crush, Xenia made her own way to the auditorium.

Back in LA, budget cuts, misappropriated funds, and an overabundance of students meant that her school had no choice but to hold assemblies such as this in shifts in the school's tiny gymnasium.

By contrast, PVHS boasted an auditorium that was a full-fledged theater in all but name. Some long-forgotten alumni had sprung for the works. Not only did the building have ample seating for the entire student body, it contained a full theatrical stage, complete with orchestra pit—facilities the school put to good use, as the stage was still dressed from a recent production of *Le Miz*.

Uninterested in the assembly, intent on resuming her interrupted calculus lesson, Xenia avoided the front rows. She had her mind set on the cheap seats.

An unwelcome icy prickle at the back of her neck sent her heart scurrying in double time. *Not now!* The last thing she needed was another hallucination, much less a panic attack, in front of a literal audience. Maybe it wouldn't be too bad—

Xenia sighed. The same old phantom of Bethany hung in the air above the upper rows. The hallucination waved and, before Xenia could avert her eyes, pointed out a seat. Her migraine halo joined the party as rainbow streamers wriggled into existence all about the illusion. *Damn it!*

Xenia knew the figure wasn't real. Still, there was no way she was going to sit next to it. Now she'd have to settle for being crammed in the middle with the other students. Dang it.

With her eyes averted from the various figments of her broken mind, Xenia failed to notice the foot. Her shin caught and she pinwheeled her arms in a desperate bid for balance. The drag of her book bag against her shoulder threatened to send her butt-first down the stairs.

Strong hands arrested her tumble before it could begin. "Dick move, Mads," said Maia. The runner stood an inch taller than Xenia, even though she was two steps lower.

In Xenia's distorted vision, Maia seethed with azure and opal fire. Xenia found herself blinking away the afterimage, even though the radiance was all in her head.

Maia's hands lingered until Xenia found her balance. Xenia was surprised at the heat of her touch. Almost as if the impossible fire she'd imagined actually burned within the other girl.

Maia scowled at Madison. "The fuck is wrong with you, Mads? You could have really hurt her!"

Madison fluttered her lashes and pursed her lips in a little moue. "Oh darling, I couldn't resist," she addressed Xenia. "You were wide open. Too easy."

The halo, Xenia saw with some dismay, had only grown in strength. Even as she withdrew her foot from the aisle, Madison seemed burned with opaline fire. The flame within the girl flickered, seemed to be on the verge of going out, which gave Xenia hope that the halo was already passing. That hope was short lived, however, as the flickered faded into a stead, annoying glow. Gracie, and the rest of the student audience, all shone with their own, inner fire. She dropped her eyes to the floor, the least glowy thing in her line of sight.

Gracie jammed an elbow into Madison's side. "Maia's right, Mads. That was too much, even for a prank. What if New Girl had fallen? Her arm's still in a cast, for Christ's sake!" She sniffed and then mouthed "sorry" at Xenia.

Madison aimed a glare at her friend, then at Maia. She

crossed her arms, sank low in her seat, and stared ahead defiantly, muttering, "No one can take a joke anymore."

Maia let loose an exasperated burst of air. She eased by Xenia. "Come on, you can sit with me."

Still dizzy from the near fall, Xenia kept her eyes glued to the steps at her feet and trailed Maia to the theater's topmost row.

"Sorry about that." Maia dropped into a middle seat. "No idea what crawled up Madison's butt and died. She used to be cool." She pulled a dog-eared book, *The Whale Rider*, from the backpack at her feet. She flipped through, then stuck her nose in the pages.

Even though they had the entire row to themselves, Xenia was unsure which seat to take. Maia had said to sit with her... did that mean she should take a seat right next to her? If she sat too many places over, would Maia take that as an insult?

Xenia split the difference between Maia's invitation and her own desire for solitude. She sat one seat over.

On the stage below, Mrs. Wedgwood strode to the center and tapped on the microphone. She regarded the student body amassed before her through bottle-thick lenses. Her expression was grave, indecipherable. "May I have your attention, please."

The student audience, if anything, grew even rowdier. A paper airplane drifted several rows before arrowing into a girl's ear. "Ow!"

"*Quiet!*" bellowed the gym teacher, Coach Fairfax. "*The adults are speaking!*" Even without the aid of the sound system, his voice cut through the chatter. One by one, the conversations dwindled away until silence ruled the theater. Following Maia's example, Xenia dug for her calculus textbook.

"Thank you." Mrs. Wedgwood nodded to the coach. "I am sorry to disrupt your day's lessons, students. I assure you that I would not have done so if it were not a matter of utmost importance."

"That's what she said about those yo-yo guys," quipped the senior slouched two rows below Xenia. Laughter rippled outward.

"Our guest today is one of Porter Valley's finest. He's here with an important message for all of you." The vice principal gestured to one of the men clustered at the stage's edge. "Captain Strauss?"

As the uniformed officer's boots clumped across the polished wood, someone in the audience oinked *sotto voce*. The police captain, who was shorter than Mrs. Wedgwood by a head, ignored the barb. The skin of his face and bald head were so ruddy that, if it weren't for his tan uniform to mellow the effect, he would have resembled a walking fire plug.

Captain Strauss plucked the microphone from its stand and gave the vice principal a sharp nod. "I am Captain Phillip Strauss of the Porter Valley Police Department. I am here to talk about a very serious issue that plagues our fair city. I am, of course, referring to the rash of copycat runaways that we have experienced over the last eight months."

Wait. Xenia looked up from her reading. *Is this because of Sal?* The phantom colors had faded while she read. Whatever satisfaction she might have had about that was dampened by her concern over her missing friend.

"I assure you, there is nothing more sinister at work here than a handful of troubled kids trying to get away from their problems, real or imagined. Not to mention the copycats who use the absence of their friends as an excuse to run off and party without supervision." The curl of his lip betrayed his exact opinion of parties, and those who took part in them. He tugged a leather notebook from his breast pocket and flipped it open with a practiced flick of the wrist. "Right from the beginning of the fall semester, when Douglass Miller failed to show for class—"

"He's catching waves in Australia, dude," chortled a voice from the middle row. More laughter followed.

"Be that as it may," Strauss plowed on, "thanks to that stunt, other teens have followed the Miller boy's example." He squinted at the notebook. "Aubrey Foster, Joseph Kaur, Trevor K...Kaujawski"—he stumbled on the surname— "Lucas Shepherd, and most recently, Salvatore Serrano have all seen fit to take leave of their classes. Not to mention causing their families no end of worry."

Sal's name sent a shivering wave of goosebumps across her arms. *Sal ran away? Why would he do that? Did he get cut from the basketball team? Why wouldn't he tell me?* As new as their friendship might be, the thought that Sal had chosen not to confide in her jabbed at Xenia's heart.

A figure in black ruffles and lace chose the seat beside hers, opposite of Maia.

Xenia ground her teeth. The colors, the halos were gone. Why was the hallucination lingering? *Fine, let's get this over with!* She whipped her head around. Glared daggers at the illusion of her dead friend.

Bethany's eyes, still graced with the winged eyeliner she'd worn the night she died, were focused on the presentation below. After a moment she seemed to grow aware of Xenia's attention. She turned and, seeing that Xenia was looking right at her, gave her a tiny smile. She spoke, but no sound emerged from the image.

Xenia mouthed, *What? What do you want from me?*

The last thing she needed was a repeat of her first day's inaugural humiliation.

Joy bloomed across the hallucination's face. Her voiceless lips shaped something that might have been, "I knew you could see me!" The torrent of words that followed were unintelligible to Xenia's poor lip-reading skills.

Xenia rolled her eyes, tapped her ear, and shook her head. She knew it was a bad idea to validate the hallucination. But at that moment, Elspeth could slap her in a straitjacket for all she cared.

Visibly frustrated, Bethany turned her eyes to the ceiling and muttered several nasty words Xenia had no trouble interpreting. Her expression sobered as she turned her attention to the stage below.

Captain Strauss had been replaced by the mother of one of the missing students. The woman implored the assembled students to please, come forward with any information they might have about her daughter, or any other missing child. Any remaining hint of joy fled the hallucinatory Bethany's face as she gave every appearance of actually listening to the speaker. She glanced to Xenia and, assured of her attention, gestured at the weeping woman.

What the frick was her brain up to with all of this? The hallucination had, so far, mostly vied for her attention. Now that it had it, it wanted her to watch the stage?

The hallucination spotted her confusion right away, just as the real Bethany would have. She fanned both hands as if to clear the air. She lifted one hand between them, fingers curled in a loose fist. As she raised each finger, she mouthed a single word. When she'd raised all five fingers she paused. Her round face appeared to be on the verge of tears. She added a sixth finger to her count. This time, Xenia was able to read the name "Salvatore" upon her painted lips.

Six fingers, six missing students. Xenia nodded her understanding.

Bethany's lips trembled as she brought her hands, her tally of the lost, to rest on the ruffles over her heart.

Xenia trembled as ice flooded her veins.

Six missing.

They were like Bethany.

All six were dead.

A gasp, thick with emotion, brought Xenia's head around.

Maia, her nose deep in her novel, scrubbed at her eyes with one hand. She glanced up, offering a sheepish grin. "Got to a sad part." She waggled *The Whale Rider*. "Gets me every time." She sniffed hard and then returned her attention to her book.

Xenia took a deep breath and waited for her heart to slow. Only then did she face the phantom her injured brain had conjured up.

The chair was empty. Of Bethany, there was no sign, as if she'd never been there in the first place.

Which she hadn't been, right?

Right?

Chapter Fifteen

Bethany, from her perch in the kitchen's box window, again cursed the existence that had denied to her all sensation other than sight and sound.

Why those two, and only those two senses yet remained was a mystery. After all, she no longer had the physical apparatus required for any sensory perception. So why could she see and hear?

If, at that moment, she was offered a trade, it would be a near thing between taste and smell. Xenia's great-aunt had spent the evening preparing a batch of the meat pies that she so clearly loved. Bethany had hovered in the kitchen, observing each step with envy. Elspeth had kneaded the dough from scratch. Mixed the lamb with herbs she'd grown in the window garden where Bethany now floated. She could identify basil, rosemary, thyme, marjoram, and oregano, thanks the to the little tags Elspeth had placed in each pot, but the row of golden flowers that dominated the back row of the window box were new to her. They were

Elspeth's clear favorite, as she grew them in every plot and garden bed that surrounded her home.

One wall of the kitchen was dominated by an ancient, cast-iron gas stove. From the oven's depths Elspeth retrieved a tray laden with tiny golden-brown delicacies. Steam hissed from vents docked in the pastry shells, and filling bubbled merrily where it had burst through.

At least, Bethany mused, Zee's appetite had returned in force. The glorious meals her guardian assembled no longer went unappreciated. As long as one of them got to sample Elspeth's cooking, Bethany would be satisfied.

Yeah, right.

In truth, more than a little jealousy seethed where her guts had been. Xenia had better start appreciating her great-aunt's efforts, Bethany swore, or she'd stop running interference on her behalf with the broken spirits that had gathered outside. Since her encounter with Lucas, two more victims of Porter Valley's monstrous serial killer had appeared at the old Victorian's gate. Both had been intent on making contact with Xenia. Drawn, no doubt, by the uncanny glow the girl emitted in their ghostly sight.

Bethany had given the both of them the same speech she'd given Lucas. So far, the lost souls had been passive enough, damaged enough, to follow Bethany's rules, and had kept themselves out of sight, down at the end of the block.

To be honest, she hadn't figured out what she would have done if one of them had ignored her and charged inside anyway. She'd float over that bridge when she came to it.

"Seek grace, Bethany Brooks," she said, in echo of her Mama's favored mantra. "Seek the positive."

So. What were the positives?

For one, Xenia had—finally!—acknowledged her existence! Okay, fine. she hadn't been able to hear her, but at least she had admitted to seeing her. They'd communicated at last, if only for a moment.

Bethany had hated to ruin Zee's day with the news about Sal, Lucas, and the others. However, warning her while she had the chance was more important than reminiscing. Her friend's intermittent ability to perceive her had fled before Bethany could convey that a single individual was responsible for the deaths. Or that said individual was very likely not human.

The strength exhibited during the horrific replay she'd witnessed had been extreme. The size and depth of the wounds had been far in excess of anything produced by a knife. A sword would have done the job. In a bodybuilder's hands, perhaps.

Before her death, Bethany would have dismissed the idea of "monsters" out of hand. They were the stuff of movies and manga. Now? She was a ghost, for crying out loud! Anything was possible!

Still, she'd succeeded at her goal of communicating, however briefly, with Xenia. Her foot was in the door. It could only get easier from here. Bethany scowled as she failed in her attempt to "knock on wood."

The assembly had borne additional fruit. Bethany had seized the opportunity to don her Ghost Detective hat once more when the police captain had produced his little notebook. By reading over the man's shoulder, she'd learned the home addresses for four of the victims. Once she was certain Xenia was no longer able to see her, she'd gone snooping. That, at least, was a task this whole ghost schtick was actually good for.

She found Douglass Miller, the first of Porter Valley's

teens to disappear, right away. The poor kid was just drifting about his own bedroom. Little more than a wisp of soul stuff, he'd exhibited zero awareness of his surroundings, much less Bethany's presence. She had no way to know if his diminished state was due to the time that had passed since his murder, or if the killer had consumed even more of him than it had of Lucas.

Bethany hoped that Xenia, should she gain control of her ghost sight, would be able to reach Douglass. Offer him some form of solace, if she could.

She trailed Elspeth about the kitchen, half-watching as the woman transferred the meat pies to a rack on the counter to cool, half-brooding over the town's killer predicament. Normally, she took care to avoid passing through other people. Basic ghost courtesy, as she saw it. Lost as she was in thought, she misjudged the woman's path when, teapot in hand, Elspeth stepped away from the counter. She failed to dodge, and the woman walked right through her. *No harm, no foul—*

Elspeth gasped. A shudder ran through her, powerful enough to send the teapot tumbling from her hands. "Dash it all," cried the woman as the porcelain smashed to pieces on the tile floor.

"Sorry, Aunt E! I didn't mean to... wait." Bethany circled the woman. "You felt that? You did! You totally felt it when you walked through me!" She pumped her fist.

Elspeth scowled into the air above the butcher block table. An uncharacteristically venomous expression crowded the cheer from her face as she peered into every corner of the room. She plucked a wooden spoon from the vase of kitchen implements. "Where are ye, nasty old boggart? I know ye've been hanging about like the nuisance that you are." She brandished her spoon before her like a fencing foil.

"You knew I was here the whole time?" Bethany backed away as Elspeth advanced. "Why didn't you say something?"

Elspeth thrust her makeshift weapon into the air four feet to Bethany's left. "Hah-*hah!*"

"Okay. You can't see me..." The follow-up grazed the edge of Bethany's ruffled skirt. "But you're aware of my general location. Got it."

Having failed to avenge her fallen teapot, Elspeth stepped over the shattered mess. She spun her weapon about her fingers with practiced ease, then returned it to the countertop vase. "I don't suppose you're of a mind to tidy the mess you had a hand in creating?"

"Frankly, I'd love to. There's just one teensy, weensy little problem..."

"Harumph, I didn't think so." Elspeth took a deep breath, smoothed her hands down her apron, and let the air out in a slow exhale. "And here I believed the iron over the door would have sufficed to keep the likes of you at bay."

Bethany drifted to the back door. There, above the lintel, hung a battered old horseshoe. "Aren't these for good luck, though? That's why the pointy bits go up, keeps all the luck from pouring out?"

Elspeth offered no reply. She fetched a broom and pan from the pantry.

"Look, I'm sorry for this, but I have to know for sure," Bethany said. She inched close as the woman began to sweep up the scattered shards of her teapot. Before she could second-guess herself, Bethany let fly with the loudest scream she was capable of.

Elspeth's wince was painful to see, and the goosebumps that crawled up her arms were clear to Bethany's eye. She immediately regretted the experiment. "Sorry! I had to know for sure." Bethany backed all the way into the dining room. From there she could watch the kitchen while staying well out of Elspeth's path.

"I know full well your kind have no love for us regular folk and just adore giving us the business." Elspeth tipped the dustpan's contents into the trash bin. "But I would be grateful if you could find it within yourself to make another household your playground. It's not for my benefit, mind, but for my great-niece. She's had a rough go of it. Your mucking about doesn't make it any easier for her to heal. So, if you would be so kind, you may find the exit on your own." She swept the dustpan toward the back door.

Bethany froze in midair, appalled. Could that be true? Had her attempts to contact Xenia only delayed her recovery?

Of course it has, you moron. How do you think Zee feels when she keeps seeing her dead best friend floating around?

"Come and get it, lassie," Elspeth called out. She paused halfway into her seat and then paced to the refrigerator, from which she plucked a carton of cream. She poured a long measure into a saucer, which she placed on the step outside the back door. By the time Xenia thundered into the room, Elspeth was in her seat, utensils in hand. "I hope your appetite's at full steam, dearie. Tuck in while it's piping." She gave the girl a wink and dug into her meat pie.

Bethany backed away from the kitchen. She didn't think Zee could see her at that moment, but why take the chance? She would give Xenia space, and time, to heal before she made another attempt to contact her.

Because, no matter how much Bethany wanted to honor Elspeth's request, she couldn't. Not for long.

A monster was stalking the students of Porter Valley High. They had to get the word out before anyone else fell to its claws, and Xenia was the only one who could do that.

Chapter Sixteen

"**Y**o, wait up."

Xenia glanced over her shoulder and found the jock, Ev something, jogging toward her. As he ran, he tugged his letter jacket over his lacrosse uniform.

Xenia instantly regretted the shortcut, which had brought her past the field. She'd tried to cut a few minutes from her walk, and look what that had gotten her. "What do you want?" Ev's laughter, and the laughter of his teammates, burned all too fresh in her memory.

"It cool if I walk with you? Just for a bit."

"What about your team? Don't they need you?" Xenia asked. Bethany would have unleashed her wit upon the jock. Something like *Don't you have balls to catch with your little stick*, delivered with perfect aplomb. Xenia didn't have anything near her friend's confidence, and the quip died on her tongue. The thought of Bethany brought last week's assembly swimming to the forefront of her thoughts. That, and the distressing hallucination she'd experienced.

He shrugged. "Eh, they can survive without me for a few minutes." He used his glance toward his team as an opportunity to toss his shaggy, blond hair. A ray of sunlight, naturally, chose that moment to pierce the clouds and lend its shine.

"Whatever." Before she could exit the school's side gate, Ev slipped by and slapped the release bar. He gave her a little bow as he swung the gate open.

Gotta be kidding me. Xenia did her best to avoid brushing the jock as she hurried through. She hoped he wouldn't follow all the way to Bits 'n' Pieces, where she'd agreed to lend Elspeth a hand after school.

Ev fell into step beside her as they crossed the street. "So."

"So?" Xenia glanced at him, then away.

"It's hard, I bet. Losing your folks like that."

Xenia stopped, eyes fixed to the sidewalk. "How do you know about that?"

"Well." Ev rubbed the back of his head and stared up to the canopy of branches above them. "Evelyn, the receptionist? She likes to gossip." He shrugged. When he spoke again, his voice held none of its usual bravado. "I know what it's like. To lose your family."

"Oh." Xenia focused on the next breath. And the one after. "I'm sorry."

"Me too." Everard jammed his hands into his pockets. The hunch of his shoulders mirrored Xenia's. "Look, I fucked up. In the cafeteria. I shouldn't have laughed at Ty's joke. I should've known better. I was a wreck when my folks died, too."

Some of the lingering outrage, the humiliation that had surfaced at Ev's presence, drained away. "When did they die?"

"I was young, like, five? I did not handle it well.

Tantrums for days. I ran away, too. Which is hard to pull off when you're too scared to cross the street."

Xenia allowed herself a tiny smile. "I bet." The smile slipped away. "How did you get through it?"

"Well, I was young. I sorta... forgot. About them, about everything."

"Oh no! That's... I'm sorry."

"It's cool. Kids are resilient. That's what they say, right? Must be true. I still had problems. Had them for a long time. Like, I was convinced that these imaginary friends I had were totally real. It was an obsession." His smile said, *Kids, am I right?* The smile vanished. "Dad stuck me in therapy for a minute. Loved to complain about the price tag. Do you know I actually heard him tell Mom that they 'got a dud'?" Hell of a way to find out you were adopted. Hearing that brought back all the memories about losing my real folks."

Xenia, stunned by the unexpected candor, walked on for several steps before she noticed that Ev had come to a halt. "That's terrible. I'm so sorry." She knew she was repeating herself, but what else could she say?

"Yeah, no. It's cool. Dad and me, we worked our shit out." Ev caught Xenia's eye, held the gaze long past the point where it became uncomfortable. "Are you working your shit out?"

Xenia dropped her eyes. "I mean, I'm getting along with my great-aunt—"

"Not what I was talking about."

"I don't understand."

Ev searched her face again for a long moment. He must have found whatever it was he sought, because he nodded. "Okay. You know those imaginary friends I mentioned? Dad let me quit therapy because I stopped talking about them. I never told him that I still see them."

155

Fear, hot and bright, gripped Xenia's heart and gave it a not-so-friendly squeeze. *Oh shit.* Before she could act on her impulse to just run, Ev went on.

"There's more. Once I stopped fighting it, stopped telling myself they weren't real, allowed myself to be me, I discovered that could do other things. Things like..." He paused. Looked up and down the residential street where they'd stopped.

The street, Xenia noted, was empty save for the two of them. She shifted her weight, ready to bolt.

Ev pursed his lips and blew a high, trilling note. A chorus of birdsong came in reply. A flock of tiny, avian bodies exploded from the trees lining the street. The sudden swarm wheeled about them, and the breeze of their passage set her hair swirling about her face.

Everard offered a hand as a perch. In seconds, birds lined his arm to the shoulder. No sooner had he raised his other arm than it too became home to its own flock.

The feathered troupe chirped and pecked at each other as they fought for space. Tiny heads darted this way and that. Beady eyes gazed with avian reverence at the one who had summoned them.

Arms spread like a Renaissance saint statue, Ev winked. A sweep of his hands sent the flock skyward. In seconds, the birds had vanished into the treetops from whence they'd come.

Xenia's mouth had gone dry. "How did you do that?" Awed disbelief had displaced the fear from a moment earlier.

"Would you believe me if I said 'magic'?" Ev flicked a feather from his sleeve.

"No."

Ev offered her a lazy, one-shouldered shrug. "Fine. I

trained a flock of sparrows to come when I whistle. Then I let them loose on this street and hoped you would walk with me before they migrated. Better?"

Xenia glared at the senior but couldn't muster any real heat. Seriously, how the hell had he done that?

"It's cool. You need some time for it to sink in. So did I, the first time." Ev reached out and, when Xenia didn't pull away, placed a gentle hand on her shoulder.

The warmth of his touch sank through her hoodie. She turned her face away as her breath caught in her chest.

"You aren't alone." Ev gave her shoulder a little squeeze. "I just wanted you to know that. If anyone around here could understand what you're going through, it's me."

The warmth from his hand sent tendrils of heat spiraling about her neck, tingling across her scalp. The whirl in her head, her confusion at Ev's bird trick, no longer seemed quite so overwhelming. Her thoughts slowed, as if caught in warm taffy. Eventually, she found her voice. "Yeah, I guess so." Before she knew what she was doing, she'd leaned into his touch.

A sudden bass note thumped from Ev's jacket. A rapper, voice attenuated by a tiny speaker at full volume, bellowed his signature line. Ev took his hand from Xenia's shoulder to fish out his phone.

It was if a sudden breeze blew away the cloud of cotton candy that had wrapped itself about her thoughts. She scrubbed at one eye with the palm of her hand.

She was surprised that Ev could afford a ΞPhone. The so-called "smartphones" were cutting edge, absurdly over-priced, and so new that she'd only seen one online.

Ev raised a finger as he held the phone to his ear. "Wassup, Coach?" He rolled his eyes, then grinned for Xenia's benefit. "Yeah, I know but—" He frowned. "Okay, fine." Ev stabbed the call off. "Gotta jet, you know how it is." He swung the phone as if it were a lacrosse stick.

Xenia nodded. Part of her wanted to follow him back. Wanted to watch him practice. Maybe, if she did...

She shook her head. Aunt Elspeth would be waiting at the shop. "Have fun hitting balls with your little stick."

Ev smirked. Held his fist out.

Xenia hesitated, then fist-bumped him. As their knuckles brushed, a tiny spark, static electricity, stung her. "Ow!" She shook her hand.

"That's right, blow it up." Ev lifted his hand, fingers waggling. "Knew you were cool." He bounced two fingers from his forehead and jogged off.

Xenia stared after him until the blue and white of his jacket vanished around a corner. When she resumed her trek toward Elspeth's shop, she hardly noticed the tiny smile dancing at the corner of her mouth.

Ev thought she was cool?

Chapter Seventeen

With spring's arrival, the sun had burned away much of Porter Valley's omnipresent cloud cover. Thanks to the digital clock/thermometer provided by the bank across the street, Xenia knew that the temperature hovered at a sweltering sixty-eight degrees Fahrenheit. A sudden gust swirled chill air down her neck, and she tugged her hood close.

She'd been so warm and cozy just a moment ago.

Xenia shook the errant thought from her head and trudged on. Ahead of her, Main Street ran more than a mile through the very heart of Porter Valley. At either end of the valley, the thoroughfare merged with the Redwood Highway. The buildings on Main came in a mix of the town's original Gold Rush era architecture and newer, post-war construction. Streetlights made to resemble old-timey gas lamps sprang from the sidewalk between shade trees and awning-covered outdoor dining. Even on a midweek afternoon, the street bustled with activity.

Xenia spied Madison and company holding court over steaming cappuccinos at The Coffee Nook. She ducked her head and hurried by before she could be spotted. The last thing she needed was more of Madison's... Madison-ness.

The scent of baked goods, chocolate, and spices drew her onward. She pressed her nose to the bakery window and drooled over the display of fresh pies, cakes, cookies, and something that looked like a croissant and a donut had relations. She had spending money, thanks to Aunt Elspeth. It wasn't a fortune, but she could afford the occasional treat.

Xenia pushed on. Main Street offered no shortage of temptations. With its selection of candy shops, bakeries, and restaurants featuring local, farm-to-table fare, there was no reason to jump at the first treat to catch her eye. She'd hardly seen half of the available shops. Even though she had to cross Main on her way to school, she hadn't spent much time exploring here at all.

She still had a few blocks before to go before she arrived at Elspeth's store. Why not look around? She needed the distraction. Ev's little trick with the birds had her stumped. Try as she might, she just couldn't figure out how he'd done it.

Then there were those imaginary friends he'd mentioned. The parallel with her own... hallucinations was clear. *That's not the same thing at all! I had a concussion!*

Then there was that thing with the wind, when that "seizure" had knocked her out. She'd been certain she'd imagined it. But, what if—

A hurtling mass missed her nose by no more than an inch. It alighted with a flutter atop the sign for an establishment called The Iron Tiki. One dark, beady eye blinked at her.

"Watch where you're flying," snapped Xenia. She gave the signpost a wide berth and picked up her pace. Bits 'n'

Pieces wasn't much farther. She could get a snack after she checked in with her great-aunt.

"*Caw*." The raven flitted from the sign to a nearby faux gas lamp. As she walked on, it flew to the next lamp, then the next. As she hurried the length of the block, the bird maintained its one-lamp lead.

Xenia had read, in biology class, that corvids were smart enough to recognize individuals. They even had favorite humans, and not-so-favorites. Especially when fed. Could this be the same raven she'd shared her snack with, in the park, all those weeks ago? If it was, its memory was impressive. "I'm out of treats today," she called out as the bird continued to pace her. "I'll bring some peanuts or something next time I go to the park."

The raven stepped from its perch. It fluttered once and plunked itself directly in her path, did a little hop. "*Caw*." The raven tilted its head to one side to better aim a glossy bead of an eye her way.

Between the raven and Ev's trick, Xenia was just about done with avian shenanigans. She edged her way around the feathered obstruction.

The raven hop-flapped across the sidewalk until it was again in her way. When she tried to go around, it spread its wings to their full extent. Xenia backed off a step.

The raven took a step toward her.

"Shoo!" Xenia lunged at the bird and clapped her hands to scare it out of her way.

The raven didn't so much as flinch. Instead, it took another step toward her. And another.

"What the hell?" The bird advanced and she retreated, and Xenia found herself herded back the way she'd come. "I don't want to kick you, but I will," she lied. She didn't have the heart to kick an animal, even if it was being weirdly aggressive. Also, that beak looked wicked sharp. Wait, did birds get rabies? Could she get rabies from a bird?

She could call for help. No. Xenia dismissed that idea out of hand. What would she say? "Help, help, I'm scared of a bird!" Her reputation was dodgy enough, and Madison was only a block away. No thank you.

The raven darted to cut off Xenia's next dodge attempt. Her back thumped against a storefront, and the bird halted its advance. Clearly satisfied with its victory, it walked in a little circle, head bobbing.

Xenia did her best to keep one eye on the avian nuisance while she checked out where she'd been herded. With any luck, they had a back door. She could ditch the bird and run for Aunt Elspeth's.

The plate glass window was smudged and more than a bit dusty, but the shop's name, Signs & Portents, was perfectly legible. A cartoon constellation of stars and comet stickers was scattered about the arch of gold leaf lettering. The display inside overflowed with bundles of dried herbs, stacks of dusty books, hanging dreamcatchers, and a handful of half-burnt candles.

"You gotta be kidding me." Xenia glared at the raven.

"*Caw.*"

Xenia feinted toward the door, then made for the open sidewalk. The deranged bird nipped at the toe of her shoe. "Fine!" At least it looked like they had books in there. Maybe she could catch up on *Armored Princess,* her favorite fantasy series. Thanks to the move north, she'd misplaced her collection.

A bell jangled overhead as she pushed inside, and again when the door closed. The air was redolent with a dry, herbaceous scent. Her nasal passages immediately rebelled, and she pinched the bridge of her nose to stifle an imminent sneeze.

"Welcome to Signs and Portents, fellow traveler. May the sun and the stars shine upon you," a laconic voice drawled from deeper in the shop.

Xenia squeezed between bookshelves groaning beneath massive, leather-bound tomes, bundled pamphlets, and stacked periodicals. All manner of crystals, tiny brass bells, replica (Xenia hoped they were replicas) human skulls, and other paraphernalia she had no hope of identifying cluttered every inch not filled with printed material. She took note of the bin of old vinyl records and wondered if her great-aunt knew of the place. Elspeth's sitting room contained a colossal collection of the old disks. The woman detested CDs and other, more digital, forms of music.

When, at last, Xenia came to the counter, she found it crammed with more oddments and knickknacks. Behind this collection, clad in threadbare, faded dungarees, one elbow propped on the counter, was the proprietor. His face was ruddy from wind or age, or both, and a shawl of burst veins draped itself across his bulbous nose. He was the same age as Elspeth, or close to, and his once-blond hair was bound up in the shaggiest mass of dreadlocks Xenia had ever seen on a white person. Watery, bloodshot eyes peered at her through the coil of smoke from the incense burner at his elbow. Stars and moons in faded blue ink adorned the knuckles of both hands. As Xenia drew close, he rose from his stool and placed both hands flat on the counter before him. "What does your heart seek, little sister?"

A way out the back? Xenia chose a more thoughtful approach. "Um..." *Brilliant.* "Are all of these"—she waved to the bookshelves at her back—"about magic?"

"Spirituality, occultism, faiths from all corners of the

globe, mytho-historical research," the man said, then grinned. "And yes. Some of them are about magic. What kind of hoodoo do you do, little sister?"

"There's more than one kind?"

The aging hippie's eyes danced with merriment as he ticked off his fingers. "We got Apotropaic magic, Druidism, Feng Shui, Fulu, Goetia, Golden Dawn, Heka, Kabbalism, Onmyōdō, Renaissance, Vodun, Wicca, and Tantric." He coughed. "No offense, but you might want to wait a few years before chasing that last one."

He sank onto his stool. "All the secrets of the universe at your fingertips. Well, most of them, anyhoo." He spun a hand in the air. "Take your time, we're open until six." He produced a wooden box from the clutter and dumped an assortment of tiny ceramic figures onto a felt mat. With one blunt finger he began to arrange them according to criteria known only to himself.

Why not? Aunt Elspeth hadn't specified a time, she could afford to loiter a bit until the bird found a new victim. She chose an aisle at random and squeezed by a metal rack piled high with cheap Halloween wizard hats. The tingle on the back of her neck arrived just as she spied the aisle's occupant.

There, in the center of the aisle, poised as if she were reading one of the many books available, was Bethany.

"Oh come on!" cried Xenia.

Bethany's calm expression turned cross. She turned, ever so slowly, to face Xenia. Raised a single finger to her lips. "Shhhh!" Message delivered, the illusion returned its gaze to the bookshelf before it.

"Everything good, little sister?"

"Yeah, fine." Xenia glared at the product of her injured brain and stomped two aisles over.

"Really?" Bethany's voice was faint, as if she were speaking from the end of a long hallway. The image popped through the shelf in front of Xenia and planted her hands on her hips. "The library ghost? I know you've seen the movie." She threw her hands up. "I know. It would've been more convincing if I could actually hold a book."

Xenia backed away. Bird or not, she was out of here.

"Zee, come on. Say something, please. I know you can see me."

The bookshelves shimmered behind a veil of tears. "You're not real."

"Yes. I am. Look, I'm sorry, okay? Sorry for scaring you. Sorry for not being there when you needed me most. Sorry for dying. Happy now?"

"Go away." Xenia screwed her eyes shut. She didn't care if the old guy heard her. Or thought she was crazy. "Go. *Away!*"

"Elspeth was right," Bethany whispered. "This was a bad idea."

Xenia took a deep breath. Thanks to the incense and dust clogging the air, she broke into a combined coughing/sneezing fit. When she'd finished dabbing the worst of the snot from her nose, the aisle was empty.

She was halfway to the exit when a copper bowl fell from above. Xenia caught it before it could strike the floor and trigger a "you break it, you buy it" policy. She scanned the upper shelves for the bowl's origin and found a familiar, beady eye staring back at her. "How the hell did you get in here?"

The raven stretched one wing, and the corresponding foot, along its body. The glossy black beak gaped in a yawn.

If the raven was inside, then the street was clear. Xenia

jammed the bowl into the nearest gap and shuffled for the exit.

The raven, having none of that, hopped from its perch. Before it could land on her head, the dark wings popped out. Xenia flinched as it wafted by her ear. A brief flutter and a little swoop later, the raven was perched atop a plastic skull with a rose clamped in its grin.

"I swear, if you say 'nevermore,' I'm throwing a book at you."

Instead, the raven hooked its clawed feet into the skull's eye sockets and leaned way out. At full extension, it pecked at the spine of a book on the shelf below. *Tap.* As Xenia backed away, each step earned a matching peck. *Tap. Tap. Tap.* When she took a step forward, the raven held its peace.

"Fine." Xenia crept close. There, almost hidden between a pair of massive star indexes, was a narrow book with the title *Practical Spells and Recipes*.

"And what, exactly, am I supposed to do with this?"

The raven fluffed its feathers until it resembled a sphere with a beak.

"I'm out of here." Xenia spun on her heel.

Before she could take a step, the raven issued a low, warbling croak. It wasn't exactly a growl. But it wasn't *not* a growl, either.

"You can't be serious." Xenia shook her finger at the raven's beak. "I'm already seeing shit that isn't there. Now I'm talking to a bird. You think some stupid book is going to help?"

The raven shook its feathers into place. The round head dipped.

"Did you just nod?"

The beak dipped one more time.

"Unbelievable." Xenia rubbed her temples. The

migraine that no doubt would follow all of this was going to split her head wide open. Before she could argue with herself, or the raven, any further, she yanked the book from its slot on the shelf.

"This is basically *Magic for Dummies*, right?" Xenia asked as she set the slim volume on the counter.

The heavyset man swept through a clattering beaded curtain into the space behind the counter. A skunky, sour odor wafted along with him. He planted a finger atop the book and slid it closer. "Harnessing Fate for one's own benefit, and the benefit of one's allies, is not something I'd stick in the 'for dummies' category, little sister." He squinted and then produced a pair of reading glasses from his overalls and squinted through them. "Huh. Don't remember this one. Well, the path finds the traveler." Blunt fingers hammered a chiming melody into the ancient brass cash register.

Xenia passed over most of the spending cash her great-aunt had given her, and the man slipped her purchase into a paper bag, along with a handful of bookmarks and a teabag sampler. He smiled. "If you should need anything else, I'm here every day but Monday. Hot yoga."

"'Kay. Thanks."

"Do give Elspeth my love, little sister. We're in the same yoga class. She hasn't stopped talking about you since she returned with you in tow."

"Oh." Well, that was only a little creepy, Xenia decided. The idea of small town life, where everyone knew everyone's business, was still new.

Xenia threaded her way between the teetering shelves and paused with one hand on door. "Hey, is that weird bird yours? It's trained really well."

"My what now?" The proprietor's puzzled face appeared at the end of the aisle.

"The raven? Over there." Xenia ducked her chin toward the bird's last known perch.

"Nope, no pets here." He blinked. "Wait, inside?" He snatched up a broom from behind the counter. "Damn thing's gonna crap all over my books!"

* * *

The moment Xenia arrived at Bits 'n' Pieces, her guardian put her to work. There was a new shipment of merchandise, and Elspeth wanted some help unpacking and inventorying the lot. The assortment of hand-printed postcards, wood carvings, and other souvenirs had all been sourced locally in Humboldt County. Xenia found the task a welcome relief from the day's insanity rather than boring.

Once the last googly-eyed wood carving was in its proper place and the last customer had been ushered out, Elspeth flipped the sign from "open" to "closed." Xenia pushed a broom around while her great-aunt tallied up the day's take. Afterward, the stroll home was brief. The old Victorian was only a few blocks over.

"Oh dear." Elspeth paused, her hand on the garden gate. She nodded across the street.

A motionless Marisol was seated on the Serranos' front porch. Her coterie of stuffed animals and dolls lay forgotten on the front lawn as she stared off into the distance. The usual pop of color in the form of ladybug barrettes was absent from her hair. Save for the ruddiness around her eyes and nose, her face was drawn and pale. Sal's basketball was perched atop her knees, a chubby hand on either side. Even from across the street, Xenia could see the shine her tears lent to the rubber.

When Xenia had first met Bug, and Sal, the girl had

been an inexhaustible font of energy. More so than even her brother. Now, the girl's eyes were listless, her expression blank. The boundless energy stilled by grief and worry.

"Marisol, sweetheart," called Elspeth. When the girl turned their way, Xenia waved.

Marisol clambered to her feet and, basketball held tight to her chest, stomped inside. The slam of the front door echoed down the street.

"The poor dear is not having an easy time of it. And who could blame her?" Elspeth shook her head and made her way inside.

Xenia spent another moment, her eyes glued to the front porch where Bug had sat. For a moment, she thought... No, it couldn't have been. Xenia followed her great-aunt into the garden and, at Elspeth's pointed look, shut the gate firmly behind her.

* * *

Xenia tumbled onto her bed. She kicked off her shoes off and scooted her way to the center of the mattress. Her vision, for now, was free from any hint of migraine halo. Absent, as well, were the unwelcome visitations.

Still, she couldn't stop herself. She whispered, "Beebs? You there?"

Xenia wasn't sure if the silence was a relief or not.

She rolled onto her stomach and dragged her book bag close to retrieve her purchase. She upended the paper bag onto the quilt. There it was.

Practical Spells and Recipes.

Xenia stuck her tongue out at the memory of the raven herding her down the street. Propping her chin in her hand, she took a closer look at what she'd been saddled with.

The book had definitely seen better days. If there had been a dust jacket, it was long gone. The fabric binding was frayed, and bits of board peeked out at each corner. Stains in a variety of colors and shapes marked every inch.

Xenia flipped to the title page. She'd never heard of "Goody Hawkes," the author. Or the "Empyrean Tech Guild," the publisher. The date of publication was 1969, which was a bit of a surprise. Xenia had assumed the book's vintage would be the 1920s, or even earlier.

Her disappointment only grew with each page. The table of contents had nothing close to the sort of flair that a steady diet of Disney princesses and Hollywood fantasy had led her to expect from a book of "magic."

"To keep a lover faithful. Spell to win a court case. Spell to prevent a wagon wheel from splitting. Spell to attract luck." The final chapter alone consisted of over thirty spells that purported to improve crop yields and the fecundity of the soil. "If that bird thinks I'm gonna zap up a pile of magic corn for him to nom, he's got another thing coming."

The chapters on divination and scrying were more interesting, which didn't say much. She had to look the terms up online. It seemed they were spells for seeing the future, or elsewhere at the present, respectively. The idea of getting a peek ahead, or watching folks on the other side of the world promised a brief thrill... until she remembered that computers and the internet did more or less the same things.

Xenia snorted. If this book was meant to convince her that magic was real. That anyone could do it, well... it had failed. Miserably. "Spell to ease the rheumatism." Thrilling stuff.

She traded the bogus magic book for her laptop and cast the spell "show me cat videos." Aunt Elspeth had gone to a lot of effort, in the days following Xenia's arrival, to have the fastest Wi-Fi available installed in her home. She'd spent hours chained to the landline phone in the hall to arrange the installation. The woman didn't even have a cell phone, much less a computer of her own, and had gone to great lengths to see the job done right. The least Xenia could do was put it to good use.

Lulled by the bottomless feed of adorable kitty antics, she found it wasn't long before sleep pulled her under.

Chapter Eighteen

Bethany elevated her nose to the precise angle required to convey how serious she was. "To thine own self be true, Mr. Findlay," she sniffed. "I must always be true to my muse." She favored Xenia with a kohl-lined wink. "You ready, Zee?"

Xenia tore her attention away from the glacier-slow traffic beyond her window. High-fived her BFFFF. "Born ready! If"—she glared at the red light that impeded their progress—"we ever get there."

Cool, salty sea air brushed her cheek.

The swollen orb of the sun shrank in the west and was gone.

Her feet, bare and calloused, drummed the packed earth as the girl ran through the camp. Her heart thundered with excitement. *Uncle was here!* She could not bear to think that she might have already missed one of the old man's stories.

She batted hanging linen away as she ducked between the wide tents used by the caravan's merchants. Ahead, a flare of flame rose in the twilight. They had already begun!

At the edge of the great circle of sitting stones, the girl stumbled to a halt. Her *Aa*, her father, had once told her of how the circle had come to be. Each year, the caravans that roamed from north to south and back again would stop here to trade and to celebrate another year of prosperity. Each time they set camp, the men would hike to the nearby mountain and cut another stone. On this night, three full rings, and part of a fourth, circled the great fire pit.

Uncle, on his stool beside the tall pyramid of logs, was easy for the girl to spot. She was in luck; he hadn't yet begun. She squeezed her way to the innermost circle and, as all of the good seats were full, sat in the dirt.

"Give us a tale, Uncle," cried one of the older boys. "Yes, a story!" The call circled about the gathered children, as a hunting pack calls when a scent has been found. The girl threw her hands up above her head and joined her voice to the call.

Uncle pretended not to hear as he scraped the last of the *tuh'u* from his bowl and sucked his fingers clean. Uncle was old, older even than the girl's father. His hair, which had long since gone white, was still thick enough to be worn in the tight waves favored by the men of the caravan. The olive oil he used to groom the snowy mass gleamed in the firelight. While his square face was well lined with age, the eyes that peered from within that nest of wrinkles were still sharp, still quick. A hint of muscle yet lurked beneath the slack skin of his bare chest.

Uncle used the wool of his kilt, fastened at one hip by a thick bronze pin, to wipe the damp from his fingers. His feet were bare. A pair of rope sandals waited beside the leg of his stool. Uncle dug his fingers into the scruff that sprung from his chin. "A story?" He gazed off over the heads of the children. "I don't think I know any stories…"

The crowd leapt to their feet in outrage, voices raised in protest. More than one sandal flew toward the old man.

Uncle smiled a rascally old smile and raised his hands. "All right, have it your way. Quiet now." He looked to the older boys, who were not yet men, to the girls not yet women, then to their younger siblings, who waited with breath bated and hands clutched, and last to the youngest, the babes in arms and the chubby-legged wanderers who'd been brought to the fire on the hips and shoulders of the others. Uncle gave a satisfied nod.

"What, then, shall it be? What tale for this night? Would you hear about the King and the Wild-Man, perhaps? Or would you prefer I speak about the time the Great Calf of the Sun threw down the Mother of Serpents, defeated, and from her bones made the world?"

"No," called a boy, "we've heard those before. A thousand times before!"

"Yes," cried another, "we want a new story!"

The girl leapt to her feet. "Tell us a new story!" She remembered the reprimand of her *Ama*, her mother, about her lack of manners. She ducked her head. "If you would, Uncle."

Uncle threw back his head with a great laugh and slapped his knee. "Since you have been so very... vigorous in your request, go. Fetch some *kaš*, and perhaps it will pry a fresh tale from this old head." One knobby finger tapped the center of his forehead.

The words had no sooner left the old man's lips than the girl was away, like an arrow loosed from a bow. Father's tent, she thought, was too far. Uncle might begin without her if she tarried overlong. Instead, she trailed the scent of fermented fish to the tent of her mother's friend. She slipped beneath a cloth wall and crept across the furs that made up the floor. Mother's good friend, who knew full well what the girl was about, pretended not to notice the diminutive burglar.

From an earthenware pot nearly tall as she, the girl dipped out a measure of *kaš,* the sweet golden beer that Uncle favored. She turned to go, then paused. With the flat of her hand held reverently before her mouth, as Father had instructed, she lowered her head. "Great are you, Ninkasi," she whispered, "who pours out the *kaš* from the jar, like the onrush of the Tigris and the Euphrates."

The girl, her prize held before her, marched up to Uncle. He accepted the offering with a grin and nodded for her to sit beside him. The girl's face ached from the breadth of her smile as she sat.

Uncle took a slow sip from his cup and gazed at the stars that shone in the heavens above. "Yes, that one will do nicely," he murmured. He exchanged the cup for the three-stringed *gishgudi* that lay atop his bundle. With the neck of his instrument cradled in one hand, he caressed the strings with his other.

"This is an old tale, older by far than any I have told you before." Uncle nodded at the girl. "When I was your age, my grandfather told this story to me, as his grandfather told him, and so on back to the very beginning. Truth be told, this tale comes from before even that time. From days when the world itself was but a newborn. Days when the Sun and the Moon walked upon the earth as we do. Great and glorious was that time. Until, that is, those sisters, the sibling Queens who ruled all of creation, found cause to quarrel."

Uncle plucked at his instrument, coaxing a simple melody from the rough strings. As the sweet notes spiraled into the air to mingle with the smoke from the fire, Uncle began to sing.

* * *

The all-too-sudden blare of the alarm clock snatched the girl from the fireside. She floundered, arms and legs wound tight in the sheets, until she prized a hand free and slapped the alarm silent.

"Huh." Xenia scrubbed at her face. For the first time in what seemed like forever, she hadn't been tortured awake by a multitude of nightmares. She'd slept the whole night through. Amazing.

What was up with that dream, though? There'd been a campfire, she thought. And a banjo? Xenia grasped after the fading thread, only to have it slip from her fingers.

Nope. It was gone.

Chapter Nineteen

Xenia took one look at the lunchroom crowd and shoved through the double door into the gray overcast outside. Today, she was in no mood for the whispered jokes, the not-so-subtle stares. The social fallout from her first day, the panic attack, had ebbed and flowed. Today, it had been extra bad.

She glared at the low clouds. Where was the damn sun in this stupid town? She missed warmth. In LA, it would be bright. Blue skies and seventy-five. Here? Gloom city.

Maia's lanky form stood out from her teammates as they ran some sort of drill on the track. Xenia hadn't spoken with her since the assembly because... wait, why? It'd just be awkward, Xenia thought, if she were to walk up now. Especially while Maia was doing track-and-field stuff.

Xenia tugged her up hood in the hope it would cut some of the chill and tromped to the row of benches at the edge of the field. She could watch, at least. If Maia noticed, she'd say "hi" then.

She was halfway through her tuna sandwich when Madison, Courtney, and Gracie headed her way. Each member of the trio carried a coffee cup; they'd left school grounds for lunch. It was against the rules to do so, but Xenia knew that Main Street's proximity made it a popular destination for students tired of the cafeteria fare. Or for those, like Madison and friends, who needed a caffeine pick-me-up.

Xenia was too much of a wuss to break the rules like that. Bethany had no problem heading up the street for her favorite taco truck back home. She'd bring back a few for Xenia and had only teased her a little bit for being such a chicken.

The trio were too engrossed in their coffee and gossip to see Xenia as they took over a nearby bench. Xenia sped through the rest of her sandwich with the intent of clearing out before she could be targeted.

The track team loped by. Maia, jogging backward, shouted encouragement and guidance to her fellows. As they passed the line of benches, Maia frowned. She tugged a cord from her ear and waved one of the others forward to take her place. Storm clouds gathered on her face as she jogged in Xenia's direction.

Is Maia pissed at me? Why? Xenia raised a hand in greeting, only for the runner to stomp right past her.

"Gracie," Maia said, "you weren't at the meet last Friday. And you're missing practice!"

Xenia sank low on the bench. She'd had no idea that Gracie was on the track team. She'd never seen the blond girl around the other runners, much less wear a uniform.

"Sorry." Gracie stared at the ground by Maia's feet.

"Look. It's not just me." Maia waved a hand at the crowd now rounding the far side of the track. "We've all been worried about you, and not just because championships are coming up. But Tamarah's been out for a week

—we need you! Is everything okay? I know your mom can be a pain..." Maia took a step closer to the other girl. "Gracie, you are a valued member of the team. You know that. You're one of the best we have—"

"Not *the* best though, right?" Madison surged to her feet and inserted herself between the other two. With a sneer she said, "That'd be you, Miss Super Legs. Maybe Gracie's tired of living in your huge-ass shadow."

Courtney tittered, then had the good sense to look ashamed of herself. She sipped at her coffee. If she had anything else to add, she kept it to herself.

"Let Gracie speak for herself, Mads." Maia took a deep breath, and the frown smoothed from her face. "Is that true, Gracie? Is this my fault? Did I do something to push you away?"

"I dunno," Gracie mumbled. Her eyes flicked from Maia, to Madison, to the ground over and over again. Her hand dipped into her purse and emerged with her phone in a white-knuckled grip.

Madison pushed into Maia's personal space. "You stomp all over your teammates. 'Oh, super Maia. Runs *so* fast, jumps *so* high.' Like you think you're better'n everyone else. So special. Well, rah, rah, fuckin' rah." She mimed a pair of imaginary pompoms as she mocked the taller girl.

Maia's lips compressed into a bloodless line. She glared at Madison who, being closer to the runner's height than anyone else, met the stare with bored eyes. "I said"—Maia's voice had become a near growl—"let Gracie speak for herself."

Gracie's voice quavered. "Look, it's not you, Maia. Or the team, or Madison." She lowered her face so that the sweep of her hair hid the tears in her eyes. She thumbed at her phone. "I'm... Mom's been..." She dragged in a shuddering breath. "Shit's not great at home. The team... it's too much."

Maia, instantly contrite, stepped past Madison. "Ah, damn it. I'm sorry. I didn't know. We'll miss you, but you need to do what's best for you."

Behind her, Madison caught Courtney's eye and made a jerking-off motion. Her smirk widened into a cruel smile. She cocked her arm and threw her coffee cup straight at Maia.

Either she'd seen something in Gracie's face or she was just that lucky, because Maia chose that moment to crouch beside her former teammate. The caffeinated missile sailed over her head and onward. Madison's malicious throw gave the cup enough distance to strike Xenia full in the face. She had less than a heartbeat to brace against the scald of hot coffee as liquid fountained across her skin and into her hoodie.

But instead of scalding hot coffee, a cascade of whipped cream and frothy tan slush poured over her. The icy brew soaked her to the skin in an instant. She sputtered bitter-sweet spittle as shivers set in.

"What the fuck, Mads?" Maia whirled on the other girl. Madison raised her hands in a gesture of feigned innocence. A muscle in Maia's jaw twitched as she bared her teeth. For a moment, it looked as if she would actually punch Mads in the face.

Instead, Maia whirled on her heel and, with an apologetic look to Gracie, ran to Xenia.

Madison crooked a finger at Courtney and Gracie. "C'mon girls. Mama needs a refill." Without looking to see if they had followed, she sauntered off. Courtney, head swiveling between the other girls and her departing friend, mouthed *sorry* before she ran off to join Madison.

Gracie rose to her feet; she spent a long moment staring after them, her face crumpled. She ran, not after her friends, but toward the school.

"Hey, you okay?" Maia asked as she dropped into a squat in front of Xenia. "Any of that get in your eyes?" Concern had replaced the fury of a moment ago. She thumbed a glob of whipped cream from Xenia's eyebrow.

"Y-yeah." Xenia pulled her hoodie close about her, only that made the chill worse. "J-just cold." At least now she had an excuse for the moisture that spilled across her cheeks.

Maia grimaced. "I'm sorry you took that bullet for me, you being an innocent bystander and all." She sighed. "I wish I knew what was going on with them, with Gracie." She shook her head. "Then again, I've met her mother." Maia's expression suggested that the meeting hadn't been at all pleasant. "Listen, if Mads gives you any shit about this, you let me know. I'll kick her ass." She gave Xenia a lopsided grin. "Unless you want to do the kicking yourself, I mean."

"N-not my thing, thanks." Xenia shook her head. Still, the idea was tempting...

"You have anything in there you can wear?" Maia glanced at Xenia's book bag. "You're going to freeze to death if you don't change."

Xenia shivered. The wind was definitely picking up. "No, just my books."

"Well, that won't work. Come on," Maia slapped her knees, stood, and held out a hand. "You can borrow my spares. Might be a bit big on you, though."

Maia's nose, Xenia couldn't help but notice, wrinkled when she grinned. Just a tiny bit. Xenia allowed herself to be yanked to her feet. She trudged along as Maia led her toward the locker room. She really hoped no one else would be in the showers, but she was sticky and freezing and—

Bethany was right next to Maia.

The hallucination was furious, as if a figment of her imagination had emotions of its own. Although Xenia was unable to hear her, the illusory Beebs was talking a mile a minute. As she caught Xenia's look, the rant trailed off. The phantom gestured after the departed Madison. Xenia was able to read her lips: *Can you believe that bitch?*

Xenia fumed. Her brain really picked the worst times to pull this crap. "Not now," she seethed at whatever inside her skull had malfunctioned.

Hurt replaced outrage as the hallucination's expression fell. She slid sideways and raised her hands in a silent apology. The illusion didn't fade, but it did have the good graces to float away on the breeze. In seconds, it was gone.

"What?" Maia paused, glanced over her shoulder.

"What?" Xenia, desperate for a distraction, spied the earbuds still clutched in Maia's hand. "What're you listening to?"

Maia offered the earphones to her.

Xenia held the tiny speaker to an ear not full of coffee gunk. She winced as an explosion of thundering bass, rumbling blast beats, shrieking guitars, and a guttural howl stabbed her eardrum. She yanked the earbud away. "What is that?" The aural overload had come close to sparking a migraine on its own.

"This?" Maia stuck the earbud in her ear for a listen. "Cannibal Corpse, 'Death Walking Terror.'" Her other hand rose, two fingers extended in a heavy metal salute. "Keeps me in the zone when I'm running."

"Really? You don't look like—"

"Like what? A metalhead?" Maia turned and stalked

toward the gym. "What's the saying about book covers and judging? Come on, it's cold out here." Without waiting, she shoved through the locker room door.

Way to go. Her hand drifted to her cast, but she pulled away before she could push a finger inside. Even if her bones hadn't healed enough to stop hurting, the tiny, self-inflicted torture no longer offered the false solace it once had.

Xenia hurried after Maia. She hoped the offer of dry clothes was still on.

* * *

Xenia stumbled to a halt. "Crap." She'd left the coffee-soaked clothes in her locker when she'd left. Now, she was almost home. The school would be locked tight by the time she made it back. If she was lucky, the bag with her clothing wouldn't be a moldy, ant-covered mess come Monday morning.

Once Xenia had scrubbed the coffee froth from her hair, Maia had come through with dry clothes. If she'd been upset over Xenia's thoughtless comment, she didn't show it.

Thankfully, the shirt she'd lent to Xenia hadn't been covered in gory, heavy metal imagery. The garment was a bit stiff, as if it were still new. The front featured a feather, or maybe it was a fern, printed in white above the name *ALL BLACKS*. When Xenia had tugged it on, the hem had fallen almost to her knees. She felt like a kid in a grown up's clothing.

"You can get that back to me whenever," Maia had told her. There'd been a bit of tension in her voice, something in her eye when she'd spoken. Was this a special shirt? Or a favorite band? Xenia was hesitant to ask and risk offending her again. Also, she really did need something to wear.

Her hand drifted to the stiff, screen-printed logo as she dithered whether to go back for her stuff. Bah. Home was just around the corner. She could always toss those clothes if they went moldy. Then again, it was her favorite hoodie...

A familiar figure at the old Victorian's garden gate brought her to another sudden halt.

"Sal!" Xenia broke into a run. It had been weeks since he'd vanished without a trace. Where the hell had he been? She had half a mind to tear him a new one and tell him in no uncertain terms how much worry he'd caused her. Not to mention his parents and, most of all, Bug! No, she decided. Sal would get plenty of that from his family. Whatever it was that had been eating at him, whatever had made him run away, she'd offer whatever support she could.

Her words of greeting died in her throat.

Salvatore Serrano stood, soaking wet, at the center of a dark puddle. His dark hair was plastered to his scalp, and his shirt clung to his narrow chest. Rivulets of water fell from his fingertips to join the growing puddle on the sidewalk.

Worse, the white picket fence was visible right through Sal's body.

Her hands flew to her mouth. "No, not you too!"

No, don't be silly. Xenia clenched her fists. *You told that phantom of Bethany to go away—twice!—and it did. This isn't any different.* Even if her brain had decided to up the ante and use her missing friend to torment her, she wasn't going to validate it by—

Sal turned toward her. Shadow filled the space where his eyes should have been. Just as with the boy she'd seen in class on her first day. His skin was a pallid caricature of its normal tan. His lips were bloodless and blue.

If this was all in her head, why didn't Bethany look like this too? Other than being a bit see-through, the hallucinations of her friend looked exactly as Xenia remembered her.

Crimson bloomed in the cloth over Sal's chest. Xenia fell back as his twitching hands rose to take hold of either side of the *Suns* logo emblazoned on his shirt. He pulled, and the shirt parted like tissue. A raw, red cavern yawned where the pale skin of his chest should have been.

Xenia's eyes burned. She longed to look away. Close her eyes. To *not see*. But she was frozen. Trapped in the vise of her sudden terror.

Within the wreckage of Sal's chest, jagged ends marked where each rib had been torn away. The space where his lungs, his heart should have been lay empty. The segmented curve of his spine gleamed amidst shreds of tissue.

What remained of Xenia's lunch burned at the back of her mouth. She fought the urge to vomit as Sal's head lolled on a neck gone slack. A second, lipless mouth slashed itself into being across the soft curve of his throat. The striated tube of his trachea bulged from the mass of gray, bloodless flesh.

"Sal?" Bug's quavering voice drifted through the evening air.

Xenia, her fear paralysis broken, tore her eyes from the gruesome spectacle. *She can see him?* Ice clawed at her heart. The sight of her brother like this would break the poor child. *No! She can't see this!*

"Bug," Xenia sobbed. She forced herself to be calm, for Marisol's sake. "Sweetie, stay there. I'm coming over." She staggered across the street, trying to impose herself between Marisol and what lay behind her as best she could.

She fell to her knees before the girl. Impossible hope shone in Bug's face. Unshed tears shimmered in her eyes. Her brother's basketball was, as always, clutched to her chest.

"Bug," Xenia murmured, "you didn't—"

"Where'd he go, Zeeny? Sal was here, you were talking..." Marisol's trembling lip jutted forward.

The girl hadn't, *thank God,* seen the horror that Xenia had. That she had even seen Sal at all... Xenia would deal with that later. For now, she opened her arms to the shivering girl. Bug wasted no time in cannonballing into her embrace. She rubbed the girl's back as the bawling began. After a moment, when she was ready, she turned to look.

The sidewalk was dry. Empty. Sal was nowhere to be seen.

Xenia allowed her tears to join Marisol's. "I miss him too, Bug. I miss him too."

Chapter Twenty

Xenia's breath fogged her bedroom window, transforming the Serranos' porch light into a hazy orange blob. Day and night, rain or shine, it had burned since the night Sal had failed to come home. Mrs. Serrano had forbidden anyone from flipping that switch until her son was home safe.

"She saw him."

In between their shared sobs, Xenia had coaxed additional detail from Marisol. Tonight hadn't been the first time, since his disappearance, that she'd seen her brother. Each time she'd approached him, to welcome or scold him for his absence, he'd vanish. The girl, in near hysterics, could not understand why Sal wouldn't stay.

If the Sal she'd seen earlier was had been a figment of her damaged brain, how could Bug have possibly seen him as well?

She stared off into the night. Thoughts ricocheted about her head, refusing to settle into anything approaching sense. The lights, the apparition her first morning in class...

Bethany... She no longer enjoyed the certainty that they all shared a common origin in her concussion.

"What is happening to me?" The question fogged the window anew. Telling Aunt Elspeth now was unthinkable. Broaching the subject had been terrifying enough when it was all in her head. Now? Tell her guardian that she might have seen an actual ghost? More than one?

Elspeth would have her in a straitjacket before she'd finished the tale.

No. She would need proof. Not just for her great-aunt. For herself. Something incontrovertible. Undeniable.

Xenia turned from the window to her desk. To the book waiting there. *Practical Spells and Recipes.* She flipped to the chapter on scrying.

Scrying was seeing, with magic, people, places, or things wherever they might be in the world. Like a camera, but without the camera.

Xenia's plan was to locate Sal, alive or... not, with one of these spells. That had to be why the raven had led her to it, right? Then, when she'd shown Aunt Elspeth the proof, she'd know for sure if any of this was real or not. For better or worse.

"Up late with your studies, dearie?"

Xenia paused in the kitchen door, glad she'd tucked *Practical Spells* under her notebook. "Kind of? Just getting a snack." *Please don't ask what I'm reading.* If Elspeth saw the book, she'd die of embarrassment right there.

"Don't stay up too late, even if you don't have school tomorrow." Elspeth covered her mouth and yawned enormously. "Woo. Past time for this old lady to heed her own advice. Ta."

"Night, Aunt Elspeth." Xenia waited by the kitchen table until Elspeth's footsteps sounded overhead. Only when she was certain her great-aunt was in bed for the night did she begin her preparations. The well-stocked kitchen had everything she required for the scrying spell.

Xenia went to the cabinet for the "bowl of dark glaze." Elspeth frequented Humboldt County's many artisans in order to secure their work for her shop. There was no shortage of hand-thrown tableware to pick from.

The next requirement was "water as fresh as can be had." The tap water had a funny aftertaste, which rendered it unsuitable in her opinion. Xenia eased open the back door to scoop a pitcher's worth from the rain barrel outside.

The sage, fennel, and other herbs were the easiest of all. She snipped a few choice sprigs from the abundance that grew in the window garden.

Lastly, the kitchen's "everything" drawer provided a box of wooden strike-anywhere matches and a chalky white candle.

She paused her arrangements as a wave of melancholy struck. It was a shame Bethany couldn't be here for this. Xenia might have doubts, but her BFFFF had been all about things creepy and occult. She would have loved to be part of the experiment.

Wait.

"Beebs," Xenia whispered, "you here?" She waited, on edge, for a handful of moments. The tick of the dining room clock was the only audible reply.

Xenia ignored her sudden disappointment. She didn't actually believe that Bethany was floating around, did she?

But Marisol had seen Sal.

Faith, *Practical Spells and Recipes* had claimed, was the key. Without it, magic was impossible. Faith that the universe would provide and, more importantly, faith in one's own self. *Fine.* She would keep her mind as open as possible.

Xenia flipped to the spell she'd chosen. Took a deep breath.

Step one: Fix your thoughts upon the place, item, or individual that you desire to see. Xenia wanted to find Sal... or his body. She pictured his good-natured, goofy smile.

Step two: With your subject in mind, place the herbs into the bowl. Spread them flat across the bottom. Add water until the bowl is near to overflowing. Xenia poured in the rainwater she'd collected. Before the bulge of surface tension could break and send water all over the table, she lifted the pitcher.

Step three: Place the candle opposite of the bowl so that you may see its reflection in the water.

Step four: Ignite the candle as you recite the following words. Xenia, match in hand, squinted at the page. The invocation had been rendered in tiny, extra-fancy letters. It implored someone named "Themis" to grant a vision of what was sought.

Step five: Behold!

Goody Hawkes had laid out her instructions in exacting detail. Despite that effort, she had failed to note how long Xenia would wait before the "vision" appeared.

Xenia kept her eyes glued to the flame's reflection, Sal's face foremost in her thoughts. Despite herself, she glanced at the clock. Fifteen minutes. She blew out the candle. Lit it again while reciting the incantation.

As the clock ticked past the thirty-minute mark, Xenia suspected she'd been had. She scrubbed at her aching eyes. Re-read the instructions. Yep. She'd done everything, gathered everything, just as the book instructed. If the spell was going to work, she would have seen something by now.

Anger flared. How stupid could she be? Magic? Really? *What did you think was going to happen? That you'd find Sal? Why? Because some dumb bird had pecked a book?* For all she knew, the old hippie had trained that crow to lure in gullible kids like her!

Xenia shoved away from the table, snatched up *Practical Spells*. In her frustration, she bumped the bowl and sent it tumbling to the floor. Shards of dark porcelain, water, and wet herbs flew across the floor as the bowl shattered on the tile. "Damn it!" She hurled the book across the room.

As fast as it had arrived, her anger fled and shame rushed in to fill the vacuum. She held her breath, eyes to the ceiling, waiting for a sign that she'd disturbed her great-aunt. *One-Mississippi, two-Mississippi…*

Silence. Xenia released the breath with a whoosh. "Good job, moron." Now there was a mess to clean up. Xenia padded to the pantry for a dustpan and whisk.

Only once she'd disposed of every scrap and every drooping wet herb, and had toweled up the water, did Xenia allow herself to look for the book. Its short flight had ended in a collision with the fridge. She found it on the floor amidst a scattering of fridge magnets the impact had dislodged.

Xenia clicked the windmill, crab-on-a-plate, and tiny snow globe back onto the refrigerator and plucked the stupid book from where it had fallen. As she stood, a loose sheet fluttered free. Xenia caught the errant page before it landed.

"Good job, you broke it." Xenia had half hoped that she'd be able to wheedle herself a refund. Not anymore. She set the book on the table and leafed through in search of any other damage.

As far as she could see, the binding was still intact. Nor

were any of the pages missing or torn. Where, then, had the loose page come from?

A second, more thorough search of the slim volume revealed a sheet of card stock glued to the inside back cover. Affixed on three sides, with the innermost side loose, it formed a pocket. The thick paper was a match for the book's binding. Xenia would have missed it entirely if she hadn't been looking. She swapped the book for the loose page.

What she'd taken for a loose page was a sheet no larger than an index card. Unlike the secret pocket, the paper didn't match anything in the book. The pages of *Practical Spells* were thin and creme in color, while this card was sturdy and white. One side was entirely blank, but the other...

In the center of the card was a drawing in black ink. More of a pattern than an illustration, it had a scratchy look. As if it had been inked by hand, with an old-fashioned quill pen. A thick rectangle bordered a handful of short lines, arcs, and small circles. Above the design, a single word had been written with the same pen.

"Lockbreaker," Xenia read aloud.

Heart thudding, she opened the book. Searched each chapter for this "Lockbreaker." Neither the word nor the drawing were anywhere to be found anywhere inside.

Why hide this inside a book of bogus spells? What was a Lockbreaker? Had it been this card, Xenia wondered, and not the book itself that the raven intended her to find?

At that moment, the idea that the raven had known what it was doing all along, that it had brought Xenia and this "Lockbreaker" together deliberately...

It no longer seemed quite so farfetched, did it?

Chapter Twenty-One

Xenia's jaw crackled like a bowl of cereal as she yawned for the third time in a minute.

"Are you not sleeping, dearie?" Elspeth looked up from her inventory list.

"Mostly." Xenia fought off another yawn. There was no way she could sleep. Not after discovering the mysterious "Lockbreaker." She'd stayed up, clicking about online in search of answers. There had been no shortage of lock-smiths, and more than a few Wicca wikis to be found. However, nothing had matched the design inked on the card. At some point, well after four a.m., she'd nodded off, face on her keyboard. Elspeth had come knocking, bright and early, with a request. There was another shipment of merchandise at Bits 'n' Pieces, and would Xenia be so kind as to lend a hand?

Xenia extracted a mass of shredded paper from a box and grimaced at the ceramic tableware within. Cousins to the bowl she'd smashed, they were far, far pricier than she'd expected. Xenia resolved to set aside some money until she could pay for a replacement.

At long last, just before lunch, the two of them had freed every bowl, plate, cup, and art piece from their cardboard-and-paper prisons. Task complete, Elspeth released Xenia into the world to enjoy her Saturday.

Xenia raced straight for home.

She paused just long enough to fortify herself with a handful of barbecue chips and a can of the electric orange soda Elspeth favored. Then she raced upstairs. There were tests to do. Experiments to be conducted.

First, Xenia held the scrap of paper up to the desk lamp, scrutinizing it for a watermark or any other clue to its origin. The lightbulb's heat should, she'd read, render any lemon juice "invisible ink" notation visible.

Negative on both counts. Xenia crossed them off her list.

The magnifying glass and magnet tests were quickly marked off when they, too, failed to produce results. Xenia wasn't ready to burn the card, or cut pieces from it, so she skipped the destructive tests.

Officially out of ideas, Xenia ensconced herself within the window nook to think. Her gaze skipped over the house across the street, and the sidewalk out front, as she mulled the problem over.

Lulled by the languorous swirl of clouds, and hastened by a mostly sleepless night, her eyelids dipped. Her breathing slowed. In moments, she'd slipped into the twilit space between true sleep and wakefulness.

The slam of a car door snapped her from her reverie. She found her room, and the world outside, alive with the streamers and auras of what she'd assumed was a migraine symptom. Her instinct was to reject the colors, to squeeze her eyes shut and keep them that way until sanity returned.

Instead, she took a deep breath and told the nagging voice of reason to take a hike.

In her altered sight, the flock of birds perched in the oak tree blazed with color that put their "normal" appearance to shame. The display was more vibrant, more beautiful than anything she'd seen in movies or on TV. Each bird was its own dainty flare of opal and carnation. When they sang, spirals of topaz and other, nameless, colors swam from their beaks. Birdsong manifest.

Even as common sense scolded her to ignore this obvious symptom of her injury, she wondered. Was this how Ev saw the world? How would the notes of his whistle appear in this impossible spectrum?

Xenia sat bolt upright.

"No way." What had he said? When she tried to recall that afternoon, walking with Ev, the memory fought her efforts, instead remaining within the depths of her mind. When at last she found the moment, it was fuzzy, incomplete.

"He said he stopped insisting that his imaginary friends weren't real. That he had to allow himself to just be himself... I think," Xenia mused out loud.

Fine. She'd cut herself some slack and pretend that the lights were real. Just for today.

With that in mind, Xenia went to her desk. Even though the ribbons of light slid from her path, she did her best to avoid them in turn. She didn't need a repeat of the last time she'd indulged her fevered imagination. Getting knocked out once was one time too many.

While every object she could see had its own internal glow, some bright, some dim, *Practical Spells and Recipes* had almost no radiance of its own. Other than a faint, blueish, fuzz about the edges, the book was entirely without aura. Xenia flipped to the concealed pocket and slid "Lock-breaker" out. "Woah!"

In Xenia's altered sight, the design shone with new life. Loops and whorls of light, no thicker than a hair, appeared to emerge from the paper. The tangled knot of light, much larger and more complex than the inked version, appeared not only above the page but extended into it as well. The effect, to Xenia's eye, was similar to one of the hologram trading cards that Bethany's little cousin had been obsessed with. When she rotated the card, the "hologram" turned with it.

Despite what had occurred last time she'd tried it, Xenia brushed one of the threads that ran along the border of the hologram. There was no sensation of contact. When she poked her finger into it, the strands failed to react in any way. The paper at the center of the design still felt exactly like paper.

Xenia dropped into her chair and centered the card on the desk before her.

"Either my imagination is running at hyper speed, or..."

Would you believe me if I said "magic"?

Xenia spun her chair around. Then again. Stuck her nose as close as she dared to the impossible hologram. She chose a filament at random and traced its path with her eyes. The pattern was dense, and the thread she'd picked doubled back on itself several times before she found the—

At the very center of the hologram, where the cluster of overlapping lines mirrored the design inked onto the paper, was a tiny, glowing, arrow. Next to the arrow, in script almost too fine to read, the words: *Start Here.*

Her arms danced with icy prickles as each hair stood on end.

Xenia fell back in her chair. The whirl of her thoughts had, for once, come to a complete stop.

She looked again. Yep, the writing was still there.

You could, suggested that nagging common sense, *pretend you don't see it. Just like you've been doing.*

Xenia ignored the impulse and swept the card from her desk. She turned it this way and that as she tracked each thread through the pattern. Even though they looped around each other, twisted into knots and out again, it seemed achievable. But in what material? Aunt Elspeth sold all sorts of string in her shop. Would that work?

Her eye went to the weird ribbons drifting about her room. The color of one, a sort of silvery orange-green but not really, was a match for the starter thread in the hologram.

"Really?" It made a weird kind of sense, if she didn't think too hard about it. She cast her gaze about the room and found a match for nearly every thread in the hologram. The missing color she located in a column of radiance twining through the air just outside her windows.

"Okay, this totally isn't nuts. Just your regular, everyday floating string of light." Xenia reached for the first color she needed to duplicate the pattern.

The string of incandescence slipped away, just as it had when she'd walked across the room. She tried again. The thread slipped from her pinching fingers like a watermelon seed.

On her fifth try, she managed to snag the elusive thread. The surface was slick, like soft glass. Unlike her earlier experience, the material was merely cool against the pad of her fingers, not frigid. When Xenia tugged, a portion came away in her grasp.

As long as her attention remained on the strand, she was

able to maintain a hold on it. The moment her focus wavered, it slipped away. She pulled a replacement from the same source.

Using the hologram as reference, she pulled on her bit of light, drawing it out into a slender thread. Bit by bit, she shaped it into a duplicate of the first portion of the glowing design. She found that, as long as she maintained contact with one hand, the string held the shape she'd imposed upon it. Like pipe cleaner art, if pipe cleaners glowed.

As she attempted to incorporate the next "color," Xenia lost her grip. Everything she'd accomplished evaporated into nothing. The tips of her fingers tingled, and a bit of pressure swelled behind her eyes. The sensation, as if someone had blown across the surface of her brain, was unpleasant enough to border on painful. In its wake, the first hints of her old friend, the migraine, began to stir.

She began again.

Over the following hour, while Xenia plucked, pinched, shaped, and twisted the strands of light, the migraine grew. The pain's advance wasn't nearly as rapid as she feared, so she pressed on. By the time she twisted the last slip of glimmering nothingness into place, sweat stuck her hair to her forehead and stung her eyes.

The result wasn't as neat and tidy as the original, and some details might be out of proportion. However, there was no doubt that the shimmering cat's cradle stretched between her trembling hands was the same as the hologram.

"Now what?" The card had shown her where to start, but that was all. "Lockbreaker. Maybe I need a lock to break?" She spun her chair around.

Aunt Elspeth had swapped out the antique knob in Xenia's bedroom door for a more modern one. Something about teenagers and their privacy, she'd said. Xenia fought to keep her hands steady as she scooted over to the door. If the lock actually broke, she might be able to get a replacement from the hardware store. The thought of concealing that she'd wrecked another bit of Elspeth's home didn't thrill her. But then, if the lock actually *broke*, she'd have other things on her mind.

"Lockbreaker, go!" Xenia threw the cat's-cradle at the little twisty bit on the knob.

The mass of lambent threads came apart as soon as she released them. In seconds, they'd fizzled away to nothing. This time, the *poof* against her brain was definitely painful. Her migraine, which had begun to fade once she'd stopped actively grabbing at threads, surged in with a vengeance. "Owww." All about her, the swirls and ribbons of light flickered in and out of visibility.

Xenia rubbed at her temples and eyed the bottle of headache medication on her desk. *What did I miss?* She was positive her cat's cradle had matched the hologram strand for strand. She kicked off the wall and rolled to her desk, where she traced the lines floating about the card with her finger.

Wait.

The lines of the hologram came together as they passed through the "window" of the paper and, at their densest, matched the design of lines, arcs and circles that had been inked there. Overlapped it, in fact. Every ink line had a glowing double.

"But not the border." Xenia exhaled, long and loud. "Right. Something needs to hold it together, like a box." She ran her finger along the heavy ink line while she thought. Did it need to be paper, or was something more durable required?

She winced as her headache bumped itself up a notch.

There was clearly a price for failure. If she could avoid doing this over and over, that would be peachy. Xenia yanked open the desk drawer and rummaged.

Among the collection of chewed pencils, bent paper-clips, and crumbling erasers, she found a tiny metal ruler. No more than six inches long, the steel was patinated with age but free of rust. *Why not?*

Xenia mopped the sweat from her forehead. Cracked her knuckles. Started again.

The migraine continued to swell as she worked her way through the pattern. With each strand of the impossible material she added to Lockbreaker's pattern, another jagged finger sawed into her head. Even as the pain surged to a level beyond any she'd yet experienced, she pressed on. Xenia knew that if she gave up now, she'd never allow herself to "pretend," to accept that the glowing ribbons of light were real, ever again. Even as her vision narrowed to the glowing skein of light between her fingers, she forced herself onward. She gritted her teeth until they groaned, braced her feet against the desk to hold herself upright as the room spun in dizzy circles. She squinted dry, aching eyes at the minute variations she imposed upon the magical thread. She'd had to work smaller, so that the final would fit the ruler. Why hadn't she chosen a larger vessel? Too late now.

Her breath was coming in great ragged gulps as she eased the complete design onto the slip of metal. Xenia's concentration narrowed to the point where impossible light met steel. When the thickest bit of the pattern, the portion that matched the inked design, lay atop the ruler, she let go.

The glowing tangle soaked into the ruler like water into a sponge. The metal shivered against her numbed fingertips and issued a single, metallic chime. In the same instant, in the manner of a fever, her migraine broke. The intolerable pain drained away until all that remained was a faint but unpleasant buzz behind her eyes. Xenia blinked her suddenly clear eyes and examined her creation.

A collection of lines, arcs, and circles, identical to those on the card, was now embedded in the metal surface. She rubbed her thumb across the ruler and found them etched into the metal.

Ruler in hand, she kicked her way back to the door. She had to pause a moment while her equilibrium caught up. "Okay." Xenia gave the tumbler a twist to assure herself it was locked. Before she could second-guess herself, she poked the knob with the ruler. "See? Nothing—"

The tumbler twitched. Gave a little rattle. Unlocked itself.

Xenia gaped at the lock, then the slip of metal in her hand. "What the hell." She twisted the tumbler again. Gave the doorknob a firm shake. Locked. She tapped the lock with the ruler.

Just as before, the tumbler rattled, then turned itself to the unlocked position.

It was conceivable that she had gone completely loco. Unlocked it herself while only imagining it had moved on its own. Sure. It was possible. Likely, even, more likely than...

She needed a better test subject. Something she didn't have a key for. Xenia spun in a circle. *Aunt Elspeth's trunk.* She kicked her chair across the room and slid to the floor.

Elspeth hadn't gotten around to relocating the old bit of luggage after Xenia had moved in. In the weeks since, it had become a convenient place for her to pile this and that.

The trunk was scratched and dented, quite deeply in some spots—proof that it had traveled as far as Elspeth claimed she had. Front and center, the lid was secured by a wide brass hasp flanked by a pair of latches. Some bit of rough handling had dented the lock. The tiny keyhole was bent and wouldn't have accepted a key even if Xenia had one. She tugged on the brass and found it secure. She set her feet to either side and gave it her best heave. It didn't budge an inch. Locked tight.

Xenia tapped the ruler—no, *Lockbreaker*—against the tarnished brass. A heartbeat later, there was a clatter from within the mechanism. A tiny *ting* of metal striking metal.

The hasp popped open.

"Holy shit."

Xenia stared at *Lockbreaker*. With a bit of reverence, she set the ruler on the floor beside her. She swept the clutter from the trunk and flipped the latches open. A heavy whiff of cedar greeted her as she forced the lid up.

The interior was full to overflowing with old document folders, vintage magazines and faded newspapers. Here and there, Polaroid photos were tucked into any space available.

The room did a little wobble and Xenia sat back on her heels. *This isn't possible.* Everything up to this point, she could explain away. Even Everard's bird trick might have had a reasonable explanation.

The trunk? Unless she'd taught herself how to repair, then pick locks, there was no way she could have opened it herself. The wood was intact, she hadn't smashed her way in.

Xenia grabbed a photo at random. The Polaroid had gone a bit purple with time, but the subject was clear.

The photographer had captured a trio of women standing arm in arm. In their mid-twenties, they wore their tie-dyed shirts knotted high to expose their bellies. The wild, windswept mass of strawberry blonde hair threw

Xenia off at first, but the impish grin on the middle woman was unmistakably Elspeth's.

Next to, and a bit behind the trio were a pair of men in black and saffron monk's robes. The taller man was much older than Elspeth was now, his face a mask of wrinkles. The shorter was barely out of his teens. Both were bald as eggs.

Behind the young Elspeth, her friends and the monks rose the tiled roof of a temple. The image was faded, but Xenia could make out the deep indigo paint, and the gold of the ornaments lining the roof.

When she shifted her thumb she found, at the very edge of the frame, someone in the background. While the stone lantern beside her was in focus, the kimono-clad woman was indistinct. Some imperfection in the lens distorted her face, angled her eyes and mouth into a vulpine leer. Xenia flipped the photo over. There, in Elspeth's tight handwriting, was "Kyoto, 1979."

Xenia flicked the photo into the trunk and fell backward onto the floor, arms wide. She stared at the ceiling, counting the tiny cracks in the plaster until her world stopped spinning.

One by one, strand by strand, the maze of glowing ribbons above faded from her sight. The auras clinging to each of the room's objects were the last to go.

It began as a tiny chuckle. A hint of merriment that bubbled up out of her gut. Before she knew it, she was kicking her heels and hammering the flat of her hands against the hardwood floor. Laughter, pure and joyous as nothing she'd felt since the accident, poured from her, bent her double with racking spasms of gleeful triumph until the muscles of her stomach ached. Once the last chortle had spent itself, she palmed the tears from her eyes and lay there, staring at nothing.

Everard had been right after all. There really was only one word for this. That would describe his trick with the birds. That would encompass what she'd done. One word that explained how a lock might be coaxed into opening itself.

Magic.

Chapter Twenty-Two

Bethany skimmed along at treetop height as she made her way to the old Victorian. She'd just pop in for a moment, she told herself: in, make sure Xenia was good, then out, before Elspeth noticed.

She was still kicking herself for squandering the opportunity in the bookstore. Zee could hear her! She should have warned Xenia about the killer right then. Instead, she'd blown it with a dumb stunt, then been chased off with her metaphorical tail between her legs.

She needed to have a serious sit-down with Xenia. It was time to convince her once and for all that ghosts were real. Bethany was real.

Before anyone else was murdered.

As if on cue, the pale form lingering before the Findlay home hove into view. If she couldn't have that chat with Zee quite yet, she'd have one with Porter Valley's newest ghost.

Bethany drifted to a halt at street level. "Hi."

Salvatore Serrano cringed away. Abject terror twisted his face into a shadowed parody of his living self. He fell away from her and tried to run, only to stumble to a halt when Bethany placed herself in his path.

"Hey, it's okay." Bethany held her hands out, doing her best to look harmless. "I'm not going to hurt you. Look, I'm a ghost too. See?" She dipped through the surface of the street, then up again. Her demonstration did nothing to lessen the fear in Sal's face, but he halted his attempts to flee.

Like Lucas, and the other victims Bethany had met, a deep pool of shadow filled the space where his eyes should have been. He was beyond pale. Even the clothing he wore had been leached of color.

Despite the fact that weeks had passed since his disappearance, and death, this was the first time they had met face to face. Judging by his panicked reaction at her presence, he had likely been hiding from her. Not that she held it against him. Hell, he wasn't even the first of the Lost to do so.

After her encounter with Lucas, Bethany had set herself the task of locating the Porter Valley Killer's other victims. She'd assumed that, like Lucas, they were stuck, unable to pass on. Her success rate was better than that of the actual police on the case. Those desk jockeys still thought they were dealing with a bunch of runaways and a domestic kidnapping. The captain, Strauss, seemed to be doing everything possible to avoid admitting there was a killer afoot!

Douglass, that poor little wisp of spirit, had been the easiest to locate.

Lucas had reappeared a couple days after his traumatic reenactment. Since then, he'd ignored her attempts to communicate. She couldn't blame him.

Trevor had just wandered onto Bluff Street. Thanks to

her police station snooping, she'd been able to put a name to his shadowed face. Trevor had gone missing over a month before Lucas and, at twelve, was the youngest of the Lost. Every time she caught sight of his pallid little face, Bethany's heart broke again.

Aubrey was, as far as Bethany knew, the only girl among the killer's victims. It had required a bit of ghost detective work, but she'd located the site of Aubrey's death. She'd found the ghost lingering, just off one of the many hiking trails that crossed the ridge north of the valley. On first sight, Aubrey had flown into a silent rage. Communication had been all but impossible, and she'd left the furious ghost to herself in the hope that, in time, she'd calm enough to join the others.

Learning of Sal's disappearance had destroyed her enthusiasm at playing detective. Maybe, if she'd actually known what she was doing, she'd have been able to warn Xenia in time. He'd still be alive.

"I'm Bethany. I'm sorry we didn't get a chance to meet while we were both still kickin'." She offered Sal a sad smile. "Thank you for being Xenia's friend when she needed it most. When I couldn't be there for her."

Sal's head came up. At the mention of their mutual friend, a fragment of the tension eased from his shoulders. The shadowed pit of his gaze turned toward the old Victorian.

"Can you talk?"

Sal's mouth opened on the same void that had claimed his eyes. His throat worked as he attempted to speak. Despite his visible strain, no sound emerged.

"I'm sorry. Charades it is."

He stared at her.

"Have you met Lucas and Trevor?" Bethany waved

toward the other ghosts who, for now, remained at the end of the block.

Sal didn't turn his gaze their way, but after a moment, he nodded.

Of course he would know them, Bethany chided herself. Even before their deaths, they would have been at the same school. Small town and all that. Bethany was the newcomer here.

"Right. So." Bethany glanced toward the window that Sal, and the others, were so obsessed with. "Xenia. She's my best friend. Since way back when we both lived in LA. I was certain, when I wound up here, that I was supposed to haunt her. But now I'm not so sure. Maybe I'm supposed to help you"—she waved to encompass all of Porter Valley's dead—"because I'm the only ghost in this bunch who can still speak. And Xenia can see me." *Sometimes*, she added to herself.

Salvatore pivoted her way, his face contorting. Fear, anger, confusion and, most heartbreaking of all, hope warred for space in his expression. His hands groped between them, as if he sought to wrench meaning from the air itself.

He staggered toward the garden fence, and Bethany interposed herself. "Hold up. She's had a rough time since her parents died. Having you guys show up... it's not helping."

Judging by Sal's stricken expression, Bethany suspected that he'd already had an encounter with Xenia. Clearly, it had not gone well.

Damn it.

"Look, I'll tell you what I told those guys. Since I can talk and I don't turn into an anatomy lesson when she's around, I'll do everything I can. Help get justice for what was done to you. Taken from you. When she's ready, I'll tell Xenia everything. All of your stories. Once the living know what's going on, they can stop it. Your families will have closure. You won't be trapped here anymore, you'll be able to move on." *I hope.* "Until then, stop getting up in Zee's face, okay? You're welcome to wait with those two." She waved at Lucas, who looked away.

Salvatore stared at her face, shoulders trembling. The ghost's empty, void mouth gaped as he tried to speak. His hands rose, fingers knotted, the gesture unintelligible. His arms fell, back bowed. At last, he nodded.

"It cool if I ask some questions?" Bethany took his silence for assent. "First off, and this is the big one, do you know who did it? Who killed you?"

Sal flinched away as if he'd been slapped. He cowered behind his arms. After a long pause, he offered a single shake of his head.

Damn. "Did you see what they looked like?"

His arms wrapped about around his narrow chest as he turned away—from her, from the old Victorian, toward his former home. His shrug was nearly lost within the shudder that racked him from head to toe. He raised one hand and then brought it down in a chopping motion.

"It happened fast. Yeah, Trevor said the same thing happened to him." She pressed on, intent on confirming what the younger ghost had conveyed by gesture. "It wasn't a person, was it, or an animal? It was something else."

Sal half turned. His lips pulled back from teeth and gums gone black as night. He shook his head, the movement so violent as to twist his entire torso side to side.

Bethany was pretty sure, based on Captain Strauss's notebook, that the killings didn't sync up with the full moon. She asked anyway. "Werewolf?" Another shake of

Sal's head. She sighed. Whoever, *whatever* was killing these teens, it struck fast. Without warning. To think she'd assumed that the ability to speak with the murder victim would make solving their case a jiffy. "This is the difficult part. Can you show me where it happened? Or where your body is?"

No sooner had the words left her mouth than Sal stumbled away from her, his arms raised as if to fend off a blow, his face a mask of purest terror.

"I know! If you get too close, you'll relive the whole thing. I'm not asking you to go through that. Just point the way and I'll take it from there. Do you think you can do that? Then, when it's time, I'll tell Xenia. You know she'll do everything she can."

The sound of their friend's name had an immediate, calming effect on Sal. He lowered his arms. The tremors eased. He looked to the glow in Xenia's window one last time and nodded. Sal turned and took one shambling step, then another, away from the Findlays' home.

During her dealings with the others, Bethany had begun to harbor a suspicion about belief, and how it pertained to the spirit. Without a body, they might not be able to interact with the material world. No amount of belief had allowed her to make contact with the physical, but there had been that moment with Lucas...

"I am so sorry, Sal. Death should have freed you of all burdens. Instead, even this was taken from you." She rose above the sidewalk. Sal stumbled to a halt and gazed up at her with as much puzzlement his ruined face could show. Bethany held out her hand. He just stared back at her.

When, at long last, Sal took her hand, Bethany did the believing for both of them.

There was the same brush of contact, gossamer fine, as when she'd reached out to Lucas. Just a hint, nothing more.

Bethany held Sal's shadowed gaze as she sent herself into the air and, just as she'd hoped, Sal rose with her. Something akin to wonder bloomed on his face. It was the closest thing to peace she'd seen in any of the Lost.

Together, the two dead teens rose above Sal's former home. Together, they sought the place where he had been torn from his life, and the lives of all who loved him.

Chapter Twenty-Three

Bethany elevated her nose to the precise angle required to convey how serious she was. "To thine own self be true, Mr. Findlay," she sniffed. "I must always be true to my muse." She favored Xenia with a kohl-lined wink. "You ready, Zee?"

Xenia tore her attention away from the glacier-slow traffic beyond her window. High-fived her BFFFF. "Born ready! If"—she glared at the red light that impeded their progress—"we ever get there."

Cool, salty sea air brushed her cheek.

The swollen orb of the sun shrank in the west and was gone.

From his stool beside the fire, Uncle plucked at his instrument. He coaxed a simple melody from the strings and, as the sweet notes spiraled high to mingle with the smoke from the fire, he began to sing.

* * *

In those times, in those distant times.

Those ancient nights, those far off years.

Amatuanki, the Divine Mother, gave birth to the Heavens above and the Earth below. About them all was the Eternal Sea.

Great was she, Mother of All. Goddess of Goddesses. Highest and most exalted firstborn of The One.

As Mothers have ever done, *Amatuanki* brought new life into the world. Twin daughters did she bear, the joy of her heart.

The Divine Mother adored her offspring so, and unto them she granted dominion over all things. All of creation was to be theirs, from one shore of the Eternal Sea to the other. In her stead, by her decree, they would rule.

Elletu, the Pure One, as the Divine Mother was also known, called her daughters to stand before her. She would judge the twins, and so divide the world between them.

One daughter, from whose eyes shone the light of day, was called *Bēlet An-Nisig*, which means "Lady of Blue Sky." Upon her brow was placed the *Kù-Sig Aga*, the Golden Crown of the Sun. All the hours of the day and the business thereof would be hers. She would rule this domain with an even hand and all the love in her heart.

The other daughter, in whose eyes swam the stars of midnight, was called *Bēlet An-Ĝíg*, which means "Lady of Black Sky." Likewise, she received the *Kù-Babbar Aga*, the Silver Crown of the Moon. The darkness of the night was hers to command, and over this domain she would rule with a firm grasp and the force of her will.

Amatuanki bade her daughters farewell. She would retire to the depths of the Eternal Sea. In time, perhaps, she would bear more children. Until that day, she would rest and contemplate matters celestial. Her daughters,

Glorious Sun and Revered Moon, would rule the world in her stead.

As time passed, the Twin Queens danced across the face of the world. The years passed through one another until they numbered more than sixty upon half-sixty.

Under the Lady of Blue Sky's benevolence, the people of the Great Continent knew no hunger. Bountiful indeed were the harvests her grace bestowed. Her tutelage brought them the arts: cures for the sick, the shaping of clay and stone, crafting lyres and pipes of subtle tone, and the means to cut the immense gemstones that sprang from the land. Judge of all misdeeds was she. No sin might be concealed from her sight.

The people rejoiced and said to their mothers, who in turn spoke to the grandmothers who, in their way, said thus to *Bēlet An-Nisig*: "Lo, you bring us great fortunes indeed, O Queen of Exaltation. Many are the gifts you have bestowed upon us. We are grateful."

At the Lady of Black Sky's command, the rains fell. Gladly she sent the waters to irrigate her sister's bounty and to slake the thirst of the people. She instructed them in the disciplines: the binding of wounds, of marking words upon parchment, the shaping of the abundant metals that grew beneath the soil, of war and tactics to drive the barbarians and Not-Men back beyond the ends of the Great Continent. Moreover, to her favorites alone did she speak her secret name. To them was granted her most subtle teachings. Punishment was hers to deliver unto those who had been found wanting under her sister's judgment.

The people became disquieted. They said to their Mothers, who in turn spoke to the Grandmothers who, in their way, said thus to *Bēlet An-Ĝig*: "Lo, you bring the flood and the tempest, O Queen of Mourning. You are stern beyond measure and drive us on without recess. War flows ever in your wake as dust rises from a footstep. You strike us down, be our misdeeds great or be they small. Strife and Sorrow are your handmaidens. Why do you set such misfortune upon our doorstep, when your Divine Sister has been so generous?"

Chapter Twenty-Four

B y Sunday evening, Xenia was half-convinced that she'd imagined the whole thing.

That was the reasonable assumption, right? There was no such thing as magic, ghosts weren't real, and ravens certainly didn't herd people into occult bookstores. Well, that last one might be possible with the right bird and some training, but whatever.

Since last night when she'd "Lockbroken" Aunt Elspeth's trunk, she hadn't seen the glowing ribbons of light, or Bethany's phantom. The trunk just sat there, mocking her. The damaged hasp made it impossible for her to relock it. Still, her doubts had lingered.

Which was how she found herself huddled in the shadows by Porter Valley High's gym door. Maia's *ALL BLACKS* shirt, which she'd washed, pressed, and folded into a tidy bundle, was in her book bag. Nerves and, to be honest, more than a little excitement set her fingers trembling so much that she almost dropped *Lockbreaker* when she drew the spelled ruler from her back pocket.

She poked the door. The lock issued a solid *clack,*

followed by the echoing crash of metal striking hardwood. Xenia winced. "Nobody heard that." She tugged the door open and stepped over the length of chain that had been the source of the racket. Despite her mounting anxiety, Xenia was impressed with the spell's thoroughness. *Lockbreaker* had not only dealt with the deadbolt in the door itself, it had opened the padlock-secured chain looped through the inner push bars. All with one tap.

She spared a glance over her shoulder. The field, and the street beyond, were free of potential witnesses. She eased the door shut and then scurried across the gym floor.

Lockbreaker made quick work of the girls' locker room door. A moment later, she stood before Maia's locker. When she found her shirt tomorrow morning, she'd have to be impressed with Xenia's ingenuity.

Or she'll be totally creeped out! Only then did it occur to Xenia that she might have gone a little overboard. *Too late now.* She tapped *Lockbreaker* against the plastic combination lock.

The dial spun a full rotation without pausing at any one number. The locker resonated with a deep *clunk*. The door popped open a half inch.

The interior of Maia's locker was sparse, all business. There were no photos, stickers, or other personal touches on the metal walls. The only contents were a duffel bag and a single pair of running shoes. The shoes were so worn, so frayed from use that the toe area of both had torn through.

Xenia set the *ALL BLACKS* shirt atop the duffel bag. She stepped back and then centered it for maximum effect. Maia would be so—

"I knew it."

Xenia's heart hammered against her sternum as if it meant to escape. She leapt away from the open locker.

The low bench in the center of the aisle caught her across the back of both knees and nearly sent her toppling to the floor. She broke out in a guilty sweat as she windmilled her arms for balance. "I'm not..." Her protest died on her lips.

Everard stood, hands stuffed into his stupid letter jacket, at the end of the row. The grinning skull of his Ed Hardy shirt declared, "Love Kills Slowly." He'd posed his Air Jordan atop the changing bench, as if he'd been there the whole time.

Xenia eased *Lockbreaker* behind her leg as she backed away. "What are you doing here?"

"I could ask you the same thing," Ev said with a lazy shrug. "Here I am, a good, law-abiding citizen who just happened to spot a B-and-E in progress..."

"I didn't break in!" Xenia's mouth snapped shut as she realized she had, in fact, broken in. "I was just returning—"

"Shyeah, right. Sunday night?" Ev shook his head. "I saw the whole thing. You tapped the lock with something and *bam*, it popped open! What was it? A magic wand?" His eyes glittered, bright and eager, in the locker room shadows.

"No! It was..." Xenia prodded her brain for a reasonable excuse. Instead, it presented her with the memory of his bird-calling whistle. *He already knows.* "It's not a wand." She raised *Lockbreaker*. "It's a ruler."

Ev's eyebrows rose. "A magic ruler that opens locks? That's basically a wand. Legit. Where'd you get it?"

Xenia forced her shoulders back. "I made it."

Ev's smirk stretched into a proud smile. "I knew you had it in you! See, that's why I like you, Xenia. You were special all along and didn't even know it."

Xenia's heart did a little *ba-dum*.

"Do it again." Somehow Ev was right beside her. He wriggled his fingers. "Do magic."

Doubt wormed its way into her thoughts. "I don't know..."

"Hey. I showed you mine, now show me yours." Ev pursed his lips and, with a wink, trilled a quiet echo of what he'd used on the birds. Warm breath puffed across her ear and sent a wave of goosebumps down her neck.

Just for a moment, Xenia considered the merits of just running. She didn't know this guy, not really. The first time they'd spoken, he'd laughed at her expense. *He apologized for that. He confided in you. He knows about magic.* Her thoughts churned and spun. A tiny voice at the edge of that inner maelstrom added, *He said he likes you.*

Xenia slammed Maia's locker shut and then rapped *Lockbreaker* against the one beside it. As the dial began to spin, she tapped the next three in rapid succession. She was absolutely not, she assured herself, showing off.

The first three lockers she'd zapped rattled themselves open, while the fourth... did nothing. "Huh." Xenia gave the handle a shake. Still locked.

"Sick!" Ev swung one door wide and grinned at the bra hanging inside. He rapped a knuckle on the door that had failed to open. "What happened? Dead batteries?"

Xenia slapped the ruler against her palm and shook it as if it were a stubborn flashlight. "Dunno." She tapped another locker, to no effect.

"Shit's dope as hell, no lie." Ev pursed his lips and favored her with an impressed look. "I can't do shit like that. How'd you pull it off?"

As ready as she was to just gush out the whole story, raven and all, part of her urged caution. "I'm not sure, really. I just... did it." Xenia turned the ruler over and over in her hands.

"You're a natural, just like me. Sweet!"

"I guess." Xenia gave *Lockbreaker* another try. This time, she was rewarded with a rattle and an unlocked door. "Hey, it's working again!"

"Told ya, batteries. Had to recharge or something."

Xenia slid the ruler into her back pocket and steadied the strap of her book bag over her shoulder. She'd have to come up with a test regimen to work out the spell's limits and capabilities. As she added a mental note to grab her soaked clothing on the way out, Xenia realized that her last, lingering doubts about magic had vanished. Everard was a perfect, mostly objective, third-party observer. If he was seeing all of this too...

Xenia closed each of the lockers that her magic—*her magic!*—had opened. Her hand lingered on the final door. "Can I ask you something?"

"Depends. Some stuff, you gotta buy me dinner first." He offered her a slow wink.

"Nothing like that, jeez." Xenia spun away. "You know about magic?"

"Obviously."

Xenia thought about the streamers of light and the auras she'd seen. The delicate threads from which she'd crafted *Lockbreaker*. "Do you see... stuff?"

"Like what, your ghost?"

"What?" Xenia's voice rose in a squeak.

"You didn't know?" Ev squinted into the air by Xenia's left. "What do you think caught my attention in the first place? Most peeps don't have their own personal haunt."

"Bethany?" Xenia searched beside her. No matter how

she strained her eyes or cajoled her brain, she could detect not a hint of her friend's presence.

"You can't see it? Huh." Ev tapped his chin.

"Sometimes I can," Xenia admitted, "but it's not reliable." She scrubbed at her eyes and gave the locker room a hard stare. "I can't control it at all. I'm sorry," she added for the unseen Bethany.

"You'll figure it out," said Everard. "I did."

Xenia gave Bethany's approximate location an apologetic smile. To Ev, she said, "Is that what you meant by imaginary friends? Ghosts?" She grinned. "You see dead people?"

Everard snorted. "Yeah, guess so. Okay, I think some were... well, I don't really know what they were. Not all of them looked like regular dead peeps. Anyhow, ain't seen 'em in a minute. They've all moved on or whatever."

"On my first day, did you see—" Xenia threw up an arm to shield eyes dazzled by the sudden light that flooded the locker room.

"Someone there? Stupid kids, I'm calling the cops," a tired, pissed-off voice called. A trio of beeps followed as he made good on his threat. Heavy footsteps and the jingle of a key ring drew close.

Ev met Xenia's panic with an amused grin. Warm breath puffed across her ear as he stage-whispered, "This way!" He nodded at the side door through which she'd entered and held his hand out for hers.

Run or surrender? The thought of Aunt Elspeth's disappointment when the police dragged her home in cuffs held her teetering on a knife's edge of indecision. Her guardian would be furious, if the shock didn't give her a heart attack first.

Xenia took Everard's hand.

Chapter Twenty-Five

"**I** knew it! You can see me!" Okay, Bethany knew that already. Hearing Xenia admit it out loud, however, was a breath of relief. The fact that this Ev guy could see her too came as a welcome bonus. At the very least, if she couldn't pass on what she knew about the Lost to Zee, he could be a fallback. She did a little curtsy in midair. "Nice to meet you."

Ev's eyes flicked to her face, then back to Xenia.

"Rude." At least Xenia finally had someone she could confide in. Someone alive alive-oh, at least. Being unable to offer any sort of comfort while Zee sank into that pit of self-loathing and despair hadn't been at all fun.

Magic, though? What the actual hell? Was that why Zee was so squirrelly lately? She almost couldn't believe it... until she remembered that she was a ghost, and that there was a no-shit monster tearing up Porter Valley's teen population. "I swear," Bethany said, half to herself, "I get just a touch occupied with ghost biz, and I almost miss the good stuff. Girlfriend, as soon we deal with one little problem, you and me are going to have some *fun*."

So caught up was Bethany in her vision of magical boarding schools and mystical journeys across wind-swept mountains that she hardly took notice of the locker room lights. Or that Zee and Ev had left her in their dust when they bolted for freedom. "Hah! The adventures have already begun!" She popped through the ceiling with a laugh.

From her vantage point above the school, it was easy to spot the two magical teens hustling, hand in hand, across the lacrosse field. Bethany grinned. "Who knew she had it in her? About dang time you made a move." Not a bad catch, either, Bethany thought. In all honesty, she'd been rooting for Sal, but that hadn't worked out the way anyone had hoped.

Sobered by the thought of the Lost at their lonely watch on Bluff Street, Bethany sped after the pair. She'd keep a polite distance until Zee was home. Now that Xenia knew for certain that ghosts were a thing, she'd waste no time in making contact. They'd just have to keep at it until it worked.

Once Bethany had a chance to fill Zee in on the danger stalking Porter Valley, showed her where to find all of its victims—once that whole situation had been dealt with, *then* they could dish.

Assuming they don't dillydally to make out. Zee was moving faster than Bethany would have expected of the lil' wallflower. She'd snuggled close, laid her head against Ev's shoulder. Not that Bethany had any objections. She couldn't help but grin as she inched closer to—*call it what it is, Brooks*—spy on her best friend.

"Look, babe," Ev said, "things'll be different now. Other than me, who could understand what you're going through?"

Ugh. Bethany gave herself a shake. *It's her choice. Let Zee do her thing.*

"Mm-hmm. Totally." Xenia's breathy reply came in a monotone, without any emotional inflection at all.

"You good, Zee?" Bethany inched close, then gasped.

Xenia's face was blank. Utterly devoid of expression. It was as if all her emotional energy had drained away. Even in the depths of her grief, her face had still been lively. Now, there was no awareness in her eyes. No recognition of the ghost's presence, or even of the street ahead. When Xenia blinked, the movement was glacier slow.

"Ev," Bethany asked, "what's up with Xenia? Why's she all blah like that?" She floated backward in front of the lacrosse player. "Cut the shit, I know you can hear me."

Ev glanced away from Xenia long enough to spear Bethany with a look so withering, so full of contempt, that she actually moved out of his path rather than allow him to pass through her. He returned his attention to Xenia. "I gotta say, I've been waiting my whole life to find someone with power like yours." He snuggled Xenia tight to his side. "You're going to be the crown jewel of my collection."

Even though she lacked the body for it, Bethany shivered in sudden fear. "Snap out of it, Zee!" She rocketed in front of her friend and bellowed, *"Wake up!"*

Xenia's mouth hung slack. A bead of saliva had gathered on her lip. She made no effort to wipe it away before it dripped to her clothing. She trembled. The shiver was so intense that Bethany could follow its course from her head to her toes.

It was the birds. Ev charmed the goddamned birds right out of the trees! Now he's doing the same thing to Zee! Anger surged into Bethany.

Everard's smirk was a monument to arrogance. He

tugged on Xenia's arm, stopping her in her tracks. His free hand slid over her shoulder, then cupped her cheek. He brushed the moisture from her lip with his thumb. Ev made a point of catching Bethany's eye and raised his eyebrow.

Bethany might have no idea how Everard's mind tricks worked but, based on every fantasy novel she'd ever read, a kiss would probably seal the deal and make his hold on Xenia permanent. Or maybe he just wanted to piss her off. Either way, she'd be damned if she'd let that jock mash his face on Zee's. "I'm warning you. Let her go. Now."

Ev waggled his eyebrows and stuck his lip out in a cartoonish pout.

"Please. I'm begging you. Don't do this."

Ev rolled his eyes and then leaned in for the kiss. His lips were no more than a hair's breadth from Xenia's when something fell from the trees above. The pale mass landed smack in the middle of his mop of blond hair.

"Augh! What the fuck?" Ev released Xenia to paw at his head. His questing fingers came away smeared with white. A viscous glob slid from his hairline to stain the shoulder of his jacket.

From the trees arching above came a single "*caw.*"

As Ev tried in vain to brush the filth from his hair without smearing it further, Xenia took a tottering step. Another followed, then another. Her eyelids fluttered as if she were emerging from the deepest sleep. Her pupils were wide, her eyes a little crossed. Her gaze focused, at last, on Bethany. "Beebs?" Xenia shook her head and rubbed her forehead. "I... I have to get home." Without another word to Everard, or to Bethany, she began to weave her way down the block. Before long, she broke into a jog.

"Right behind you, Zee," Bethany called out, floating

backward. She offered the jock a nasty grin of her own, accompanied by both middle fingers.

Everard had produced a tissue from one of his pockets and was scrubbing at his hairline. He paused to scowl at Bethany. When their eyes met, his blazed with an inner, sapphire glow. The luminous, faceted orbs vanished behind a blink. Once again, regular, human eyes glared at her. He dropped the useless tissue, and his hands curled into fists. One corner of his mouth twisted in a sneer. Despite the distance between them, Bethany had no trouble hearing his words.

"Next time, dead girl. Next time."

Chapter Twenty-Six

Xenia scratched her head. She'd spent the last ten minutes working to make sense of what she'd written. Her AP Calculus notebook held page after page of figures, notes, and homework assignments. Until, that is, she reached the current week. Those pages were a mess of nonsensical figures, scribbles, and a doodle that might have been a cow in a top hat. None of which had anything to do with math. She racked her brain to recall what Mr. Druszcz's lessons had been and came up empty. She could clearly picture her other classes. First period, however, remained a blur.

Maybe she wasn't getting as much sleep as she'd thought. Those weird dreams had been a welcome change from her nightmare, true. But if she was still tired enough to sleepwalk through calc...

"Ugh." She'd just have to reread every one of the chapters she'd zoned out on. So much for the weekend. Xenia slid a pencil under the edge of her cast and scratched the persistent itch with the eraser.

She'd barely read half a page before her attention

drifted to the drawer where she'd stashed *Lockbreaker*. Every time she thought about it, she got a little *zing* up her spine. *Magic! Real magic!* She had no clue how it was even possible, but she'd done magic. Cast a spell. Proven it was all real Sunday night when she'd...

Wait.

She'd gone to the school gym? On a Sunday? Why? Try as she might, Xenia was unable to coax the purpose of the excursion out of the depths of her memory. If anything, the night was a bigger blur than the week's calc classes.

For so long, she'd been terrified that she was losing it, that her head injury had left her permanently damaged. Crazy. *But Ev doesn't think I'm crazy.* It was nice, knowing that there was someone else who knew about magic. Someone who'd have her back. Just the thought of it, of him, made her guts go a bit wobbly.

The warm fuzzies took a back seat as a swarm of icy goosebumps swept across the back of her neck.

Xenia took a deep breath. Held it. Blew it out in a slow, controlled exhale. Only when she was as ready as she could possibly be did she turn to face her visitor.

There, perched at the edge of her bed in all her gothic finery, was Bethany. Just like her other visitations, Xenia could see the swirling, flowery wallpaper through the substance of her friend.

A tiny, hesitant smile crept over Bethany's lips. Her mouth moved, but no sound reached Xenia's ears.

She quashed the habitual urge to reject the image. To deny the evidence of her eyes as she'd done since she'd surfaced from her coma. Ev had seen Beebs with his own eyes. Plus, *Lockbreaker* was real. So this really was Bethany.

"I see you." Xenia's voice cracked. Tears of joy and loss drizzled across her cheeks.

A smile of pure glee bloomed on Bethany's face. She leapt into the air... and hung there. She pumped both fists as she spun in a little circle.

"Missed you too, Beebs." Xenia held up a hand to forestall a torrent of silent words. "Can't hear you, though. No clue why."

Xenia stood as Bethany descended to floor level. The ghost held out her hand. When Xenia matched the gesture, her fingers passed through without resistance. Disappointment flickered in the ghost's expression. She mouthed, *Ghost, remember?* As long as she spoke slowly and enunciated, Xenia found she could pick up the gist of her words.

"Oh my God, I want to give you the biggest hug." Xenia held her arms out but then dropped them. "It doesn't hurt, does it? Being..."

Dead? Bethany asked. She shook her head. *No pain at all.*

"Oh, thank God. I was worried you were like, constantly suffering because of the..." Xenia shook her head. "Even after the hospital, I had the worst headaches. Glad one of us is pain free." She sank into her chair.

Bethany took a seat, or pretended to, on the edge of the bed.

"Please don't get mad, but I have to ask," Xenia said. "Why are you here? Instead of, you know." Xenia pointed to the ceiling. She had to swallow the lump in her throat before she could ask the next bit. "Mom and Dad? Are they here, too?"

Bethany's smile crumbled. She shook her head. Shrugged. Xenia picked out the words "not sure" from whatever she was saying. The ghost shook her fist at the heavens above, with an added glare for good measure.

"How can you not know? You didn't get like, Saint Peter or your grandma or someone to greet you?"

Bethany's head dipped, and her shoulders began to shake. For a moment, Xenia thought she'd crossed a line... until the ghost threw her head back with a howl of silent laughter. Bethany threw her hands up and mouthed, *Nope!*

"Well, that sucks. I was hoping to get a few answers."

You and me both, girlfriend! Bethany seemed to think for a moment, then pointed two fingers at Xenia.

"Me? My parents?"

That got a nod. Bethany crossed her hands and fluttered them like wings. Once she'd fluttered them above her head, she spread them apart.

"I don't... oh! You're here, but Mom and Dad flew off? Went to heaven?" That got another nod. Relief crashed over Xenia like a wave. She'd been worried, utterly terrified, that whatever trick of her mind that allowed her to see Bethany just wasn't working on her parents. The idea that they were right here, but invisible, would have been too much to bear. Knowing that they were well and truly gone, but had passed on to... heaven or whatever, was more of a relief than she expected. It meant that one day, in time, she might see them again. "I'm sorry you're stuck here. But I'm glad you're stuck here with me." Xenia grinned through her tears.

Bethany stuck out her tongue and smiled back.

"Sorry for all the 'you're not real' stuff—"

Bethany waved off the apology. Her torrent of words eluded Xenia's poor lip-reading skills.

"I didn't get any of that." Xenia sighed. "Is that why you're the only ghost I've seen? Everyone else..." She copied her friend's "passing on" gesture.

Bethany nodded, then tilted her head. *Not everyone.*

Xenia's stomach dropped. She'd hoped that those other

visits actually had been hallucinations. Then she remembered: *Marisol saw him too.* "Oh, shit."

The grief on Bethany's face matched her own as she
gave silent voice to a name. *Salvatore.*

Xenia bit down on the tremble in her jaw.

I'm sorry.

Xenia scrubbed at her face. When her eyes cleared, she
recoiled from the dread, the sorrow, that twisted her friend's
expression. "What? Beebs, what is it?

Oh, Zee. It's bad. Bethany spoke slowly so she could
follow. *Worse than you could imagine.* Before Xenia could
speak, the ghost drifted from her seat on the bed. She came
a floating halt beside the window nook and then beckoned
for Xenia. At the window, Xenia followed her pointing
finger and gasped.

Sal, clearly visible in the noonday sun, stood at the end
of the block. His shadowed eyes met hers, and he twisted
away.

The pallid ghost wasn't alone in his vigil. Beside him
stood the boy Xenia had seen in class that first day. With
them was a younger boy, barely into his teens. Beyond them,
as if unwilling to join the group, was another ghost. This
one, a girl in her mid teens, seethed with unbridled rage.
She spared not a glance toward the other ghosts, or Xenia, as
she paced back and forth in the middle of the street.

Unlike Bethany, whose spirit was as vibrant in death as
she had been in life, the sad cluster of souls below were
pallid, drained of color. Each had the same shadowed pits
where their eyes should have been.

Xenia recalled how her previous sightings had gone and
backed away from the window before a horror show could
begin. "Bethany, why are they here? How did they die?"
The assembly at school, the one that had followed Sal's

disappearance, swam into her thoughts. That was the day Bethany had delivered her dire message, which Xenia had immediately put out of her mind. "They're not runaways at all, are they? Someone killed them." Xenia sank into the cushions at her feet. "Do you know who did it?"

Bethany sat beside her. Nodded. She curled the fingers of one hand into claws and yanked them across her throat.

"Freddy did it? Come on, be serious."

Bethany glared at her and then turned the glare into a parody of a snarl. With both hands raised as imitation claws, she stalked about the bedroom.

"You are serious. A monster killed them?" Xenia couldn't keep her disbelief from coloring her voice.

Bethany pinned her with a look. She crossed her arms and descended through the floor. A moment later, she dropped through the ceiling and came to a stop in midair. She pointed at herself with both hands. *Hello? Ghost?* She aimed an imperious finger at Xenia. *Magic!*

"Okay, okay." Xenia wrapped both arms around her knees. After untold slumber parties where Bethany insisted on scary movie after scary movie, the fact that she'd stuck around as a ghost really wasn't out of character for her. As for magic? Well, Xenia had touched it. Felt it.

Monsters, though? That was a tough sell.

"So," Xenia said once she'd had a moment to process the notion, "what are we going to do about it?"

Bethany staggered in midair. Relief crashed over her expression like a wave. She steadied herself and assumed a cross-legged seat in the air. Her dark eyes roamed over Xenia's face, searching.

"Of course I'll help!" Xenia pointed toward the spectral audience outside. "Nobody knows they are actually dead! Sal's parents think he's coming back, any day now." She fought back her tears; she could cry later. "You think I'm gonna sit on my ass while they're stuck out there? Trapped here?" Xenia tapped her chin. "What do you think, would finding their killer be enough to solve their 'unfinished business'? Let them pass on?" She was winging it. Everything she knew about ghosts came from Bethany's movie collection.

Bethany met her eyes. *It's really, really bad, Zee.*

"You said that already. I can handle it." She held up a hand when the ghost opened her mouth. "I'm not gonna fight whatever it is. Sheesh, what am I, Wonder Woman? As if." Xenia jumped to her feet and scooped her hoodie from the back of her chair. "If I know you, and I so do, BFFFF o' mine, then you've already snooped out the clues." The look on the ghost's face told her she'd hit the mark. "You show me, and I'll tell Aunt Elspeth everything. Knowing her, she probably has friends in the Army. Let them handle the monster."

Bethany made no attempt to hide her satisfaction as she drifted toward the door.

"You jerk! This is what you've been waiting for this whole time, isn't it?" Xenia grinned as she stuck her head beneath the bed in search of her shoes. "Let's do this thing before I chicken out."

* * *

Xenia trudged to a halt as her spectral guide raised a hand. She dabbed at her forehead with the sleeve of her hoodie. Of course the weather would warm up today!

Their conversation, charade-based as it was, had lagged as they crossed Main Street. Xenia was just a bit wary about talking to thin air where anyone could see.

Xenia's other concern was that Sal, and the other ghosts waiting at the end of her street, would tag along. The impulse wasn't her at her most empathetic, but... honestly, they creeped her out. Even though Sal was her friend, Xenia couldn't bring herself to meet the hollows of his eyes. But when they'd left, Bethany had a few words with the cluster of lost souls and, to her relief, they had stayed put.

It came as no great surprise when, half an hour later, the two of them arrived at the rambling green space of Riverside Park.

You're sure you want to do this? Bethany enunciated.

"Let's just get this over with."

Bethany nodded and led Xenia on toward the water's edge. When she reached the bench where Xenia had spent so many afternoons feeling sorry for herself, she doubled back along the jumble of rocks that served as a beach. There, between the ridge that marked the western edge of the park and the river, grew a dense snarl of bramble. There was a path, little more than an animal trail, squeezed in between a bush and the hillside. Xenia had only progressed a few steps before the wall of bramble swallowed all sight of the park behind her.

The farther she progressed, the higher the ridge at her side grew. Up top, she knew from her walks, was the residential neighborhood that surrounded Porter Valley High.

The tangled web of branches and weeds grew dense. Twigs and thorns caught her sleeves as she pushed along the water's edge. Here, in the shadow of the hillside, the air grew chill and heavy with moisture from the river.

The trail and bramble dwindled away to nothing. Now Xenia was forced to pick her way across slick, water-smoothed stones and mud. Just ahead, Bethany came to a halt above to a tall outcropping of stone. *Here we go.*

Anxiety burned acid-hot at the back of her throat as Xenia slipped and stumbled across the damp rocks. The slab ahead was half again her height where it thrust itself from the bluff. It thinned and lowered as it reached out into the river's flow. Spume and froth, white where the spring sun caught it, leapt into the air where the water boiled around the obstruction.

The barrier of stone entered the river at sharp angle, an elbow bend where the water halted its mad rush to the Pacific. A slow gyre, neither whirlpool nor calm, turned within that space. The barrier had trapped a mishmash of fallen wood and trash from the park and farther upstream. A smattering of leaves turned a lazy orbit about the outer edge of the whorl.

Xenia placed her feet with care as she eased to the water's edge. When she looked to Bethany for guidance, the ghost pointed at the tangle of branches.

At first, Xenia thought the mass in the water was no more than another jumble of shattered wood. Unbidden, her hand rose to her mouth as her brain unpacked details she'd missed upon first glance. What she'd taken for branches weren't anything of the sort.

They were ribs.

The rush of the river fell away beneath the thunder of her heart. Her foot slipped, came down in a puddle. Xenia hardly felt the shock of cold as her sock drank up the winter runoff.

Below the surface of the water, tattered fabric billowed about the basket of bones. Xenia's eye followed the curve of a shoulder. An arm emerged from a sleeve. The flesh was pale, bloated, and, in places, split to reveal gray meat within. Above the ruin of a chest was most of a face. Something, either submersion or the attack that had killed him, had emptied the eye sockets. The jaw, half denuded of flesh, yawned wide in a final, endless scream.

Fire clawed at Xenia's gut, burned its way to her throat as she vomited her breakfast onto the rocks at her feet. The spasm held her in its vise, bent double, until long after she'd purged all she had to offer. She staggered away from the grisly tableau. Tears and snot poured across her face. She'd recognized all too well the Phoenix Suns logo on that shirt. The shirt that Salvatore Serrano had worn nearly every day.

"Oh God. Fucking hell, *what did that to him?*" Xenia's shriek echoed from the bluff across the river. Her foot turned on a wet rock and she landed hard amongst the mud and stones. "Sal. I'm sorry."

Bethany hovered by Xenia's side as she wept.

When she had cried herself out, Xenia nodded and levered herself upright. "I'm okay." She glared at the sky, which, after months of dreary gray, had chosen this day to shine a dazzling blue. How dare today be beautiful, while Sal lay dead. Mutilated. "Get it together, Findlay," she muttered.

Eyes averted from the ruin of her friend, Xenia scanned the ridge above her in search of a landmark. A point of reference with which to orient herself.

A wall of familiar red brick extended a few hundred yards in either direction. On the other side of that wall, she knew, would be a lacrosse field. Without realizing it, she'd traversed enough of the river's edge to loop back below her school.

"Let's go." Xenia turned and began the long, wet, slog back to the park. *I should have taken Aunt Elspeth up when she offered to get me a new phone.* She added that to her mental to-do list. When she burst through the thicket by the water's edge, Xenia made for the first adult she saw. It was a shame to ruin the nice family's picnic, but Sal had waited long enough.

It was only after Mr. Davidson, the man whose phone Xenia had borrowed, corroborated her claim that the police dispatched a cruiser to "have a look-see." Of course! Why would they take a silly teenage girl at her word? It had been satisfying, in a grim sort of way, to watch as the rookie officer stumbled out of the brush with fresh vomit down the front of his uniform. Now, they would believe her. Now, finally, Sal could go home.

She'd been questioned, of course. There, in the park and again at the police station by city hall. How had she known where the body was? How had she known the Serrano boy?

Xenia had, of course, omitted the part where his ghost, and the ghost of her friend, had dropped in for a visit. "I've only lived in Porter Valley a month," was her answer. "I was exploring."

At least they'd given her a bottle of water to rinse the taste of vomit out of her mouth.

Later, while holding down the bench that she'd been told, not asked, to stay put on, she observed as the cadre of desk jockeys exploded into motion. From what little she was able to overhear, the diver who'd gone in to recover Sal had found additional remains on the riverbed beneath him. They weren't sure how many bodies were there, but it was more than two.

Great-Aunt Elspeth swept into the police station like a tsunami clad in paisley cotton. Her brogue was in full force as she tore new orifices in all and sundry for holding her great-niece without cause. Why, if anything the girl was a hero, finding a body like that! When, she'd added with a glare, the police themselves had failed to do so!

"I am so sorry you had to see something like that, dearie," Elspeth said as she parked in front of their home. Xenia wasn't sure if she was referring to her outburst at the station or to the body. "Have I told you of late," Elspeth added, "how very proud I am of you?"

"What? I didn't do anything! I was just wandering—"

"You kept your head, and that's not nothing. And don't think I haven't noticed how hard you've been struggling. Aye, I've seen how far you've come as well."

"Really?" As far as Xenia was concerned, she hadn't done anything since she'd been foisted off on Elspeth. She poked at the vomit dried on her hoodie. "I'm a fucking wreck." Xenia grimaced. "Sorry, Aunt Elspeth."

Elspeth waved the apology away. "Psht. Just know, my love, that I will do anything in my power to help you. To keep you safe."

Xenia paused, her hand on the door handle, and almost... *almost* told her guardian everything right then and there. Bethany, magic, the truth about how Sal had died. Instead, she launched herself across the bench seat and wrapped her great-aunt in a great hug. "Thank you," she whispered into the kaftan-wrapped shoulder. "I don't think I could have done this without you."

Elspeth blinked hard and sniffed as she rubbed the girl's back. After a moment, she took Xenia by the shoulders and eased her back toward the opposite side of the car with a grin. "As much as I appreciate the love, dearie, you've gone a bit ripe. Might I suggest a shower?"

"I may or may not have blown chunks," Xenia said. She focused on the moment she'd had with her guardian, and the love she'd found in her new home, to hold the tide of grisly images at bay. Sleep would not come easy tonight, she knew.

Before the two of them could make their way inside, a pair of police cruisers, light bars flashing, screeched to a halt in front of the Serrano home.

"Lands, I don't envy a soul in that house tonight. Come on, while you make yourself presentable, I'll cook us a proper meal and a cuppa. Then, we shall offer what comfort we can."

Xenia hesitated on the garden path as Elspeth fished for her house keys. The street was empty of any sign of Bethany... or Sal, or the others she'd seen. In the all of the confusion at the station, she'd lost track of her ghostly friend. Her ability to see spirits was so spotty and uncontrollable, there was no way to know when she'd see them again.

"Sal," she whispered to the night, just in case. "I'll do whatever I have to. Whatever it takes. I won't let this happen again."

Chapter Twenty-Seven

As Xenia made her way through the halls Monday morning, it was clear the news had arrived with all the subtlety of a bomb. From the students clustered in the hallway between class to the teachers in their lounge, word that Salvatore's body had been found dominated every conversation. In the school's back yard, no less!

Mr. Druszcz fought the good fight in the name of education and math. Even his unbridled enthusiasm for calculus failed to hold the attention of his students. He listed the required reading for the week on his beloved whiteboard and then retreated to his desk to bury his nose in the pages of a tawdry romance novel.

Xenia kept her head down and hid behind her textbook as she awaited the inevitable moment when she was called out as the one who'd found the body. Bodies, plural now. The divers from the county had confirmed additional remains in the pool below Sal.

Notable, too, were the absences. Madison, Gracie, and Everard were the most obvious of the AWOL students. Everard, Xenia assumed, had taken the discovery as hard as she. *Did he know Sal? They weren't on the same team, but they probably knew each other. Lucas, though, he was on the lacrosse team.* The longer she fretted over Ev's empty desk, the more the butterflies in her stomach grew.

Ms. Rixx, Xenia's English teacher, shelved her plans to analyze *A Midsummer Night's Dream* in favor of the AV cart. With the help of a more technically inclined student, she tuned into the local news station. Captain Strauss glared at them through a rain of technicolor static. A cadre of men in various uniforms, and one in a rumpled department store suit, stood at his back.

The police captain cleared his throat a number of times. "This press conference is for the dissemination of what we currently know. I will not be taking questions once I've completed my statement." He took a sip from the glass on the podium as a dissatisfied murmur rose from the off-screen crowd. "At this time, we can confirm that three bodies, each displaying varying levels of decomp, have been recovered from the Eel River some six hundred yards west of Riverside Park. As the families of two of the three have been notified, I am able to release their identities. They have been positively identified as Joseph Kaur and Salvatore Serrano."

The girl next to Xenia gasped and clapped her hands over her mouth. Xenia wondered which of them she had known, and if they'd been close.

"It is my belief, and that of this department," Strauss went on, "that the three deaths were not the result of foul play."

What? Xenia nearly shouted aloud. *How could he possibly think that? Sal was almost torn in half!*

"Based on the"—Strauss coughed—"massive tissue loss that appears to have been inflicted perimortem, we believe that the deaths of all three individuals were caused by one of northern California's numerous predator species. While it is certainly unusual to see a black bear within the limits of our fair city, or for one to attack a human being, both have been known to occur. With the recent drought exerting pressure on the inland mountains and Central Valley areas, animal populations are migrating west. One or more hungry, desperate mountain lions may have followed." Captain Strauss waved one of the uniformed men to his side. "Fish and Game will be coordinating with our department, and the county, as we search for the predator responsible."

You didn't think they'd come right out and say a monster killed them, did you? Xenia wished she'd gotten more from Bethany before her "ghost sight" fizzled out.

Monster movies were more Beebs's thing than hers. But, thanks to her friend's obsession, she'd seen her fair share. While some films depicted their monsters as ravening, mindless beasts, she didn't think that was what they were up against. A mindless beast didn't try to hide the bodies.

As far as Xenia could determine, the victims had all been teenagers. The bodies had been no more than a stone's throw from the school. Right over the back wall, in fact. It was likely that the killer was here, in school. Hiding in plain sight. Werewolves were just people who changed into monsters, right? Or it could be demonic possession, or some other creature everyone assumed was a myth?

Fear slid its cold finger down her spine. She studied her fellow students out of the corner of her eye searching for any hint of the beast that might be lurking within.

"Scratch that, I'll take that one." On screen, Captain Strauss pushed his way back to the microphone. "No, I do not see a link between what happened to the three in the river and the rash of copycat runaways." He shuffled through his notes. "Both Aubrey Foster and Douglass Miller were in their own homes on the nights of their respective disappearances. There were no signs of forced entry, nothing indicative that an animal had been on either premises, nothing to connect the cases at all. They are, and will continue to be handled as, separate events. That is all." Strauss aimed a final glare at the camera before he surrendered the podium to the man in the rumpled suit.

"Good morning. My name is Mathew Bergdorf. I'm with the mayor's office here in Porter Valley. The city council and the mayor both agree that, for the time being, certain protective measures are required. With the assistance of our fine police department," Bergdorf said, giving Strauss a pained side-eye, "the city of Porter Valley will be imposing a curfew on all minor persons, effective tonight. Thank you for your understanding and cooperation during these extraordinary times."

The classroom erupted in chaos.

* * *

For the remainder of the day, Xenia endured her classes and ignored her fellows' curfew bellyaching as she mulled over what little she knew. When the final bell at last warbled, she made for the gymnasium. She skirted the lacrosse field and went to the rear of the building, where the school had laid out the remainder of its sports facilities. As all of the team practices had been canceled, thanks to the curfew announcement, she had the basketball courts to herself.

Sal had been taken from here, she was sure of it.

It had rained twice since the night of his disappearance. Xenia held little hope that physical evidence like blood would yet remain on the blacktop. Unsure of what she was doing, or even what she was looking for, she made a slow circuit about the trio of courts. For the first time, she found herself wishing her "magic sight" would put in an appearance. Who knew what might be visible in that alternate spectrum?

Beyond the basketball courts, the school grounds came to a literal end. The red brick wall she'd seen from the river ran along the bluff's edge, then around the far side of the school. There, it was replaced by a more modern chain link fence. Xenia paced along until she reached a point that corresponded, she thought, with the location of Sal's body. She peered at the scuffed concrete, poked at the mortar between the bricks, squinted at the wrought iron points running along the wall's upper surface. Frustrated at the lack of anything at all, she was ready to give up when something caught her eye.

It was difficult to see from her angle, but the bricks above her looked damaged. Four small divots had been punched into the fired clay, about which radiated a web of cracks. A handful of red bits, too large for the rain to wash away, lay scattered at her feet. Fragments of the busted brick? Xenia held one hand up at arm's length. The divots almost looked like finger holes—

"New Girl, whassup?"

Xenia's shoulders came up in a reflexive hunch. She forced herself to unclench, to breathe. "I have a name, Madison. It's Xenia, remember?"

"Yeah, yeah." As usual, Courtney and Gracie flanked their ringleader. "My bad, 'kay?" Madison stood there, snapping her gum and twirling a lock of mahogany hair about a finger until Courtney elbowed her, none too gently, in the side. "Ow, okay!" Gracie looked up from her phone and peered through the curtain of her hair long enough to make uneasy eye contact with Xenia.

Madison charged on. "*Any*-hoo, I wanted to make amends"—she air-quoted the word—"for the thing. You know. With the coffee. And for tripping you." Something that resembled but was not actually contrition passed over her features.

"Okay." Xenia's prior experience with people like Madison—popular, conventionally attractive, more than a little spoiled—suggested they were not prone to offering honest apologies. There was always an ulterior motive. Always a self-serving reason for a sudden self-effacement. Then again, that had been in LA, where enormous egos were a dime a dozen. Maybe things were different in small towns. "Thank you?"

A smile, radiant and perfect, exploded across Madison's painted lips. "See, all good in the hood." She turned to Courtney. "Yes?" To Gracie. "Good?" Back to Xenia. "Me and you are going to be such good friends now. You're gonna love it. All the best parties. We can show you where the good shopping is, it'll be awesome." She planted a fist on each hip and tossed her hair back. "I didn't want you to think I was just this awful bitch, m'kay?"

Courtney beamed at Xenia, visibly pleased that her efforts as peacemaker had succeeded. By contrast, Gracie's discomfort grew all the more obvious, even as her nose remained fixed to her phone's tiny screen.

Xenia stared at the trio, at Madison. *Well, if she's actually serious about this...* Xenia could make the effort, could put the whole "frappening" behind her. Maybe be a bit more open-minded about other people.

Madison snapped her fingers. "New Girl." She paused, and her smile grew even more saccharine. "Xenia. What are you doing right this instant? I mean, other than dying of boredom. I stole a fuckton of weed gummies from Trophy Mom's stash. You are totes coming over to hang with us." She flicked painted nails at the girls beside her. "You can tell us all about your little adventure. Come on, I'm driving."

"Adventure?"

Madison added a conspiratorial edge to her voice. "You're the one who found the body. Right?"

Greasy sweat sprang up across Xenia's forehead as she fought down her gorge. No way in hell. Madison was the last person she wanted to share that with, or vomit in front of. In sheer defensive reflex, she said the first thing that came to mind: "You should apologize to Maia." Now that she'd raised the subject of the runner, Xenia realized that she hadn't spoken with her in days. She hadn't even followed up after returning her shirt. *What the hell, Zee?*

The smile vanished from Madison's face as if it had been slapped off. "What?"

"You said you wanted to make amends, didn't you? You might have hit me with your coffee, but you threw it at Maia. And the things you said to her were pretty crappy." Xenia forced herself to stand up straight. "I don't know what history you have with her, but she deserves an apology too."

Madison's voice was flat. "I don't think so."

Courtney rolled her eyes and threw her hands up. "Oh, just fantastic."

Gracie shot another furtive glance to Xenia, then at Madison's back. She took a step away. Then another. Without saying a word, she turned on her heel and ran. Before either of her friends had noticed, Gracie had vanished around the corner of the gym.

"Now look what you've done." Madison glared at Xenia. "Never mind, New Girl. I don't want to get high with you anymore." She gave a haughty sniff and then stalked after Gracie. Without looking, she snapped her fingers.

Courtney's shoulders slumped. She muttered, "Sorry," before she scurried off in Madison's wake.

Xenia stared at the empty space where they had stood. The wind picked up. She shivered. Thanks to the unwanted encounter, she'd almost forgotten her find. She scooped one of the fragments into her pocket and paced off the steps from the damaged brick to the turn of the wall so she could find it again if needed.

It might be a good idea, Xenia mused on the way home, if she learned more magic. *Lockbreaker* was handy, true, but it was of limited utility. Also, it wasn't that cool. Magic should be cool, in her opinion. Flashy. *Ev thought it was cool.* Xenia shivered at the thought. If he thought that silly little spell was impressive, just wait until she showed him some real magic.

Chapter Twenty-Eight

Xenia stopped in her tracks. An all-too-familiar black bird had perched atop the streetlamp ahead. She looked around to assure herself that no one was close enough to overhear. "What do you want?"

The raven cocked its head. Hopped the length of its perch. Swiveled to track the passage of a wind-blown candy wrapper.

"Oh, you're just a bird." Confident that another bird-led adventure wasn't in store, Xenia allowed herself to relax. Then again, if it had been "her" raven, he might have led her to a second lesson in magic. Dang.

Since the imposition of curfew, Aunt Elspeth had been insistent that Xenia spend her after-school and weekend free time at the shop. Even though home was no more than a couple blocks away, Elspeth drove them rather than walking. She hadn't said much, but Xenia could tell that the news had her guardian spooked. Xenia had agreed to the request without argument. After all, there really *was* something stalking the town. Also, with lacrosse practice canceled, she'd lost the opportunity to watch Ev do his thing on the field.

Elspeth had demonstrated the operation of the old cash register, and now with Xenia at the counter, Elspeth was free to focus on the myriad preparations required for Porter Valley's upcoming "Gold Rush Days." In little more than a month, four blocks of Main Street would be reserved for pedestrian traffic. Tents and awnings would fill the street. There'd even be a stage for live music in front of city hall.

"The name is a tad ironic," Elspeth had explained. "The Porter Family Mine, from which our quaint little hamlet derives its moniker, was actually a silver mine. The city council put its foot down, and I have to agree. 'Silver Rush Days' just doesn't have the same zing!"

Regardless of the nomenclature's accuracy, the festival was as vital to her shop as the holiday season. Once the tourists rolled in, they could expect sales three times greater than on the average week. Bits 'n' Pieces, with its eccentric inventory of utensils and tableware hand-carved from local (ethically sourced!) redwood, do-it-yourself leather craft kits, beading supplies, jewelry and articles of clothing from local artisans, ceramic goods, and other colorful items Xenia couldn't categorize was perfectly positioned to eke a sale from nearly everyone who wandered in.

The news of the "animal attacks" had yet to put a dent in the usual weekend traffic. Xenia rang up sale after sale until, just after one, Elspeth took over at the register. She gave Xenia a handful of bills and a mission to retrieve lunch from Henry's Deli. "Just a salad for me, dearie. Oh, and one of those black-and-white biscuits, perhaps."

Henry's was the next street over, right in the middle of Main's busiest block. Close enough, Xenia knew, that

Elspeth was confident that she could make the trip without being pounced on by a mountain lion.

Xenia stuck her tongue out at the raven and crossed over to the next block. At Henry's, she ordered a salad and the last two remaining black-and-white cookies. For herself, she ordered the number ten hoagie, full size, not half, with extra provolone. Even with the enormous breakfast her great-aunt had prepared, Xenia's stomach had grumbled all morning. She dropped onto the bench outside to wait. The raven, she was pleased to see, had effed off.

With time to kill, Xenia worked on her elusive "magic sight." Since she'd created *Lockbreaker*, there had been only two moments when she could perceive the magical spectrum. Neither by choice. If she hadn't wasted so much time rejecting the "migraine halos," she might've learned how to do this on command by now! She thumped her leg in frustration.

Bethany, and the other ghosts, had also remained invisible. Xenia wasn't sure if seeing ghosts and seeing magic were the same thing or two separate skills. She'd done both at the same time and independently. Again, it would have been nice if she'd just accepted it all from the start.

Her jaw ached, and she realized that she'd been gritting her teeth. She forced her jaw to unclench. What if she couldn't do this? How was she going to learn more magic? *What would Ev think of her if she couldn't do magic?*

"You need to relax."

Xenia blinked her eyes into focus as a boy clambered, one-handed, onto the bench beside her. In his other hand was balanced a towering double-scoop ice cream. Every bit of his attention was focused on getting himself seated without tipping the cone.

"What?" Xenia asked the boy.

He chomped into the top scoop. Chewed. Gave her a chocolate-smeared grin. He took a second bite and then thrust his lower lip out, his brows knit in a parody of deep thought, or perhaps constipation. He crossed his eyes and pointed at his face. "This is you."

"Thank you. Very flattering." Xenia turned to see if her order was ready.

"You are," the boy said between bites of ice cream, "a yurt and a tipi."

"What?" Xenia stared at the boy. She snapped her fingers as understanding struck. "Two tents. I'm too tense. Har-har."

The boy clucked his tongue and shot her with a sticky finger-gun.

"Just what I've always wanted. Unsolicited advice from a total stranger. Thanks, lil' dude."

"You're not a stranger." The boy crunched into the sugar cone. "You shared your fern... tart, thing with me. Kids aren't supposed to accept treats from strangers, so that makes you a friend!" His wide, gap-toothed smile was free of guile.

"I don't think it works that way, kid." At least that explained the nagging sense of familiarity. She scanned the sidewalk crowd. "Your folks nearby?" *Who lets their child run around with animal attacks in the news?*

The boy shrugged and popped the final bit of cone into his mouth. "Close enough." His eyelids sagged with bliss as he savored the mouthful.

"How can we be friends if I don't know your name?" If this kid's parents didn't show up soon, Xenia figured it'd be best if he came to the shop with her. Too risky to leave him to fend for himself.

The boy licked a smear of mint and chocolate from his hand. "Guess my name." He peered at her through the sweep of his hair.

"Like I'd know." Xenia had never been particularly good at this sort of thing. She gave him a quick once-over but, unfortunately, he wasn't wearing a name tag. "Michael. Thomas."

The boy shook his head.

"Oscar, Richard, Jayden, Levi?"

With every wrong guess the boy turned his head and his dark hair whipped at her shoulder.

"Harry, Sebastian, Branson."

The boy's eyes flew wide, as did his grin. He slid from the bench to jump in front of her, nearly capsizing the double armful of coffee carried by a passing pedestrian. He held up his hand, his finger and thumb a hair's breadth apart. "So, so close." He winked. "But no cigar. See you later, Xenia."

There was a rap on the window behind her; when she looked, Harry himself waved her in to claim her order. She gave him a thumbs-up, and then turned to invite the boy to wait for his folks with her at Elspeth's store.

The rascal had, of course, already run off to who knows where. Xenia peered up and down Main Street, but he was long gone. She tried not to worry as she collected her lunch. His parents had to be local. Maybe Elspeth knew them? Maybe they worked on Main Street too.

Xenia delivered Elspeth's salad and sat beside her at the counter. She peeled the wrapper from her hoagie. Took a deep whiff. Harry's was right next to a bakery and got their bread fresh from the oven. Her sandwich was still warm and smelled *divine*.

She opened her eyes on a world ablaze with the ebb and flow of magic.

"Frick yes!"

Chapter Twenty-Nine

Bethany retreated into the ceiling as Everard spun to high-five a passing teammate. *I might have become a bit too accustomed to ghost invisibility.* She eased her nose through the acoustic tile. Ironic that, the one time she needed to remain unseen, it was to follow the one guy who could actually see her!

Bethany thought it unlikely that Ev would do anything overt while in class. Then again, she had no clue what the scope of his power was. It had appeared that whatever he'd done to Zee required physical contact. Then again, the birds had come at no more than a whistle. For all she knew, Ev could make the whole school dance a jig with a snap of his fingers.

Despite his threat, Ev had yet to take another go at Xenia. For two weeks, he hadn't followed her after school, hadn't tried to communicate with her in any way. In the single class they shared, he had entirely ignored her. Bethany really wanted to believe he'd given up.

At the start of calculus, Xenia went straight to her desk. Ev, who had been at the back of the room chatting, chose that moment to head to his seat. As he squeezed by Xenia, the back of his hand brushed her shoulder. If Bethany hadn't been looking right at her friend's face, she would have missed it. In the instant of contact, Zee went all moony-eyed. *Shit. Has he been doing that every morning? How did I miss it?* While Xenia seemed to snap out of it by third period, Bethany was still concerned. And angry.

Whatever weird, psychic groundwork Everard was laying in Xenia's mind, it hadn't prevented her from agreeing, no, volunteering to follow Bethany to "find" Salvatore's body last week. Xenia was still herself. Well, mostly. She'd begun to hang about after class to watch lacrosse practice, but the curfew, thankfully, had put an end to that.

Needing to learn more about her new adversary, Bethany had begun to tail Everard. With any luck, she'd be able to fill in a few blank pages in her mental notebook.

Four periods in, other than the nudge in calc, Ev had done little more than drift through class. He gave the teachers the barest minimum of his attention and received high scores and glowing praise in return. He high-fived his way through the school's social order, appeared to know just about everyone in the building, and even drew an affectionate smile from the usually dour Mrs. Wedgwood.

At the ring of the final bell, Bethany discovered that lacrosse practice, and *only* lacrosse practice, had been reinstated. The special exception to the curfew had Everard's smell all over it. Xenia, she assumed, had yet to hear the news because she'd gone straight to Elspeth's shop after the bell.

In contrast to the low-effort cruise through his scholastic endeavors, lacrosse seemed to extract Ev's full attention. By the end of the opening drill, he was no less drenched in sweat than his teammates. *Might be that this is the only thing he has to actually work at,* Bethany mused. After all, he'd have to touch everyone in the bleachers if he wanted to fake his way to sports excellence as he had with his grades. If this was something he honestly enjoyed, without the trickery, it might be why Ev hadn't been trailing Xenia home. *Or maybe he just likes being the center of attention,* she thought as Coach Fairfax heaped praise upon his star player. Ev was clearly basking in the acclaim as he swept his lacrosse stick in an exaggerated bow.

Even before her involuntary relocation to Porter Valley, Bethany had no experience or interest in the sport. Until practice ended, she whiled away the time atop the school's belfry tower. At long last, Coach blew a long blast on his whistle and sent the team packing.

PVHS's student body, for the most part, walked, biked, or skateboarded to school. A handful rode the ancient yellow bus in from the farm community that occupied the valley's eastern half. A few had their own cars. Everard, naturally, was one of those few.

Bethany stayed high, out of her quarry's line of sight, as Ev approached the cherry red muscle car parked at the very end of the lot. A girl Bethany wasn't familiar with waited there, hip propped against one mirror-finished fender. His sigh was audible even at ghost height. "What do you want, Jane?"

Jane crossed her arms and glared daggers at Ev. "Don't you give me that attitude, you cheating dick!"

Oh, I like her. Bethany eased a bit lower, the better to eavesdrop.

"Six months, Ev! Six months since prom. Since we started dating. That's how long I was willing to give you the benefit of the doubt. Every time you were late, or blew me off, or just plain didn't answer my calls, I brushed it off. Just part of dating a 'star lacrosse player.'"

Bethany wished she had some popcorn.

Ev popped the Charger's trunk with his fob and pitched his duffel in. Jane stomped her foot.

"I had to hear it from Raffy that you've been chasing other girls." Jane glared down her nose. "And a freshman? Really?" She made a show of shaking herself in disgust. "I thought you were better than that, Everard Ambrose." She spun on her heel and sniffed. "I certainly am. We're done."

Woo! Bethany pumped a fist.

"That's what this is all about?" Ev rolled his eyes and slammed the trunk. Fury darkened his expression. "We're done when I'm done with you."

You sack of shit!

"Oh, is that so?" Jane's heels clacked on the pavement as she stomped over to Ev and poked him in the chest. "And what's stopping me from dumping your cheating ass, huh?"

Bethany hurled herself at the pair as Ev raised his hand. Jane flinched as, instead of striking her, he cupped her cheek.

The instant his fingers made contact, Jane wilted. Her arms fell to her sides, her fingers uncurling from their fists. The righteous anger that burned in her eyes flared out as every hint of the girl's personality drained away. She swayed on her feet, and were it not for Ev's hand on her cheek, she would have fallen in a heap.

"Knock it the fuck off, Ev," Bethany snarled.

The jock's eyes didn't so much as twitch. His lips curled in a nasty smile, and he stroked Jane's cheek with his thumb. "You really thought I'd let the best chest in school just walk away?"

Bethany's lip curled in contempt. "Of course you're a pig, too."

Ev ignored her as he drew Jane's face closer to his. "I still need your daddy's beach house, Jane. Big party tomorrow night. You don't want to make me miss out, do you?" His thumb made little circles on her skin.

"No," Jane said after a long moment. Her voice was dull, no more than a whisper. She blinked once, the movement a stutter.

Bethany jammed her arm between Ev's face and Jane's. "I said knock it off. Let her go, Ev!"

Everard's eyes flicked to Bethany, "Go away, dead girl."

"Oh, now you hear me. Back the fuck off!"

"Or what?" Ev asked, amused. He returned his attention to the ensorcelled girl. "Jane, you're going to forget all about that freshman girl. You didn't hear any rumors. If Raffy mentions it again, you're not going to believe a word she says. Understood?" He tightened his grip. The skin below her eye indented under his thumb. "You are my girl, Jane, and I am the only man in your life. No talking to other guys. You don't even see them, got it?"

"Yes." A string of drool slipped from the corner of Jane's mouth.

Bethany recoiled in horror. If Everard was so jealous that he would command her loyalty even as he cheated... Had Sal been too friendly with the wrong person? Lucas had been Ev's teammate—could he have done something to draw Ev's ire?

The ability to charm with a touch was just the ticket if you wanted to get away with murder. How many inconvenient deaths had Everard commanded Jane to forget?

Bethany stared at the jock and searched his face for any hint that a literal beast dwelled within.

Why couldn't I be a poltergeist? In the movies, ghosts were able to crap all over the living. If she had those abilities, Bethany would have dropped Ev's stupid muscle car on his stupid head.

Jane's eyes fluttered as Everard withdrew his hand. "What... what was I saying?" She rubbed the center of her forehead.

The menace vanished from Ev's face, replaced in a blink by a mask of boredom. "Something about your folks being out of town this weekend."

A sly look crept across Jane's face. "You still have that connection, right? If you can get a keg and a lil' sumthin, we can party at the beach house!" Jane whipped out her phone as she slid into the Charger's passenger seat. "I gotta let the girls know it's party time."

Bethany fumed, helpless, as Ev gunned the car across the parking lot. "How could you just stand there while he screwed with her mind, Beebs?" *How was I going to stop him? I can't fucking touch anything!*

Bethany hurled herself after the Charger. She might not be able to punch Ev in his smug face, but he could see and hear her. She was going to haunt the *fuck* out of him all weekend.

Bethany's plan, such as it was, came to a crashing halt as Ev's Charger roared onto the Redwood Highway. She slammed into the unseen barrier that confined her to Porter Valley. "God damn it, not now!" She flung herself higher until she reached the barrier's vertical limit. The cherry red gleam vanished around one of the highway's innumerable curves.

Everard had, with no more than a touch, erased Jane's memory. Rewritten her fury into willing compliance. *He's got the same thing planned for Xenia. Or worse.* Even without a stomach, Bethany felt sick.

Yet he'd backed off, even though he could have crushed Xenia's mind with no effort. Why? What did he even want with her, when he could have anything he desired?

The answer was obvious, really. The same thing had made Zee a beacon for the Lost.

Xenia could do magic.

Ev, in all likelihood, wanted her new abilities to develop as much as possible. That way, she'd be a bigger prize in his "collection."

She might be a jerk for thinking it, but she hoped that Zee wouldn't learn any more magic. At least, not until Bethany had the chance to fill her in on the threat Ev posed. Forewarned, and armed with the locations of his victims, Xenia might be able to spur the police into action and focus their scattered attention on the actual killer.

Until then, it was unlikely that Everard would do to Xenia what he'd done to Sal and the others. Not while he still had a "use" for her.

Unless, of course, he killed to satisfy an entirely different craving.

Chapter Thirty

Xenia giggled as she read the name she'd scrawled on the diary page.

Xenia Ambrose.

She slapped the diary shut. "You are such a head case," she told herself. Xenia fitted the metal strap into the tiny, heart-shaped lock on the diary's cover.

The book had been a gift from Bethany on her ninth birthday. She'd dutifully logged her every thought, every night, until she'd lost the key. Only sentiment had made her pack it with the rest of her things when she'd moved in with Aunt Elspeth.

When she'd discovered it that morning, the tiny lock had yielded to *Lockbreaker*'s touch. She'd pored over the clumsily penned memoir of school assignments, slumber parties, visits to Disneyland and Knott's, and, most embarrassingly, the brief phase where she'd imagined herself as Armored Princess's sidekick.

When she'd arrived at the first blank page, the reasonable thing was to give her poor, neglected diary an update. Instead, she'd doodled and daydreamed of the day when she finally learned a new bit of magic... and how impressed Ev would be when she showed him. At some point during this flight of fancy, she'd tried on the name.

She shoved the diary across the desk. Before she could do any of that, she had to get her eyes to cooperate. Or her brain, or wherever her ability to see magic originated. Since the day she'd crafted *Lockbreaker*, she'd been able to summon the ability only once. Maybe she should sniff another hoagie? Xenia blew a long raspberry at the thought.

She changed tactics. Hands raised like a conductor, Xenia brought her fingers together, slowly, and imagined the strands of magical energy she couldn't see trapped between them.

Nada.

Well, those weird ribbon-things always avoided her when she walked through them. Maybe seeing magic was a prerequisite to grabbing on? Otherwise, people would be bumping into the stuff willy-nilly. Everyone would be chucking magic around all the time. Or passing out from the contact.

Xenia's eyes went to *Lockbreaker* and then the card that held its design. Someone else could see magic. How else had they made that card? And why had they hidden it inside the book? Xenia held the scrap of paper up to the light and, for the thousandth time, scrutinized it for any clue she'd missed.

Maybe there are more of these hidden in other books? Xenia dismissed the idea of scouring Signs & Portents. If there were more out there, they were likely scattered to the wind. She'd have to come up with a way to track them down first.

"Why *Lockbreaker*, though?" Xenia mused. Why not a spell that would, for instance, light a candle? Wasn't that the usual first lesson in fantasies? She swapped card for ruler and tapped the lock on her diary. The heart-shaped lock *snicked* open. She secreted the spell card within its pages and snapped the lock tight before she tossed the diary atop her stack of schoolbooks. One corner of *Practical Spells and Recipes* mocked her as it peeked from the bottom of the stack.

No way. Could it really be that simple? Xenia extracted the faux spell book from the pile and centered it before her on the desk, swallowing hard. "Just do it," she scolded herself. She gave the book a poke with *Lockbreaker*.

A sharp *pop* echoed about her bedroom. There was a sound not unlike a deck of cards being shuffled as the book unfolded from within itself. The decidedly non-Euclidian movement made the inside of Xenia's eyes hurt.

"Holy crap."

Practical Spells and Recipes was gone. In its place sat an old-fashioned document folder, similar to those she'd found in the steamer trunk. The heavy card stock was the color of sand and, just like the book that had concealed it, bore the stains of travel and time on its surface.

Xenia's fingers trembled as she unwound the red string fastener. The thick paper crackled as she flipped it open. She used one hand to ease the contents onto her desk as she upended the folder.

When Xenia unfolded the topmost sheet, an electric *zing* rushed through her. The page was covered in swirls of black ink and, at the top, was a name. *Ghost Flame.* She read aloud: "A candle in darkness." The next sheet of paper held another, *Ring of Knots*, "to bind that which is yours," and the next, *Bone Weave*, "to turn the blade aside." While *Ghost Flame* was in the same handwriting as *Lockbreaker*, each of the others appeared to have different authors. The fourth spell—and these *had* to be spells—had been inscribed on a page so large Xenia had to unfold it like one of her father's old road maps. Where the first three each had a single pattern inked in the center of the page, the map-sized spell held no fewer than five of the intricate drawings, the fifth of which took up the entire bottom half of the sheet. Whatever this spell did, it had to be a *doozy*.

The nature of the enormous spell, or spells, however, was even more of a mystery than the first three. The author had filled the space in between the diagrams, and the as-yet invisible holograms they no doubt represented, with a text-book's worth of notes in tiny, crabbed handwriting. Unfortunately, neither the notes nor the spell's name were in English. Chinese was Xenia's best guess. She had no experience with the language, or any writing system other than the alphabet, really.

Still, four new spells! Xenia carefully folded the massive sheet back to its original size and set it aside with its companions.

The next item from the folder was a slim, leather-bound journal. Each of the narrow pages was filled, top to bottom, in looped handwriting. The script was tiny and nearly impossible for her to decipher. The one phrase she could make out, *Nacht Königin*, suggested that the writing might be German. Xenia didn't speak that one either.

Beneath the journal was a single, waxy sheet of something stiff and translucent. Parchment, maybe? The material crackled in her fingers as she held it up to the light. There was no marking, no writing, on either side. The parchment was utterly blank. "Hmm."

The last of the folder's contents was a bundle of tracing paper. Each sheet had been used to take a rubbing from a carving, or relief. The strokes of charcoal revealed row after row of tiny triangles. Something about the geometric patterns struck Xenia as familiar, but she couldn't quite put her finger on it. She set the tracings beside the other items and fished around in the folder for anything she'd missed.

The search proved fruitful. She slid a single sheet of typewritten paper into the light.

Congratulations, whoever you may be, for divining the unseen and mastering Lockbreaker. Know that we are kindred spirits. Fellow seekers into the true nature of the world. While I have walked this road for many years, your journey is at its beginning.

To that end, I offer you both encouragement and a warning.

Magic is not for the faint of heart, nor the weak of spirit. The road ahead is fraught with peril. Not only is magic dangerous in its own right, its use will attract all the wrong sort of attention. Keep your head low and your secrets close. For very good reason, magic remains, for the great majority of humanity, the stuff of legend.

I fear I must press you, fellow traveler, for a great favor. Watch after these notes. I failed to heed my own advice, and my delving into the secret history of the world has placed me firmly in the crosshairs of exactly those I sought to avoid. In time, should I escape the fate I fear awaits me, I shall reclaim them. If not, I charge you thus. Keep them secret, keep them safe.

As recompense, and to aid you, I have included a selection of basic spells. I wish I could offer you more, but as you will find, magic can be fickle. Best that you begin small. Master these spells, and yourself, and the path to even greater magics will open before you.

I wish you luck. May your fortunes be better than mine.

Quentin Flagstone
Empyrean Tech Guild - 1981

Beneath the grandiose, looping signature was a smeared thumbprint. While the mysterious Quentin had penned his note in blue ink, the smear was a deep umber. When Xenia prodded it with a fingernail, a bit of the dark material flaked away. She dropped the note. *Is that blood?*

What the flipping hell had she stumbled into?

No, she thought, *not stumbled. I was led.* "Thanks a ton, bird."

Xenia took care to avoid touching the dried blood again as she packed everything, save the spells, into the folder. When *Lockbreaker* failed to reverse its effect and turn the folder back into *Practical Spells* again, she settled for slipping it beneath a stack of blank composition books in a drawer.

Xenia did her best to ignore the queasiness that the ominous note had kindled in her gut. She reached for the first of the new spells, *Ghost Flame*. The visible pattern, which the notation referred to as a "glyph," appeared to be only a bit more complex than *Lockbreaker*. However, until she succeeded in controlling her magic sight, the spell's true complexity remained hidden.

Minutes later, her eyes aching from another fruitless attempt to see into the magical world, Xenia tossed the page down. Until she got control over herself, the new spells were completely out of her reach. If she wasn't able to learn magic and build up her skills, how was she going to impress Everard?

Chapter Thirty-One

Bethany orbited the belfry tower in an attempt to keep each of the roads to school in view. She'd spent the entire weekend fretting, from the moment Ev had roared off down the highway with the brainwashed Jane in tow, to now. She'd bounced between the Ambrose household, which Ev hadn't returned to, Xenia's home, and the various places that Lost frequented when they weren't camped out on Xenia's doorstep. No matter how she tried, she couldn't be everywhere at once.

"There you are, fucker," Bethany growled. The cherry red jockmobile chirped its tires as it swung into the parking lot. She pulled up short as, alone, Ev swaggered off to class. "Where are you, Jane?" *Oh, shit.*

Once Ev was out of sight, Bethany passed through the Charger's interior. Ghosts might not breathe, but Bethany still sighed with relief as she found the trunk empty of bodies. Overall, the car was free of any signs of mayhem. She arrowed across the lot and into the school.

She avoided Ev, and Xenia, in AP Calc as she made a lightning circuit of the hallways. At last, she located Jane.

The senior girl gave every appearance of being in high spirits as she chatted with friends. The "kegger" had run from Saturday night well past Sunday morning. The bell rang, and the group dispersed to their various destinations.

While Jane took her seat, Bethany searched her face for any clue, any signal that the real Jane was in there, somewhere, struggling to break free. If a battle raged within the girl's head, not a hint showed on her face.

"Hang in there, okay?" Bethany knew Jane couldn't hear her, but she said it anyway. "We'll stop him. Somehow."

Disgusted at herself, at her ineffectiveness, Bethany flung herself through the ceiling.

"I've been doing this all wrong," Bethany groused as she rose above the school. A motley assortment of jays, sparrows, doves, and one enormous raven were perched along the peak of the roof. She wondered, for a moment, if any of them had been in the flock Ev had called to his arm. "I have to break through to Xenia. Today." *Before she ends up like Jane.*

Or Sal.

When the next bell sounded, Bethany ducked into Xenia's class and perched on her desk. She waved as her friend hurried into the room. "Yo, Zee. What's good?"

Xenia dropped her books through Bethany and sat.

"Crap."

If the dreamy look on Zee's face was any clue, she'd been tagged by Mr. Brainwash in AP Calc.

"Double crap."

Bethany wasted the remainder of the day in one attempt after another to get through. She maintained an endless stream of chatter, jokes, and outright pleading, all to no avail. Xenia just wasn't in tune today.

At least, Bethany knew that her walk home would be clear. Everard had his precious lacrosse practice. Xenia would go straight to her great-aunt's shop. "No, wait. It's Monday. Aunt E's closed on Monday." Even better. Xenia would head straight home.

The two of them made it to Bluff Street without incident, much to Bethany's relief. Oddly, Sal and the other Lost were absent. *They better not be inside!* She needed Zee calm, not all freaked out. As bottomless as her sympathy was, their apparent inability to control their gruesomeness didn't help. If they were inside, she would be polite but firm in shooing them out.

As Xenia banged through the garden gate, Bethany floated ahead to do a quick scan for the others. "See you in a minute, Zee."

Halfway up the porch steps, Xenia paused. Turned. Tilted her head to one side, as if listening.

"Hey, you heard me! Sweet." Even better, none of the Lost were inside. *Wonder where they got off to?* No matter, she'd find them once she'd had a talk with her BFFFF.

Bethany's elation dissolved as the all-too-familiar rumble of Ev's car filled the air. A moment later, the Charger screeched to a halt in front of the old Victorian.

"Ah, shitballs." Bethany dropped to garden level and took a position in front of Xenia.

"Yo," Ev called as he bumped the Charger's door shut. He hopped up onto the sidewalk. "Got a minute?"

"What about practice?" Xenia answered from the porch. She was, to Bethany's dismay, far too eager. She brushed a lock of hair behind her ear and skipped down the steps.

"Coach had a 'personal emergency.'" Ev tilted a hand

by his mouth, miming a swig from an invisible bottle. "Called practice early."

"Isn't that convenient," Bethany snarled.

Ev ignored her and strolled through the open garden gate. "I didn't get a chance to ask. How's the magic coming along?"

"Zee, don't—"

"Oh my God, you have no idea!" Xenia walked straight through Bethany to meet Ev in the center of the garden. She clutched her book bag in both hands and bounced on her toes. "I found what I needed to learn more spells!"

Bethany sighed. "Come on, Zee, don't do this. Please don't fall for his crap." The hunger in Everard's face was so clear, so obvious. How could Xenia not see it? *Because, stupid, he's been zapping her every day to keep her on the hook.*

"Dope! Show me," Ev said.

Xenia's eyes fell. "It's not ready yet. I have to figure out some details. It's not... it's not easy for me, like it is for you."

Ev tapped his chin. "Maybe I should show you a few things after all."

Eyes wide, Xenia gazed up at the senior. "You'd do that? You'd help me learn magic?"

"Yeah, sure. Folks like us have to stick together."

"Like us?"

"Special, like us."

Bethany rolled her eyes. "Oh barf."

Ev went on, "You think just anyone can learn magic?" He laughed. "If everyone did it, it wouldn't be magic! It'd be, I dunno, math or something."

"I guess." Xenia dug the toe of her shoe into the ground.

"Here, let me show you," Ev held out his hand.

Bethany darted to Xenia's side. "Zee, don't! He'll—"

Xenia, without hesitation, took Everard's hand. As before, the instant they touched, all of the liveliness, the personality animating her face, drained away. She swayed on her feet. Only Ev's hand on her shoulder kept her from tipping over. Her book bag tumbled to the grass as her arms fell limp.

"God damn it, Ev. Let her go!" Bethany shoved her face into Everard's.

He raised an eyebrow as he deigned to acknowledge her. "Or what?" He chuckled. "Seriously, I'm just dying to know what it is you think you can do."

"I'll... I'll possess you!" She had no idea where the thought had come from. She'd just blurted out the first thing to pop into her head. She bared her teeth in what she hoped was a fearsome snarl.

Ev tossed his head back and bellowed with laughter. "I'd like to see you try!" He narrowed his sapphire eyes, and his voice was thick with contempt as he said, "Dead Girl, you have no idea what I am, or what I am capable of." He drew Xenia under his arm with a chuckle. As she pressed herself to his side, she echoed his laugh. The sound was flat, devoid of emotion.

Rage boiled through Bethany and she flung herself at the jock. She didn't know if it was even possible. Not to mention that, on any other day, if someone had suggested possession, she would have refused. Stealing someone's body, invalidating their autonomy, was no better than what Ev did. But now? To save her friend? Bethany was going to fucking well give it everything she had.

She was a heartbeat from the blue and white of Ev's jacket when his mask of bravado wavered. His free hand darted between them, and Bethany slammed to a halt. No matter how she strained and fought, she was unable to cross those final few inches.

Ev extended his arm, and the barrier moved with it. Bethany was shoved from the garden, out into the street. Away from Xenia.

Worse, for the first time since she'd awoken as a ghost, Bethany was fatigued. As if Ev's defense not only held her at bay but sapped something vital from her.

Is this what he did to Sal? To Lucas? Had they fought on, beyond death, only to be damaged by Ev's magic? Bethany screamed her frustration and flung herself away from the invisible wall, sending herself skyward until the sense of draining stopped. "Zee! Sweetheart, you have to fight him! Snap out of it!"

As Ev's mocking laughter followed her, Xenia's vacant face rose. A hint of frown creased her brow. "Beebs? What are you doing all the way up there?" Confusion slithered across the blank of her face. She shook her head.

"That's it! Fight!" Bethany flipped double birds at Ev.

Everard turned from her and took each of Xenia's shoulders in hand. She blinked, her eyelids out of sync, as he began to whisper in her ear. What little personality she'd managed to exert vanished.

"Shit!" Bethany flew in a wide arc and sought the edge of Ev's defenses. *There's no time!* The instant Ev thought he had Xenia locked up, he'd steal her away to who knows where. *I won't let that happen!*

Out of time, out of ideas, Bethany hurled herself over the curve of Everard's barrier and through the roof of the old Victorian.

Chapter Thirty-Two

Xenia drifted as the heat of Everard's touch burned into her. She wanted nothing more than to lose herself in that fire, forever. The tension she'd carried since the hospital had eased. The muscles of her back and shoulders unclenched as that heat spread through them. If she were to fall, Xenia knew that Ev would be there to catch her.

The words he whispered in her ear eluded understanding, but that didn't concern her. Only his breath on her ear, on her neck, was important now.

His thumb left a burning trail across her skin as he cupped her chin. Tilted her face to meet his. The sapphire of his eyes filled her vision. His lips, fever hot, were so close. Her first kiss, less than a heartbeat away. Would the sear of his mouth on hers burn her, reduce her to ashes? Xenia welcomed it.

The crack of Great-Aunt Elspeth's voice halted Ev's lips a hair's breadth from her own. "Take yer bloody mitts from my Xenia, Mister Tall Britches!"

Xenia blinked as Ev flinched away. Her eyes were

gummy and refused to focus. "What?" She turned her head, that simple movement almost beyond her, to see what had upset her great-aunt. The woman's brogue came and went with her moods, but Xenia had never heard it this strong before.

Elspeth stood atop the porch steps with a fist planted on each hip. Although she swam in and out of clarity, the sheer fury on her face was unmistakable.

Why is Aunt Elspeth dressed like that? The thought rose through the cotton candy–stuffed hallways of Xenia's mind. She squinted. No, she'd been right. All of her guardian's clothing, from the peasant skirt to the loose flowery blouse, was on inside out. As if that weren't outlandish enough, she appeared to wear a golden crown.

No, Xenia realized, *those are flowers. Why is she wearing a garland on her head?* A second loop of golden blossoms dangled from one of her great-aunt's wrists.

Pure malice blazed from Elspeth's eyes as she stalked through the garden. Her march took her in a wide arc around Xenia and Everard to the open garden gate. With a sweep of her hand, she slammed it shut. Her reversed skirt flared as she turned to face them. "I'll not be asking again, lad. Release my Xenia, or there'll be hell to pay!"

Xenia shrank from her guardian's rage into the comforting curve of Ev's arm. *Did I do something wrong? Why is she so angry?* Not once since coming to live with Aunt Elspeth had Xenia seen the woman lose her temper. Even when her favorite teapot had broken, Elspeth had brushed it off with a laugh.

Everard tightened his arm about Xenia's shoulders. "Let's get out of here. Your old lady's creeping me out."

Xenia nodded. Clearly Elspeth was out of line. This

sort of anger was totally uncalled for. Her fingers found Ev's. He squeezed her hand as she took his.

"If you're set on leaving with that villain, lassie, don't be forgetting your keys." Elspeth lobbed something dark toward Xenia.

I already have my keys... Despite the sugary fog slowing her thoughts, Xenia lifted a hand in time to catch the keyring.

Everard tore himself away as her fingers closed about the object Elspeth had thrown. Her skin burned cold at the contact, but the sensation was refreshing rather than painful, the chill of a brisk winter with the promise of cocoa ahead. The lethargy of her thoughts, the blur of her vision, began to fray under that crisp rush.

Xenia opened her hand and found, rather than a set of house keys, a battered, square-headed nail. "What?"

Before she knew what was happening, Elspeth was in front of her. In a blink, she had the hoodie up over Xenia's head. With a brusque movement, the woman inverted the garment and dragged it back onto her. Like a child, Xenia allowed her arms to be threaded into the sleeves.

With that bizarre task accomplished, Elspeth set the second wreath of golden flowers atop Xenia's head. An aroma, not unlike lavender but even more grassy and sweet, filled her nose. The cotton candy that had clogged her thoughts and slowed her mind blew away on that perfumed rush. The tempo of her thoughts became a torrent. She swayed on her feet, but Elspeth caught her arm and steadied her before she could fall.

"Yer safe now, lassie. That villain'll have no more of ye." Elspeth glared at Everard. "That is, if he knows what's good for him."

"Villain? Ev?" When Xenia turned, she found Ev backed almost to their porch. When she looked at him, really looked, the sight of his sky blue eyes, the artfully tousled mop of his blond hair, the lean, muscular physique... meant nothing to her. Hadn't he, just a moment ago, been her whole world? Why had he seemed so important? So much larger than life? Her stomach did a slow, queasy roll about her insides.

Everard returned Elspeth's glare and raised his hands, bringing them together in a slow, melodramatic round of applause. "Oh bravo." His lip curled in a sneer. "Old Lady Hero saves the day." He spread his arms wide. "You ain't saved shit."

Xenia's mouth went dry. There were, by her estimation, far too many teeth in Everard's mouth.

"I can wait," Ev went on, "until tomorrow, or next week, or even next year. I have all the time in the world. You, grandma, hardly have any left at all. I'll have the witch girl, and her power, for my own."

Witch girl? What the fuck?

"Yer off yer head if you think I'll allow you another go at Xenia, boyo," Elspeth's voice lashed out, though the hand on Xenia's shoulder was gentle. "Ye show yer age, or lack of it, ye wee numpty changeling!"

Ev's jaw dropped. "How—"

It was Elspeth's turn to laugh. "Look about, lad. Ye came calling at my home, intent on stealing *my great-niece*, and not a thought did you give as to what was all about!"

Everard's mouth closed with a snap. His eyes darted to the rows of planting boxes on either side of the stone path he stood upon, to the tangle of bushes and shrubs growing along the white picket fence, which bordered the entire property. Clusters of gold bloomed through it all. Yellow flowers, the same that Elspeth had twined into the garlands they both wore, grew in every corner of the garden.

The color drained from Everard's face. A tiny cry escaped his lips. He spun on his heel and tried to mount the porch steps, only to backpedal from something Xenia couldn't see. As he launched himself down the garden path, Elspeth, her arm firm on Xenia's shoulder, guided them both into the space between planters.

Everard ignored them both as he seized the gate latch. There was a sharp *hiss,* like bacon on a pan, and he snatched his fingers away. Ev clutched his hand and stumbled. His heel caught the edge of a paver, and he went down hard on his ass.

Xenia gasped and shrank against Elspeth's side at the sight of Ev's hand. The flesh of his fingers was burnt. A wisp of greasy steam trailed from the injury.

"Aye, lad. Cold iron." Elspeth's grin was fierce as she nudged Xenia. "All around the fence, do you see it?"

Xenia had noticed the line of nails protruding from the topmost fence rail. She'd dismissed them as yet another of her guardian's half-finished projects. When she examined the nail Elspeth had tossed to her, she found it a match for those in the fence.

"I built that fence with my own hands." Elspeth shrugged. "I'll admit a carpenter would have done a better job of it. But I wouldn't have been sure that every last inch was ash wood if I had. Ash is important, dearie," Elspeth murmured. She nodded to the tangle of spiked brush that grew along the fence. "Thorn as well, and oak. You'd do well to remember that."

Everard cradled his injured hand as he rose to a crouch. "I am going to rip—"

"Shut it!" Elspeth snapped. Xenia couldn't help her

own flinch at the ferocity in her guardian's voice. "It's nothing you'll be doing, lad. Not if you wish to avoid another handful of iron." When Elspeth raised her free hand, she held one of the iron nails.

Ev flinched away and caught himself before he bumped the fence. He sank lower into his crouch, his muscles taut beneath the denim of his jeans.

Xenia looked from Ev to the nail in her great-aunt's hand. She set her teeth and aimed her own at him, brandished it as if it were a tiny dagger.

Some of the bravado, the ferocity, slipped from Everard's face then. "Look, Xenia, I..." He turned his eyes to the clouds above, as if the right thing to say might be written there.

"Don't you listen to a word that villain says, lassie. Not a word out of him can we trust. His folk, to a one, are peddlers of deceit and illusion, and I'm not speaking entirely about men!"

"His folk?" Xenia took care to keep her nail aimed at Ev when she looked up at Elspeth. "I don't understand, I thought he was... that I..." Her shoulders slumped. "I don't know what I thought." Anger swirled through her, taking the last of her uncertainty with it. She set her shoulders back and glared at Everard down the length of her iron nail. "What do we do now, Aunt Elspeth? How do we deal with" —*what did she call him?*—"a changeling?"

Elspeth patted Xenia's shoulder. "While we cannae trust a word out of that one's mouth, there's one thing we can be sure of. If we get his oath on it, he won't be able harm you. His kind can no more break a promise than I can flap my arms and fly to Edinburgh!"

Sweat had transformed Everard's styled mop of hair to a

sodden mass. He mashed a hand across his face to clear his eyes. As his balance teetered, his shoulder brushed the row of nails behind him. Even through the wool of his jacket, the sizzle of his flesh was clear. He yelped and shuffled away from the fence, only to nearly topple into one of the thorn bushes. Wide, panicked eyes darted from iron, to thorn, to Elspeth. His head dropped even as he raised both hands in defeat.

"That's more like it, lad. I'll be hearing that promise, now. Promise you will release any hold, any glamour or enchantment, you have on my great-niece, Xenia Findlay. Swear that you will seek no quarrel and attempt no injury, be it by action or subterfuge, with Xenia, with me or with any of the lass's friends... or their families, for that matter. For all the days of your misbegotten life, however long they may be."

As Elspeth laid out her demand, fire had crept back into Everard's eyes. When she spoke the last of it, he bared his teeth in a snarl.

Elspeth signaled for Xenia to stay put and stomped over to the changeling. One trembling, sapphire-blue eye tracked the point of her iron nail as she brought it right up to his face. A fat bead of sweat slipped from his hair to drip from the tip of his nose.

"Swear it, lad, or so help me—"

"I swear! Everything, just like you said!" Everard's throat bobbed as he swallowed in fear. His eye never wavered from the nail.

"Nay, speak the whole piece. Just as I said it."

Everard swallowed again. "I promise that I will release Xenia Findlay from all my glamours and enchantments. I swear that, as long as I live, I will seek no quarrel with her." The nail twitched closer. "Or with you, Elspeth Findlay! Or

Xenia's friends or their families!" His voice climbed one octave and half another as he spoke.

"What was that, lad?" Elspeth cupped her ear. "Once more, if you don't mind."

Everard repeated the promise, word-for-word.

"I'm afraid my hearing isn't what it used to be. Let's have it again, shall we?"

The last shred of defiance oozed from his face as he shifted his weight. He licked his lips and slid his foot on the stone paver beneath him. "I promise... I swear..." His lip quavered as he tried to force the words out, then peeled back in a snarl. "I promise nothing!"

Elspeth stumbled away as Ev's body uncoiled like a spring. Xenia caught her great-aunt before she fell even as her eyes tracked his course through the air. His knees came up into a backflip that carried him over the gate's trellis and the thorn and iron affixed there. He landed in a feral crouch on the sidewalk outside, hands and feet braced wide on the concrete.

Icy fear slithered down Xenia's spine as Everard growled. Actually growled, his chest rumbling like an animal's. His eyes met hers and, in that instant, he was something else. The face was the same, in the broad strokes, but the skull beneath the skin was too long, and far too narrow, to be human. The overlarge orbits of his eye sockets now contained spheres of glittering crystal. Motes of cobalt and turquoise danced in the core of each alien eye.

Behind his sideburns grew long, pointed ears. So long, in fact, that the angular tips nearly met behind the curve of his skull. The snarl of his mouth was overcrowded, packed corner to corner with a multitude of tiny needle teeth. A dark, barbed tongue flicked out to wet the colorless lips.

Everard shimmered, like heat haze in the desert, and

was himself once more. Just a regular teenager. Same old arrogant, lacrosse-playing Ev.

He backed away, his eyes never leaving Xenia's. He popped the door to his Charger and slid behind the wheel. The engine rumbled to life. Rubber screamed against pavement as the muscle car peeled away. A moment later, car and changeling were gone.

Elspeth dusted her hands. "Well. That might have gone a tad better." She cupped Xenia's face. Hazel eyes bored into Xenia's. "How are ye, lass? Head clear?" Elspeth's composure cracked at last. Tears spilled across her face as she threw her arms around Xenia.

Stunned, Xenia returned the embrace.

"I'm so sorry, lass. I should have seen the signs before today," Elspeth sobbed into the top of Xenia's head. "I was just so happy you were making new friends, and it seemed as if you were finally on the mend. If only I'd known..."

Xenia eased herself free and gazed up at her great-aunt. "Aunt Elspeth," she said, when she found her voice.

"Aye, lass."

"You. Were. *Amazing!*" Xenia threw her arms around Elspeth again. "How did you do that? How did you know all of that, what to do?"

Elspeth rocked her in her arms for a moment. "Well, my Granny had these stories she would tell, you see. All manner of fables and tall tales. She'd put out a saucer of cream for the brownies, or honey when she had it. I suppose I picked up a thing or two from her."

"All right." Xenia had no idea what a brownie was. "But how did you know I needed help? Right now, I mean."

Elspeth looked at her a bit longer and then rubbed the side of her nose. "That's an easy one, lass. Your wee ghostie told me."

Chapter Thirty-Three

Xenia stared, aghast. "You knew Bethany was here? This whole time? Why didn't you tell me?"

Elspeth clucked her tongue and shooed her toward the house. "Now, lass, it's not as if I knew who was buzzing about my home. You were having a hard enough time of it, without your batty old great-aunt going on about ghosts and the like." She paused in the doorway and turned to the now empty garden. "You might as well come in and join us, lass." Elspeth waited a beat and then shut and locked the front door. Once they were in the kitchen, she waved at the table. "Have a seat. I'll put the kettle on."

While her guardian busied herself at the stove, Xenia half fell into her usual chair. A familiar set of goosebumps ran down her neck. "Beebs, that you?" She turned, and found the ghost hovering in the dining room.

Bethany waggled her fingers. "Hey, how's your head?" If her expression was anything to go by, she didn't expect to be heard.

Xenia sat bolt upright. "I can hear you!"

Elspeth paused in making a selection from her extensive assortment of tea. "Have you not been able?"

"I've only been able to see her sometimes," Xenia said. "But now... Wow, you're clearer than ever!" Her stomach turned sour. How much had Ev's machinations interfered with her new abilities? "I'm sorry," she said to Elspeth and Bethany alike, "I should have said something. I just couldn't believe it... I thought you were wishful thinking, that something was wrong with me. Because of the accident." She rubbed her cast. "Have you seen a lot of ghosts, Aunt Elspeth?"

Elspeth swept the kettle from the burner at the first hint of a whistle. She tipped the boiling water into the pot, added the tea strainer, and wrapped a knitted blue tea cozy about the whole affair. She fetched three cups and three saucers from the cabinet, along with a tube of McVitie's, her favorite "digestive." Only once she'd arranged everything on the table and had taken her favorite chair did she speak. "Don't be rude, lass. Pull out a chair for your friend."

Xenia goggled at her for a moment and then hopped up to drag out the chair beside her.

Bethany's smile was bright enough to light the room. She arranged herself to appear as if she were sitting rather than floating. "Thank you, Aunt Elspeth." She shot a look at Xenia. "Ask if it's okay for me to call her that!"

"What? Oh! Bethany says 'thank you' and wants to know if it's cool if she calls you 'aunt'?" Xenia dropped into her chair with a giggle.

Elspeth waved away the question, "You're practically family, lass. Suit yourself. Now, to answer your question, I can't see you, Bethany, and I've only a notion when you're speaking. It's just a feeling when you're about. An itch I can't scratch, or a buzz in my ear. It's a relief to learn that you're not a boggart, or worse." Elspeth filled the three waiting cups and slid two across the table.

Bethany looked as if she would explode with joy as she leaned over the steaming cup. "I can't actually, you know, drink it. I can't even smell it. But tell Aunt E thank you for including me."

Xenia passed the message along and sipped at her tea. Whatever Aunt Elspeth had brewed, it had a heady, herbaceous scent.

"Seriously, Zee, she's a frickin' legend!" Bethany cupped her hands about the cup, as if to warm herself. "I was freaking out while that slimeball was getting his hooks into you. Your face was all blank, total zombie-ville. I couldn't stop him, and he knew it." Her lip trembled. "I thought I was going to lose you. That you'd end up like the others. He knocked me away, somehow. I was desperate, so I did the only thing I could think of. I screamed in Aunt E's ear. Sorry, Aunt E." She paused as Xenia mopped at her eyes and then translated for Elspeth. "I thought she'd just chase him off with a broom, or call the cops. No, she took one look out the window and *bam!* Off like a rocket. I thought I was losing my mind when she started turning her clothes inside out, though."

"I had no idea what was going on. My brain was all foggy..." Xenia rubbed her forehead. "Actually, it's been foggy for a while. I don't know when it started. I couldn't think straight. There were thoughts in my head, but they weren't mine. I was me, but not me."

"Aye, lass. That was his glamour." As Elspeth paused to sip her tea, her other hand clenched until the knuckles went white. "That's what the Gray Neighbors do. They get in your head." She saw the question in Xenia's eyes and added, "Fairies, lass. Sprites and brownies and so forth. I do believe that villain was a changeling. An elf-born child left in a crib after the fairies have stolen the wee one for their own. Snatching people up, that's their very bread and butter."

"How did you know what to do? To make him stop?" Xenia's fingers first brushed her forehead and then the wreath of golden flowers she still wore. At her guardian's nod, she set the garland on the table. "Why was he so scared of a nail?"

"I know that one!" Bethany, in her excitement, was half through the table. "Cold iron, the fae can't abide its touch."

"Aye," Elspeth confirmed, once Xenia had passed the comment along. "A turned coat, cold iron, and St. John's wort. Just the ticket to break an enchantment. Then there's oak, ash, and thorn to keep them at bay and out of your business." She slapped the table and scowled. "We'd be quit of that one, if I'd been able to squeeze a third promise out of him." Elspeth took a deep breath and nibbled at a biscuit.

"Two wasn't enough?" Xenia asked.

"Thrice spoken is thrice done, Granny used to say. There's power in threes, much more than something done once. It might be that he'll be held to his word, but I won't bet our lives on it. Not without that third promise." Elspeth bit her biscuit in half and washed it down. "Granny, she... now that I think of it, that whole side of the family had a touch of the sight. That'd be the Findlays, lass," she added for Bethany. "Granny might have had rather more of it than most, because she was the only one who could see the brownies and sprites dancing about in the fields. The farm she grew up on, to hear her talk, had a bit of a boggart infestation. Now, back in her day, it wasn't quite as unusual to hear someone talk about such things, not like today. Still, she raised more than one eyebrow." Elspeth fished another digestive from the tube. "Since I was younger than you are now, lass, I've had some awareness of these things. That there's more about us than meets the eye. For the most part, it hasn't been a bother, but sometimes... well, my teeth itch something fierce." Her gaze flitted between the girl she could see and the one she could not. "For better or worse, lass, you've got the family gift. A bit of a surprise, that. Your father, rest his soul, had nary a tick. The lad wouldn't have known a brownie if it bit him on the boll— if it bit him."

"Well. I'm real, clearly," Bethany said with a grin. "Even if I didn't believe it myself at first." The grin was replaced by something darker, something wary. "What else is out there? Other than ghosts and changelings?"

"Just about anything and everything you've heard a story about, I suspect," Elspeth said, "and some you haven't. Oh, I'm sure they're not exactly like the fairy tales and myths. Certainly not in the numbers they must have once enjoyed before we went and filled the world with our cities, our cold iron and our guns. But they're out there. Like that horrid wee goblin of ours, they hide in plain sight. Or in places we won't, or can't, go. After all, we're not such very good neighbors ourselves."

"We're not good neighbors?" The rush of outrage came out of nowhere. Xenia reached for her teacup and found she'd drained it.

"You're old enough to have seen how people treat those who only look a wee bit different, lass." Elspeth topped off both Xenia's cup and her own.

Xenia blew the anger out with a long breath. "Yeah." She took a cookie for herself. "Have you seen anything like him before? Other, um, supernatural things?"

"Come now, lass. Do you think I spent all those years wandering about this grand old planet of ours, poking my nose wherever I fancied, and not see something that beggared explanation?" Elspeth chuckled. "Truth be told, it wasn't all that often, and it's been ages since the last." Her eyes lost focus as she poured over her memories. "It must have been Japan, I believe. I'd fallen in with a pack of do-gooders, you see, and we were out volunteering wherever needed. Spent a summer restoring one of those delightful temples they have over there. Did you know they build them without any nails? Anyhow, there was a lass who'd hang about just outside the temple grounds. Right queer feeling I got from that one. I couldn't begin to guess what she might have been, but she was something all right. Well, one night, one of the lads took her out for a drink and that was that." Melancholy touched Elspeth's face as she spread her hands wide. "Not a one of us saw hide or hair of them ever again."

"Da-yumn," breathed Bethany.

Xenia nodded, awestruck.

"The world, for all of its wonder and beauty, can be an unforgiving place," Elspeth said.

Xenia nodded again. She'd just received her first unpleasant lesson on that subject. "You said I had this 'sight,' like your Granny? And that's why I can see Beebs?" She decided not to mention, for the moment, the other ghosts she'd seen.

"That's right."

"Could any of the Findlays see more than that?" Xenia wasn't sure how to phrase her question.

"Like the future? Well, if we could see that, I'm sure old Uncle Angus might not have stumbled in front of that lorry!" Elspeth slapped her knee with a cackle.

"Maybe I should show her." Xenia said to Bethany. Before either of them could speak, Xenia dashed upstairs.

She gathered up what she needed and returned to the kitchen at full speed.

"I swear, lass. I have no clue how a slip of a girl like that manages to sound like a whole herd of wildebeests on those stairs," Elspeth said to Bethany. Her grin, when she turned to Xenia, held no shame.

"Oh my God, I love this woman," Bethany gushed.

"Since I woke up in the hospital, I've been seeing more than just Bethany." Xenia swallowed the sudden pang of grief and pushed on. "I thought it was a migraine symptom, like the doctor warned me about. But then, I wound up in this weird shop." She sketched out her encounter with the raven and how he had led her to *Practical Spells.* "Sorry I chased you away, Beebs. Made you miss that part."

Bethany did an "aw, go on" wave and smiled.

"I found this hidden in the book." Xenia set the card inscribed with *Lockbreaker's* design on the table.

"How curious," Elspeth said. "What do you suppose it is?"

"Oh, that's where you got that! I've been dying to ask!" Bethany abandoned any pretense of sitting and rose above the table for a better look.

Xenia set a heavy padlock she'd found in the kitchen's everything drawer beside the card. She pulled *Lockbreaker* from her pocket.

Elspeth peered at the lock. "That old thing? I lost the key ages ago—"

Xenia tapped the padlock. There was a sharp *click-clack* from within, and the lock popped open.

Elspeth's jaw dropped.

"I can do magic," Xenia said. "Real magic. Those lights and things I saw? That"—she pointed at the card—"showed me how to twist and tie that light into this." She held up

Lockbreaker so that Elspeth and Bethany could both see the glyph etched into the metal.

As Elspeth's eyebrows continued their climb, Bethany did a backflip in midair. "That is so frickin' cool!"

"It's a magical key." Xenia waggled the ruler between her fingers. "And it can open any lock. Well, I don't know if it'll work on electric locks or whatever. It's opened everything I've tried. As long as I let it rest up between the big ones. Then, I asked myself 'Why this spell, why not a fireball?' It's such a random thing." Her grin turned fierce. "I used it on that book, *Practical Spells and Recipes*." Xenia held up the folder. "And the book turned into this!" She dumped out the contents for all to see.

"Crivvens!" Elspeth, eyes gleaming, lifted the topmost sheet from the pile. "*Ghost Flame?* Now doesn't that just sound marvelous!" She turned to Bethany's empty chair. "Would it have something to do with your state of being, do you think?"

Xenia's heart lurched as raw, desperate hope bloomed on her friend's face. "I don't know," she said. "I can't see magic whenever I want, so I haven't been able to try that one yet." She tapped the glyph inked in the center of the page. "When I can see it, though, these are like holograms. Three-dimensional instructions on how to make a spell. You have to weave a bunch of different colors—types? I'm not sure what they are—together to make it work. But if I can't see it, I can't touch it. It's been slow going." She met Bethany's eyes. "If it's something that will help you, I'll make it work. Promise."

"Holding you to that, BFFFF," Bethany said.

A gasp from Elspeth brought Xenia's head around. Her great-aunt held one of the odd, charcoal rubbings from the folder up to the light. Aghast, she traced a finger over one of the tiny triangles. "I believe," she said after a moment, "that there's something you both should see."

Xenia looked to Bethany and got a shrug in return. The two of them trailed Elspeth from the kitchen, down the hall and into the sitting room. There, Elspeth stood before the "forbidden" cabinet, the one she'd asked Xenia not to pry into. She fished a key from about her neck and then paused. "On second thought, why don't you do the honors, lass?"

"What?" It took a moment before Xenia's brain caught up, and she ran back to the kitchen for *Lockbreaker*. When Xenia tapped the tiny brass keyhole set in the wood, she was rewarded with a *clickety-clunk* from inside. At her guardian's nod, she swung the door open. Inside, the most scandalous thing waiting for her tender eyes was a complete set of commemorative *Star Trek* plates. The shelf below that held a glossy, lacquered box filled with small, woody objects, each in their own twist of cellophane.

"Whoopsie!" Elspeth slapped the box closed. "Not that one, dearie. This one." She ran her hand along the underside of the middle shelf. There was a tiny *click*. Elspeth grasped the shelf and gave it a solid tug.

Xenia stepped back, jaw agape, as the entire cabinet swung away from the wall on silent hinges.

* * *

The only detail Xenia could discern within the shadowed portal was the first riser of a staircase descending into the darkness beneath the house.

"Oh, snap! Zee, this is the good shit right here." Bethany gave Elspeth an appraising look. "Is there a level above 'bad ass'? Aunt E has to be, like, four steps over that."

"I haven't had a reason to go downstairs in quite some

time." Elspeth's expression sobered as she twisted the antique Bakelite switch. The *tink-tink-tink* of fluorescent lights igniting echoed from below, and dim, greenish-white light replaced shadow.

"What do you think," Bethany asked, eyes wide and eager. "Vampire coffin, mummy sarcophagus, or werewolf in a cage?"

"Shut up," muttered Xenia. "Aunt Elspeth? Why is there a secret door to a secret basement in the sitting room?"

"'Tis a long story, lass." Elspeth began to pick her way down the stairs. "Years ago, when the old wanderlust still had its teeth in me, I met a lad..."

"Now we're talking," crowed Bethany.

Xenia glared at the ghost and then followed her great-aunt.

"I was in Prague, such a lovely place, when I met Quentin."

At the mention of the name, Xenia paused on the stairs. *No way!* She held her tongue, intent on hearing all of Aunt Elspeth's story before she spoke.

"I couldnae have been more than twenty-three, twenty-four at the most. He was the most dashing, interesting man I'd ever met. We danced, wandered the city until dawn, then parted ways. I ran into him in Singapore, two years later. Before I knew what had happened, we were spending all of our time together. Oh, we still had our own interests, our own travels. But, like magnets, we'd always find each other. For the first time in my life, I thought about my golden years, and knew I wanted to spend them with him." Elspeth's chuckle was full of affection. At the base of the staircase, she patted the wall. "Which is why I bought this old place. I had a mind to settle down, one day."

Xenia gaped as she stepped into the tiny basement. The

single room occupied perhaps a third of the Victorian's foot-print. The pale plaster of the walls was stained with water and time, and here and there, it had cracked and fallen away to reveal the stone blocks beneath.

Row after row of shelves, cabinets, and glass display cases filled all but a narrow aisle's worth of the room. Every shelf was overloaded, cluttered, with a menagerie of old books, boxes of wood and metal, figurines tiny and not, and items beyond Xenia's ability to identify.

Bethany was aglow with excitement. "Zee! You know what this is? It's one giant cabinet of curiosities! The whole room!" She squinted at a fist-sized carving of a four-armed elephant man. "I am so, so jealous right now."

Xenia nodded absently. She followed Elspeth deeper into the room.

"Just as he and I were getting serious, Quentin dropped off my radar. Six months slipped by without a word. Then, out of the blue, he appeared! I was in Cairo, being an abso-lute tourist I'm afraid. Camels, pyramids, the whole bit." Elspeth gazed into the past. "I was too distracted by the adventure of it all to truly pick up on Quentin's mood. He was agitated, on edge in a way I'd never before seen in him. He gave this to me."

She brushed the dust from the upper facet of a cube carved from white marble. Veins of pale gold twisted through the stone's surface. "He asked that I hold on to it for safekeeping. It seems he'd made some sort of discovery, him and his cronies. That silly 'guild' of his. Absolutely mental, the lot of them. It was going to change everything, he said, once they'd put all the pieces together. There were men looking for him, and this, he said."

Elspeth moved on to the next row. "It was all so very exciting, you have to understand. So very Hollywood!

Secret societies, hidden cults, international intrigue." She tapped the alabaster ear of a dog-headed canopic jar. "A wee bit of smuggling." Her smile was twin to the one she'd worn in the photo in the trunk upstairs.

Xenia turned in a circle, trying to estimate the collection's size. "This is all stuff he wanted you to keep for him?"

"Aye, lass. Each and every one of these was another world-shaking discovery of his. 'Keep them secret, keep them safe,'" Elspeth paraphrased. Her smile slipped away. "Then, one day, the letters stopped. As did the phone calls, the telegrams, all of it. I didn't worry so much at first. It's not like I hadn't gone off the map myself, from time to time. The months became years and still, there was nothing but silence. I realized, after far too long, that Quentin's delving into the shadows had caught up with him. It was nearly as long before it struck me that, if they could catch up with him, they could certainly catch up with me!" She patted the head of a waist-high bronze idol. "I had myself a proper panic, believe me. I set aside my grief and made a mad dash to all the corners of the world where I'd squirreled away Quentin's treasures. I brought them here, to the house I'd purchased in the town he'd grown up in." Elspeth's eyes shimmered in the fluorescent glare.

Xenia threw her arms around Elspeth. The two of them stood there, each supporting the other.

Bethany made a throat-clearing noise. "I don't want to be rude, but... was there something specific down here you wanted us to see?"

"Aunt Elspeth? Bethany wants to know, is this what you wanted to show us? This collection? Or was there something special?" Xenia dabbed at her eyes with her sleeve.

Elspeth nodded and led the way across the room. "Ah-hah." She plucked a fan-bristled brush from a jar full of them.

Xenia coughed as her great aunt raised a cloud of dust from the first of a row of tablets. The blocks of ancient clay had a shelf of their own, and ranged from over twelve inches wide to less than four. The surface of each tablet was packed, edge to edge, with tiny, triangular markings.

"Woah, are those—"

Before Bethany could finish her thought, Xenia was off at a run. When she returned from the kitchen, she had the stack of rubbings. She hesitated by the tablets. Elspeth nodded for her to continue.

Xenia shuffled through the sheets until she found one that was close in size to the nearest tablet. She rotated it, squinted, then shifted to the next. The rubbing and the clay inscription were a perfect match. She spun to Bethany and shook the bundle of tracings. "It's them! These are the originals!"

Elspeth took half of the pages from Xenia. The two of them matched each rubbing with its respective tablet. When they were done, there was only one left uncovered. "Huh," Xenia muttered. She ran a hesitant finger across the rough clay. Her nose filled with the heady aroma of roasting barley, sea salt, and campfire smoke. She sneezed, and the moment passed. All she smelled now were cobwebs and dust.

"Is there a catalogue for all of this?" Bethany asked.

"Nay," said Elspeth, once Xenia had passed the question on. "I burned as much of the paper trail as I could find. After Quentin..." She swallowed. Blinked hard a few times, and not from the dust in the air. "Nay, lass. The only catalogue is up here." She tapped her forehead. "Not that this old brain would be of any help, Quentin was the expert on all of this, not me."

Xenia dug in her back pocket. When she'd gone up for the rubbings, she'd also grabbed the note that had accompanied them. "This was in the folder too." She handed the scrap of paper to her great-aunt.

Puzzlement clear on her face, Elspeth scanned the few lines the note had to offer. When she reached the signature, and the blood-smeared thumbprint, her face crumpled. She pressed the note to her chest as tears spilled unchecked down her cheeks. "You daft bugger. You damned fool."

Xenia took her great-aunt by the elbow and led her upstairs. In the kitchen, she sat Elspeth at the table and set about preparing a fresh pot of tea. The basement, with all of its mysteries, had waited this long.

It could wait a bit longer.

* * *

It was several hours, more than one pot of tea, and a delivered pizza later before Xenia at last went to bed.

It seemed that Elspeth had intended to cope with the long-delayed news by rushing herself through each stage of grief in one sitting. In the end, she focused on the good times, her favorite moments with the love of her life. She'd regaled Xenia and Bethany with the time she and Quentin had hiked the mountains of Tibet. With each word, her strength returned. She described how Quentin had lost his sole pair of trousers to an overly curious and hungry yak. How he'd spent the next two days wearing a blanket knotted about his waist, until they'd made it to the next village.

"Would you look at the time! Why, it's past midnight!"

Elspeth slapped both palms against the table and stood. "I do believe I'll treat myself to an extra day off. And why not? It's my shop, after all. A woman's entitled." She hid a titanic yawn behind her hand. "In the morning, I'll call the school, lass, and let them know we've all come down with just the worst case of the flu. After what you've been through, no doubt you could do with a day off of your own!" With that, she bid both girls a good night and tottered up the stairs.

"How are you holding up, Zee?"

Xenia's jaw cracked as she echoed her great-aunt's yawn. "I'm okay. I'm going to crash too, if that's cool?" The thought of sleeping now, when she'd just reunited with the friend she'd lost, was unbearable. Not to mention Beebs would have to just... hang around while everyone slept. But if she didn't go to bed soon, she'd be in trouble.

Bethany made a shooing motion. "Go, go. I can keep myself entertained while the mortal world sleeps." She winked, then waved a hand before her eyes. "Do you think you'll still be able to..."

"I don't know. Honestly, I'm surprised it lasted this long. I've only been able to see you in bits and flashes before. Maybe because I'm not fighting it? Not insisting you're not real? Or maybe it was—" Xenia bit off that line of thought. "Just don't give up on me, if I lose it while I'm asleep. Okay?"

"Never!" Bethany blew her a kiss and then slipped through the wall.

Xenia stared after until the next yawn sent her upstairs.

Once she was safe in her room and had assured herself that the alarm clock was off, Xenia burrowed under her blankets. Then, hidden from all prying eyes, she stopped fighting the inevitable.

The trembling began in her hands. It spread, quickly, through the rest of her. Tears followed in a rush.

Since Elspeth had released her from Everard's "glamour," revelation after revelation had followed. The torrent of discovery had afforded her no time to process what she'd endured.

She'd told Aunt Elspeth and Bethany that her memories of the changeling's hold on her were fuzzy, incomplete. That she couldn't remember most of it. That had been a lie, to save them from worry.

Xenia could remember every moment of it.

She remembered all too well the thoughts he'd thrust into her head and the emotions he'd inflicted upon her. The artificial feelings that had compelled her to follow him like an eager puppy. An instant crush, out of nothing. She hadn't had a crush on anyone, ever. He'd stolen that first from her. Poisoned it. Then there were the urges...

Xenia clamped her teeth about the edge of her pillow. Bit down the muffle her torrent of sobs.

That hadn't been the worst. No. Everard had stolen her pain.

From the moment she'd emerged from her coma, learned that her parents, that Bethany, were dead, she'd been... gutted. Her emotions had seethed raw, unchecked. In her short time with Elspeth, they'd become manageable, if only a little. But her mother and her father were still gone. Bethany had been gone. The first new friend she'd made in Porter Valley, Sal, was gone. Even though Bethany's return suggested that there was a place for the departed, Xenia knew she would never see her parents again. Not in this life. Knowing that was worse than any pain from her injuries.

Everard had, with a touch, stolen all of that from her.

Snuffed out her pain as if Mom and Dad, Bethany, Sal... as if they'd never existed. Like they didn't matter.

Thanks to the candy fog Ev had stuffed into her head, Xenia had missed Sal's funeral. It hadn't been important to the changeling, so it hadn't been important to her.

Now, in the still of the night, without a flood of improbable discoveries to hold it at bay, grief had come crashing down upon her. She welcomed that tempest because it was hers, and hers alone.

Xenia didn't know if she spent minutes or hours curled about herself beneath the quilt. She clenched her fists. *Stop crying! Enough! It's not over, and Everard is still out there.* A nail, Xenia knew, wouldn't save her a second time. She couldn't wear her clothing inside out, or a flower garland, all the time. Great-Aunt Elspeth, as wonderful as she might be, couldn't be everywhere.

She'd have to do this herself.

She hugged her arms about her and squeezed until the worst of the tremors ceased, then padded to the bathroom to blow her nose and wash her face. When she clambered back into bed, she carried one of the spells from Quentin's collection. From the notes he'd written around the glyph, she knew it was meant to follow after she'd learned *Lock-breaker*.

"*Ghost Flame*, a candle in darkness," Xenia whispered.

She'd been able to see Bethany earlier without trying. It had just... happened. But it had been days since she'd last seen the ribbons and auras of magic. Why was it that she could see one, but not the other? Were her abilities to see magic and to see ghosts two different things? Or two sides of the same coin? Xenia thought back to that breathless moment when Aunt Elspeth had revealed that Bethany had warned her. To the kitchen, when she was at last able to see and hear her friend's spirit. She closed her eyes.

"Two tents," she murmured as the boy's piping voice popped into her head. Xenia smiled and opened her eyes on a world ablaze with magic.

Her bedroom swarmed with color and light. Twining through the air were ribbons and streamers in shades and hues possible and impossible. Her bed, the walls, her desk, each object in the room glowed with its own inner light. Her hand, when she raised it, burned from within with opaline fire.

On the page before her, *Ghost Flame*'s magical hologram bloomed above and through the ink diagram. The weave of the spell was denser, more intricate, than *Lockbreaker*. Xenia peered into the webwork of light until she found the tiny, glowing notation that denoted where she should begin.

"Thanks, kid. Next ice cream's on me."

As Xenia reached for a ribbon of light that matched the one indicated by Quentin's notes, the spectrum of magic flickered. She blinked, and it was gone. "Shit!"

Xenia took a deep breath. Smoothed the paper flat against the quilt. Waited for her agitated heart to quiet itself. Closed her eyes.

Even if, when she opened them, she was still unable to see the magic she needed to craft *Ghost Flame*, Xenia would try again. And again. She could sleep later. She'd slept enough under the changeling's spell. She had to be ready.

Because Ev was still out there. He was coming for her.

Chapter Thirty-Four

U ncle's fingers danced across the strings as the firelight began to ebb. The older boys, entranced by the old man's song, had forgotten to stoke the campfire.

* * *

The Lady of Black Sky raged.

Lightning snapped at the parapets of her temple. Thunder crashed within its long halls as the Mistress of Storm vented her fury.

The acolytes cowered within their chambers. The temple boys fled to the stables and hid beneath the hay. The Grandmothers, the great Thearchs through whom the Goddess of Night spoke her will, remained steadfast at the altars, even as their unease grew.

The Queen of the Moon stormed the length of the great hall. "Have I not given the people knowledge enough? Have I not taught them the lore of the stars, that they may voyage across my mother's sea? Advised them as they crafted their great engines, and instruments of power? Do I not grant them largess from below, draw up the fine metals and precious stones so that they might have their pots and their plows, the ornaments with which they adorn their bodies?"

The Grandmothers, who numbered six, shared their mistress's disbelief at the people's lack of piety. Long had it been since last a strong ox or fine fish had been laid upon an altar in offering. Lax had the people of the Great Continent fallen in their worship of the goddess who commanded one-half of all creation.

"If they would have me not," declared *Bēlet An-Ĝíg* in a voice that was thunder, "then they shall have me not!"

Mistress Night shut her heart to all the world. She rescinded the gifts she had bestowed. As punishment was hers by divine right, so did she punish the Great Continent's peoples for the insult they had given.

And so, even though the Lady of Blue Sky did bless the land with her radiance, the stalk and the branch withered before the fruit ripened, or the flower bloomed, for no rain now fell to water them.

The deep places of the earth, the caverns and mines below the land, likewise ran dry. The rich veins of copper and iron were no more, for without *Bēlet An-Ĝíg*'s blessing, fresh metal would not rise in place of that which the people had mined.

The blessing of her protection, too, was no more. The people who had no cause to fear the night, to hide from the shadows, now shut themselves away behind locked doors and shuttered windows. The horrors that the Lady of Black Sky had long held at bay now roamed unchecked.

As the Great Continent suffered beneath the wrath of Night, their defenses did falter. The coasts and harbors swarmed with barbarians, and the Not-Men dragged parent

and child alike to the slaughter. Famine stalked the country-
side, and only *Bēlet An-Nisig*'s grace kept pestilence at bay.

For sixteen upon sixty nights, *Bēlet An-Ĝig*'s retribution
endured. Time slaked not the fury that burned within her
breast.

The Lady of Blue Sky knew, as no other, her divine
sister's temperament. Despite her love and sympathy for her
sibling, she could stand idle no longer. An emissary was
sent, bearing a scroll in the Bright Lady's own hand. "The
people abase themselves, sister mine. Be at peace. Let their
punishment be at an end."

Bēlet An-Ĝig closed her heart to her sister's plea. Her
thirst for vengeance was yet unslaked, her fury unsated. She
would cease her punishment when she saw fit. No sooner.

In reply, the Lady of Black Sky sent unto the Temple of
Day a box of fine wood bound in silver. Within the chest lay
the head of the messenger.

The people flocked, in their desperate, hungry numbers,
to the eastern plateau, where the great Temple of Day rose
like a conch of gold above the cliffs. There, they fell to their
knees and cried, "O *Ṣayyaḫatu*, Smiling One, we beseech
you. Raise up your hand betwixt us and the Lady of
Vengeance. Spare us from her wrath and her woe. Grant us
succor from the discord she has wrought upon all."

Bēlet An-Nisig heard their plea, and wept.

Angered by her divine sibling's rebuke, the Bright
Queen turned to her own Thearchs. "I have implored sister
mine to quell her fury, to end the castigation of the people.
She would hear me not. What remedy might I offer? I am
barred from her domain, as she is from mine. So did our
mother decree when she raised us up above all things."

For six days did the Queen of the Sun confer with the
Grandmothers who served the Day. Six days in which,

while not possessed of divine wisdom as their mistress, the six high priestesses offered what thin counsel they might. Where a divine entreaty to sisterly love had failed, if Midnight's heart could not be swayed, then mortal action must need suffice. If the Sun was forbidden to stand in Night's presence, then the Sun must send one who was not so forbidden.

In every corner of the Land, birds of golden feather and bright eye did alight upon branch and beam. At noonday, this scattered flock raised their heads in song. In pure crystal harmony, they sang the message they had been given. The Bright Queen's command was thus:

"Hear me. Send unto me a warrior."

From every corner of the Great Continent, they came. Soldiers and sportsmen. Scholars and smiths. All flocked to the summons, ready to serve the Queen of Day.

From among these hopefuls, *Bēlet An-Nisig* selected the most astute, the most comely, the bravest and strongest of them all. From him she took his name. In its place she bestowed the title of Champion.

Upon his shoulders she placed armor of gilt. To the sandals laced about his feet she granted celerity, that he might reach the lofty throne of Midnight. Into his hand she gave her own spear, within which burned a fragment of the Sun's golden flame. Upon his head she placed her blessing, that she would bear upon her own flesh the brunt of any blow to land upon his. For without that protection, the Champion was doomed, for no mortal may stand in battle with the divine and live.

At last, and with great sorrow, the Lady of Blue Sky gave her Champion purpose. "From my sibling's brow you must pluck the *Kù-Babbar Aga*, the Silver Crown of the

Moon. Into my hands you will deliver it. Only then might I lift my sister's wrath from the Land."

Even as the Champion strode into the West to confront the very Night itself, the Lady of Blue Sky wept. For to relieve her people of their suffering, her only sibling must fall. To restore balance, she must defy the word of their Divine Mother.

Bēlet An-Nisig would bear the burden of both Day and Night, though it would surely cost her all.

* * *

A mighty yawn stretched the girl's mouth. The hour had grown late, and her chin dipped to her chest. To rouse herself, she pinched her leg. Not a moment of this wondrous tale would she miss, she vowed.

Uncle paused his song long enough to drain the last of his *kaš*, and the girl's eye drifted about the circle of stones. There, at the edge of the firelight, stood a woman unfamiliar to her.

Tall as she was, and noble of bearing, the woman belonged to neither of the caravans camped at the crossroad. The ivory pale of her hair was wound into a spiral mass atop the crown of her head and descended to the nape of her neck. Jeweled pins and combs of fine wood gleamed from those pale tresses. Gemstones dotted the lobes of her ears. Linen finer than any the girl had seen, finer even than that woven by her own mother, draped the woman's shoulders. Equally fine was the wool of her kilt, which, as it fell to her ankles, marked her as a woman of stature. Here, far from the great cities, she was a rare thing to behold. Consort to one of the more successful merchants, perhaps, or a priestess on a pilgrimage. As she had no attendant or guard by her side, it was unlikely that she was highborn.

Despite the ivory of her hair, the woman's face was yet firm with the blush of youth, her bosom pert. This newcomer held remarkable beauty, free of mark or blemish. So fine of pore was her complexion that she might have been carved from the finest alabaster. *Most certainly a consort or concubine*, the girl thought to herself.

The woman observed the mass of children seated about the fire even as the girl examined her. When the woman's dark eyes alighted upon her own, a chill deeper than any winter night slithered along the girl's spine. A delicate line, the only such on the woman's face, formed between those perfect eyebrows.

Another yawn forced its way from her, and the girl pinched herself again. She must stay awake! As Uncle sang on of the quarrel that had brewed between Sun and Moon, the matter of the strange woman slipped from her thoughts.

Chapter Thirty-Five

"Got a minute?"

Xenia turned from the window. She'd been brooding, again, over the changeling situation. The time she'd spent ensorcelled by Ev still burned bright in her memory. The thought of losing herself like that again... Xenia shuddered. "Yeah, what's up?"

Bethany's face betrayed a worry that was twin to her own. The ghost perched at the edge of the bed. "It's about Everard."

"You too, huh?" Xenia wiggled herself into a more comfortable posture amongst the cushions. At least her ability to see Bethany, to see ghosts, appeared to have stabilized, now that she was no longer under Ev's power. "Hit me."

"There's no easy way to say this, so I'm just gonna. I think Ev killed Sal."

Xenia fought down her nausea as images of that gruesome afternoon by the river intruded. "You're serious. Why?"

"I think he's responsible for all of the missing teens, Zee. Lucas, Tamarah, Joseph, Aubrey, Douglass... everyone." Bethany gazed out over Xenia's head. "I'm not sure where they've gone off to, I haven't seen any of them since before..."

"Before Ev tried to take me," Xenia finished. She peered through the window. Just as Beebs had said, the entire street was devoid of the spectral audience. Part of her was glad for their absence, and guilt seeped in hot on the tail of that relief. It was hard enough to process the circumstances of Sal's death without his empty-eyed ghost lurking outside her home.

"When Ev was trying to take you, the power he used to block me... I think it scared them. Bad enough that they don't want to come back, even though they're drawn to you."

Xenia wound her hands about a cushion to hide the growing tremble in her fingers. "Why would they be scared? They're already dead."

"You saw what Sal looked like. And Lucas. They're all like that." Bethany looked away. "A few are worse. Parts of them are missing. Not just because they were torn apart when they died. Parts of *them*, their essence, their souls have been ripped away. Eaten. Not one of them is whole. That's why, I think, they're trapped here. Why they can't talk. They don't know how to move on. They're scared, Zee, that he'll take what little they have left."

"Oh God." Xenia twisted the cushion until a seam popped. "You're not—"

"I still have all my bits." Bethany offered her a thin smile. "Normal death for me, remember? Still no clue why I'm stuck here. It's got something to do with you, though.

Might be that whole magic thing." She flapped a hand as if to suggest it was no big deal.

"I'm sorry. You shouldn't have to be stuck here for all of this."

"Zip it. It's cool, okay? I'm good with it."

Xenia sank deeper into the window nook and tried not to think about Everard. *Too many teeth.* "What are we going to do about it? About him?"

"Okay, under normal circumstances I'd be the last one to suggest dropping a dime, but..."

"Sure. 'Hello, police? My friend the ghost told me that this handsome dude is a killer! By the way, don't let him touch you, because he's a changeling and can control your mind. You have to wear flowers and wear your uniform inside out to stop it.' That'll totally fly."

"You don't tell them that part, dum-dum! Aunt E should be the one to call. She's an"—Bethany affected a stuffy voice—"established member of the community, after all."

"Also not a teenager. Still, even if they do listen to her, they still have to touch him to arrest him. Or to do the fingerprint thing."

Bethany shot her a look. "Zee. What are handcuffs made of? And jail cells?"

Xenia sat up. "Oh! Well, maybe it'll work after all. Hey! How come he can drive a car? That thing has to be a ton of steel, and it's all around him."

"Fuck if I know. All-leather interior?" Bethany drifted away from the bed. "We have to stop him before anyone else gets hurt. Or brain-zapped. Jane, his 'girlfriend,' accused him of cheating. Tried to dump him. So he—"

"...did the same thing to her he was doing to me." Bile burned at the back of Xenia's throat.

"You find anything in Quentin's notes that might do the trick?" Bethany waved at the spells stacked on Xenia's desk. "Blow him up real good, maybe. After all, you're a magical girl now."

"Blow him up? You mean kill him?" Xenia heart stuttered. "Beebs, I can't do that. How could you even—"

Bethany crossed the space between them in an instant. Her face, inches from Xenia's, was a mask of anguish. "Zee, he was going to *eat you!*" She backed away. "You saw what he did to Sal, to Lucas. They were *lucky*." She spat the word. "Douglass, what's left of him... he's not even a person anymore. Just a thimble of memories, if that. He's gone." Her eyes bored into Xenia's. "What if he did that to you? There's nothing I could have done to stop him!"

"Now you want me to go after him?"

"No!" Bethany spun around. "I don't know. You have magic now. That has to count for something, right? You know what he is now. How to defend against his magic."

"One spell, Beebs. I know one stupid spell!" Xenia surged to her feet. "I haven't even cracked the next one, much less the rest. Even if there is something in there to 'blow him up,' I couldn't use it if I wanted to!" Xenia stood there, heart pounding, and glared at her friend. *Wait.* "We know what he is, now!" Xenia began to pace across the hardwood. "First off, you're right. We get Aunt Elspeth to call the cops, or whoever she thinks can handle him."

"Hell, she probably knows someone at the CIA and MI6," Bethany said.

"While that's in motion, there's something else we can do."

"What's that?"

"Scare the herd off."

"What?" Bethany asked.

Xenia scooped her hoodie from the back of her chair. "I have to get to school."

"What?" Bethany repeated. She dashed through the wall, followed Xenia down the hallway. "Why now? Aunt E got you excused for the whole week!"

Xenia paused at the top of the staircase, a wicked grin on her face. "We're going to start a nasty rumor."

* * *

Xenia barged through the side gate onto the athletic field just as the bell signaled the start of lunch period. She leaned against the bench where she'd been doused by Madison's coffee and scanned the wave of students surging from the school. "Where is she?"

On their way over, Xenia had detoured to Main to check each of the spots a student might hang out while cutting class. No Madison. Other than the calculus class they both shared, Xenia had no clue what her schedule was. Her plan hinged on Madison's love of rumors and gossip. Xenia and Bethany had worked out the perfect blend of fact and lie to build a rumor that would, she hoped, render Everard Ambrose persona non grata amongst the student body. The tale was so juicy that Madison wouldn't be able to resist spreading it to every ear and cell phone in the valley. No one would allow Ev within arm's reach after that!

A cluster of students, a few clad in the school's blue and white, began to gather at the center of the lacrosse field. When a familiar, tall runner joined them, Xenia made for the group. "Maybe Maia will know where she is." Even if she didn't keep tabs on the school's premier gossipmonger, Xenia should at least warn her away from Ev. "Hey, Maia!"

The tall girl waved back. She said something to her teammates and then loped across the field. Xenia was surprised, and pleased, to see her wearing the *ALL BLACKS* shirt she'd returned via magical burglary. She stomped, hard, on the memory of what had followed and plastered a smile across her face.

Maia jogged to halt and plucked at the hem of her shirt. "I never got the chance to thank you for bringing this back. Nice trick, by the way. How'd you get it into my locker?" She gave Xenia a nose-crinkling grin.

"Uh." The warning-disguised-as-a-rumor on Xenia's lips evaporated. "A magician never reveals her secrets?"

"Nice. I like a little mystery. Been out sick? Ain't seen you in a minute."

"Something like that."

Bethany, shaking with laughter, drifted behind Maia. Xenia suppressed the urge to flip her off.

Maia hooked a thumb over her shoulder. "You want to hang with us?"

"Do you know Everard?" Xenia blurted. Mentally, she kicked herself.

Maia's smile faltered. "Ev? Ambrose? The lacrosse guy?" Her eyebrows rose. "Doesn't everyone? Why?" Her eyes searched Xenia's face. "Oh, you're into him. Cool, I guess. Just be careful, he's with Jane Parker now. Of course, he was dating Aubrey right before that, so maybe you'll get your shot." She spun on her heel. "Not my salsa, not my burrito."

"What?" Xenia's mouth hung open. "Oh God, ugh. Yuck, no." She reached for the runner's arm, paused, dropped her hand. "He's dangerous. Like, for real. I think he's hurting people." Her carefully plotted rumor lay in shambles. She pushed on. "He's the reason that Sal and the others were—"

"I think you're mistaken." Maia stopped in her tracks, spine ramrod straight. When she turned to Xenia, her eyes were distant. Blank.

"Oh shit," Bethany said.

Xenia took a step back. "Maia?"

Maia's left eyelid fluttered. The spasm went no further. Her face remained blank and still. Eerily so.

"Did Ev touch you—"

"Everyone knows that Everard Ambrose is the best long stick middle that the Banana Slugs have ever had. We're a total lock for the championship." Maia's eyelid twitched again. "Fourth year in a row."

One of Maia's teammates—Xenia didn't know his name —wandered over. When he was close enough to catch the last of Maia's bizarre statement, his face went slack. "That's right," he said in a voice devoid of inflection. "Ev's going to bring that trophy home."

Maia rubbed her eye. Just like that, she was back to her usual self. "Hey." She glanced at the sophomore boy who'd joined them and nodded. "Look, Xenia, we were going to get some laps in, so..." She backed up a couple steps. "Good luck." She turned and walked with her teammate to the group waiting for her. As the circle closed about her, Maia shot a final, indecipherable look over her shoulder.

Xenia turned. Trudged across the field. Shouldered her way through the gate and made her way home.

Bethany trailed above and behind her, a balloon of worry. "Zee, what about the plan? You could still find Madison—"

"There's no point, Beebs. He already thought of that." Xenia spit onto the sidewalk. "He's had years to prepare.

More than enough time to make sure no one can ruin his bright future. Cops too, I bet."

"But..." Bethany fell in beside Xenia. "Shit. Now what?"

"No clue." Xenia made no attempt to disguise the hopelessness that filled her from head to toe. "I have no frickin' clue."

Chapter Thirty-Six

Over the next few days, Xenia tried and tried again to warn her peers of the danger Ev represented. Without fail, any mention of the senior's name in connection with anything remotely negative spurred the same vacant expression, the same thousand-yard stare. The line Maia had recited, that Everard was "a lock for the championship" would come, verbatim, from whomever she'd approached. Even the school counselor and Mrs. Wedgwood, when pressed on the school's golden boy, recited the same line. Aunt Elspeth reported a similar experience after a trip to the police station. Everard had been a busy little beaver indeed.

Back to the drawing board.

Elspeth and Xenia set about bolstering the old Victorian's defenses. A rotten fence post was uprooted and replaced. They tapped into Elspeth's dwindling supply of iron nails to fortify each window and door. The beds of thorn bush and St. John's wort were weeded and watered. Elspeth sewed up a few sachets, each containing a handful of the golden blossoms. "Keep one with you at all times, lass," she'd admonished Xenia, with an apology to the ghost who was unable to carry anything.

As long as Xenia had a nail and a sachet in her pocket, Elspeth assured her, Everard would be unable to glamour her again. Xenia knew that wouldn't stop "Mr. Tall Britches" from having a go at her, should he catch her alone. There was no mistaking the worry in the woman's eyes when Xenia at last returned to school. The flu excuse was only good for so long.

Xenia had redoubled her efforts with *Ghost Flame*. While her ability to see ghosts had stabilized, her magical sight left something to be desired. Each time she'd tried to weave the spell, her magical vision had crapped out. Her fingers still stung from the morning's failures.

According to Quentin's notes, *Ghost Flame* would build on what she'd learned from *Lockbreaker*. He'd selected each spell with a mind for their "educational" value. If Xenia could master them, Quentin's notes assured her, she would be well on her way to devising spells of her own.

It was both reassuring and more than a little daunting to find that Aunt Elspeth's very own lost love was the one who'd left the magical care package for her to find. Well, to be led to. There was a sense of things coming full circle. Xenia wondered if Quentin had known the raven. Perhaps he was the one who'd spelled the bird, charged it with that mission. Why her, though? Was it because she was a Findlay? Or just the first person in Porter Valley to display magical ability since who knows when? Shame she'd never have the chance to ask him in person. She allowed the pang of sorrow, an echo of her great-aunt's grief, to pass through her.

Elspeth reopened Bits 'n' Pieces and, again, requested that Xenia spend her after-school hours, and weekends, with her in the shop. That way, they could watch each other's backs.

The torrent of weekend customers came as a welcome distraction for them both. "This is nothing, lass," Elspeth commented following a particularly taxing busload of tourists. "Gold Rush Days are just around the corner, and then there's Independence Day! You'll not be able to see the sidewalk for all the bodies."

Xenia rang up the customers while Elspeth, somehow, managed to be in every corner of her shop at once. She would chat up each intrepid soul who ventured inside, then lead them to the perfect bit of art, the exact knickknack, that had them reaching for their wallets. If this was nothing, Xenia marveled, what was Christmas going to be like?

At long last, Elspeth flipped the sign to "closed." "Phew! Let's not dillydally, lass. I'd like to avoid being out after dark. We have that silly curfew to worry about as well."

Xenia and Elspeth both knew that the real threat wouldn't come in the form of a mountain lion skulking in the shadows. Ev did his hunting out in the open, at school. Still, there was no telling when, or how, he'd come after "the one who got away." With that in mind, Elspeth would drive them the few blocks home in her battered station wagon.

As Elspeth counted out the cash from the day's sales, Xenia pushed a broom down each aisle. She paused by a shelf of hand-crafted toys. "Aunt Elspeth? Would it be okay if I took this one?" She brought the subject of her interest up front.

Elspeth peered over her reading glasses. "Aren't you a tad old for such things?" She held out her hand for the subject of Xenia's interest.

One of Porter Valley's woodworking artisans had sanded and oiled a zigzagging length of wood to a mirror finish. Affixed to the narrow end was a five-pointed star carved from pale, fine-grained wood. Colored ribbons trailed from the point where star met twig. Elspeth gave the wand an experimental swoop and set the streamers fluttering.

Xenia lowered her voice, despite the absence of prying ears. "The spells, as far as I can tell, need to be put in or on something. Keeps them from unraveling. That's why I stuck *Lockbreaker* in that ruler. I figure, why not? Might as well make a real magic wand!"

"Say no more!" Elspeth thrust the wand into Xenia's hand. "Have at it, lass." She packed the envelope of cash into her belly bag, which she hid beneath a fold of her eye-watering paisley kaftan. "In all of the excitement, I do believe I nearly forgot! Your cast is due to come off this week. First thing Monday morning, we're off to the doctor in Eureka. While we're there, what say you to a leisurely sushi lunch? I know just the place."

Xenia tucked the wand into her book bag and held up her cast. "I say 'more spicy tuna,' please!"

* * *

"What'cha doon?"

Xenia blinked the sweat from her eyes, "One sec." She couldn't afford for her attention to slip, not now. She was deep in her fifth attempt at *Ghost Flame* that afternoon. Her "second sight" was cooperating, for once, but the sudden absence of the cast was throwing her off. She hadn't been all that pleased, either, with the scar that marked the spot where her arm bone had poked through. At least the headaches that had plagued her up until she'd succeeded with *Lockbreaker* were gone. Now all she had to deal with was the blowback when a spell failed.

Ghost Flame called for even more varieties of magic than *Lockbreaker* had. Xenia still didn't know what the differing textures and hues represented, other than the "wind-blue" from her inaugural experience. Thanks to that, trial and error would be her very last resort in identifying the seemingly endless varieties. What she really needed was a magical encyclopedia.

Xenia ignored the eager ghost hovering at her shoulder as she looped and tied the glowing, hair-fine strands into the star at the end of her wand. There was a tiny crackle as the spell's glyph etched itself into the pale wood. She blew out a long breath and sagged in her chair. "Magic really takes it out of you," she said, mopping at her soaked forehead. She rolled her head against the headrest. "Where've you been?"

"Doin' ghost stuff." Bethany took up a reclining pose above the bed. "Keeping a lookout for you-know-who, looking for the others." She frowned. "Ev really has them spooked. I was only able to find Douglass, and only because he never leaves his bedroom. He's too far gone to be scared, I think." She shook herself. Forced a grin. Pointed at the wand. "What'cha doing?"

Xenia aimed a finger at herself. "Magical Girl, right?"

"Right."

"Well, every magical girl needs a wand."

"Shut up!"

"Well, that's my idea, anyhow. You remember that show you wanted me to watch? You bought all the DVDs when you were in Japan?"

"*Hai.*"

"Unlike that magical girl, there's no eldritch plushie on my shoulder to hand me a wand. I had to make my own." Xenia presented one side of the wooden star to the ghost. "Also, it's an experiment. I wanted to see if I could put more than one spell on the same object." She pointed to a glyph. "*Lockbreaker.*" She spun the star. "*Ghost Flame*, which I just now finished."

"All I saw was you wiggling your fingers."

Xenia frowned and waved her hand at the magic that surrounded them both. "You don't see any of this? At all?"

"Girl, all I see is you. Then again, to me, you look like you bathed in glow-stick juice." Bethany drifted over. Her eyes nearly bugged from their sockets. "You're seeing magic right now?"

"Yeah."

"Your eyes, Zee!"

"What?" Xenia scrambled to the mirror mounted on the closet door. At first, she didn't see what had Bethany so agitated. She put her face right up to the glass, and gasped. Both eyes now sported a thin, glowing ring about the iris. The effect was faint; if she hadn't been looking, she might have missed it. She blinked a few times. Honestly, the effect was pretty cool. "Wild. Still doesn't explain why a ghost can't see magic. You're probably made of the stuff!"

Bethany shrugged. "Maybe I'm on a different wavelength."

Xenia approached her friend. "Can I try something?"

"Sure?" Bethany raised an eyebrow.

Xenia held out her hand and, when Bethany matched the gesture, attempted to touch the ghost. As with every other time, her hand passed through without resistance. Xenia shook her head and forced herself to relax. Touching magic required her to focus right on it and hold that focus steady. *What if...*

As Xenia fixed her attention upon her friend's hand,

the glow of magic around her dulled. The streamers and auras didn't vanish, not entirely. Instead, they lost their intensity. The substance of Bethany's ghost flesh sprang into clarity. Patterns and textures were now evident on the surface, and within. Xenia, moving slowly, reached for Bethany's hand.

"Ow! Fuck, what the hell!" Bethany whipped her hand away and backpedaled through the air. She stopped, eyes wide, staring at her hand. "What the hell," she whispered.

"You felt that?" Xenia asked. Despite her focus, when her fingers had brushed Bethany's, there had still been no sense of contact.

"Yeah, it hurt. A lot. Like being jabbed with a needle and touching a stove at the same time."

"I'm sorry!" Xenia rushed to Bethany's side.

"No, Zee, don't be." Bethany's grin was fierce, triumphant. "I felt it! I haven't felt anything since I died. Okay, I'd prefer not to feel pain again, but I'll take it! It means—"

"It means I might be able to help you," Xenia said. "Assuming I learn the magic for it."

"And the others. Sal and Lucas and everyone. They need it more than I do." Bethany drifted to the window. She gave her fingers a little wiggle. When she turned back to the room, hope shone in her eyes. "So. *Ghost Flame.* What's it do?"

Xenia pushed aside her wonder. One more amazing discovery to work on. She'd have to tread carefully, lest she cause Bethany more pain. "I'm not sure. Quentin's notes didn't really describe it. Only that it would 'react to my intent,' whatever that means." She fetched the wand from her desk and thrust it before her.

"Whoah." Bethany held her hands up. "You really want

to test something with 'flame' in its name here? In your oh-
so flammable bedroom?"

Xenia blinked. "Right. Kitchen?"

"Kitchen."

One mad dash down the staircase later, Xenia held her
wand at arm's length over the massive cast iron stove. With
no real idea of what to expect, she mentally asked *Ghost
Flame* to do its thing.

A thumb-sized, electric blue flame popped into existence above the wooden star. The tiny flame flickered and
danced just like its cousin, the stove's pilot light. "Heck
yeah!" Xenia fist pumped her free hand.

"Sweet!"

Xenia passed her hand over the tiny flame. There was
no sensation of heat on her palm. "Intent, hmm." She held
the wand still and pictured the flame in motion. Just as she'd
imagined, the tiny spark hopped from the end of her wand
to hang in the air above the kitchen table. She sent more
mental images to the spell. *Ghost Flame* shrank to a
pinpoint, swelled to three times its original size, then
danced a sprightly figure-eight above the tabletop. Grinning
wide enough that her cheeks ached, she recalled the mote of
light to her wand. "Beebs, hand me a sheet of paper?"

"Sure thing." Bethany crossed through the table to the
stack of paper Xenia had brought with them. She passed her
hand through the paper, and the table below. When Xenia
glanced over, she crossed her eyes and stuck out her tongue.

"Sorry! Sorry, I was too excited." Xenia shook her wand.
She retrieved a slip of paper and touched the magical flame
to the edge. The azure glow flickered and danced through
the paper, which remained pristine, unburnt. "Huh." Xenia
licked the tip of her little finger and poked the flame. There
was no heat, no cold, no sensation of contact at all. Just like

with Bethany. "Oh, I get it. 'Ghost Flame.' Light, but no heat. It can't burn anything." She stuck her whole hand through the fire to demonstrate.

"Groovy." Bethany narrowed her eyes. Before Xenia could stop her, she stuck her own hand into the flame. Her face fell. "Damn."

"Were you hoping to burn yourself?"

"Hey, if it did, that would be another connection, right? More proof that your magic can affect us materially impaired type peeps." Bethany did a poor job of concealing her disappointment.

"Well, just be careful. How was I supposed to put you out if you'd caught fire, huh? I don't have Ghost Water!" A sudden wave of fatigue sucked the heat from her outrage. She braced a hand against the table until the dizzy spell passed. Right on cue, her stomach made a growling demand for sustenance. "Woof, magic *really* takes it out of you." Reluctantly, she doused *Ghost Flame*. She dragged open the fridge to search for the protein and carbs the growl in her belly demanded.

"Hey, Zee. I'm going to go. Ghost stuff," Bethany murmured. She floated toward the window garden.

Xenia, her arms laden with leftover chicken and a slice of lemon pie, called out, "Beebs, be careful, please. We don't know where—"

Bethany was already gone.

Chapter Thirty-Seven

"**D**amn it." Bethany kicked at the rooster-shaped weather vane atop the old Victorian's turret. As always, her foot passed through without effect.

It's not that she wasn't happy for Zee. If anything, she was thrilled she'd discovered a talent for real magic. How amazing was that?

That didn't mean she didn't have the tiniest little worm of jealousy gnawing at her heart, though. Even though she was a ghost, she couldn't perceive the magic Xenia claimed was all about them. She was as shut off from that as she was from the plain old material world. Even though Xenia had discovered she could "tune in" to Bethany's spiritual frequency, or whatever, the brief contact had caused awful, searing pain. It had only been for a moment, but the memory of that touch made Bethany reluctant to allow it again.

Xenia had lost both of her parents and her best friend. Well, halfway on the best friend. It seemed only fair for the universe to toss her a magical bone by way of apology. *But what about me?* Bethany couldn't help but think. *I frickin' died!* Her "gift" was to be trapped, unable to pass on and unable to interact with the world. Hooray.

Bethany immediately felt worse as she remembered Sal and the others. How dare she feel sorry for herself? They had suffered far, far more than she.

She glared at the unfeeling stars. "Like I said, a few instructions would be the least you could do. A Post-it with bullet points, maybe?"

It couldn't just be her and the Lost, could it? There had to be others who'd met whatever obscure criteria trapped the soul on this side of the hereafter. That criteria had to be stringent, Bethany assumed, otherwise she'd be ass-deep in fellow specters. At least meeting Cleopatra, or Amelia Earhart, or even Johnny Cash would have eased the dire prospect of being stuck forever.

She had come to dread the day when Xenia would, inevitably, die.

Even if Zee made it through this whole changeling ordeal and had herself a totally boring life, she would die, eventually. What would happen then? Would she pass on, like her parents had, and leave Bethany here? Trapped in Porter Valley? Or, would the force that had bound her to this side of the veil dissipate with Xenia's life? *It damn well better. I do not want to spend eternity bound to my BFFFF's moldering bones!* She kicked at the weathervane again. "Being a ghost suuuuucks!"

"*Caw.*"

"Oh, it's you again," she said to the rotund corvid perched on the rooftop. "Have another book recommendation for Xenia the Magical Girl, do we?"

The raven ruffled its feathers. Preened its belly. Ignored her completely.

"No, of course. You can't see me either." Frustration

seized her, and she threw herself at the bird, arms raised in proper ghost fashion. She cut loose with her fiercest "Grawr!"

The raven fell backward off its perch. It fluttered about until it regained its balance and then alighted at the far end of the roof. It fussed with its wings as it attempted to regain some semblance of avian dignity.

"Holy crap! You can see me!" It didn't seem that weird, now that she thought about it. "Of course, the bird who led Zee to a magic book would be, itself, magical." She drifted over as non-threateningly as she could. "Dude, you should've said something. Big apologies for taking out my woes on you. It's been a day."

The raven met her eye for a moment and then rubbed his beak along the edge of his perch.

Bethany sat beside the raven. "So, which one are you?" She racked her memory for every mythical bird she'd ever read about. "Hugin, or Munin? Hey, don't roll your eyes at me!"

The raven reshuffled his wings. Settled his belly feathers over his feet. Closed his eyes.

"Fine. Be that way. See if I care." Bethany gazed up at the clouds. She'd found someone else who could see her, and it was a bird. *Whoopie.* The improvement, she decided, was infinitesimal. "Don't suppose there's a book on ghost shit you could lead me to, eh?"

One beady, black eye cracked open. If she didn't know better, Bethany would have said the bird was thinking it over. For all she knew, maybe he was.

Having apparently reached a decision, the raven burst into the air in a swirl of feathers. *"Caw!"* He wheeled about the roof of the old Victorian and, when he passed in front of Bethany, dipped his wing.

"You want me to follow? For real?"

"*Caw.*" The raven flapped higher, banked into a wide turn, then flew off toward Main Street.

"Well, Brooks, it's not like you had plans for the evening." Bethany launched herself after the bird.

When she caught up, she found the raven circling the chimney of a ranch-style home identical, in all respects, to the dozens of others visible from her altitude. She came to a halt above the shingled roof. The raven alighted upon the chimney beside her.

"Okay dude, now what?"

The raven gave the brick he was perched on three distinct pecks.

"What, go inside?" Even though she'd fancied herself, briefly, as a ghost detective, the prospect of trespassing within a random stranger's home didn't sit well with the girl her mama had raised.

Tap, tap, tap.

"Fine. If people start screaming, 'Eek, a ghost,' just remember this was your idea."

* * *

When Bethany dropped through the ceiling, she found herself in the house's master bedroom. Where one might have expected a king-size bed, there was instead an articulated, hospital-style bed, similar to the one Xenia where had spent the long weeks of her coma. An array of IV stands, heart monitors, and other devices Bethany couldn't name crowded the room.

At the center of all that medical attention was an elderly woman. Pain had carved deep lines into her face, more vivid than those from mere age. Snow-white hair spilled across the pillow and over her shoulders. Whatever ailment the woman suffered had rendered her dark skin sallow and thin as paper. A cluster of tubes linked the woman's nose and arm to the nearby machines.

Beside the bed sat another woman. She wore hospital scrubs, and snow streaked her braided, midnight-black hair. Although she was decades younger, she bore a clear resemblance to the ailing woman. If that hadn't marked them as relatives, then the grief she wore, and the gentle manner with which she cradled the older woman's hand in her own would have left no doubt. A daughter, Bethany thought.

When the moment arrived, there was no fanfare, no clamor from the medical devices. Between one moment and the next, the sick woman simply failed to take her next breath. The daughter squeezed her mother's hand. Quietly, she began to weep.

When Bethany had died, she'd missed the moments immediately after. Spiritual trauma from being ejected from her body, perhaps. Thanks to those moments of non-being, she hadn't witnessed the passing of Mr. and Mrs. Findlay. She'd assumed, had hoped, that they had indeed gone on to whatever came next.

Here, now, Bethany had another chance.

A small sound, a tiny sigh, drew Bethany's attention from the grieving woman. Beside her stood the woman in the bed. While her face still bore the lines of age, the cruel furrows carved by pain were no more.

Somewhat to Bethany's surprise, the woman was clad not in the nightgown she'd died in but in an elaborate emerald-and-purple sari. The snow white of her hair now hung in a thick braid that fell below her waist. Bethany had assumed that, based on herself and the Lost, that a ghost would wear whatever they'd died in. Perhaps, she considered, she'd taken entirely too much for granted.

The woman smiled at Bethany, then knelt beside her weeping daughter. "Goodbye, Rahi, my sweet. You were the joy of my life. From the day you were born, you brought nothing but love into my life. I have been, and will forever be, so very proud of you." She brushed her lips across her daughter's cheek and then rose to her feet. With a nod to Bethany, she rose through the ceiling.

When Bethany joined the woman in the air above her home, she wasn't surprised to find that the raven had flown off.

The newly dead woman turned in a slow circle, her expression calm. She gazed off across the treetops, watched the glow of Main Street, and then regarded the mountains that ringed Porter Valley. Her eyes came to rest upon the glorious vista to the west as, beyond the valley's end, the sun sank into the Pacific. When the last scrap of daylight vanished behind the horizon, the woman gave a little nod. She turned to Bethany.

When she spoke, her voice carried a lilting, musical accent. "Thank you for allowing me to say my goodbyes. To my Rahi, and to my home. I am ready to go with you, now."

"With me? Where are we going?" Bethany asked, confused.

The woman blinked. "Are you not..." Her gaze traveled across the dark ruffles of Bethany's dress, the ribbon-laced corset, the leather boots buckled to knee height and the black lace that adorned it all. Her smile crinkled her eyes. "Considering your manner of dress, I was concerned you might be one of Yama's, here to take me to Naraka. Perhaps the Devas are having a bit of amusement at my expense."

The laugh lines in the woman's face deepened as she smiled.

"Sorry, no. Just a regular ghost with an extra helping of style." Bethany offered the woman a tiny curtsy. "I was passing by and happened to catch your big moment." Bethany wasn't sure how to explain the raven. She decided he could handle his own introductions.

"My big moment? Oh." The woman chuckled. "My death." She held her arms in front of her and examined her sari. "It was time. I had a good life, and a long one. I brought two daughters and a son into this world, and now I have more grandchildren than I can count. Two husbands, each who proceeded me on this journey. I had been sick for a very long time. Too long." She met Bethany's eyes. "I was ready for it to end."

Bethany fought down the envy the woman's words had kindled within her. She hadn't even made it to college before she'd been booted out of her life! *Don't be a jerk, Brooks.* She offered the woman her hand. "Bethany. Glad to finally meet another dead person." This woman, she decided, was much too nice to be burdened with the tragedy of Sal and the others. At least for now.

"Naira," said the woman. "I am delighted to be met."

When Bethany had taken Sal's hand, there had been only the faintest inkling of contact. With Xenia, it had been excruciating. When Naira took her hand, Bethany felt it. It wasn't like the hand of a living, flesh-and-blood person, but the sensation of fingers closing about her own was unmistakable. She squeezed back and, reluctantly, let go. "So. Got any plans for the next hundred years? Any sightseeing you didn't get around to? You can go anywhere you want, now. Sky's the limit." She demonstrated by pirouetting in midair.

"Tempting as that thought may be, I have already lived

this life for nearly a century of my own. I am ready for the next one."

"Next what?"

"Life, Bethany." Naira tilted her head to one side. "The cycle of birth, death and rebirth? I have done the first two, I am ready for the third."

Panic flared within Bethany. The very first ghost she could have an actual conversation with, and she wanted to leave right away?

Her desperation must shown, because Naira drifted close and held out her hands. When Bethany took them in her own there was, again, that sensation of contact, of pressure. If anything, it was even stronger. Bethany treasured the moment, that sense of connection. "I thought you'd be here for a while, like me. I don't think I can do that. Be reborn, I mean. I'm stuck here."

Naira's eyes searched Bethany's face. "What does your faith tell you? Are you a Christian?"

"Mama is. Me, not so much." Bethany lifted her eyes as the first stars emerged from the twilight. "None of it felt right. Mama's church, Dad's... well, he didn't talk about God stuff that much. He left that to Mama. Over the last couple years, I read all the books. I was searching, I guess. The Bible, the Koran, the Torah. Nothing gave me a sense of connection, of belonging. Maybe I should have kept reading. Or talked to someone about it. Of course, before I had a chance..."

"You died."

"Yeah."

"Has it been very long?"

"A few months? Maybe more. I'm losing track."

Naira nodded. "When I was a little girl in Jaipur, Dada would sit me on his knee and tell me wonderful stories.

Stories from the Vedas. He was very old, my dada, and I think that was his way of preparing me for what was to come. He taught me death is every bit as natural as birth. That Lord Krishna tells us, just as we rise in the morning, shed the attire of yesterday, bathe ourselves and dress for the new day, so too does the soul don a new body." Naira's face glowed with love as she gazed at the house below them. "You and I, we have certainly shed the attire of yesterday. Is it not time to don the new?" She squeezed Bethany's hands in her own.

Bethany marveled at the warmth in the woman's touch. "How are you doing that?" If she'd still been capable of tears, her face would have been drenched. "I haven't touched anything, felt anything like this since I died."

Naira looked to her hands, then to Bethany's face. "None of us are physical beings. We are all the same, where it matters. Each of us comes from the same place, the same divine source, and to it we shall all return." Naira's smile grew even wider. "When I first laid eyes on you, I believed you had been sent to guide me into the next life. Perhaps, it is I who will guide you." She pressed both of Bethany's hands between her own.

"How? I'm stuck here."

"Do you not feel it?" When Bethany shook her head, Naira gave her an appraising look. "Then I will follow it for us both. Come, we'll go together."

Bethany's hesitation didn't stem from fear, at least not for herself. If she left now, who would watch Xenia's back? *She has Aunt E, and she has her magic. She'd have to get over you anyhow, if things were normal.* If she didn't go now, she might never have another chance. "Goodbye, Xenia," she whispered. To Naira: "I'm ready."

Naira moved, then, and drew Bethany along with her.

She didn't pull them higher above the Earth, or fall below it. Instead, they traveled a path that had nothing at all to do with the world of the living.

Bethany, via her hand in Naira's, became aware of what the woman had spoken of.

It wasn't a sensation like the wind on her face, or the pull of gravity. A gentle knowledge had made itself known at the very core of her being. A sense of where she must go. "Home is this way," that awareness told her

Porter Valley faded from all perception. But there, at the very edge where she knew her journey would be irrevocable, she was halted. "No, not now!" The same force that had drawn her to Porter Valley, that had kept her from returning to her family, held sway over her existence even on the border of the hereafter.

Sympathy and compassion beyond anything Bethany had ever experienced shone in Naira's face. "It is not your time, is it, Bethany?"

"I... I think maybe there's something I still have to do. Before I can join you." She wasn't surprised when, here at the very edge of eternity, for the first time since her death, tears spilled from her eyes.

Naira drew her into an embrace that was every bit as warm and comforting as her mother's. "Go. Do what you must." Naira's voice was no longer only her own. Her words echoed with the voice of Bethany's grandmother. Mr. and Mrs. Findlay were there too, and so many others. "We will be here for you, when the time comes." Naira brushed her lips against Bethany's cheek.

"Thank you," Bethany said between sobs, "for everything."

She let go.

As Naira vanished beyond the limit of her perceptions, Bethany called out, "Have fun being a baby again!"

Bluff Street, the old Victorian and Porter Valley snapped into clarity about her. As it did, the damp on her cheeks became nothing but memory. As she drifted toward her friend's home, Bethany discovered that the thread of connection to the hereafter, that ineffable compass needle, still existed within her. She turned her face to the stars above. "Thank you," she called to Naira and whoever else might be listening. "I know why I'm here, now."

"*Caw.*"

Chapter Thirty-Eight

D espite the hours she'd spent crafting *Ghost Flame*, Xenia found herself unable to sit still. She'd devoured every leftover the fridge had to offer. She was ready to charge into the next spell in Quentin's primer. However, her fingers and head still ached from the failures that had preceded her success. Best if she took a break, no matter how much she yearned to master every one of the spells.

Instead, she decided, she'd have a go at Aunt Elspeth's secret archive.

With Aunt Elspeth's arsenal of cleaning supplies at her disposal, she swept up the dust and cobwebs filling the basement. With that done, she began to clean the collection itself. Xenia took extra care while wiping dust and grime from the various oddments. Who knew what might be unleashed if she were to drop the wrong item.

Or maybe she'd seen too many movies.

Even though her eyes stung and watered from the dust she'd stirred up, Xenia gave each item a thorough once-over with her magical vision. For once, that esoteric skill was cooperating.

Three rows in and not one of the knickknacks Aunt Elspeth had stashed away showed the least bit of magical potential. While Xenia was aware she didn't have the experience to determine what form that potential might take, she assumed her second sight would show her *something*! After all, when she examined her new wand, she could make out the weave of spells within, even if the wood's own aura obscured the patterns somewhat.

"Here we go." Xenia wiped dust from an orb of dark glass and held it up to the fluorescent tubes overhead. At the exact center of the smoky sphere was a winged shape. It might be a butterfly, or a moth—the glass prevented her from making out the detail. In her second sight, a tight web of magic had been constructed about the insect. A spell? Or a cage meant to hold the bug in place? Xenia was extra careful in returning the orb to the velvet cushion where she'd found it. She jotted down a brief description of the item, along with its location in the archive, in the composition book she'd brought for the task.

She struck gold again on the next row. This time, her find was a medieval-style lockbox. Thick straps of dark metal wrapped the box, secured by rivets the size of her thumb. Xenia traced the seam of the lid but found no keyhole or mechanism with which to open the box. The hinges, if there were any, had been mounted on the inside.

Xenia pushed and prodded at each of the rivet heads, attempted to wedge her fingernail beneath the metal bands, all to no avail. If this was a puzzle box, the secret eluded her. On the magical side of things, it was encased in a dense weave of light. Each thread dipped in and out of the metal, like stitches. Whoever had crafted the spell had been extremely thorough. There were no gaps in the coverage she could find.

Xenia noted the box and its location down in her notes. She'd dusted half of the next shelf before her brain delivered belated inspiration. "A-doy, Xenia." She slapped her forehead and grabbed her wand from the side table where she'd left it.

When she tapped the box with the *Lockbreaker* side of the wooden star, there was no click, thump, or other audible clue. However, now she could raise the lid without effort. The inner surface of the box was bare metal, without lining. The only item inside was a bundle of letters bound by a rubber band. As she lifted the bundle, the ancient rubber crumbled at her touch. Xenia smiled a tiny, sad smile when she found the letters addressed to Quentin Flagstone. Each letter had been sent to a different city, all return-addressed to Elspeth Findlay, in an equally disparate number of origins. She set the bundle of letters aside for her great-aunt and returned the box to its place on the shelf. When she shut the lid, it was once again locked tight.

Icy prickles danced over the back of Xenia's scalp. She shivered. "Beebs, that you?" Her words emerged as a plume of wintry vapor. The basement had plummeted to arctic temperatures in less time than it had taken for her to speak. While spring in Porter Valley ran colder than her native Los Angeles, it shouldn't have been this cold. She rubbed her arms and scanned the room in both visible and magical spectrums for the source of the chill.

"Bethany, if this is you figuring out how to do real haunt stuff, that's cool and all but enough's enough." Xenia's ears and the tip of her nose had begun to ache in the frigid air. "Come on, this isn't funny." She flexed fingers gone stiff and rubbed her arms in a futile attempt to warm herself. *I hope this is a ghost prank, and not some new trick from a certain changeling.* Xenia made for the staircase and then paused.

She'd left the cabinet door open so that Elspeth would know where her great-niece had gotten off to. The sitting room lights should be visible up the stairwell. Instead, the entire staircase lay in darkness.

Xenia slipped her wand from her back pocket and ignited *Ghost Flame* with a thought. She sent the tiny azure flame into the darkness where the staircase should have been. As soon as it passed the shadowed door frame, the flame vanished. Xenia conjured another, to identical results.

Movement stirred within the rectangle of night. Only when her back rattled the glass of a cabinet did she realize she'd run out of space to retreat.

Each of the ghosts Xenia had seen so far had retained at least a hint of the color they'd possessed while alive. Bethany, in her gothic finery, was the most vivid. The Lost might have been less vibrant, but there was still plenty of color in Sal and Lucas, especially when their injuries were on display.

The figure that lurched from darkness was beyond pallid. Hair, face, and clothing were rendered in the hues of bleached bone. Like the other Lost, the spirit's movements were clumsy, its steps a stumble, as if it was still beholden to gravity. Unseen currents set the pale hair adrift about the ghost's head. As with the others Xenia had seen, shadow filled the space where her eyes should have been. Even through the shadow, and the unnatural pallor of her skin, Xenia had no trouble recognizing her visitor.

"Gracie, not you too." Xenia bit her knuckle. This was her fault. If she hadn't fought off Ev, denied him his prize, there would have been no reason for him to vent his rage on Gracie. That she herself, in all likelihood, might have been the one lurching about as a ghost was no comfort whatsoever.

The ghost wore the uniform of the school's track team. Death had leached all color from her garments as it had her phantom flesh, the blue and white now only shades of bone and gray. Even the single shoe she wore was chalk white.

The shadowed pit of Gracie's gaze met Xenia's. Her lips parted on a matching void, a window into nothing. Her scream was voiceless yet shook the basement with its fury. Cracks shot through the cabinet glass beside Xenia. The mute howl sent spikes of pressure into Xenia's ears. She fell against the cabinet, hands clapped to either side of her head in a futile attempt to block that unbearable silence. The first stirrings of a migraine, the first she'd had in weeks, began to curdle behind her eyes. "Gracie, stop! Please stop!"

The scream's end was as abrupt as its beginning. Xenia's ears rang in the aftermath. She'd clenched her eyes against the pain. When she opened them, the ghost had crossed the length of the basement to stand before her.

Gracie's head lolled on a neck gone boneless. The phantom skin in the hollow of her throat dimpled. Flesh and fabric alike parted like tissue as the ghost was rent from neck to belly. The cavity within her chest lay empty, devoid of heart, lung or other organ. The inner curve of each rib was scored, carved deep by multiple strokes of an enormous blade. The ragged ends of arteries and connective tissue swayed in the same current as her hair.

Bile burned at the back of her throat as she fought her gorge. "I'm sorry," gasped Xenia. "We should have stopped him! Everard escaped from the garden before Aunt Elspeth could—"

The ghost's head snapped upright. The curve of her

neck worked as her pale lips gaped. Her fingers, bent and broken, pawed at her throat as Gracie tried to speak.

"Yeah, he attacked me too." Xenia forced a confidence she didn't feel. "I will stop him, I promise. I might not know how, but I won't let Everard do this to anyone ever again." As the first stirrings of outrage joined her horror, Bethany's earlier suggestion of simply "blowing him up" no longer seemed at all objectionable.

Gracie wrenched her head from side to side. The motion sent an obscene wave through the exposed flesh of her chest cavity. Her face twisted in desperation, raw and ragged.

Xenia reached out, intent on offering what little solace she could. Even though she they couldn't touch—

Cold fingers clamped about her wrist with the force of a vise. The phantom flesh burned where it met hers, and Xenia cried out in pain. She fought to wrench her arm free, but Gracie's grip was as unyielding as iron. The stygian cold crept into Xenia's flesh. The jab of an icy dagger within her arm told her that the unnatural chill had reached the pin the surgeon had set in her ulna.

"Gracie, let go!" No matter how she struggled, Xenia was unable break the ghost's hold. The fingers of her left hand went numb. She batted at Gracie with her wand, only for it to pass through without effect.

As the numbness crept to her bicep, the ghost's fingers began to regain some of the color they'd had in life. Gracie's hand and arm grew more real, more *there*, as her touch sapped something vital from Xenia's living flesh.

What little humanity Gracie had retained vanished as she bared her obsidian teeth in a feral snarl. A second set of arctic fingers clawed at Xenia's face, only to clamp about her right arm when she tried to fend off the grab.

Xenia shrieked in pain as jagged blades of icy cold tore into her.

Footsteps hammered the basement stairs. Elspeth burst into the room, brandishing a massive railroad spike in one hand and a bouquet of St. John's wort, torn from the window garden, in the other. "Hands off my Xenia, you son of a—" Elspeth stumbled to a halt, eye wide as saucers. "Crivvens! What on earth..." She squared her shoulders, dropped the bouquet, aimed the railroad spike like a sword, and charged at the ghost. As with Xenia's wand, the spike passed through Gracie's head without resistance. As her hand entered the specter, Elspeth cried out in surprise and pain. The spike dropped from nerveless fingers to clatter on the floor.

"Don't touch her, it's not safe!" Xenia gasped.

"I see that now, lass," Elspeth edged around Gracie to Xenia's side. Grim determination shone in her eyes as she thrust her own arm before the pallid face. "Take me, spirit! Let my great-niece go, and I won't fight you for it. I might look as if I'm at the end of my days, but there's life enough in these old bones to satisfy the likes of you!"

"No!" Xenia planted her feet and hauled against Gracie's hold. Not to free herself, but to pull the specter away from her guardian.

"Here!" Elspeth thrust both arms before the ghost's face. Black teeth snapped at the offering, and Elspeth stepped back. Gracie lunged after, releasing one hand as she did so. Xenia found herself dragged along by her left arm. The numbness was slipping into her shoulder now, and her fingers no longer responded to her efforts to move them.

Bethany's voice echoed down the stairwell, "Seriously, where is everyone? Zee?"

"Bethany!" Xenia gasped. "Down here!"

Bethany drifted down the staircase, "You are never going to guess what I just—the fuck?" She crossed the basement in a heartbeat, passing through Elspeth as she went. She caught Gracie's neck in the crook of her arm and wrenched the ghost's head back before the ebon teeth could rip into the woman's arm. Strain shone in Bethany's face as, bit by bit, she dragged Gracie away from Elspeth.

The hungry ghost released her hold on Xenia to batter and claw at the arm around her throat. The instant contact was broken between raw spirit and living flesh, the creeping chill halted its advance. Xenia fell backward onto the floor. At Elspeth's urging, she crawled under the struggling ghosts. Elspeth hauled Xenia to her feet. Together, they retreated to the dubious safety of the stairwell.

"Your friend has put in an appearance, I take it?"

Xenia nodded. "Wait, you see Gracie but not Bethany?"

"Only that nasty bugger, I'm afraid."

Gracie clawed and spun about, desperate to free herself. Ebon teeth gnashed at the air. She snapped the hand Bethany used to brush the floating hair from her face. Bethany's furious expression calmed. With a tenderness that surprised Xenia, she shifted her headlock into an embrace. She whispered in Gracie's ear. The hungry ghost slowed, then stopped fighting. She hung there, in Bethany's arms, unmoving.

"It's okay now," Bethany said. "I know you didn't really want to hurt anyone. Not after what you've been through. You just want the pain to stop, don't you? I can help with that."

A heaving shudder ran through Gracie.

"We won't let this happen again, isn't that right?" Bethany met Xenia's eyes.

Xenia glanced up to her guardian, then back to the

ghosts. She took a deep breath. Drew herself upright. Did her best to put the lingering pain out of mind. "That's right. We'll stop him. I promise." She might not know how she would keep that promise, but she meant it with every fiber of her being.

"Aye, lass. We'll bring this to an end." Elspeth slipped her arm about Xenia's shoulders. "Don't you be worrying any longer."

"See, Gracie? There's no reason to linger," Bethany said. "Isn't it time for your pain to end? Don't you want to be at peace?"

The shadow of Gracie's eyes rose to meet Xenia's. After a moment, the pallid head dipped in a nod. When she spoke, her voice was less than a whisper, no more than the memory of a word spoken in an empty room. "Yes."

Bethany looked to Xenia and Elspeth. "I was so excited to tell you what I'd learned. Now, I can show you." Her smile was a beacon of love and, in that moment, Bethany was more beautiful than Xenia had ever seen her.

"Show me what?" An anxiety she couldn't place twisted in Xenia's heart.

Bethany rose into the air and Gracie, in her embrace, rose with her. "Oh, don't go all worrywart, Zee. You're stuck with me. I just have to give Gracie a little guidance. A little nudge to start her on her journey." She rubbed the ghost's pale shoulder. "I'll be right back. Best friends, right?"

Xenia nodded. "For fuckin' forever. Yeah. I'll be waiting."

"I know," Bethany said. She snugged her arms tight about Gracie. "Come on. Time to go home."

Between one heartbeat and the next, they were gone.

Elspeth rubbed Xenia's shoulder. "Have no fear, lass. There's work to be done ,and that one doesn't strike me as the type to shirk responsibility. If it turns out she cannae return after all..." Elspeth's sniff was heavy. "Then have faith she'll be in good company."

"Yeah," said Xenia. She examined her arms. Red welts in the shape of handprints marked where Gracie had grabbed her.

"That's a nasty bit of work," Elspeth said. "Let's get you to the kitchen so I can have a proper look." She ushered her great-niece up the stairs with a gentle hand in the small of her back.

Xenia paused by the cabinet and nodded that she'd join Elspeth in a moment. Once her guardian had left the room, she turned to face the staircase. "Come back soon, Beebs," she whispered. "I still need you." She winced as she braced her shoulder against the cabinet and leaned into the push until the secret passage was hidden from view.

Xenia stabbed at her pint of ice cream and cringed as the effort sent a bolt of pain sizzling from the center of her fore-arm. Even though Aunt Elspeth had slathered her burns with creams and aloe, the pin in her bone had yet to release the last vestiges of the unnatural chill Gracie's touch had kindled.

She wriggled herself deeper into the knitted orange comforter and slurped a fragment of frozen strawberry from her spoon. Beside her, beneath the other half of the comforter, Elspeth dug into her own pint of banana-and-chocolate ice cream. Both wore their versions of comfort attire: Xenia in her PJs and hoodie, Elspeth in a faded purple robe and a pair of fuzzy bunny slippers.

The sitting room television, the only one in the house,

had been wheeled out in front of the couch. The ancient tube spent most of its time in the corner beside the cabinet of mysteries. Two hours had passed since the encounter with Gracie, and Bethany had yet to return. Elspeth had clicked on the tube in the hopes of distracting an increasingly distraught Xenia. Instead, they'd found the same story on every channel.

"The body was discovered," the windbreaker-clad woman said into her microphone, "in Postage Square just after eight this evening. The Porter Valley Police Department has declined to release any further information on the victim's identity until the family can be notified. However, Channel Ten News has confirmed that the body does, in fact, belong to a Porter Valley High School student." The woman half-turned toward the tiny park behind her, where a disorganized mob of uniformed and plain-clothed officers milled under the glare of portable lights. "At this time, city officials refuse to comment if they believe this death is connected to the so-called 'mountain lion attacks' that claimed the lives of Salvatore Serrano, Joseph Kaur, Aubrey Foster, and one as-yet unidentified victim. Nor have police offered any explanation as to how such a grisly crime could take place in direct view of the town's busy Main Street without a single witness. I will remain at the scene in Porter Valley to bring you developments as they come. Coraline Connors, Channel Ten News."

"It's not your fault, lass. You had no way to know that villain would vent his spleen upon that poor girl." Elspeth exchanged the empty ice cream carton for her tea.

"But I did know." Xenia paused to fight the wail that threatened to displace her words. "Bethany and I knew he killed Sal and the others." As Elspeth had tended to her burns, Xenia had filled her guardian in on her run-in with the other ghosts. "If I'd believed what I was seeing or had told you right away, then Gracie... and Sal, might still be alive."

"Pah! Xenia, look at me."

Xenia didn't know if she'd find accusation or empathy on her great-aunt's face. Instead, steely determination flashed in the older woman's hazel eyes. "You bear no guilt for that girl's death, Xenia Findlay! Or for Salvatore, God rest his soul. That guilt belongs entirely on that bastard Everard!"

Xenia flinched away from the intensity of Elspeth's voice, her eyes.

"Are you with me, lass?"

"I... I guess." Xenia shrank into the blanket. After a moment, she nodded. "Okay. You're right. I didn't kill them. Even if I'd let him... get me, that doesn't mean he wouldn't have gone after Gracie anyway."

"Aye." Elspeth's voice softened. "You weren't the first to catch that villain's eye, and you certainly wouldn't have been the last. Once a body's acquired a taste for that sort of bloody business, they don't stop. Not on their own." She shuddered and set her teacup on its saucer. "Taste is certainly the word for it, judging by the state he left that poor girl's spirit in." Her face twisted in a mix of disgust and sympathy before she patted Xenia's knee. "It's not as though I don't understand. I know that feeling all too well. That there must have been something you could have done, or something that would have warned you. If only you hadn't overlooked it."

Xenia nodded.

"That look on your face, lass, I know as well. I've seen it in my own mirror. That's the look that sent me out into the world with naught but the clothes on my back and a handful of coins in my pocket. I had no clue what I would be getting myself into. It's only luck and happenstance that carried me through until I learned what I was about." Elspeth clucked her tongue. "I wasn't facing a literal man-eater out of the storybooks, however. I'm not saying we'll allow that villain to stay his course just to save our own hides, lass. I'm telling you that it's not your fight to stop him. Magic or no, I won't have you chasing after him!"

"But—"

"But nothing! Would the thing we saw disguised as a high school lad be laid low by a lass armed with no more than a magical key and a blue candle that doesn't burn?"

Xenia bit back her initial retort. "No," she admitted.

"What we will do is keep our wits about us." She patted the railroad spike weighing down the comforter between them. "We stay armed, vigilant, and, at the first sight that the bastard is near..."

"I run," Xenia mumbled, unable to meet her guardian's eye.

"We run," Elspeth corrected. "I'll be keeping the char-iot"—she meant her old station wagon—"topped off and ready to go. At the first sign of trouble, we'll have ourselves a nice holiday. The men with badges and guns can handle him. After all, it's not as if you're the only one the lad has a beef with."

"Beef?" Xenia half-laughed.

Elspeth's smile was tight and brief. "If you find yourself cornered, though..." She gazed into the space above Xenia's head and then gave a sharp nod. Elspeth slipped from under the comforter and padded upstairs. Just when Xenia was about to follow, to see what her great-aunt was up to, she returned. In her hand was a small, dark object.

"When I was heading out into the big, bad world,

Granny slipped this into my pocket. Now it's time, I believe, for you to have it."

"What is it?" Xenia accepted the unexpected gift, which turned out to be a small knife. The leather of the sheath was worn shiny with age and use. The blade, when Xenia pulled it free, was short, no more than four inches in length. One side had been sharpened to a wicked edge, while the other was scalloped along half its length. A design had been carved into the wood of the handle, but the touch of many hands over many years had worn it down until no more than a hint remained. The knife was well balanced. When Xenia's fingers closed about the handle, it felt as if it had been made for her hand.

"A *sgian-dubh*, lass. Men like to wear them in their socks when they've got their kilts on." Elspeth's eyes danced with merriment. "This sharp fellow saved my bacon more than once. I'm confident he'll do the same for you. I trust you to be sensible with it. No flashing it about, no showing off. A last resort, only."

Xenia slipped the blade into its sheath. "Thank you! I'll keep it with me, but I'm not sure I could—"

"Damn! Aunt E is the best!"

"Beebs!" Xenia threw the comforter aside as she leapt to her feet. "You're back!"

"What? I was gone for, like, a minute..." Bethany drifted to a halt above the coffee table and took in the spread of tea and snacks. "Huh."

"It's been hours." Xenia turned to Elspeth. "Bethany's back!"

"So I gathered, lass." Elspeth smiled at the space to Bethany's left. "Been on a journey, have we? I'm for bed, but these old bones need a proper soak in the tub, first." She saluted the girls with her cup and then made her way upstairs.

"Beebs, I wasn't sure if you were coming back. If you'd even be... allowed back." Xenia sank onto the couch.

"I told you, you're stuck with me." Bethany drifted over to the seat Elspeth had vacated. Her grin slipped away. "I'm serious, actually. I can't leave. There's a barrier or something that keeps me in Porter Valley. If I try to fly out, or pass on"—she turned her eyes to the sky beyond the ceiling—"*poof!* I'm right back here, in front of the house. How do you think I found you, after you moved up here without leaving so much as a note?"

"I thought you'd followed us." Guilt prodded Xenia. Despite the fact that she'd only been able to hear her friend for a few days, she should have asked about this sooner.

"I didn't even know you were moving!" Bethany's smile took the sting from the words. "I was at home, trying to get through to my folks. To Mama." Worry crossed her face like a shadow. "She wasn't doing too great at dealing with, you know. I wanted to give her closure. Let her know that, even though I was dead, I was still kicking. Next thing I know, I'm up here with my head spinning!"

"All right. The second Ev's dealt with, when we've stopped him from hurting anyone else, I'm going to figure out why you're stuck here. Fix it so you can go home. I could call your mom—"

"Nuh-uh!" Bethany held up her hand. "The minute you tell Mama that you believe in ghosts, she'll have Pastor Jim chasing you around to preach the devil out of you." Her eyes crinkled in a smile. "I appreciate the thought, but I know why I'm stuck here. It's you, dum-dum."

"What?"

"I told you, to my eyes, you glow. The others see it too.

That's what draws them here after they..." Bethany sighed, aimed a finger skyward. "Either some joker upstairs is having a laugh, or..."

"Why me?" Xenia took care not to dislodge the gauze wrapped about her arms as she examined her hands. "When I look at myself with my magic vision—"

"Okay, we need to workshop a better name for that."

Xenia stuck out her tongue, then continued. "I see an inner glow, but it's the same thing I see in every living thing. Dogs, cats, people. Everyone glows."

Bethany framed Xenia with her hands. "Well, something's up with you, because you got a whole golden radiance thang goin' on."

Xenia sagged against the couch. "Do you think that's why Ev was interested in me? Does everything supernatural see me glowing? Why do I glow, Beebs?" Panic edged its way into her voice. "Is this going to keep happening, even if we stop him?" She buried her face in the nest of her arms. "Is Gracie okay?"

"She is. I took her as far as I was allowed, but she kept going. She's home, Zee. At peace. Before I lost sight of her, she..." Bethany's smile was radiant. "I don't know if she was whole again, if she got back what had been taken from her, but she was healed. I don't pretend to understand it, but her suffering was at an end. She's where she needs to be." The smile vanished, and she rose into the air. "I have to go, Zee."

Xenia knew exactly where her friend was off to. "Sal. Lucas. All the others. Say goodbye for me."

"I will. They've suffered long enough. Too long." Bethany paused at the window, "I don't know where they're hiding, but I'll find them. I have to." She blew Xenia a kiss and then disappeared into the night.

Xenia padded to the window and gazed up to the wisps

of cloud draping the starlit sky. If Bethany could find a way, despite being dead herself, to help Ev's victims, then what was her excuse? It couldn't be coincidence that Bethany had been bound, somehow, to Porter Valley just as she'd discovered her own aptitude for magic. It was clear, despite what Aunt Elspeth had said, that it was her responsibility to deal with the other side of that bloody coin. She would have to stop Ev, once and for all.

Xenia ignored the clutter on the coffee table and made her way upstairs. She could clean up in the morning. The longer she waited to master the magics she'd been given, the more freedom Everard would have to prey upon her friends.

Chapter Thirty-Nine

Xenia sucked on the tiny cut and glared at the cleaver that had nearly severed her finger.

The experiment might have been a resounding success. However, Xenia vowed to proceed with just a teensy bit of additional caution in the future.

The burns from Gracie's arctic touch had all but faded. A long, hot soak in Elspeth's claw-footed bathtub had eased the lingering ache in her left arm. Whatever vitality Gracie had siphoned off didn't appear to have caused any permanent damage. The fatigue had lingered for a couple days, but Elspeth's cooking and a good night's sleep had set that right.

Xenia had spent every waking moment pursuing her magical research. Her second sight, or at least her ability to summon it, was improving. While it didn't respond one hundred percent of the time, she'd been able to get some work in on *Bone Weave*, the spell Quentin had suggested as a follow-up to *Ghost Flame*.

While her long-lost mentor had provided ample notation for *Flame*, *Bone Weave*'s author had not. All she had to go on was the cryptic phrase "to turn the blade aside." Once she'd worked out its labyrinthine patterns, she'd applied it to the haft of her wand. For whatever reason, the spell refused to respond to her will as *Ghost Flame* had. No matter how firmly she thought at it, nothing happened.

Bethany had provided the vital insight. "Maybe it's like *Lockbreaker*? You don't have to control that one, it's just on, all the time." Bethany's effort to guide Ev's victims into the peace of the hereafter had stalled out. While she'd had no difficulty locating Douglass and Aubrey, Sal and the others were nowhere to be found.

Inspired by both her friend's suggestion and the spell glyph's resemblance to chain mail, Xenia suspected "turn the blade aside" might be literal. To test this theory, she'd gone straight for the biggest blade in the house, the massive cleaver Aunt Elspeth kept on a magnetic strip over the kitchen counter.

At first, she'd taken a timid, careful tap at the spelled wood. The cleaver was heavy enough that the minor effort should have left a divot in the wood, but the wand was unmarred, without so much as a scratch. Even though it suggested that her assumption was correct, that the spell offered a form of protection, Xenia found her attempt... unsatisfying.

Enthusiasm relegated common sense to the back seat. Xenia had raised the cleaver, which was as long as her arm, high above her head. She'd grinned at Bethany even as she brought the blade down with everything she had.

When the cleaver struck the wand, there had been a clear, bell-like *ting*. The handle twisted in Xenia's grip as the blade glanced from the wood. The cleaver, still moving at full speed, embedded itself in the butcher block table. The errant blade had narrowly missed the hand with which she'd braced the wand, shaving off a tissue-thin strip of skin from the edge of her finger.

"Works as advertised," Bethany quipped from her perch in the window garden. "That blade turned right aside. No doubt about it."

"Har-har." Xenia breathed through the thrum of a belated adrenaline rush. "Aunt Elspeth's going to crap a frog when she sees this." She tugged the cleaver free, wincing at the giant notch it had gouged. She could fit a finger into it!

"Nay, lassie!" Bethany's impression of Elspeth's brogue was more than a bit exaggerated. "Jus' be honest and forth-right w' her!"

"Be nice."

"Bitch, please. I have nothing but love for Aunt E." Bethany crossed her arms. "Hell, I want to *be* her. Who knows, maybe when all of this is over, I can reincarnate into someone just like her. Chill, Zee, not right away."

Xenia smoothed the panic from her face. "Add that to the list." She held her wand up to the light and sighted along its length. The wood was as smooth as the wood-worker had left it. "Just as soon as we—" A familiar, icy tingle danced across the nape of her neck. "Company!"

"About time! Maybe Sal will stop giving me the runaround." Bethany drifted to Xenia's side. "Just let me handle whoever it is, okay?"

"Yeah. If it is Sal..."

"Don't worry, you'll have a chance to say goodbye."

Xenia shook her head. "No, I mean for Marisol. She needs the closure much more than I do." Assuming, of course, that Sal could keep from going all gory in Bug's presence.

As the tingling spread across her scalp, Xenia wondered why Bethany no longer triggered the shivery reaction.

Familiarity, perhaps? One more item on the ever expanding list of "magic crap Xenia doesn't know."

"Over there." Xenia pointed to a curl of light in the dining room. A webwork of glowing strands, the ghost, if that's what it was, was little more than a wisp.

"Aw, no. Douglass was the first one I helped cross. That's someone else, someone we missed. Damn, there's hardly anything left." Bethany circled the wisp and held up a hand to forestall Xenia's approach. "Hold up, I don't think there's enough here to go all *The Grudge* on you, but better safe than sucked dry." To the fragmented spirit, she added, "Hey, it's okay now. I know what you're going through, and I can help. Let's get you home, bring an end to your pain."

The curl of spirit twisted away from Bethany's offered embrace and swirled to a halt in the kitchen doorway. Xenia skipped back a step as a sound, little more than a sigh, issued from the ghost.

The web of ghost light began to fold in on itself. The tenuous streamers of which it was composed gathered into a common center. The mass thickened until Xenia could almost make out a hint of a face. The arch of an eyebrow, perhaps, or an inkling of a nose.

"Don't you want her help?" Xenia asked. "Isn't that why you're here?"

The suggestion of a face swung to one side, then the other. It dipped toward Xenia. Bethany leapt at it, tried to catch it, but the ghost fragment darted around her hands.

Xenia rose from her crouch. "I don't think it's here to hurt me, Beebs. You don't want to do that, do you?" she asked the wisp.

Again, it shook its head.

"Do you want my help?" That received a partial nod.

"Why me, though? Bethany's the one who can help you cross over. Aren't you in pain?"

The answer was unmistakable as the wisp exploded into trembling streamers of vapor. Everard may have torn away, and consumed, everything this poor soul had to offer, but what remained was more than capable of suffering. Over the next few minutes, the ghost gathered itself until it was as whole as it could be. When the hint of a face was again visible, it darted around Bethany and floated through the dining room to the front door, where it bobbed up and down.

"Oh, it wants me to follow," Xenia said. She scooped her wand from the table and slipped it into her back pocket.

Bethany winced. "That's a terrible idea, Zee. It's late, and who knows, Ev might be prowling around—" At the mention of the changeling's name, the spirit again convulsed and burst apart.

"It came to me for help, Beebs." While the ghost re-formed, she shrugged into her hoodie. A tiny voice in the back of her head scolded, *Three spells, none of which will stop him.* "I'm going." Her hand went to her neck. She felt past her mother's necklace to the iron nail she'd hung on a bit of string. Which reminded her... Xenia tugged her hoodie off and tugged it on inside out. "There, safe." She gave Bethany a defiant glare.

"Yeah, until he skips the glamour and just rips your fuckin' guts out," Bethany snapped.

Xenia ignored her and addressed the waiting spirit. "I'm ready. You lead, I'll follow. I'm not sure how I can help, but if I can, I will."

That appeared to be enough for the wisp. It slipped right through the door. Xenia eased outside and held the doorknob to keep the door from slamming. She ignored the sudden sense of foreboding as she crossed the front garden. *It's fine. I got this.* It occurred to her, then, that she should have roused Aunt Elspeth, or at least left a note to explain what she was up to. If she went back inside to do either now, she'd lose her nerve. Not to mention Aunt Elspeth would absolutely forbid her from venturing out at all. *She did give me that knife, though. She'll understand.*

"I still think this is a terrible idea," Bethany said from above.

"Oh hush." Before she could second-guess herself any further, Xenia followed the wisp into the night.

* * *

Xenia ducked behind a bush as the patrol car cruised its way down the block. The curfew was still in effect—one more thing to worry about while sneaking around. At least Bethany had agreed to provide "overwatch" and warn her before she could be spotted. Once the coast was clear, the unlikely trio continued their trek toward what Xenia was certain would be the site of the poor, unfortunate soul's demise.

The wisp led them down Bluff Street, parallel to Main, into a neighborhood Xenia hadn't yet explored. A handful of blocks farther on, the street came to an end. There lay one of the city's innumerable green spaces. The tiny park was just enough to hold a doggy-doo bag dispenser, a covered trash can, and a bench. On the far side, beyond a safety rail, the ground fell away.

Xenia hooked a foot into the railing and peered over the edge. "Dang. Hella deep." Scrub brush and the occasional stunted tree grew from the cliff face below her. Fifty feet below that, maybe more, a canopy of a dense wood filled the canyon as far as her eye could see. If she squinted, she could make out a few scattered lights on the far side of the geological rift. To her right, perhaps a half mile away, Main Street crossed the canyon via a hefty concrete bridge.

"Let me guess," Xenia asked, "we're going down there?"

Beside her, the wisp bobbled once.

"Bad idea," Bethany said from her other side. She pointed at the mountainside capping the canyon's end. "Down there? That's where Lucas was killed."

"Figures. No doubt Ev has a favorite spot to... yeah." Xenia gnawed on her lip. Forced her breathing to slow. Reached for the calm she needed to summon her second sight. For once, her new skill cooperated. The night air bloomed with magic.

In that uncanny spectrum, the forest below was an ocean of verdant energy. A mass of emerald and topaz, and colors that had never been named, roiled and surged across the treetops. The sheer variety and intensity of the magic below put the stuff puttering about her bedroom to shame.

Then again, it made a certain sense. This must be what the natural magic of the world was supposed to be like when there weren't a bunch of buildings and people to muck it all up.

She hopped from the rail and searched for a way down. Half a block away, the city had built a narrow staircase, handrails and everything, into the cliffside. They'd even installed a convenient, if sparse, map of "Porter Canyon" and its trails.

"Zee..."

"It's fine! I can handle it. Even if this is where Ev does his dirty work." Beside her, the wisp grew agitated. Xenia offered it an apologetic smile. "Why would he be there now?"

"Because this might be a trap?" Bethany peered at the wisp. "We don't know who this was, or what they really want!"

Xenia looked from her friend to the fragmented spirit. The mote of soul had grown, if anything, even wispier while they'd argued. "I'm going. I have to learn how to handle this stuff if I'm going to do this magical girl shit, okay?"

Bethany crossed her arms.

"Then help me stay safe. I'll go low, you go high?" Xenia mimed looking through binoculars. "If you see anything. A bear, a mountain lion—"

"A changeling."

"Yeah, that. If you see anything, yell! Then go wake up Aunt Elspeth so she can call the Army."

Bethany searched Xenia's face and then heaved a huge, theatrical sigh before she jabbed an imperious finger at Xenia's nose. "I say run, you fucking run."

"Deal."

Xenia began her descent. The wisp darted ahead while Bethany paced alongside, keeping to the treetops. Xenia wished she'd grabbed a jacket before charging out into the night. The night air was cold, and her hoodie wasn't quite up to the task. Better shoes, too. Her high-tops were comfy but were nearly worn through.

Xenia was pleased to find the trail at the bottom wide and well maintained. The half moon peeking through the cloud cover provided just enough illumination for her to navigate. She assured herself that Bethany was still overhead and then trailed her spectral guide into the canyon.

The trail cut a winding path through the trees and, eventually, merged with another. A cheerful little creek burbled alongside. Idle curiosity had Xenia wondering what sort of fish might live in those waters.

The trees closed in as Xenia followed the wisp deeper into the canyon. Before long, she'd lost what little light the moon had provided. She added a flashlight to the list of things she should have grabbed, then slapped her forehead. "Magic, dummy." She drew her wand and willed *Ghost Flame* to life. She raised the wand, and the tiny azure flame, overhead like a torch and marched on.

"Hey, Beebs, how close are we to where Lucas..." Xenia stumbled to a halt and scanned the canopy overhead. Neither the sky nor Bethany were visible through the overgrowth. "Shit." Time to call this off. She could return in the daytime or, even better, have Aunt Elspeth ask the police to search for whatever the wisp wanted her to see.

When Xenia turned to retrace her steps, the wisp darted to block her path. The mote of light zigzagged before her face and then extended a tiny filament of light. "We're here?" asked Xenia. The wisp bobbed once.

Just a quick look, then. Xenia gave the canopy overhead a last glance before stepping over the chain that marked the trail's end. She followed the mote of spirit into the trees.

A muted roar grew at the edge of her awareness, a distant rush of falling water. When she at last emerged from dense wood, she found herself beside a jumble of rocks. Here, the creek she'd seen earlier rushed about the base of those massive stones. Her foot squelched into the mud, and she winced as an icy trickle found its way through her sock.

Beyond the creek-bound boulders rose a sheer wall of granite, the very end of the canyon. At its base, looking for all the world as if someone had kicked a hole into the granite, was the mouth of a cave. The stream vanished right into that darkness. Here, then, was the source of the falling water she'd heard. "Yeah, sorry, little guy. I ain't going in there."

The fragmented spirit looped about her head and pointed its filament away from the cavern. There, where woods met canyon wall, was a narrow footpath. Xenia made her way over and paused as the wisp remained at the water's edge. "You're not coming?"

The wisp shivered and broke apart. In a handful of seconds, the delicate threads of soul-stuff had dissipated like smoke in the wind.

"Ah, no." Xenia hoped the poor thing could pull itself together so that Bethany could help it find the peace it deserved. She scanned the night sky for her friend, but Bethany was nowhere to be seen. She chewed on her thumbnail. "Just a quick peek." After all, she'd come this far. She willed a bit more light into *Ghost Flame* and, against her own better judgment, set out upon the narrow path.

The trail proved to be short. As she emerged from the scrub and saplings, the crescent moon likewise emerged from its shroud. The irregular space before her was overgrown with grass and dotted with wildflowers. In daylight, Xenia thought, it might be quite charming. Now, though, the moon's pale light had rendered the glade in a foreboding palette of blue and umber shadow.

Pale stone gleamed ahead. A wide boulder, cousin to those in the stream, poked above the knee-high growth. A dark, wet stain marred one side of the granite outcropping.

Xenia pushed her way through the grass and raised *Ghost Flame*. Even though the stain ran black in her magic's cobalt glow, she knew blood when she saw it.

There was so much blood. So much.

The grass beside the boulder had been battered flat over an area wider than she was tall. The splash of dark matter coated more than half the stone's surface and soaked the nearby grass into the dirt.

There was no body, at least none she could see, for which Xenia was grateful. She'd had her fill of gory corpses when she'd found Salvatore's body. However, without one, there would be no way to identify the wisp.

Xenia crept to the very edge of the trampled grass, taking care to avoid the bloodied stalks as she held her wand out to illuminate the scene. A sliver of pale material, a fragment of bone perhaps, or a tooth, gleamed in the foul mud.

Everard had savaged Sal, Gracie, and the others. From the state of their ghosts, she believed Bethany's theory that he also consumed parts of their very souls. If all that remained of Ev's current victim was a splash of blood and a few bone chips... No wonder it had been the merest fragment of a soul. "I'm sorry, whoever you were," she whispered to the night.

The clouds swallowed the moon and plunged the glade into shadow. Xenia raised her wand higher, both to improve visibility and as beacon for Bethany. The magical light revealed a dark mass slumped at the far side of the trampled, bloody grass. It wasn't nearly large enough to be a body but—Xenia swallowed—it might be part of one.

She sent *Ghost Flame* over to illuminate the object. The tiny blue flame revealed not the severed head she'd feared but a sodden mass of cloth. Xenia sidled over to join her spell's flame. She held her breath as the copper penny reek filled her nose and then prodded the lump with the tip of her wand.

The lump collapsed with a squelch that nearly had Xenia puking up her dinner. Here was a curve of white rubber, part of an athletic shoe, and shreds of what might once have been jeans. A strip of material, miraculously free of gore, fell free of the clump. She hooked it with her wand and dragged it close.

The strip was a bit of white wool. The tufts of blue clinging to the edge at last granted recognition. A collar, torn from a Porter Valley High varsity jacket. She flipped it over with her wand. Just as she'd hoped, a name had been written on the inner label.

Ambrose.

Ice flooded Xenia's veins as she fell into the grass. *We were wrong.* She scrambled to her feet. She had to get out of here. Before she'd taken more than a step, she backed into a barrier that hadn't been present when she'd entered the meadow.

Xenia spun, wand raised. A wall of armored muscle filled her vision. Row after row of overlapping indigo scales, save for a band of pale green across the middle, armored the massive torso.

The creature stood on its hind legs, towering seven or more feet in height. Twin streams of vapor jetted from the beast's muzzle as it scented the air. A pair of curved fangs overhung the jaw, prominent in a mouth overflowing with razor teeth. Clawed hands flexed. Layered muscle shifted beneath the scaled armor of its arms. Twin horns curved from its brow, arched above the enormous skull. Below them, slit-pupiled, reptilian eyes gleamed with an inner light.

Unprompted, her brain offered up a tidbit from last year's biology class: *Vertical pupils imply excellent night vision.*

Xenia screamed.

Without thinking, she thrust her wand at the beast's muzzle, pouring all her fear, her sudden burst of adrenaline, through her link to *Ghost Flame.* The tiny spark exploded into an azure sunburst.

The creature threw an arm across its eyes. Monster

spittle spattered her face as the creature bellowed in shock and pain. It stumbled away from the intolerable light, tripping over its own tail. As it tumbled, a clawed hand swung and struck Xenia's wand. *Bone Weave* fulfilled its purpose, and a metallic *ting* rang out across the glade. While her wand remained unbroken, the shock of impact was transmitted to Xenia's hand. Her only weapon, such as it was, spun from fingers gone numb. *Ghost Flame* guttered out as its link to her will was broken. Xenia, her eyes dazzled by her own spell, was plunged into darkness.

The sound of heavy breathing and tearing earth filled her ears. She turned, put her head down, and ran.

Xenia knew she had no hope of outrunning the creature. The instant it regained its balance, it'd be upon her. Her only chance, slim as it was, would be to lose herself amongst the trees and to hope, against all odds, that it was too massive to fit between the trunks.

She plunged into the forest at the meadow's edge. Branches clawed at her face, her eyes, and she raised her arms to ward them off. If anything, the darkness was even more cloying within the trees. She caromed from trunk after trunk as she hurtled through the night. Her imagination painted an all-too-vivid picture of the moment when those claws, those teeth, tore into her. She'd seen the ruin they'd made of Sal... and Ev.

How could they have been so wrong?

The changeling might have been arrogant beyond measure, but arrogance wasn't proof of murder. She, and Bethany, had just assumed his guilt. In all likelihood, he was little more than a spoiled, self-indulgent asshole. Whatever abuse he had inflicted upon Jane, and Xenia too, he'd paid for it in blood.

With Elspeth's help, her new magic, and Bethany,

Xenia had been confident she could outsmart and outmaneuver the changeling. But the creature that even now stalked her was of another order entirely. In the face of that monstrosity, she might have had no magic at all.

"Zee?"

Xenia sobbed between ragged gasps. "Help! I'm lost! Where's the trail? I don't know— *Something's chasing me!*"

"Here!" Bethany arrowed through the canopy into her path. She waved her on, a beacon in the darkness. Xenia slammed into a tree trunk. A spike of pain lanced into her arm as it took the impact. She raced on, eyes glued to Bethany.

Her breath burning in her lungs, her heart hammering in her chest, Xenia ran to preserve not only her life, but her very soul.

* * *

Xenia's toe caught on the topmost step and sent her headlong into the dirt. She clawed at the ground and scrambled into the grass beside the trailhead. Desperate for air, she dragged breath after breath into burning lungs.

"I don't see anything," Bethany said from above. "You're sure it was chasing you?"

"Yes!" Xenia rolled to her hands and knees. "It's not Ev," she gasped. "He's dead. Ev was the wisp."

"What?"

"That thing that killed Sal and the others... it got Everard."

"What the hell..."

"There was so much blood, but no body. Just shreds. Scraps. There was nothing left. I read a name tag." Xenia knew she was babbling, but couldn't stop. "Those teeth..."

"Okay, okay. Just take a breath, sweetheart. Then get up. We gotta get you home, tell Aunt E—"

The crunch of a footstep from below brought their heads around. Bethany put a finger to her lips and waved Xenia into motion.

Xenia spun around, desperate for refuge. *There!* No more than a block away, the light of an all-night gas station was a beacon in the night. Xenia threw herself toward that glow.

An acne-studded young man looked up as she barged inside. "Are you okay? Should I call someone?"

Xenia looked down at herself, then to her reflection in the nearby window. Her inside-out hoodie had been shredded in her headlong flight. She'd lost a shoe. Her face was a web of scratches, and a bird's nest of leaves filled her hair. "M'fine," she muttered, crouching beside the magazine rack.

The cashier stared at her for a moment longer and then shrugged. He turned his attention to the massive textbook open on the counter.

"There," Bethany said, pointing.

A shadowed figure, just beyond the station's pool of light, followed the course they'd fled along only a moment earlier. Xenia blew out a breath of relief. Rather than the hulking, armored thing that had pursued her, the street's sole occupant was entirely human.

A rather familiar human, at that. Maia wandered into the station's light. The tension ran out of Xenia in a shuddering rush, and she had to brace a hand against the shelf beside her.

Maia was either the most dedicated member of the track team ever, or she suffered from insomnia. Either way, she was a sight for sore eyes. For her night run, she'd donned a hi-vis, neon-yellow spandex top and black leggings with matching, reflective stripes. A ball cap, with a reflective stripe, completed the ensemble. Clearly, Xenia mused with an exhausted chuckle, Maia wasn't at all worried about breaking curfew.

"Why's she out so damn late?" Bethany asked. "I mean, *you* have an excuse. You're dumb as hell."

"Maia's on the track team, Beebs." Xenia sank to her heels. "She runs like, all the time. Every time I've seen her." She hardly felt the smile playing about her lips. "Maybe we could walk home together. Safety in numbers—" A new surge of terror froze her voice in her throat.

"What?"

Xenia swatted at the air and whispered, "Get down!" While the ghost sank halfway into the floor, Xenia folded down the corner of a magazine and used the gap to confirm what she'd seen.

Maia had wandered close to one of the pumps. The annoying screen on its face ran a video extolling the insane prices to be found on the corn dogs and frozen drinks inside. A close-up of a blue slush cup had bathed Maia in a spill of light that was a close match to *Ghost Flame*. In that cobalt illumination, Maia's yellow top had flared green.

The same green she'd taken for a stripe across the creature's chest.

"No..."

As she passed the window, Maia adjusted her top. No longer skin tight, it hung from her shoulders as if, recently, the spandex had been stretched beyond its limits.

Xenia clapped her hands over her mouth as a tiny whine slipped out.

Maia paused. Turned her head.

Xenia shrank lower. There was no way she could have heard that, right?

The runner tilted her head. Lips parted just a bit, she sniffed at the air.

She's tracking my scent! Considering the fear sweat she was drenched in, it'd be a wonder if the cashier couldn't smell her, let alone Maia.

Luck, at last, was on Xenia's side. Either the wind had shifted or gas pump vapors had run interference. Maia gave a little shrug, tugged her top into place, and jogged into the night.

Xenia hunkered down behind the magazine rack. She stared, unseeing, past photos of aspirational yachts and muscle cars until the first blush of morning graced the eastern sky. To her everlasting gratitude, the night cashier continued to grant her the courtesy of ignoring her.

Battered by her headlong flight, covered in innumerable scratches and exhausted by bout after bout of sheer terror, she stumbled out into the dawn. As the rising sun spilled her shadow before her, Xenia ran for home.

Chapter Forty

Guilt and fear had fought a prolonged battle within Xenia over the course of the morning. Fear had won.

Lacking a reasonable explanation for the scratches covering her face and arms, she'd had to time her efforts with the precision of a bank heist. While Elspeth cooked breakfast, she'd dallied in her room. Only once her guardian had eaten and gone up to her own bedroom did Xenia rush downstairs to wolf down what she could. There was magic to be done, and she desperately needed the fuel.

She'd raced ahead of Aunt Elspeth in a performative hurry. By the time her great-aunt had locked the front door, she was already at the end of the block. There, she had loitered, out of sight, until Bethany signaled that the coast was clear. Then it was back to her room, where the plan was to decipher what she could of the largest of Quentin's spells. Even though the notation was in a language unfamiliar to her, Xenia was certain that at least one of the five glyphs on the map-sized page would provide what she needed to arm herself.

Bethany, once again, proved to be the key. All thanks to her fledgling skills in Japanese, which she'd picked up on the same family trip that had changed her wardrobe.

Two hours of intense, internet-aided translation later, Xenia had assembled a rough understanding of the spell. *Mahō Fuyūjutsu,* or *Magic Floating Technique,* was revealed to be a treatise on utilizing magic to impart movement to objects. Not quite the "fireball" she'd hoped for, but she'd take it.

Before she could implement her ideas, she would require the proper materials.

"Where are you going?" Bethany asked, as Xenia burst through the back door. The ghost had put herself on lookout duty and was keeping a wary eye on the surrounding streets, lest a certain running enthusiast put in an appearance.

"Shed," Xenia answered. While Aunt Elspeth had planted the same variety of fairy-repellent growth around the back fence as she had in front, the center of the old Victorian's back yard had been given over to her vegetable and herb garden. Row after row of planters and trellises overflowed with salad greens, tomatoes, basil, rosemary, and other kitchen staples. How the woman could coax such enthusiastic abundance from the botanical menagerie with so little effort was a mystery.

Beyond the vegetable garden, but within the fence, sat a tidy little shed. Here, Elspeth kept her gardening supplies and all the other implements required to maintain her home. A pile of offcuts, wood scraps, and other leavings were piled beside the shed.

Xenia circled the scrap pile. She had an idea of what she needed and hoped to find it within. In the midst of a knotty tangle of branches and broken fence pickets, she found a near-perfect candidate.

The branch was free of cracks, splits, and rot. It was too long for her to handle easily, and too heavy, but she wouldn't need all of it. Not for what she had in mind. Xenia dashed to the shed and returned with a small handsaw. In a jiffy, she had herself a proper length of wood.

"Wand 2.0?" asked Bethany.

"Yup." Xenia shooed a tide of spiders from the shed's workbench and set her prize atop it. Despite her lack of woodworking know-how, the assortment of tools her great-aunt stocked made easy work of stripping the twigs and bark from her branch. She sawed a bit from each end and used the sandpaper she found in a drawer to render her candidate as smooth as possible.

When she was done, she had a shaft of wood just over two feet in length. The thicker end fit her hand perfectly. The wand-to-be tapered hardly at all along its length but wasn't so heavy that she couldn't hold it easily. And it was just hefty enough to pack a wallop.

The final step of her preparations was to slice a thin disk from the base of the wand. Now that she had her materials, the real work could begin.

* * *

"You around, lass?"

Xenia blinked awake as Elspeth tapped on her bedroom door. *What time is it?* "M'here." She scrubbed at her eyes. It had taken her hours to weave each spell into her new wand. She must have dozed off.

"I was a mite concerned when you failed to show up after school, lass. You didn't answer when I called the house, so I came a-looking." Elspeth's frown of concern eased as she saw the notebooks and *Mahō Fuyūjutsu's* instruction sheet spread across the bed. "Struck by a bit of magical inspiration, were we?" Aunt Elspeth's enthusiasm for her great-niece's occult discoveries nearly exceeded Xenia's own. "I understand your enthusiasm, lass, but next time give us a call."

Xenia stomped on her surge of guilt. "I made a new wand." She waved at the paper covering the bed. "I figured out one of the new spells."

Elspeth scurried to Xenia's side, her concern forgotten. "Let's have a look-see. What's it do?"

Xenia held her new creation up for inspection. Every inch of the pale wood was laced with the fine, dark scribing of spell glyphs. Elspeth's eyes glowed with excitement as she examined the wand.

"We should probably go outside," Xenia said. She scooped a plastic toy ring from her desk. Aunt Elspeth fell in behind her as she marched downstairs to the back door.

"You finished it?" Bethany asked from above. Xenia waved her down. The ghost took up a position beside Elspeth.

Xenia ran to the shed and propped her wand by the door. "With Bethany's help"—she nodded to her friend as she mounted the porch stairs—"I was able to decipher some of *Mahō Fuyūjutsu*. It's more of a lesson plan than a spell. Most of it is theory, but one of the examples was super useful."

Elspeth gestured, somewhat impatiently, for her to get to the good stuff.

Xenia slipped the toy ring onto her finger. "Right. What's the one thing every magical weapon should do?" Without waiting for a response, she spun to the yard. "Return to their wielder!" She held out the hand with the ring and snapped her fingers.

The wand burst from its rest as if fired from a cannon. A buzzsaw whine issued from the length of wood as it raced across the yard. Xenia jerked her head aside before her own creation took her head off. The wand passed clean through Bethany and slammed into the old Victorian with a *thud* that shook the whole house.

"Crivvens!" Elspeth stumbled back a step.

"Was that supposed to happen?" Bethany asked, her voice sweeter than honey.

"Hold on, my math was off." Xenia crouched with the wand across her knees. Once she'd calmed her racing heart, she cajoled her second sight into cooperation and plucked at the threads of magic embedded in the wood. Once she was satisfied with the fix, she replaced the wand at the shed.

Elspeth took two rather large steps off to one side.

Xenia raised her hand. Managed to flinch only a tiny bit when she snapped her fingers.

This time, when her wand leapt into the air, it proceeded at a reasonable velocity. It met Xenia's outstretched hand with a meaty *smack*. She pumped her hand overhead. "It works!"

"Well done, lass," Elspeth applauded. At her side, Bethany cheered.

Xenia spun on her heel, her grin fierce, and flung the wand like a javelin. Before it could land, she snapped her fingers. Obediently, the wand flew to her hand. "Woo! Check this out!" She held the length of wood out for inspection. Elspeth and Bethany crowded close. "I put *Lockbreaker* and *Ghost Flame* here and here. *Bone Weave* to reinforce the whole thing." As she spoke, a fist-sized blue flame sprang into being above the wand, then vanished. "You know the first two. *Bone Weave* makes it nearly unbreakable. Nothing, not claws, knives, or swords, will be able to cut my wand now."

Elspeth's eyebrows nudged together in the first hint of a frown.

"*Mahō Fuyūjutsu*, at least the parts I understand, is what brings it to me." Xenia showed off the toy ring on her finger. In the setting where once had been a plastic gem, she had glued the disk cut from the base of the wand. "Since these were once one piece, the spell brings them together." She dropped the wand and then snapped it to her hand before it could strike the ground. "That's not all! I even made up my own spell!

"Shut up!" Bethany cried.

"Yep! I wanted something with a little more oomph. Okay, back when I didn't know what was going on, didn't know that magic was real, I got tangled up in some wind magic. You remember, the day I got knocked the heck out?" Xenia paused as the memories rose. How Sal had helped Elspeth look after her. She pushed on. "Well, I wanted to get back on that horse, if you get me. I cribbed from Quentin's notes and came up with this." She pointed to a quartet of glyphs about the base of the wand. The tiny black symbols were notably less ordered, less refined than the others. "It's called *Gale Hammer*, to send your foes a message!"

"Ooh! Copying Quentin's style, are we?" asked Bethany.

Xenia tapped her nose.

"And what message does this spell send, lass?" Elspeth folded her arms. The last hint of amusement had vanished from her expression.

"This!" Xenia aimed the wand at the clouds above. With a thought, she triggered *Gale Hammer*.

The wand exploded from her hand on a thundercrack of displaced air. Xenia's hair and clothing fluttered in the blowback. Before the wand had traveled too far—Xenia could just see it smashing through a neighbor's living room on its way back—she snapped her fingers. The length of wood dropped out of the darkness into her waiting hand. She gave the wand an inexpert twirl in her fingers. "Ta-dah!" She obliged Bethany's raised hand with a careful high-five.

"It's all quite impressive, I'll grant you that, dearie." Storm clouds had gathered in Elspeth's expression. "But I cannae help but wonder why you might be worried about claws and swords all of a sudden. Didye not think I'd cotton to the fact that ye've made yerself a weapon? And where, I might ask, is yer other wand? Would its absence, and your sudden obsession with what you call 'oomph' have something to do with last night's midnight excursion? The one you thought I wasnae aware of? Or these?" Elspeth cupped Xenia's chin and brushed her thumb over one of the many scabbed abrasions.

Xenia was unable to meet her guardian's eyes. She twisted the wand in her hands.

"Oh shit, busted!" Bethany gave Xenia a knowing "told you so" look and then drifted toward rooftop level.

Elspeth pinched the bridge of her nose. "Jings, crivvens, help ma boab." She thrust a finger at the door. "Inside," she snapped, "the both of ye."

Bethany froze in midair. Her shoulders drooped. She fell in behind Xenia as Aunt Elspeth marched the both of them into the kitchen.

* * *

Try as she might, Xenia's efforts to plead her case had fallen on deaf ears. "But—"

"But nothing, lass!" Elspeth slammed her hand onto the kitchen table. "I'll not have you taking on that... whatever she may be. Not on your own, not even with an army at your back! I forbid it!" If Elspeth had possessed the same talent for magic as Xenia, her glare would have reduced the girl to ashes. "It's bad enough you were wandering about after curfew, chasing ghosts. You knew that changeling has... had your scent in his nose and revenge on his mind! Did you not stop to think he might have sent that spirit? Have you never heard of a will-o'-the-wisp?" She threw her hands up in frustration.

The fact that Elspeth had at no point paused her castigation to put the kettle on was scarier than the yelling. Xenia had never seen her this angry, ever.

"But—" Xenia's mouth snapped shut as her guardian pinned her with another glare. She shook her head and pushed on. "I thought you, of anyone, would understand! Why'd you even give me the *sgian-dubh* if I was supposed to sit on my hands? People are dying, Aunt Elspeth. My friends are dying! No one is stopping it!"

Elspeth's eyes were wide with anger and, if Xenia managed to look beyond her own outrage, fear. "Ah, lass..." She set her chin and nodded once. "You're right, this is my fault. I'm the one filling your head with stories. The one who put the knife in your hand, trusting you'd be mature enough to know the difference between preparation and foolhardiness. Perhaps I should have set more boundaries, more structure for you, once you arrived. I didn't want to overwhelm you, lass. You were so lost."

Elspeth sagged in her chair. Some of the fire ebbed from her eyes. "It's not as if I don't understand. I was your age, once. I've known loss. Lost more friends than I can count. Wanted to take on the world too, when it happened. But you're my responsibility now. What would your parents, God love them, say if I'd lost you just when you'd been placed in my care? There's nothing for it." Elspeth crossed her arms. "You're grounded."

Xenia shrank into her chair. In all her life, she'd never warranted a grounding. Not that she was perfect, no. It was just that the worst punishment she'd earned had been a weekend without TV.

Then again, she'd never snuck out in the middle of the night to chase a ghost before, either.

Elspeth jabbed her finger at Bethany. "Don't think I've forgotten about you, lass. I may have invited you into my home, true, but there's a responsibility in accepting that invitation. I know I might as well try to ground the wind for all I could curtail your comings and goings, so it's your love for Xenia I'll be relying on. If you wish to remain welcome in this house, it's Jiminy Cricket you'll be playing from now on. You're to be the wee nagging voice in her ear when I cannae be." Elspeth's expression brooked no argument.

"Yes, ma'am," Bethany mumbled. She sank so low in her chair that she wound up halfway through the floor.

"You're already spending every moment not at school, or home, at the shop with me, so your grounding'll need sharper teeth if the lesson is to sink in."

Xenia's stomach plummeted. Surely she didn't mean—

"There's to be no more magic, lass. No spells, no exploring the basement. Not until I'm sure you've learned your lesson. Not until I'm convinced the danger has passed us both by."

Xenia's jaw dropped. "That's not fair!" She leapt to her feet, not caring that she'd sent her chair clattering off the wall behind her. "You can't do that! I need it! How am I supposed to—"

"Ye're supposed to mind yer elders," Elspeth snapped. She stood, more carefully than Xenia. "I know yer father taught you as much. What did you think would happen, if you'd been caught?" She charged on over Xenia's protest. "Not by that beastie. There's a curfew on! Did ye forget that I only have custody over you thanks to your parents' will? If I prove to be an unfit guardian, if ye're out defying my wishes and the law, I'll lose you, lass! They'll take you away faster than either of us could blink. Put you in a foster home, with strangers. And if that thing had caught you, then what? You'd be dead, and I'd be all alone again. What would I do then?" Tears poured, unchecked, from Elspeth's eyes.

Xenia longed to run to her great-aunt, to throw her arms about her. But pride rooted her in place; anger and outrage held her fast. Elspeth hadn't seen what she had. Felt what she'd felt. The sickly, cotton candy leash of Everard's will. Gracie's cold, life-stealing touch. The wreckage of flesh and spirit left behind after that... *thing*... had feasted upon Sal. Her hands, low by her sides, curled into fists.

Elspeth went on. "It won't be forever, love. I'd not steal away the wonders of the world. My only concern is that you to stay out of sight and out of mind until that girl, whatever she may be, turns her attention elsewhere." She sank into her chair. "I'll not be leaving her to wreak havoc on your classmates, mind. Since the changeling's no longer in the picture, I know a body or two on the city council. They'll send someone to that meadow for a proper investigation. A word in the right ear will have them prying into her affairs and whereabouts. It'll be handled, lass. In a proper fashion."

"The police won't be able to stop her," Xenia sniffed.

"The bobbies are a damn sight better equipped to handle a nasty creature in the woods than a girl barely into her teens," Elspeth snapped.

Xenia bit down and trapped her rancor behind her teeth before she flung it at her guardian. Instead, she spun on her heel. Stormed from the kitchen. Trampled the stairs beneath her feet. Slammed her bedroom door. Before the last echo had faded, she'd fallen to her bed and crumpled into a puddle of misery and tears.

Chapter Forty-One

When Xenia arrived at school the next morning, the student body still reeled from the news of Gracie Collins's gruesome death. Even though it had been only a day or so, thanks to her experience in the canyon, it felt as if weeks had passed. Then again, the fact that the atrocity had been discovered less than a block from the town center gave it a staying power that the "simple" disappearance of Lucas and the others had lacked.

As Gracie's death was determined to be foul play, the investigation was only now, and begrudgingly, expanded to the other missing students. At no time during his latest press conference did Captain Strauss allow the words "serial" or "killer" to be uttered in proximity to each other. As Aunt Elspeth had explained, admitting that a serial killer might be stalking their fair town would have a negative impact on the Gold Rush Days revenues. With only weeks to go, the city council would brook no interference.

The curfew had been mere days from its scheduled end. With this latest, and most public death, city officials expanded the ban. Since the killer appeared to prey, for the most part, on teenagers, all minor persons were now required to be indoors, or accompanied by a parent or guardian, between 7:00 p.m. and 7:00 a.m..

Instead of outrage at this fresh indignity, the announcement roused little more than a perfunctory protest from Xenia's peers.

Most of the laughter, boisterous conversation, shouted greetings, and hormone-fueled bluster had vanished from the between-class hallway scrum. A pall descended over the lunchroom crowd. The chatter was stifled, hushed. The gathered students had taken on the hunched posture of mice in the field, wondering where next would fall the hawk's talons.

As Xenia worked her way through a PB&J, Coach Fairfax burst into the lunchroom. What little hair the man still possessed stood from his skull in greasy clumps. Wide-eyed and frantic, he went from table to table, asking, "Have you seen Ambrose? Where's Ev? Where is he?" No one, it seemed, had laid eyes upon the Banana Slug's star player in days. Even worse, the special dispensation the team had been afforded to hold their practice, despite the curfew, was no more.

Xenia nodded to herself. It made sense. Whatever glamour Everard had used to get his way had died with him. *I should ask Maia what she thinks about him now.* No sooner had the thought occurred than her mouthful of peanut butter became dirt on her tongue. She shoved her lunch away.

At least the spectacle unfolding before her would serve as a distraction from all things Maia. She was witnessing in real time the death of Coach Fairfax's dream of a fourth championship. Right away, she dismissed her urge to tell him what she'd found in the canyon. Doing so would only put the spotlight upon herself, and the last thing she needed was to give Maia another reason to target her. She had no choice but to trust that Aunt Elspeth's "friend" in city hall would carry the investigation forward without her.

"Coach? I saw something. At Ev's house, I mean," said a girl at the next table over.

The fires of hope blazed anew in Fairfax's eyes. "Spit it out! I'm dyin' over here!"

The poor girl brushed a lock of hair behind her ear and swallowed hard as she found every eye upon her. "So, um. Last night? I heard his parents shouting. Like they were having a big argument." The girl flinched as the coach's wild "go on" gesture clipped the head of the boy sitting across from her. "They were loading stuff into their SUV. Like they were going on a trip or something. Just throwing everything in. I mean, for real throwing their shi— stuff in. When they drove off, they almost hit Mom's car. There's burnt rubber all down the street."

Xenia couldn't blame the elder Ambroses. One could only imagine the hell a teenage boy, granted the ability to command obedience, could inflict upon his adoptive parents.

Clearly, this was not the news Coach Fairfax had hoped for. He stared at the unfortunate girl, mouth open in shock. When the phone in his hand rang, his flinch nearly sent the device across the room. Without another word, he exited the lunchroom at the same speed with which he'd entered.

* * *

Xenia excused herself from class to avail herself of the "good" restroom. The school's layout set the auditorium far enough from the average classroom to render its facilities too inconvenient for most. As long as she could get a hall pass, she would have the leisure to relieve herself in peace. It was just what she'd needed when she was still a new arrival, with no control over her tears.

It was only when she arrived at the secluded restroom that she realized that solitude was not the best idea for one being stalked by a super-predator. Best to pee as fast as she could, then get back to class.

A faint weeping froze her in place. While she realized the proper thing to do would be to find the nearest teacher, her better nature prevailed. First, she'd determine if immediate help was required. If not, she'd leave whoever it was to grieve in solitude.

Xenia crept along the line of stalls. The weeping was coming from the last in the row, the door of which hung open. She eased an eye past the sheet metal partition.

Madison, face cradled in her hands, was slumped on the toilet seat. Her shoulders shook as she clamped a hand over her mouth to stifle her sobs. Mads, for the first time Xenia had seen, was without her usual fashion-forward attire. In its place she wore a stained T-shirt printed with a faded cartoon sundae and a pair of plaid felt lounge pants. The entire ensemble looked as if it hadn't been washed in days. Nor did Madison. Her mahogany hair hung in a limp, greasy mass about her face.

To be sure, the senior girl's own actions had kept her off of Xenia's list of favorite people. That didn't mean, however, that she wasn't deserving of sympathy. Gracie had been one of her best friends. More than anyone, Xenia knew exactly what that sort of loss would do to a person.

"I'm sorry, Madison," Xenia said. "I know you and Gracie were close. If there's anything I can—"

Madison's head snapped up. Her eyes, red and swollen, flared with rage. "Who fucking asked you? The fuck you know what I'm going through, *New Girl*." She literally spat the words; Xenia had to skip back to avoid the spittle. The grieving girl's lip curled in a contemptuous snarl as she slammed the stall door in Xenia's face.

She stood there, blinking, a handful of fluttering heartbeats longer. She nodded her acceptance. Her experience wasn't a perfect match for Madison's, but she recognized the shape of it. Rage was easy to come by in times like these. When she was ready, if she wanted, Xenia would be there for her.

Until then, she had a responsibility. Before anyone else lost their lives, their friends, their family, Maia had to be stopped. The police were still looking in all the wrong places. No one had the slightest clue that a beast lurked beneath the runner's skin. No one, except her and Bethany. It was up to Xenia to bring Maia's reign of terror to an end.

Even if she must defy Great-Aunt Elspeth to do it.

Chapter Forty-Two

U ncle raised his cup. A small, rueful smile passed over his lips as he found he'd already drained the last of the *kaš*. He settled the *gishgudi* in his lap. His fingers crawled over the strings in search of the melody. Music filled the night air as the old man's voice rose above the circle of sitting stones.

* * *

Bēlet An-Nisig, the Lady of Blue Sky, retired to the depths of her temple as twilight fell across the world. Her Gilded Champion journeyed to the west, to the Temple of Night, with but one goal in mind: to lay low *Bēlet An-Ĝíg*, the Lady of Black Sky.

The Champion knew that he would not be allowed to enter the presence of the Night Queen with weapon in hand. Sly must he be, and cunning.

The Champion draped the finest linen about his armor. Likewise did he bind and adorn his spear that it might be taken as little more than a staff. Lastly, did he paint his lips and color his cheeks, anoint his hair with perfumed oil, that he might be taken as a courtesan.

Thus was the temple guard deceived. The acolytes brought the Champion into the presence of the Night Queen herself. Low did he bow before the goddess. "I am a gift," said the Champion, his brow pressed to the stone floor in obeisance. "Your divine sister sends to you her love. She bids you enjoy me as you will." He raised his head, unbidden, and offered the goddess his most comely smile. "Loosen your combs, my Lady. May we spend sweet nights in the pleasures of love."

Intrigued by her sister's ploy, the Lady of Black Sky bid the Champion approach. For, in truth, she did find his appearance pleasing. Long had it been since she had taken a lover to her chambers.

The Champion rose and approached the Goddess. Before her divine eyes could pierce his deception, the Champion struck! In the darkness of the temple hall, his spear shone like the sun itself.

The Dark Queen, alas, was no stranger to guile. Quick as serpent's strike did she evade the blow.

Into battle did the Lady charge. She struck at the Champion with all the force of the winter tempest. The Champion was as nimble as he was strong, and so he evaded the sweep of her ebon blade. For once, he had served *Bēlet An-Ĝig* herself. Along with his brothers and sisters he had been tutored in the art of war here, in this very temple, that they might stand between the Great Continent and its foes. So now did he stand between his people and the tyranny of the Night Queen.

Such was the Champion's skill at arms that the Lady of Black Sky was driven from her own hall. Enraged, her ferocity knew no bounds. Lo, first blood was hers to claim.

The blessing laid upon the Champion by his mistress held, and she accepted the blow upon her own flesh. Thus was the mortal spared from death. Even as his skin ran gold with the blood of his goddess, he struck in return.

The conflict soared to the very vault of the heavens as the land below knew its first rain since the onset of the Night Queen's punishment. Liquid gold and flowing onyx fell across the world. Beneath this divine deluge, it was changed.

At dawn, when the world must pass to the Bright Queen's reign, as decreed by their Divine Mother, *Bēlet An-Ĝig* plummeted into the deep places of the earth, the Champion, as ever, at her heel. Through cavern and tunnel they skirmished, until the hour of Night's return was upon them. Into the sky did those adversaries rise, to do battle among the clouds.

For six upon six nights and days did the battle rage. The Champion harried his foe across land and over sea without landing a decisive blow. The Lady of Black Sky stalked her enemy through sky and cavern, yet she could not pierce the mortal's heart.

With neither rest nor refreshment, the adversaries grew weary.

Even with his matron's blessing, the Gilded Champion was yet mortal. He knew that if he failed to secure victory ere long, he would fall. The fatigue that even now dogged his heels would see to that.

The battle had carried the foes far beyond any land known to song or legend. Neither divine nor mortal had yet laid eyes upon the forest over which they now fought. The timber of those colossal trees, when shattered by an errant blow, ran as red the morning-kissed horizon.

It must be here, the Champion knew, that the fight would, nay, *must* come to its conclusion.

The Bright Queen's golden spear was the only weapon that might bring the Dark Queen to defeat. Only that sun-bright blade might break her armor and pierce her ebon heart. He had fought with weapon fast in hand, unwilling to hurl it at his foe. For, should he miss, he would be naked before her fury.

The Champion's vision wavered, and he knew that his end was nigh. In desperation did he devise a ruse that might grant him victory.

From his shoulders, the Champion shrugged his armor of gilt, allowing it to fall to the forest below. The metal, brighter than any mirror in its finish, caught the light of the Moon as it fell.

The Night Queen, fatigued beyond mortal ken, mistook that gleam for her challenger. Without hesitation, she pressed her attack.

With a final prayer to his Mistress, the Champion spent the last of his strength to hurl the spear at his foe.

Thus was the Queen of Darkness struck from the sky.

The goddess plummeted to the land below. Such was the force of her impact that forests fell, rivers were torn from their beds and the very stone heart of the land was rent asunder.

The Champion turned to salute the rising sun and cried, "It is done! My Lady, it is done!" Having expended the last of his mortal vitality on the throw, he fell to his end upon the rock below.

Bēlet An-Ĝíg did not meet her end that dawn.

The wound inflicted upon the Lady of Black Sky was grievous indeed. Yet the golden spear had not found its mark within her ebon heart. Even as it had rent the black armor of Night, the weapon had shattered into innumerable shards of golden metal.

There, deep within the earth, concealed from the eye of the sun by the tomb her impact had carved, she lay as a broken thing. Diminished by battle and injured by the Champion's blow, her glory was all but gone.

In those depths she would wait. In that abyss, she would slumber. The night would come, vowed the Dark Queen, when she would reclaim that which was hers by right. No forgiveness would there be on that eve. No mercy. Until the hour of her reckoning, she would marshal her strength. Her dreams would be dreams of her domain renewed, of vengeance, and the means by which she would take them both.

Bēlet An-Nisig, the Lady of Blue Sky, was no less diminished by the battle. As her blessing upon the Champion bid her accept his wounds as her own, she too, fell to slumber.

In the absence of the Twin Queens who had ruled all, the land was left to its own devices. The rains began, at long last, to fall once more. Only now, without the hand of their mistress upon the tiller, the tempest blew as it alone desired. So, too, did the world find new balance. The people had not the means to navigate this new order. When they spoke to their mothers, who turned to the Grandmothers who, in their own way, beseeched the Twin Queens for guidance, only silence answered their prayers.

The years passed, as they do. In the gulf of ages that followed, the seas would drink down the Great Continent. Gone with that mighty land was all memory of the Gilded Champion, the Twin Queens, and the battle that had raged between Sun and Moon. Empires rose and fell in the manner of sea tides.

Of *Bēlet An-Nisig*, Lady of Blue Sky, no more may be spoken. Of her sister, *Bēlet An-Ĝíg*, Lady of Black Sky, only this:

In darkness, she waits. In darkness, she will return.

* * *

The young woman breathed out a long sigh of relief. She wiped the sweat from her brow and read again the words she had written. As her finger traced each line, she took care not to smudge the damp clay.

Not so long ago, she had begged Father, entreated him, to send her to the *Edubba*, for she wished to learn the art of writing. Because she was his only child, he had admitted, after an evening when *kaš* had rendered him forthright, he had allowed her to be educated. Still, he had made no effort to disguise his pride, or hide the width of his smile, when she had returned. He had not attended the House of Tablets in his own youth, and thus had been forced to spend far too much of his meagre profits on a scribe.

The woman smiled at the memory and ran her finger across the golden disk of the pendant given to her by her grandmother. The old woman, had she lived to see this day, would have been even more proud of her.

Here, upon these tablets, the young woman had recorded what she recalled of Uncle's tales. She missed that old drunkard dearly. That night, at the great circle of stones when he'd sung of the quarrel between Sun and Moon, had been his last. None had laid eyes upon him after that night.

The girl had told and retold Uncle's stories to the other children, and to any who would stop and listen. In truth, it had been her need to preserve those tales, and not a desire to become a scribe, as she had told her father, that had sent her begging to attend the *Edubba*.

Allowing the girl, now a young woman, to learn cunciform had been one of Father's better decisions. Now that his own daughter was a scribe, he was assured of his records and their accuracy. As a result, his fortune grew, and grew again.

It had been many winters since her family had been required to travel the caravan routes. Father now owned a fine estate outside of Kish, and Mother had a servant to weave the linen for her.

It had taken her many long nights, and many cups of *kaš*, but the young woman had finally transcribed all of Uncle's tales. Here, before her, was his last. Her favorite. It might have been nothing in the balance of things, but she could take pleasure that the old man's tales would not pass into the darkness as he had.

"He has done it to me again!" Father raged from the corridor. The young woman tucked her grandmother's pendant away beneath her tunic; the old woman had charged her not to allow her father to take it as his own. When Father at last strode into her chambers, a storm cloud raged upon his brow. "I have been cheated, yet again!"

The young woman smiled and plucked a fresh reed as a stylus. "Another missive to Ea-nāṣir, Father?"

Chapter Forty-Three

Bethany stared at her friend in disbelief. "That's the worst idea in the history of bad ideas, Zee."

"Noted," Xenia said around a mouthful of tuna sandwich.

Since Elspeth had handed down her sentence, Bethany had redoubled her efforts to help the Lost cross to the hereafter. She might be as grounded as Zee, but that didn't absolve her of that responsibility.

When she'd died—well, once she'd accepted the concept—Bethany had wanted nothing more than to make peace with her family and assure herself that they'd move on as best they could. Then, she could go wherever it was that souls went. Reincarnation, heaven, didn't matter. She was trapped here, and she wanted to go where she was meant to.

Since her encounter with Naira, she'd had a nagging suspicion that this, right here, was where she was supposed to be. That this, not some heavenly cloud, was her actual afterlife. That she, Bethany Brooks, was meant to guide the lost and the trapped into the afterlife that they, themselves, could not reach.

It was an interesting idea. The more she thought about it, the more it felt like she'd hit the nail on the head. After all, even if she ushered all of Maia's victims into the beyond, what's to say there weren't other monsters out there just like her? Vile predators who left a trail of broken, tattered souls behind them. Souls who needed a guide, so that they could at last know peace.

If that was the case, then the barrier that held her in Porter Valley might be more akin to training wheels. Meant not as a trap but to keep her in "in school" until she learned the ropes. Accepted her destiny.

She could live with that, so to speak. *Bethany Brooks, psychopomp.* Okay, that needed some workshopping.

At least she was dressed for the part.

One by one, she'd located Lucas, Tamarah, and the others and helped them find the peace they so desperately needed. Now, only Salvatore remained. The poor, terrified soul had continued to evade her. Bethany hoped he was just good at hiding and that he hadn't dissipated entirely, as Everard seemed to have. Since that night in the canyon, there'd been no sign of the changeling's fragmented spirit.

Her search for the wayward Sal had come to an end when she'd spied Maia at school. Since the encounter in the canyon, the runner had been absent, citing her grief at Gracie's death. If Maia was back, Zee would need her ghost bestie watching her six.

At lunch, Xenia had gone straight to the benches at the edge of the field. There, the two of them could speak without interruption while also keeping an eye out for a certain runner.

"You should have seen what a wreck Madison was,"

Xenia said. "Hell, everyone's messed up. Everyone's lost a friend, or a friend of a friend, thanks to her."

"I know you miss Sal, Zee. That doesn't mean it's up to you to handle this. Come on! Aunt E said—"

"What, I'm supposed to just sit around while the cops maybe take a look, just cause Aunt Elspeth asked? Hah!" Chips flew in every direction as Xenia tore open her bag. She scowled. "Maia has all the freedom in the world to chow down on anyone, whenever she wants to."

Bethany opened her mouth in protest, but Xenia held up her hand. "Look, I ain't gonna fight her! Hello! Monster Maia's gigantic!" She turned haunted eyes to the ground. "I'm just saying. We're the only ones who know the truth. That she's the killer. So, we watch her. From a safe distance." Xenia fished a notebook from her bag and flipped through, pointed to a page. "Look. The interval between the disappearances, the killings, is shrinking. Douglass Miller was the first. It was more than two months before Aubrey Foster vanished. If this keeps accelerating, we have one, maybe two nights before she goes for her next victim. If we keep her in our sights, we can warn whoever it is she… hunts. Then, we can call the cops in—"

"To do what?" Bethany interjected. "Shoot her?"

"What else is going to stop her?" Xenia's voice was thick with emotion, but she met Bethany's eyes without flinching.

Bethany glared back at her well-meaning but idiotic friend. Playing spirit guide had offered her a measure of peace even as she'd ushered the Lost on to the real thing. Having to do the same for Xenia would assure that Bethany never knew a moment of peace ever again.

But then, she didn't want anyone else to fall to Maia's appetite either. Even if it was her destiny to be a spirit guide, she didn't love the circumstances that made it necessary. "Fine," Bethany said at last, "but I'm the one who'll do the following. You're on telephone duty, got it?"

Xenia's smile was devoid of humor as she offered a thumbs-up. "Got it."

Bethany nodded once and then sped off to the gym. Sure enough, she found Maia inside, amidst her unsuspecting teammates. Unlike Everard, the runner hadn't shown any signs she was aware of Bethany's presence. However, considering the state of her victims' souls, she thought it best to be prudent and assume the monster girl could perceive things beyond the physical. She'd need the same tricks she'd used to tail Everard.

At the end of the day, she stuck to Maia. Xenia, if she knew what was good for her, should already be halfway to Bits 'n' Pieces. Since, as a ghost, she couldn't exactly pick up a phone, it was imperative that Xenia stick to her schedule. Otherwise, Bethany couldn't inform her of any changes on the surveillance front.

With all extracurricular activities canceled, it seemed as if Maia was heading for home. Perfect. Not only would this give her the monster girl's address, but she'd have a chance to snoop around. It might just be the true crime documentaries talking, but she hoped Maia was a trophy taker. A severed ear or bloody sock was just the excuse needed to send the cops in with guns blazing.

"Maia!"

"Aw, shit. Woman, what are you doing?" Bethany muttered as Madison and Courtney hustled after the runner. Madison, when Courtney elbowed her, waved for the runner to wait.

Maia scowled and crossed her arms.

Bethany drifted as close as she dared. With any luck, the trees along the fence would keep Maia from seeing her.

"What do you want, Mads?" Maia made no effort to conceal her distaste for the other girl. "I have to be home by curfew."

Madison rolled her eyes. "That's not for hours."

According to Xenia, Mads had been a wreck just the day before. There was no sign of that now. Mads was back to her usual overcaffeinated self. Only the hint of red about her eyes and nose betrayed her grief.

"Look, Maia." Madison knit her fingers together. "I know we don't get along that well. It's probably my fault..."

Maia snorted.

"Fine! Yes, it's my fault." Madison offered up a tiny shrug. "I don't know why, okay. It's just... whatever." She fanned the air between them, as if she could clear away the bad blood. "Gracie was your friend long before she was mine."

The muscles in Maia's arms jumped as her fingers clamped into her biceps. Some of the severity slipped from her expression, though, and she nodded.

"Even so, she was my friend too."

"And mine." Courtney spoke for the first time. Her voice was toneless, miserable.

"Even if you and I don't get along, Gracie loved every one of us like family. I wish we could have been one big happy bunch just like she wanted. I'm sorry." Madison took a deep breath. It was clear even to Bethany how difficult this was for her. "I'm sorry I got in the way of the friendship Gracie wanted for us."

"Gracie was good like that." Maia's voice cracked.

Madison pushed on. "So, Court and I were thinking—"

"Fuck the curfew!" Courtney stomped her foot. "We're going to hold a vigil for Gracie, candles and everything. Tonight, where she was..." Courtney burst into tears. Madison pulled her close and began to rub her back.

"I was wrong to nag her about being on track." Madison's eyes began to fill, and she blinked hard to clear them. "I can't change what I did, what I said. Can't undo fucking up your relationship with her. All I can do now is try to make amends. With her teammates. With you, Maia. We can get the whole team together, make it a real vigil. We can all say goodbye to Gracie together."

Oh hell no, Bethany thought, *that's a terrible idea! Just offer everyone up on a silver platter, why not?* It took everything she had not to yell at the two stupid but well-meaning teenagers. They wouldn't hear her, but Maia might.

Maia's shoulders slumped and she allowed her arms to fall. Eyes heavy with crocodile tears, she said, "I think Gracie would like that. Thank you, Madison." She held up a hand before the other girl could speak. "Tamarah's been missing for weeks now. They're saying that whoever killed Gracie might have gotten her. I want the vigil to be for her, too."

The balls on this bitch!

Courtney's nod sent her scarlet hair flapping. "Yes, absolutely. She and Gracie were on the team together. It's the right thing to do." She produced a wad of tissues from her purse and blew her nose. "How about nine? That's late enough. No one around to mess things up, right?"

Madison nodded. "Yeah, this is our vigil. The last thing we need are some stupid cops busting it up. Could you"— she turned to Maia—"maybe invite the whole team? You know them better than I do and... I don't think they like me very much."

Maia's lips quirked. "They'll come. We all miss them, so much."

Okay. Maybe this isn't a worst-case thing. Bethany thought the situation over. *As long as everyone stays together, Maia won't go all monster mash. Probably. No, why would she risk it? What if someone got away? Her cover'd be blown. More likely, Murder Bitch'll just follow someone home for dinner afterward. Shit.*

Courtney tugged at Madison's sleeve. They nodded and then made their way to the parking lot. After a few steps, Courtney waved to Maia. Maia, her expression clouded, returned the gesture.

If Bethany hadn't been watching Maia's face, she would have missed it. A look of pure, unfiltered hatred flashed across her face the instant the other girls' backs were turned. There for a fraction of a second, then gone. Swallowed by her mask of grief. "Bitch," Maia whispered. Tears spilled from her eyes. She scrubbed at her face with both hands and then shook her arms out. She reshouldered her backpack and shoved through the gate.

Bethany hung back, keeping to the treetops while she shadowed the monster girl. There was no doubt in her mind that she'd just had a glimpse of the beast lurking within, before the grief returned. That grief might seem genuine, but who knew for sure? If it had been an act, who was it for? As far as Maia had known, she was alone. Was it possible that she actually felt remorse for the lives she'd taken? For the souls she'd torn apart?

Would it have mattered if she did?

Stick to the plan. She'd follow Maia home. The runner would likely, hopefully, stay there until the vigil. Bethany would use that opportunity to tell Xenia what she'd learned from that split-second revelation.

Maia's next victim would be Madison.

Chapter Forty-Four

Time slowed to a snail's pace as Xenia waited on Bethany's return. News of the "Porter Valley Killer" had reached the major media outlets, and Main Street's crowd had dwindled to a trickle. Bits 'n' Pieces was all but empty. The uneasy silence and lingering tension from her argument with Aunt Elspeth hadn't helped the time pass any faster.

"It's just a slow day, dearie, nothing to fret about," Elspeth said as Xenia stared out the front window for the millionth time.

Of course, Xenia had been on the lookout for a certain ghost in knee-high boots and lace, not prospective customers. *Where is she?* Had the monster girl caught her? *Maybe I should— Oh thank God.* Xenia sagged in relief as the ghost dropped into the store. She excused herself to the restroom so she could converse with Bethany without tipping off her great-aunt.

"That's a horrible idea," Xenia said, once she'd learned what Madison and Courtney had planned for the evening. "What the hell are they thinking?"

"That's what I said!" Bethany shook her head. "What do you think, snitch 'em out?"

"You mean call the cops?" Xenia considered the idea. "It might work. Better that they get arrested, or whatever, than torn apart. Then again..." She thumped her knee in frustration. "If the cops show up, a few are bound to panic and run. Then they're out in the dark, alone..."

"And you just know Maia couldn't pass up that opportunity. Right. Plus, they'd just have the vigil again tomorrow night, and we're right back where we started."

"So we stick with Plan A, then."

"I hate that plan," Bethany groused. "It puts you right in the line of fire. Line of teeth? Bah, you know what I mean."

"If you've got a better idea..." Xenia waited, but the ghost indicated that she had nothing to add. "Fine, you stick to Maia. Make sure she doesn't show up, or leave, early. Then, when everyone's getting ready to go, I'll run in and say 'the killer' is chasing me. That'll keep everyone together." At least, Xenia hoped it would. Best case would be everyone piling into one or two cars for the trip home. Based on the palpable dread hanging over the school, the odds were in her favor. Maia had taken pains to keep from compromising her cover. The last thing the monster girl desired would be to out herself before witnesses.

"Okay. I hate it, but I can't think of a better plan," Bethany said.

"Great. Now get out of here, I actually have to pee."

* * *

As the hour of curfew drew near, Aunt Elspeth closed up early. "If no one's seen fit to drop in so far, they'll not be doing it after curfew." No sooner had Elspeth driven them home than Xenia was off and running for her room. "Dinner in an hour, lass," Elspeth called after her.

Once her bedroom door was firmly shut between her and her guardian, Xenia slithered under her bed. Due to the "no magic," clause of her punishment, Aunt Elspeth had confiscated all of Xenia's preternatural paraphernalia. This had included Quentin's folder of spells, as well as Xenia's own notebooks on magic.

Fortunately, Xenia had managed to "overlook" *Bone Weave* when she'd handed the lot over. She'd tucked the spell sheet into the frame of her bed for just this moment.

This time, her second sight gave her no problems. *Bone Weave*'s hologram burst into visibility.

Her headlong flight through the canyon had left her favorite hoodie in tatters. She rooted through the still-unpacked boxes that filled her closet for a replacement and unearthed another, a black one with the store tags still attached. Her preferences ran toward lighter shades, pastels and grays. The black hoodie had been Bethany's idea, but she'd never gotten around to wearing it. Tonight, however, black would do just fine.

Xenia smoothed the fabric flat on her bedsheet and set *Bone Weave*'s instructions beside it. She took a deep breath and attempted to cultivate the calm she required to touch magic. Anxiety—that Aunt Elspeth would come barreling in, that she would fail and Madison would die—was making this more difficult than usual.

Although she failed to achieve anything close to "inner peace," Xenia was at last able to capture the first of the many threads the spell required. Beads of sweat sprang from her brow as she began to loop the glowing threads together.

"Soup's on, lass! Get it while it's piping," Elspeth called

from the kitchen. Xenia ignored the answering growl of her stomach as she wove the final segments of the spell's repeating pattern into the cloth of her hoodie.

Bone Weave's author had designed the spell so that it could be repeated any number of times. That way, it could be applied to objects of any size. Every inch of the hoodie was now armored in overlapping instances of *Bone Weave*. Just as she'd hoped, the fabric's dark hue all but concealed the glyphs that would have otherwise betrayed its presence.

Xenia raced to the kitchen and did her best to smile and nod as she ate. *See? Everything's normal.* Once she'd washed and dried the dishes, Xenia politely turned down Elspeth's invitation of a game of bridge. "Homework," she lied. "Big essay for history class." Even though she was still steaming mad at her punishment, guilt at the deception turned the meal to mud in her belly.

Back upstairs, Xenia packed quickly as she could without alerting her great-aunt. Better shoes, thicker socks. An extra layer under her hoodie to guard against the chill. Into her book bag went a bottle of ibuprofen, the first aid kit from the hall closet, and, even though she knew they were probably of no use, a sachet of St. John's wort blossoms.

The opening beat of "Crosstown Traffic," one of Aunt Elspeth's favorites, thrummed from the sitting room below. Now or never. Xenia tiptoed into the hall and sighed in relief. Elspeth's bedroom door was ajar. If it had been closed, or even locked, she might have lost her nerve right then and there. She hoped that Aunt Elspeth hadn't hidden her magic stuff too well.

Luck was with her. She found her wand among the umbrellas and walking sticks in a metal urn beside the hulking great wardrobe. She slipped it into her satchel, where it didn't quite fit. The bit that stuck out, Xenia decided, would allow her to "quick draw" the wand if needed. She found the dagger, the *sgian-dubh* Aunt Elspeth had given her and then taken back, on the dresser next to the ring she needed to call her wand to her hand. She swept the plastic bauble into her satchel and slipped the knife into her waistband. Just in case.

Xenia sent a silent apology to her guardian and tiptoed through the homey clutter. She eased open the bedroom's French doors and slipped out onto the balcony. Once or twice, she'd joined her great-aunt at the balcony's tiny metal bistro table for a sunrise cup of tea. Dismissing the pleasant memory, she leaned out over the balcony rail.

When she'd worked out the escape plan in her head, the distance from railing to ground hadn't seemed quite so... insurmountable. *Not like you have a choice.* The staircase and front door both lay in clear view of the sitting room. Aunt Elspeth wasn't likely to doze off any time soon, either. At least, not while Hendrix was blaring.

Xenia dropped her satchel over the side and swung her leg up over the rail. She lowered herself over the edge until she was hanging by her fingers. It was a great deal harder to let go than she'd expected. "Don't look down, don't look down," she whispered. The moment she forced her fingers open and gravity took over, Xenia realized she'd failed to verify that her target bush wasn't one of the thorny kind.

Her luck held, and she remained free of unwanted piercings. Xenia stayed low as she scuttled through the side yard. A squealing guitar rose to a fever pitch as she passed the sitting room windows. She held herself in the awkward crouch until she exited the garden gate. A thumb on the latch kept it from rattling when she shut it behind her.

Senses on high alert for curfew enforcement, or the sound of claws on pavement, Xenia broke into a run.

Chapter Forty-Five

"Where are they?" Xenia asked the empty park. Wasn't the vigil supposed to be here? Save for the light of a lone streetlamp and a toenail clipping moon, Postage Square lay in shadow. Absent was any sign that a crowd of candle-wielding teenagers was, or had been, present.

Xenia slammed her fist against her thigh. The run to the park had wasted more time than she'd expected. A patrol car had taken its sweet time cruising the block next to her own. She'd been stuck in the bushes for what had seemed like forever but had been closer to fifteen minutes. The big clock in front of city hall read 9:12. The vigil should have started at nine. They couldn't have wrapped up already, could they? Had the cops rousted them before Xenia had arrived? Madison could already be in danger.

Xenia made a quick circuit of the park, just to be sure. Nothing in the tiny, landscaped square suggested that a vigil had occurred. The only sign of activity was the flutter of yellow crime-scene tape around the fountain where Gracie's body had been discovered.

Winded from her mad dash, Xenia sank onto a park bench. She fished out a bottle of water and cracked it open. *You need to work on your cardio*, she scolded, draining half the bottle in a gulp.

A familiar black, feathered acquaintance fluttered to a landing atop the opposite armrest. The raven's round head bobbed as he settled his wings into place.

"I don't supposed you know where the hell they are?" Xenia waved at the empty park.

A beady eye blinked at her.

"Didn't think so." Xenia bent to stuff the water bottle into her bag.

"Aren't you scared?"

Xenia jumped at the unexpected question. The water bottle went skittering across the pavement. There, on the bench beside her where the raven had been, sat a boy. Her breath caught in her throat as she recognized the round, young face. He wore the same faded black T-shirt, black jeans, and sneakers that he'd worn in the park, and on Main Street. The same face that had been smeared with ice cream now grinned at her in the wan moonlight. His dark eyes sparkled as he met her stare.

"What, no. I mean, yes, a little. I'm just..." Xenia needed a moment for the whirl of her thoughts to slow. When she'd achieved as much calm as she was going to, she faced the boy, or raven, or whatever he truly was. "I just want to help. If I can stop her from hurting anyone else, I will. I'll do whatever it takes."

The boy's smile slipped away. The solemn expression seemed out of place on a face that young. "Sometimes people get hurt, no matter what we do."

Xenia just stared. Anger began to curl through her. "Fuck that! Look, I have no clue what I'm doing. While I appreciate the book, really I do, I'm going into this with-out..." Her fingers carved at the air as she struggled to match the words to her boiling resentment. She yanked her wand from her satchel and willed *Ghost Flame* alight. "A fire that doesn't burn. A magic key. Ooh, scary. Totally what I need to fight a giant monster." The cobalt flame guttered out as she shoved the wand back into her bag.

"Would you abandon it, then?"

"What, magic?"

The boy nodded. "If giving up magic meant that you were free of what was to come, would you part with it?"

"In a heartbeat!" If it meant she never had to face down Maia's bestial alter ego, never had to experience again the fear that had almost paralyzed her in the canyon, never had to see another ghost wearing the wounds that had killed them...

She would never see Bethany again.

"Even if the price of your sanctuary were the deaths to come, tonight and every night after?" The young face sorrowed as he gazed up at the sliver moon. "You would trade every soul in this valley, and beyond, for your happiness?" He turned to regard her. The movement of his head was abrupt, avian.

Bile burned the back of her throat as the boy's words sank in. *It won't stop with Madison's death. It's only going to get worse after tonight.* She allowed her head to fall. "Mom and Dad raised me better than that. What would they think, if I let that happen?" A lone teardrop slid from her eye, hung at the tip of her nose. She scrubbed it away. "I don't want that. If I can save Madison and Courtney and all their friends, I will. Even if I don't have the slightest clue how to do it."

The boy's raucous laughter came out of nowhere. He

met her glare with his wide, gap-toothed smile. "You already have everything you need, Xenia." He tapped his temple with a chubby finger.

Xenia shook her head in disbelief. "Sure."

The boy pursed his lips and, for a moment, appeared lost in thought. Eyes distant, he clambered to his feet atop the bench. One hand came to rest on his chest, fingers tented over his breastbone. His half-lidded eyes gazed at a point somewhere above Xenia's head. He took a deep breath and then began to sing.

Whatever language the boy gave voice to, it was nothing Xenia had ever heard in her life. And yet the words were familiar. Hauntingly so. Somehow, somewhere, she'd heard them before. Without understanding how she could possibly know its meaning, the song's message unfolded from the depth of her memories.

In those times, in those distant times.

Those ancient nights, those far-off years.

Amatuanki, the Divine Mother, gave birth to the Heavens above and the Earth below. About them all, there was the Eternal Sea.

Great was she, Mother of All. Goddess of Goddesses. Highest and most exalted firstborn of The One.

How could she have forgotten that dream? It had been weeks since her nightmare had last plagued her and forced her to relive the night of the accident. The weird dream about the old man at the fire pit had replaced it. Despite that, she hadn't recalled any of it until the boy's song called it from the depths of her memory.

Her mind raced ahead of the boy, to the very end of Uncle's tale. Ice slithered down her spine. How could she possibly fight *that*?

"Zee! What the heck are you doing here?"

Bethany's voice snapped Xenia from her reverie. She turned as the ghost raced through the air toward her. "He was just..."

The bench beside her was empty.

"Of course," Xenia muttered. Belatedly, now that she'd missed her chance, she realized she should have examined the raven-sometimes-boy with her second sight. *Dang it.* She waved at the snarl of crime-scene tape. "You said the vigil was here, where Gracie was killed."

"No, I said it was at the school! Where the track team practices? Gracie was going to rejoin the team?" Bethany urged Xenia into motion with a wave of her lace-gloved hands. "The vigil is very nice, very respectful. Everyone's getting along. A little bit of singing, a lot of crying. Now get moving. They were close to wrapping up when I left to look for you!"

Xenia slung her bag over her shoulder and scanned the sky above for the raven. Nothing. She shook her head and ran. Toward the school. Toward Maia and a battle she had no hope of winning.

Chapter Forty-Six

Xenia staggered to a halt before Porter Valley High's front entrance. She braced her hands against her knees and focused on dragging in one ragged breath after another. The pair of windows in the belfry tower, lit from within, glared down at her in disapproval.

She'd planned to enter via the side gate, to catch anyone leaving early. Instead, caution had sent her around to the school's front.

When she could at last breathe, she began to mount the long staircase to the triple doors. *Lockbreaker* would grant her entry, and she'd approach the vigil from the lunchroom. Only, one of the doors was already ajar. Had they moved the vigil inside for some reason?

Xenia dug in her satchel for her ring and slipped it onto her hand, just in case. "I'll go in this way." She nodded at the open door. "You go over the top. If they're already leaving, or you see Maia trying to get someone off alone, raise a ruckus."

"A ruckus?" Despite the gravity of their situation, Bethany grinned.

"Whatever." Xenia proffered her fist.

Bethany bumped her phantom knuckles to Xenia's. She gave a jaunty wave and then arrowed toward the belfry's crenelated top.

Xenia gripped the base of her wand and climbed the remainder of the wide, concrete staircase. She froze, one foot still in the air, as the coppery tang of blood hit her. "Oh crap." Whoever had opened the door had used a white athletic shoe to keep it ajar.

The shoe was not empty.

A ragged stump jutted from the high-top. Bone gleamed at the center of the raw, shredded meat. Xenia fought to keep her dinner inside her as she whispered, "Beebs! Bethany, get down here!"

The ghost descended from her belfry perch. "What's up —Oh *fuck!*"

"We're too late," Xenia moaned. "She's already killed Madison. If only I'd—" She yanked the door open and then jumped away as the severed foot tumbled toward her. Inside, in a heap next to a wide pool of blood, was the foot's former owner. "That's not Madison."

The boy, one of Maia's teammates, had been ripped from belt to throat. Most of his insides were now splashed across the school's trophy case. Both legs were severed mid-shin, but only the foot used as a doorstop was visible. The other one was nowhere to be seen.

A random thought: *I should have put* Bone Weave *on my jeans, too.*

"Okay that's it. You're out of here, Zee. Go get—"

"Fuck that." Xenia sent a silent apology to the boy she had failed to save. She drew her wand. The hallway ahead was dark, much darker than it should have been. When she'd snuck in to return Maia's shirt, there had been night lighting. Now, even the tiny red lights in the smoke alarms were out. Xenia willed *Ghost Flame* to life and sent it on ahead to light the way.

"Let me go first," Bethany said. "We don't know where she's lurking."

"Oh, I think Maia's way past lurking now, Beebs."

Another body, a girl Xenia didn't recognize, lay crumpled at the center of an intersection between hallways. A fresh candle, the base wrapped in foil, was still clutched in her hand. A few feet beyond that, the custodial cart waited in the center of the hall. Xenia instantly regretted her peek into the trash receptacle. The emptied eye sockets of the custodian's severed head were there to greet her.

Anger shouldered her fear aside. The ember of rage that had been kindled in the aftermath of Ev's manipulations now burned hot and bright in her gut. Whatever guilt she would no doubt feel over her failure to save these latest victims, she could wallow in it tomorrow. If there was a tomorrow for her. Right now, the goal was to stop Maia before she killed everyone.

While Xenia wrestled with her inner turmoil, Bethany had drifted on. The ghost stopped and then stuck her head through the wall. She raced to Xenia's side. "Zee!" she whispered. "Survivors! In the counselor's office!"

Relief crashed through her. She wasn't too late after all! She raced to the counselor's office. The door handle was twisted, crushed into the jamb with monstrous force. *Saving them for later? Or are they bait?* Not that it would stop her from getting them to safety. "Watch my back."

She wasn't sure if *Lockbreaker* would work, given that the doorknob and lock were ruined. Well, it'd worked fine on Aunt Elspeth's trunk, hadn't it? She poked the door with her wand. The *scree* of metal scraping metal echoed down the hallway. When it ended, the door popped open.

Xenia paused, one hand on the knob. Quentin's written admonition to keep her secrets close echoed through her head. She tugged her hood up and set *Ghost Flame* just behind her shoulder, where it would cast her face in shadow. She yanked the door open.

"Get the fuck back!"

Xenia skipped away as a tall boy in the school's track uniform jabbed at her with a chair. His wide eyes darted to *Ghost Flame*, then to her wand, every inch of which was covered in arcane glyphs. His shoulders sagged and he lowered the chair. "It's not her," he called out, then, to Xenia, "How'd you get the door open? She did something to the lock. Told us to wait until she came for us." He shuddered. Behind him, three girls, also in their track outfits, and a younger boy in a black button-up peeked from behind the counselor's desk.

"Who's that?" asked the boy in the button-up.

Xenia ignored the question. "Did any of you call for help?"

One girl raised her phone. "I can't get any bars."

"And this one's dead," said another. She jiggled the desk phone's receiver.

"Get out of here." Xenia backed out of the office and pointed her wand down the hall. "Don't stop, don't look around. Just run. Go as far as you can, then call the cops. Tell them they need to send everything they have. The SWAT team, if Porter Valley even has one." It would take every gun in Humboldt County to take down Maia. Even with that, she had her doubts.

"Thank you," said the boy who'd tried to stave off a

monster with an office chair. He stepped aside to allow the other survivors to slip into the hall.

The younger boy stopped in front of Xenia. His pale face gleamed in *Ghost Flame*'s light. "Is that magic?" he asked, eyes wide with wonder.

Xenia put a finger over her lips. "Shhh."

The boy solemnly mirrored the gesture, then nodded. One of the girls grabbed his hand, and the two of them ran after the rest. Xenia was glad to see her cover the boy's eyes as they passed the human wreckage by the exit.

"Think they'll make it?" asked Bethany.

"They have to." Someone had to survive. Otherwise... Xenia couldn't finish the thought. She sent the tiny blue flame ahead as she resumed her march. In the lunchroom, she found another pool of blood, but no body. Crimson smears trailed across the floor to the rear exit.

A scream cut through the night air, and Xenia broke into a run. Words followed the outburst, too garbled to make out. Xenia shoulder-slammed through the lunchroom exit just as the speaker's terrified words ended in a wet gurgle.

"*Maia!*" Xenia bellowed. "Stop! Let her—what the fuck?" She tripped over her own feet as she tried to process the tableau before her.

What little remained of the candlelight vigil lay crumpled in a circle at the center of the lacrosse field. Eight bodies, maybe more, had been arranged as if on display. Only, Maia wasn't the one who stood triumphant at the heart of that carnage.

It was Madison.

Madison, who even now held her own best friend aloft, hand clamped about Courtney's throat. Madison, who'd thrust her other arm elbow deep into Courtney's abdomen. A waterfall of scarlet poured from that obscene junction.

For one horrible moment, Courtney's pleading eyes met Xenia's. Blood bubbled from her lips as she begged Xenia to save her. Before the would-be magical girl could move a muscle, the light left Courtney's eyes. Her arms fell to her sides as her struggles ceased.

Madison released her grip and allowed her former friend to crumple at her feet. As the body fell, there was a nasty, wet tearing as it slid from Madison's arm. When her hand emerged, she held Courtney's heart clutched in her grasp.

Madison's lips parted to reveal a shark's mouth of jagged metal teeth. There was a faint crackle as her jaw stretched wider than humanly possible. She devoured the heart in two swift bites.

Xenia doubled over as her guts rebelled. Vomit burned its way through her throat and stung her nasal passages as she emptied her stomach. She staggered to her feet and dragged a sleeve across her mouth.

Madison hauled another body from the ground and raised it into the air with her hand about their throat.

Maia!

The runner groaned. Even though she was taller by a good two inches, in Madison's clutches her feet had left the ground. Maia's eyelids fluttered as she fought to regain consciousness.

Maia's still alive! Not only that, Xenia had been wrong, *again*. Maia wasn't the killer. She really had only been out for a run that night. Her presence at the gas station had been coincidence, nothing more. It had been Madison who'd chased Xenia through the canyon.

No matter. As long as Madison stayed in this mostly human shape, Xenia had a chance. Her spells might be enough to keep Maia alive until the police arrived.

"Oh good," Madison's voice rose in a malignant purr. "Another guest for my coming-out party." Her head lolled on a neck gone inhumanly boneless. She grinned through a smear of blood. Her eyes twitched to the space above Xenia. "Your plus one is a dead girl? How gauche."

"Aw, shit," muttered Bethany.

"I wanted to save this one"—she shook Maia—"for dessert. But now, I think it would be more fun to watch your face while I devour everything she has to offer. *You* can be dessert."

"Why? Madison, why are you doing this?" *Stall for time*, Xenia thought, *force her to drop Maia*.

Madison stroked Maia's face with her free hand. The gesture left the girl's skin streaked with gore. When she looked to Xenia, the glint in her eyes doubled, then doubled again. The space between her eyelids became a window into a void, within which shone an infinity of starlight. At the center of each eye, where her pupils had been, were two brighter stars. Madison raised her bloody hand, fingers bent. Her fingernails, already far too long and impossibly sharp, cracked and splintered as blades of dark metal burst from the flesh of her fingertips. "Let me show you why." She raised her clawed hand to strike Maia's face from her skull.

"No thank you." Xenia leveled her wand, aligned it with the Madison-thing's face. *Gale Hammer* sent the chunk of wood hurtling into that jagged smirk. *Two left,* she counted. She'd only set four charges of the spell on her wand. There'd been no time to replace the one she'd expended while showing off for Aunt Elspeth.

She'd either caught the monster girl off guard, or Madison was too arrogant to dodge. A hollow *thunk* sounded as the two feet of ash wood impacted her skull. Madison's head snapped back as the wand pinwheeled off into the night. She went over backward, dropping Maia as she fell. A reedy, keening sound echoed over the field as she cradled the ruin of her face.

Xenia rushed to Maia's side, offering silent apologies to each of the fallen, especially Courtney, she passed. She couldn't save them, but she'd be damned if she'd let Madison finish the job. She hauled Maia's arm across her shoulders. When she tried to stand, she nearly pitched over into the gory mud. Maia was *heavy*.

"Get her out of here," Bethany said from above. "I'll distract She-Beast long enough for the cavalry to arrive."

"Beebs, you're not safe!" Xenia almost tripped as Maia staggered. The runner caught her balance, then took her weight from Xenia's shoulders. "You saw what she did to the others! Besides, you can't touch her!"

"She doesn't know that!" Bethany whispered in Xenia's ear. "I'm fast and, if I have to, I can dive underground. Now *go!*" The ghost ended the argument by flinging herself at Madison, who was even now rising to her feet. "Back the fuck off!"

Madison backpedaled. There was no sign, now, of the damage Xenia's wand had inflicted. The monster girl's lips twisted in a bestial snarl as she spun to keep the ghost in sight.

Encouraged by Madison's flinch, Bethany began to loop and dart about her. Untethered by gravity, she evaded Madison's claws with ease. Even as a second set of blades burst from the creature's other hand, Bethany's face shone with a fierce grin. She ducked and weaved as she lured Madison away from Xenia and Maia.

"You with me?" Xenia asked. Maia gave a weak nod. She slung the runner's arm over her shoulders again; together, the two made their way toward the nearest gate.

With each step, Maia's strength returned. As their exit drew near, she no longer relied on Xenia to stay upright. Still, her arm lingered on the magical girl's shoulders.

"How'd you pull that off?" Maia asked. "The stick to the face thing, I mean."

"What, my wand?" Xenia couldn't keep the dizzy grin from her face. She snapped her fingers, and her wand leapt out of the darkness. Without taking her eyes from Maia, she snatched it out of the air. "It's just magic. No big."

Maia's jaw dropped. "It was you—"

Bethany's piercing shriek turned Xenia's blood to ice: "*ZEE!*"

Chapter Forty-Seven

Xenia spun as another shriek tore through the night. At the center of the field, Madison spread her arms wide. Her shark mouth hung open, eager. Something glimmering clung to one hand. She brought her claws to her mouth and lapped at the glowing substance with a long, dark tongue.

Bethany had retreated high above the field, out of the Madison-thing's reach, her face twisted in agony. The wobbling path of her flight made it clear that something was very wrong. A trail of glowing flecks, the same substance as on Madison's claws, streamed from the ruin of her knee.

"Oh shit," Maia said. "She hurt your ghost friend."

"Beebs? *Bethany!*" Xenia hurled herself across the grass. *Can't lose her, not again!*

Up close, the wound in Bethany's leg was even worse than she'd first thought. Madison's iron claws had torn a rent in whatever it was ghosts were made of. Sparks fizzled from the wound as it burned itself larger, like paper touched to a flame.

Bethany gasped as she pawed at the laceration. Her

efforts to stanch the smoldering edges were in vain as her hands passed through. She was as insubstantial to herself as she was to everything else. The wound's frayed edge crumbled. Larger chunks of ghost matter tumbled away as the decay accelerated.

Through Bethany's transparent form, Xenia spotted Madison. The monster girl spread her bladed hands wide as she stalked across the grass toward them both. Xenia's lip curled in a snarl. *Gale Hammer* sent her wand rocketing into the monster girl's gut. Quick as her reflexes might be, the wand struck Madison on the hip with enough force to send her spinning away.

Xenia returned her attention to Bethany as her entire leg below the knee collapsed into a shower of spectral embers. One by one, the dancing points of light winked out. The wound continued its smoldering climb through the matter of Bethany's thigh.

"I'm scared, Zee," Bethany sobbed. "It's not supposed to hurt now. Why does it hurt so much?"

Panic had Xenia's heart thundering in her chest. She did the only thing she could think of and summoned her second sight. Ignoring the blaze of magic about her, she narrowed her focus on Bethany. In the same manner that she grasped the strands of magic, Xenia took hold of the wound in Bethany's leg.

The ghost shrieked as Xenia worked to seal the rupture. "Sorry, sorry," Xenia cried. But no matter how she pressed or pinched at the ever-expanding lesion, she could not halt its progression. "It's not working! Why isn't it working?" She fell back in horror as a portion of Bethany's leg came away in her grasp. In a heartbeat, the fragment had sizzled away into nothing.

"I'm dying, Zee," Bethany gasped. "For real this time."

Her eyes, saucer wide, met Xenia's. "I'm sorry. Looks like I won't be keeping that BFFFF promise after all."

"No! Shut up! You're not, you *can't!*" The scar that Bethany's first death had left in Xenia's heart ripped itself wide open. There was still so much she wanted, needed to say to her. She'd assumed, like a fool, that her return had given them all the time in the world.

The color had gone from Bethany's phantom skin, her spectral attire. Just like Sal and the others, she was a pallid shadow of herself. The wound had burned its way into her abdomen now. "It's okay, Xenia. I'll always—" Whatever assurance she'd been about to offer went unvoiced as, all at once, Bethany came apart in a rush of glittering embers.

"*Bethany!*" Xenia grasped at the swirling cloud, all that remained of her best friend. One by one, the tiny motes of light winked out, until only a single spark remained. Xenia cupped her hands about that point of light. She brought her hands to her chest and focused with everything she had.

A white-hot needle lanced into the flesh at the base of her left thumb. Xenia peered through a curtain of tears. There, where the last of Bethany had guttered out, was a tiny scar. Xenia raised her palm to her lips long enough to whisper, "Love you, Bethany."

"How sweet."

Madison's guttural voice was her only warning. With no more than an instant to spare, Xenia caught the iron-dark claws on the spelled fabric of her hoodie before they could strike her head from her neck.

To her eternal gratitude, *Bone Weave* held. Madison's claws glanced from Xenia's sleeve with a nails-on-chalkboard *scree*. But while the spell fulfilled its promise to turn the blades, it did nothing to dissipate the force of impact.

A flare of pain joined the damp-wood *crack* from within

her left arm. One, or both, of the bones were broken again. She curled around her re-injured arm as the blow sent her reeling across the grass. Strong hands arrested her tumble. Maia steadied her until her head stopped spinning.

"Sorry," Maia said. "Bitch Prime caught me off guard. Sucker-punched me." She rubbed the massive shiner about her eye. "I'm sorry about your friend. Bethany? She seemed pretty cool."

"The coolest."

Maia patted Xenia's shoulder and then stepped away. She braced a hand against the opposite shoulder, then worked to stretch the joint. As she repeated the move with her other arm, she scowled at the scattered bodies. "She had to take me out first. I would've stopped her cold before she did this. Payback's all I've got left, now." Maia shook her head. "Keep her off balance with your magic. I'm going to wreck her shit."

Xenia blinked. "W-what?"

Maia shot her an amused look. "You thought you were the only one with a little magic?" Between one blink and the next, her pupils stretched to vertical lines. Blue, shot through with quicksilver, filled her eyes.

Xenia fell onto her ass. Cradling her broken arm, she scooted across the grass.

In one smooth motion, all at once, Maia changed.

She was already the tallest girl Xenia knew. Now she towered seven or more feet in height. Her hair burst from its braid even as it flushed from walnut brown to a deep, metallic blue. A pair of horns rose from within the mass of beryl hair, curved from the edge of her brow up over her elongated skull to razor points. The lean, runner's musculature swelled, filled out until it would put a powerlifter to shame. Each major joint was now armored by heavy, overlapping scales. The bony plates gleamed with a nacreous, pearlescent sheen. Short, wicked claws gleamed platinum at the tip of each finger, and larger cousins curled from each toe. A fine patina of scales covered every inch not protected by the armored bone. A tail, its upper curve ridged in jagged, pearly plates and ending in a serrated spike, lashed the air behind her.

Maia's face had become something between a predator's muzzle and her human visage. The long jaw held row after row of daggered teeth, the longest of which overlapped in front. While the delicate tracery of scales shone in hues of pearl and alabaster, a pattern of whorls and lines in a deep indigo graced her chin and throat. The design flowed across her neck to disappear beneath the collar of her distended spandex top.

Xenia gaped. She'd been wrong, doubly so. "It... it was you." Even as Madison staggered to her feet across the field of bodies, Xenia could not tear her eyes from Maia's transformation. Both teens had concealed an inner self from the world, from Xenia, but they were nothing alike. Madison was a nightmare of shark's teeth and gore-soaked claws, a perversion of her once lovely appearance. A monster in truth.

Maia, though... Xenia blinked as the light of the crescent moon danced across the iridescent, reptilian form. Maia's transformation might have been more startling, and had left little of her human self visible, but Maia was...

Maia was magnificent. Beautiful.

"Hey." The rumble was still Maia's voice, even if the bass undertone rattled Xenia's teeth. "For the record, I wouldn't have hurt you, the other night. I was tracking a blood scent. You took me off guard with that light thing. I mean, until Mads went all Hellraiser, I thought *you* killed

Everard. Blew him up or something. That's why I've been avoiding you."

"What?" Xenia voice climbed an octave. "Me?" She tried to stand, only to sit down hard as a stab of pain from her arm sent her off balance.

An enormous, clawed hand filled Xenia's vision. She only hesitated a moment before she took it. Xenia marveled at how soft those scales were. Smooth, too, like silk warmed in the summer sun. With no effort at all, Maia drew her to her feet.

Madison's claws clattered in mocking applause. "So very sweet," she gurgled. "I knew there was something in your scent, Maia. I had no idea it could be this glorious, though. You will be so much more delicious, now that your power has come out to play." As she spoke, the growl of her voice gained an odd harmonic. It was as if another spoke with her, voicing the same words, but not quite in the same cadence.

A deep growl throbbed from Maia's chest. "Not gonna happen." The glow of her eyes found Xenia's. "She killed my friends, and yours."

"She killed Salvatore. Everyone who's gone missing over the last year. It was her."

The cobalt glare of Maia's eyes narrowed. "She dies. Right now." Her spiked tail thrashed behind her. "If you can't handle that..."

Xenia regarded the new scar on the palm of her hand and then slipped her injured arm into her hoodie's front pocket. As slings went, it left a lot to be desired, but it'd do. A snap of her fingers brought her wand arcing to her good hand. A thought set *Ghost Flame* burning above her left shoulder. "No," she said at last. "I'm good with that."

"Well," Madison said in her strange, dual voice, "since

you're both showing off, why don't I?" She bent, the movement sudden, convulsive. The flesh beneath her skin writhed as her muscles appeared to twine about each other. Her spine curved as a spasm bent her over backward, then forward again.

For an instant, before her face vanished behind the sweep of her hair, Madison's eyes were suddenly, unexpectedly, human. Fear shone in her face. When she spoke, it was without that unnatural dual timbre. "Maia? What's happening?" asked the terrified teen.

Another wave of spasms sent Madison to her hands and knees in the bloody grass. Her back arched, the bones of her spine prominent through skin pulled taut. The fabric of her dress parted under the strain. Her flesh too gave way with an unclean, wet tearing.

Xenia's feet, of their own volition, carried her a step, then another, away from the obscene spectacle. A mass, dark and pulsing, heaved itself free of Madison's ruptured back. At Xenia's side, Maia matched her step for step.

At first, Xenia had thought that, like Maia, Madison would transform herself. Instead, the evil lurking within had chosen to shed the girl entirely. As more and more of the obsidian form extricated itself, it became clear that there was so much more of it than should have ever fit within Madison's slender frame.

Chapter Forty-Eight

As the creature liberated itself, it unfolded. When the last of it was free, it towered over the lacrosse field. All that remained of Madison, little more than an empty sack of skin, lay crumpled on the grass.

Xenia couldn't begin to guess at the segmented creature's size. Each section was half as long as she was tall. She tried to tally how many there were but, as the body began to writhe, she lost count at fifteen. Black chiton armored the body, and a pair of jointed limbs, each ending in a wicked spike, sprouted from each segment. Twin spikes, bladed along their inner edge, thrust from the terminal end. They scissored together with a flat, metallic *clack*.

Four segments reared from the ground, counterbalanced by the long body. Atop that arthropodal pillar was an all-too-human, and disturbingly feminine, torso. Here, the ebony chiton was shot through with veins of silver and overlapped at shoulder and waist. A grievous wound, only partially healed, disfigured the left side of that torso. Rent as if by some great impact, the armor was split from shoulder to waist. The flesh within that breach was, if anything, darker than the jet of its armor. Nor had the injury spared the creature's face. From jaw to hairline, it had been laid open to the bone. The exposed socket now served as a wider portal to the same sea of stars that were its eyes.

Despite the severity of the damage, the face gazing down at them was still exquisite, inhumanly so. Despite herself, Xenia was saddened that such an affront had been visited upon that beauty.

A circlet of pure silver rode the creature's brow. Simple in form, the unadorned sweep of metal was complete save for a gap above the bridge of that perfect nose. From each end, twin arcs of metal rose. Waxing and waning crescents about an empty circle.

As the creature reared high above the field, the waning moon broke through the clouds. Xenia's breath caught in her throat as it opened like an eye, bathing all of Porter Valley in the glow of an unnatural full moon.

As Xenia wrestled with the fear threatening to freeze her in place, she reached for her second sight. The field, the trees and mountains beyond, glowed with the natural magic that she'd come to expect. The thing that had pulled itself from Madison's shell, however...

Every living thing that Xenia had examined with her magical sight had burned with an inner, opaline fire that represented, she assumed, the fire of their life or spirit. At her side, Maia blazed in hues of pear and cyan, too intense for her to view straight on. In sharp contrast, the creature before her was a void. That ebon armor drank in, or concealed, any hint of the fire that should have shone within.

More disturbing was the ambient magic's reaction to its presence. Each nearby ribbon and thread had become snagged, tangled about the spines of its armor. As it moved, more and more of the local magic was drawn in, wound tight about its form. If Xenia was a rock in the stream of magic, this thing was a nettle. A briar that captured all it could reach. As the flow of magic came in contact with the surface, it was absorbed.

"Still think we can take her?" Xenia asked. She'd had her doubts while it was still Madison sized. How the hell could they possible defeat this? Why couldn't Quentin have put some real magic in his notes? She'd give anything for a fireball or lightning bolt right now.

"Sure," Maia said, though her voice lacked the confidence of her words. "No sweat. We got this."

"Foolish children." Nothing of Madison remained in that resonant, honeyed contralto. Nor had it spoken English. The spill of liquid, alien syllables forced their meaning into Xenia's awareness. "Why resist the inevitable? The power that ye hast stolen, I shall reclaim. So, too, shall I retake my throne. Such is the shape of destiny."

Corded muscles tensed beneath the scales of Maia's leg. "Stolen? Fuck you. I was born with this. Watch my back," she added to Xenia. Sod exploded from clawed feet as she threw herself at the creature. Platinum claws struck sparks of jet and quicksilver from ebon armor as the creature deflected the blow with its arm.

Xenia tugged the spelled fabric of her hoodie up about her face, even though she knew it offered little protection. While *Bone Weave* would stop those claws, any blow from that creature would reduce her to pulp.

The segmented body twined through the grass. Insectile feet churned the body of a fallen student to crimson mud as the creature and Maia circled one another. Each of Maia's attacks was deflected or dodged as it cut a sinuous curve across the field. Dark teeth glinted in the half ruin of its face.

Is that thing having fun? The battle shifted her way, and Xenia had to break into a run to avoid being trampled.

Now it was the creature's turn to press the attack. Maia bobbed and weaved like a prizefighter as she evaded slash after slash. To Xenia's eye, despite the size difference, they seemed to be a match for each other. Neither could land a decisive blow.

That is, until the creature fell back, the legs on each segment twisting in their sockets to carry the tail forward in a strike from below. The bladed tail snapped shut and Maia, off-guard, was caught. The pincer's edges, sharp as knapped flint, bit through Maia's armor. Her blood was as red as Xenia's against the pearl of her scales. Her roar of pain was half beast, half her own voice. She scrabbled at the blades, but the chiton, slick with her blood, offered no purchase.

The creature chuckled low in its throat. The long body flexed, drawing Maia in close. "Lament not, little godling. This power was never meant for such as thyself. It only returns, at long last, whence it came. Fear not, thou shall not be forgotten. Thy legacy is no less than the restoration of mine own dynasty." Again, the words forced their meaning into Xenia's mind. She ran sideways, desperate for an opening

Maia grunted in pain as the pincers bit another inch deeper. She hammered and pried at the tail but was unable to break its grip. The arthropod body began to wind itself about her while the creature tapped its chin in thought. No doubt deliberating which morsel to sample first.

There! In restraining Maia, the creature had twisted. The gap in the human torso's armor had flexed wide. Xenia spent a handful of heartbeats to align her wand before she triggered *Gale Hammer*'s final charge.

Twenty-four inches of ash wood slammed through the gap in the armor with all the force of a hurricane.

Its shriek of agony was loud enough to strip the paint from a car. The segmented tail convulsed, flinging Maia across the field. She tumbled head over actual tail until the cinder block wall of the gym arrested her flight.

The thing that had been Madison writhed, twisting like a worm under a magnifying glass. In seconds, the long body had wound itself into a protective knot about the humanoid torso.

Xenia kept her distance as she circled the squirming mass of spines and armor. She found Maia slumped beneath a pile of shattered cinder block, halfway through the gym wall.

She'd only managed to pull a few bricks away before the inhuman shrieking ceased. She turned in time to see the knotted body uncoil like a spring. In half a heartbeat, the exquisite ruin of the creature's face was inches from her own. It seized her shoulders, then rose to its full flight. She gasped as her weight hung from its grip and her broken arm objected to the motion.

Below the human torso, a segment twisted to bring a jointed leg forward. A shiver ran through the chiton, and the needle end split into a wicked pincer. But rather than slicing into her belly, it gripped the wand protruding from the creature's abdomen. With a delicacy belied by its appearance, the pincer extracted the length of ash. With the help of another limb, it turned her wand end over end. The sea of stars that passed for the thing's eyes examined Xenia's handiwork.

The scarred face rose to regard Xenia. The sole eyelid

blinked once. "This is thy craft? Speak true, child." Below, the segmented limb waggled her wand.

From their appearance, Xenia had expected the armored hands to be rough, abrasive, and unpleasant to the touch. Instead, while the grip was unyielding, its hands were warm, its touch oddly comforting. Too reminiscent, by far, of her own mother's hands. "Yes," she answered, when she found her voice. "That's my wand. I made it." She met that starry gaze and tried like hell not to flinch.

Midnight hair spilled across the silver of its crown as the creature tilted its head. From head to toe, it examined first Xenia and then the azure flame that burned above her shoulder. "It is indeed. Is it not?" As the pinprick stars in its eyes bored into Xenia's, pressure began to mount at the center of her skull. The sensation was deeply unpleasant, and somehow familiar. It was the same mental influence Everard had used, albeit without the sugar coating. Where the changeling had used his abilities as a candied battering ram to get his way, this creature exerted its will with subtlety yet with an infinitude of power beyond anything the changeling had been capable of.

Xenia strained against the intrusion even as she recognized her willpower was less than an ice cube in a volcano before that power. If the creature had desired, it would have already crushed her mind like a bug.

"Serve, thou wilt, in another fashion," the creature declared. "When I have reclaimed the godling's stolen power, I will have the strength to make my presence known anew. Thou shalt be the herald of my return, as the first and most high Thearch of my temple. Tis true thou art too young for the role of Grandmother, but it matters not. Mine own need is paramount. Thou shall learn at *Bēlet Kaššāpāti*'s knee, where the true magics of the world shall be revealed. No need wilt thou have for these petty trinkets." The grasping limb twitched, and Xenia's wand sailed off into the night. Above her shoulder, *Ghost Flame* guttered out.

The pressure within her skull redoubled. The name, *Bēlet Kaššāpāti*, echoed through the halls of her mind. A distant memory, from a dream half remembered, suggested that *Bēlet Kaššāpāti*, Lady of Sorcery, was the secret name of *Bēlet An-Ĝíg,* the Lady of Black Sky.

"Through me, thou shall move mountains. Through me, thou shall topple empires." The intact half of her mouth curved into a smile. "I shall even tutor thee in the means, if thou ask it of me, by which thy *gidim*, thy ghost servant, might be restored."

The promise of magic, of power beyond anything she might have learned on her own, had not tempted her. Accepting that offer, Xenia knew, meant abandoning Maia to *Bēlet Kaššāpāti*'s appetite. Saving Bethany, on the other hand, had blindsided her. *Restore? She's not gone for good? She can be brought back? To life?*

A pinprick of cold fire pulsed in the palm of her left hand. Even if she accepted and became this "Thearch" and brought her back, Bethany would never forgive her. Not after everything this creature, this *Bēlet Kaššāpāti*, had already done.

No. If Bethany could be saved, if it was at all possible, then she would discover the means to do it on her own.

Even as she made her decision, the nature of *Bēlet Kaššāpāti*'s presence in her mind changed. The rhythm of her heart began to slow. Her limbs grew heavy, and the darkness of the night sky gained new depth, new detail. Pain flared in her broken arm as she clenched her hands. She focused on that pain, using it to form a barrier between herself and whatever change the Lady of Sorcery had in store for her.

"Come now, child. Even my sister's Gilded Champion failed to oppose my will. What hope hast thou? Submit, thou shall, and gladly."

Gilded Champion. In the back of her mind, a boy's piping voice: *You already have everything you need, Xenia.*

"Even if you kept your promise, taught me how to bring Bethany back, how could I live with myself?" Xenia forced her words to the forefront of her mind even as she fought not to remember. "How many other kids did you tear apart? How many more will die after tonight?" She rubbed her hands together as if to banish the creeping cold, and used the motion to elicit another spike of clarifying pain from her arm.

The beautiful, horrible face shook in disappointment. "Tsk. The potential of years unspent, the vigor of battles-not-yet-fought, were all required to rouse me from my torpor. Such a small sacrifice indeed for my greater glory. Their memory will be honored for all time, within my temple. The temple that thou shall build, child."

Xenia shivered, and not just from the cold the Lady of Sorcery had set into her flesh. The taste of hot pennies flooded her mouth as her chattering teeth caught the edge of her tongue. "Hard pass," she snarled through the tremble of her jaw. Xenia twisted until her hand closed about the hilt of the *sgian-dubh* sheathed at the small of her back. Pinned as she was, she couldn't muster the leverage she wanted. The bones of her arm screamed as she jammed the blade into the creature's undamaged eye.

A scream, impossibly loud, battered Xenia's eardrums. Distracted by the knife in her eye, *Bēlet Kaššāpāti* had ceased her assault on Xenia's mind. Xenia braced her good hand against that armored chest and pushed with everything she had as the grip on her shoulders faltered. For a moment, she feared those hands would tear her in half before she could break free. She levered a leg up to add its strength to her push.

The fingers of her right hand caught in the fissure marring *Bēlet Kaššāpāti's* armor. As she tumbled free, her ring snagged within and was pulled from her finger.

The grass offered little cushion to her fractured arm, and her cry of agony joined that of the fallen goddess. She shoved herself across the slick grass with her feet until she was clear. Her head throbbed as she staggered to her feet. As she stumbled to Maia's side, the unnatural cold winnowing its way into her limbs faded until all that remained was the ordinary chill of night air.

"Maia!" Xenia slipped her injured arm into her hoodie pocket again as she jogged the beast girl's shoulder with her foot. "Get up! I have a plan, but it won't work without your help!"

"Five minutes, Dad," mumbled Maia. "Promise I won't be late again..." Scaled eyelids fluttered. Slitted pupils narrowed into focus. "Whuhappend?"

Xenia hopped away from the spiked tail to avoid collateral damage as Maia levered herself upright. A clawed hand touched an armored side and came away scarlet. "I'll heal, don't worry about it," Maia said. "What'd I miss?"

Xenia glanced to the writhing goddess at the center of the field. "I might know a way to kill that thing, once and for all."

"How the hell do you know that?" Maia favored Xenia with a bit of reptilian side-eye.

"A little bird told me. Look, I need to find my wand. She threw it over there somewhere." Xenia nodded at *Bēlet*

Kaššāpāti. "I need you to keep her occupied while I look for it. My plan won't work without it." Xenia grabbed Maia's scaled arm. When the beast girl leaned in, she cupped her pigmented chin. "Don't die, okay? No getting eaten by the monster."

Maia froze. Beneath Xenia's hand, the scaled jaw trembled. The beast girl nodded and took Xenia's hand in both of her own. "No dying. Got it."

Chapter Forty-Nine

Reluctantly, Xenia pulled away. Together, the fledgling magical girl and the shapeshifter turned to face *Bēlet Kaššāpāti*.

Where the fallen goddess had writhed in agony, the bodies of the fallen students were caught up and churned into so much gory mud. The serpentine body rose from the charnel pit it had created, striped and spattered in filth. The Lady of Sorcery shook her humanoid torso, and the shiver carried along the entire length of her arthropod body, shaking the gore from the dark chiton as it passed. The regal face regarded the two teenagers. Something akin to disappointment passed briefly across her features.

"So be it. Thou would have commanded legions. Enjoyed power second only to mine own. Known years beyond the measure of mortal life. Now thou shall share the godling's fate." Needle feet hammered the earth as she coiled about herself and spread her arms wide. Blades of iron, eager to rend flesh from bone, glinted at each finger. The long body uncoiled as the goddess launched herself at her prey.

Maia set a hand in the small of Xenia's back and shoved her clear. She spread her own arms wide, curving her platinum claws to catch the moonlight. The earth trembled as she slammed her taloned foot down once, twice, three times. Eyes wide, her forked tongue thrust from gaping jaws. Maia bellowed, *"HAAAAHHH!"* as she charged to meet the goddess in battle.

With all her heart, Xenia wanted nothing more than to witness the fight, to assure herself that Maia would prevail. That, she knew, would be folly. As powerful as Maia might be, the goddess was... well, a goddess. She had to find her wand *now*. Xenia tore her eyes from the battle. Holding her broken arm against her middle, she ran. The rasp of claw against chiton, the crack of iron on bone rang out as she hurled herself toward where the length of ash wood had fallen.

Maia's battle cry rose, became a squeal of pain as a great tearing echoed through the night. Xenia stumbled. Nearly went to her aid. *You have a job to do, stupid!* Bare-handed, without a ready spell, she'd die even faster than Maia would. The warrior-girl would have to hold out for a few more—

There!

The pale length of ash wood, wreathed in the scribing of her spell's glyphs, gleamed in the too-bright light of the moon. Propped as it was within a shrub near the fence line, it looked for all the world like someone had dropped an enormous lollipop.

Xenia fell to her knees and caught the wand up in her good hand. She balanced it in the crook of her broken arm while she slipped her hand into her shirt. Her fingers slid along the chunky metal links as she felt for the clasp. She worked it loose, and her mother's necklace pooled in her hand. The precious metal gleamed against her skin as she allowed herself one last look at the memento. She whispered, "Thank you, Mama," as she brought it to her lips.

Winding the length of chain about the end of her wand with only one hand was nearly her undoing. No matter how she braced it, the necklace slipped from the wood. What she wouldn't give for a bit of tape right then, or even a bit of string. *Magic! Duh!* Xenia plucked at the wood, using a strand of its own *woodiness* to bind the necklace in place. Once the final inch of her wand gleamed with gold, Xenia shoved herself to her feet and ran like hell.

Maia was on the ropes. The fight had gone south a lot faster than either of them had hoped. Her scales were striped in crimson gore, and her left arm hung useless at her side. Still, she fought on. Maia slapped the pincered tail away with her good hand, scoring a hit on *Bēlet Kaššāpāti's* side, just above the junction between humanoid waist and the arthropod body. Splinters of obsidian armor erupted as her claws bit deep. She ducked the counterattack and circled her foe, eyes sharp for an opening.

"Maia!" Xenia stumbled to a halt well outside the range of those thrashing tails. She gripped her wand in her left hand and, despite the flare of agony raised by the move, braced it across her right wrist. Now she could sight down the wand's length and keep her right hand free. The instant the gilded tip aligned with her target, she screamed, "*Duck!*"

Without hesitation, Maia plummeted, opening a path between Xenia and *Bēlet Kaššāpāti*.

Xenia had already expended all of *Gale Hammer's* remaining charges. Even if she'd had her notes, it took an hour or more just to craft a single charge. Though she no longer had the wind's own force to deliver her wand, there was one spell remaining to do the job.

Xenia hadn't allowed her ring, the second half of her "come home" spell, to slip from her finger by chance. When she'd heaved herself free, she'd purposefully jammed her hand into the fissure in *Bēlet Kaššāpāti's* armor. A fissure that ran directly over the goddess's black heart.

Xenia snapped her fingers, and the wand leapt from her hand. Aimed right where it needed to go, the length of ash flew without tumbling. It shot through the air, straight as an arrow, to join the ash "jewel" of the ring.

Quick as a serpent's strike, the goddess snatched the wand from its path, halting its flight. Not, however, before the wand's golden payload kissed her ebon armor.

At the touch of the proscribed metal, the living symbol of her lost sister's power, the chiton boiled. Her good eye, already healed of the damage Xenia had inflicted with the *sgian-dubh*, went wide in horror. Her mouth gaped in a soundless scream.

Bēlet Kaššāpāti's strength wavered, just for an instant. The wand, eager to complete its journey, slipped another inch toward the ring in her chest. Amber light speared from the point of contact, burst from the jagged cracks that sprang across her armor. Her other hand joined the first but, weakened by contact with the gold, she was unable to draw the weapon away.

"Maia!" Xenia jogged to her friend's side. "Get it into her heart! It has to destroy her heart!"

The shapeshifter groaned as she rolled over and levered herself upright with her good arm. She fended off a blow from the pincered tail that would have taken Xenia's head. Planting the flat of her hand against the base of Xenia's wand, with a resonant grunt, she leaned into the push.

Inch by inch, the wand slid through *Bēlet Kaššāpāti*'s grasp. Black steam seethed from the wound as her chitinous armor vaporized. The moment the precious metal at last grazed the goddess's heart was clear, for her spine went rigid. The long, segmented tail froze mid-lash. Her hands released their hold on the wand.

Maia heaved, and the gold slid into the very center of *Bēlet Kaššāpāti*'s ebon heart.

Golden rays of light, every bit as warm and glorious as the noonday sun, speared from every crack, every gap in that armored body. The rumbling hiss from within rattled Xenia's teeth.

She stumbled away from the fallen goddess. In her second sight, every bit of magic, every ribbon, every dancing mote as far as she could see was being drawn into the golden conflagration that burned where the creature's heart had been. It swirled about them as if a stopper had been pulled, and all of that energy was now being sucked down the drain. "Maia, I think—"

"She's gonna blow!" Maia pivoted on a taloned foot and scooped Xenia over her shoulder. Long, loping steps carried them away from the goddess's imminent demise.

From her sack-of-potatoes position on Maia's armored shoulder, Xenia was the sole witness to the anguish on that horrible, beautiful face. In the sky above, the unnatural orb bled away until only the proper waning crescent remained. In a voice racked with pain and loss, *Bēlet An-Ĝíg,* The Lady of Black Sky, spoke her last: "*Ama—*"

The goddess detonated.

Maia curled about Xenia as the shock wave swept them from the ground. Cinder block shattered as Maia took the impact with the gym wall across her armored spine. Floorboards splintered as they bounced. Xenia was torn away when Maia tumbled to a halt.

She slid across polished hardwood and shuddered to a halt, the crown of her head mere inches from the far wall. A flare of pain from her broken arm, and everywhere else, halted her attempt to rise. Only just audible through the fading echo of the Lady of Sorcery's destruction were the strident wails of Porter Valley's first responders. *About fucking time.* Then again, she hoped those she'd freed from Madison's impromptu larder had run all the way across town before they'd stopped to call 911.

As the edges of her vision wavered, Maia's reptilian face filled her sight. Between one stuttering heartbeat and the next, the runner regained her human form. Her mouth moved, but whatever she said was lost to the surge of stars and darkness that carried Xenia away.

Chapter Fifty

ethany!

Xenia struggled to rise. The flare of pain in her arm and the gentle pressure of a hand on her shoulder stilled the attempt.

"Easy, lass. You've been through the wringer," Aunt Elspeth said. "Again. Despite my attempts to keep you safe."

Xenia cracked an eyelid and found herself in the old Victorian's sitting room. She'd been laid out on the couch, the comforter pulled up to her chin. Elspeth sat by her side, on a stool she'd set beside the couch. Concern, relief, and no small amount of anger cycled across the woman's face.

Oh. Right, I was grounded. Her exit via the balcony might have been a thousand years ago. "Aunt Elspeth." Xenia's voice was a dry croak. She paused to sip the water offered by her guardian. "How did I get home? I don't—"

"Hey, girl," Maia called.

Xenia turned her head and winced as the whole room wobbled. Maia slouched in Elspeth's favorite comfy chair. The lacerations inflicted by the Night Queen's iron claws were all but gone, now no more than scratches. As impressive as that feat of healing was, every visible inch of the runner was a patchwork of bruises. The shiner about her eye had turned a particularly nasty shade of purple-green. Her left arm was bound up in a makeshift sling. She grinned through her obvious discomfort. "We won. Oh, and check this out." She wiggled her injured arm. "Twinsies."

Xenia offered a wan smile, then, "Madison?"

Maia's smile slipped away. "Gone. I think she was the first one that thing ate."

Xenia allowed her head to fall. She'd had a faint hope, foolish as it might have been, that Madison had still been in there somewhere. That slaying the monster would have, like in the movies, set her free.

Real life, of course, wasn't nearly that kind.

"How many died? Before we stopped her?"

Maia shrugged. "I lost count. Jenna, Cath, Ryan, Liz, and her little brother got away. They almost knocked down some old lady's door. The cops found Eric and Rosa hiding in a classroom after we..." She rubbed her forehead. "I didn't think it was a good idea to hang around. Too many questions, y'know?"

"And weren't you a sight to behold! This one"—Elspeth nodded at Maia—"shows up at the crack of dawn with you slung like a sack of tatties over her shoulder. The both of you absolutely doused in gore." She cupped Xenia's chin, tilted her face. "You, lass, are not out of the woods with me just because you happened to save the world. Once you've had a chance to mend, you'd best believe you and I will be having a few words."

Xenia sank into the couch. "It doesn't feel like I saved anything. She'd already killed so many." *Bethany. Sal.*

Maia rocked forward in the chair, eyes intense. "You

saved my life. You got Jenna and the others out of the school while I was out cold. You knew, somehow, how to kill that thing. From what it said, it wouldn't have stopped after eating me. That was all you, Zee."

Elspeth glanced between the two girls. "Now that sounds like one hell of a tale. I cannae wait to hear it."

"She was total badass," Xenia and Maia said in unison. They shared a look before howling with laughter.

"Oh God, don't make me laugh," Maia groaned, hand at her ribs. Which, of course, only made them laugh all the harder.

Once the giggles had run their course, Xenia filled Aunt Elspeth in on what had occurred following her balcony escape. Recounting the moment of Bethany's second death was difficult. When she reached the bit where Maia had transformed, a tiny shake of the head indicated the runner's preferences. Xenia embellished the tale to avoid outing her friend's supernatural nature.

"You should've seen her, Ms. Findlay!" Maia chimed in. "She stabbed that thing right in the fucking eyeball." She mimed the move with her good arm. "So cool. Ah, crap. I waited to be sure it was all the way dead, then took a quick look around. I couldn't find your wand or your knife. Sorry."

Despite the pain, Xenia struggled upright. "Crap! I lost the *sgian-dubh*."

"Pish, lass. It did what it was meant to. Granny would have been proud of you, as am I. A knife can be replaced. A great-niece? Why, there's no replacement for you, my love." She patted Xenia's knee. "I am very sorry to hear about Bethany. She was a good friend."

Xenia ran her thumb across the tiny scar on her palm, which was warmer than the skin around it. "She knew that, ghost or not, that thing could hurt her. She threw herself at it anyway, just so I could get away." She mopped at her eyes with the comforter's edge.

Maia slapped the armrest of her chair and kicked the footrest down. "Almost forgot. I found this in the crater when I was looking for your stuff." She grabbed a bundle from the floor beside her and set it on the coffee table. "I didn't think it was a good idea to leave this for the cops," she explained as she unwrapped the shreds of her sweatshirt.

The skin of Xenia's arms pebbled as the glint of silver shone within the bundle.

Maia pulled the last bit of cloth aside to reveal none other than the crown that had adorned the Lady of Black Sky's brow. The circlet showed no sign of the cataclysm it had survived. The delicate crescents at the forefront were unbent, unmelted by heat.

From her dreams, unbidden, the crown's name rose to her lips. "*Kù-Babbar Aga,*" she whispered, ignoring the look from the other two. "The Silver Crown of the Moon." Dread, cold and clammy, coiled about her heart. Her hand, of its own accord, drifted to the circlet. Deep within her mind, where the Lady of Sorcery's will had imposed itself, a voice whispered.

Xenia snatched up the tatters of the sweatshirt and wrapped them about the crown until none of the precious metal remained visible. She flung herself onto the couch and dragged the comforter up to her chin.

"I might not know the story behind that bauble, but I know temptation when see it," Elspeth said with a nod. "Well done. What, now, shall we do with it?"

"We keep it safe, and hidden." Xenia met her great-aunt's eyes, then Maia's. "No one will get their hands on that." A newfound determination lent its steel to her voice. "Ever."

There was a flutter in the tree beyond the window. A large, glossy raven fluffed its feathers against the breeze.

"*Caw!*"

* * *

At Elspeth's insistence, Xenia spent just over a week in bed. While she recovered from her ordeal, she waited for the axe to fall.

She'd been certain that, any moment now, there'd be a knock at the front door. Men in black suits who, having heard of the events in Porter Valley, and her role in them, wanted to "ask her a few questions." She'd be disappeared to some government facility and that, as they say, would be that. She'd never be heard from again.

No such knock had come.

A fresh blue fiberglass cast once again enclosed her left arm, thanks to the fracture she'd received while fending off Madison's attack. The break was located in the same spot as her prior injury, but it wasn't as severe. Her doctor was confident she'd heal with no complications and be out of the cast in a month, tops. Other than that, she'd suffered no major injuries, which Aunt Elspeth had regarded as a minor miracle. "Someone upstairs has their eye on you, lass," she'd said.

Upstairs? Xenia doubted that. The tree outside? Perhaps.

What little remained of the semester had been canceled. The district had made a few official noises about bussing students over to Eureka for the duration. However, in consideration for those who'd lost their lives in the "incident," that plan was discarded in favor of allowing all involved time to recover in their own way. The blame for the "homemade bomb," and the deaths it had caused, was laid at the feet of one Everard Ambrose. With his whereabouts unaccounted for, it was assumed that the would-be terrorist had perished alongside his victims. Even though the survivors Xenia had rescued knew the real story, or parts of it, not one came forward to dispute the official version. Soon, rumors began to circulate that the "Porter Valley Killer" and the school bomber had been one and the same.

When Xenia considered the way the changeling had abused the abilities he'd been gifted, she didn't feel all that bad about this misapplication of blame.

Once she had convalesced enough, she forced herself into motion. There was work to do. Still a bit wobbly, she settled for unpacking the long-neglected stack of moving boxes crowding her bedroom closet.

To her surprise, the pile of clothes, toys, pop music CDs, souvenirs from Disneyland and other SoCal attractions—all the things she had once considered to be her "treasures"—held none of their old appeal. It wasn't that she disliked them now. It was just that too much had changed, *she* had changed, since she'd packed for the move north. She just... didn't need them anymore. She hadn't stopped grieving for her mother and father, for Bethany. She missed them terribly and always would. Even with Bethany's second death heavy in her heart, Xenia found that the old pain no longer held that overwhelming purchase on her soul. She set aside a handful of mementos and some family photos while the rest, with Aunt Elspeth's help, went into the charity bin at a local church.

She asked for, and received, her great-aunt's permission to introduce Maia to the secret collection in the basement. Together, they finished the job that Xenia had begun and that Gracie's hungry spirit had interrupted. Each item was dusted, inspected, and catalogued. Other than the cuneiform tablets they couldn't read, Xenia found no other clue that might explain why the fallen goddess had been here, in Porter Valley.

Then came the matter of the collection's latest addition.

Even in her human form, Maia was strong enough to make short work of sledgehammering a hole into the concrete floor. They took turns with a shovel until they'd excavated sufficient space. This they lined with a fresh pour of concrete, under Elspeth's watchful eye.

Xenia's grounding was given a brief stay. She used this reprieve to puzzle out the purpose behind *Ring of Knots*. The spell would secure any container with a barrier, which the notes called a "ward." This would prevent anyone but the spell's caster from accessing the contents. As the cubby's fresh concrete lining cured, she wove her new spell into the material.

Elspeth dove into her abundant supply of hobby goods to sew up a padded bag. As she stitched the velvet shut around the silver crown, which they'd wrapped in plastic to prevent accidental contact between skin and metal, Xenia stitched *Ring of Knots* into the fabric itself. She added *Bone Weave* as well, to render the bag as un-cuttable as possible.

With her great-aunt's blessing, she'd put Quentin's magical lockbox, the one he'd kept Elspeth's letters in, to the test. Whatever spells he'd laid into the metal rendered it impervious to every cutting implement they could throw at it. Elspeth had even garnered the assistance of a local artisan friend, one who specialized in welded scrap metal sculptures. Even after a lengthy application of his cutting torch, the metal was cool to the touch. The box even passed Maia's transformative crush test with flying colors. Quentin, Xenia had to admit, had really known his stuff. The crown, in its protective bag, went into the lockbox.

After they'd completed every preparation they could think of, Xenia knelt at the cubby's edge, lockbox in her hands. Even through all the layers, and all the spells she'd woven about it, she could still hear its whisper in her mind.

Take me up, the crown urged. *Lay me upon thy brow, become* Bēlet An-Ĝig, *the Lady of Black Sky. All the power of Night shall be thine. Become* Bēlet Kaššāpāti, *the Lady of Sorcery, and rule.*

"No," Xenia said and dropped the box into the hole they'd prepared for it.

With a grunt and a fierce grin, Maia upended the wheelbarrow of concrete onto the box. Side by side, the two of them troweled the surface flat. The new concrete, Xenia knew, wouldn't match the original floor. When it was cured, she'd put a fresh coat of paint over the whole room.

Once the work was done, and all that was left was the cleanup, the three of them, Xenia, Maia, and Great-Aunt Elspeth, took a moment to breathe and regard their handiwork. Maia's fingers found Xenia's. With care for her cast, she squeezed Xenia's hand.

Before she allowed herself to relax, to return the gesture, Xenia closed her eyes. Listened.

Nothing. The crown was silent at last. For the first time since the battle with *Bēlet Kaššāpāti*, the only thoughts in Xenia's head were her own.

Epilogue

Xenia paused at the sidewalk's edge. A "for sale" sign had sprung up in the center of the Serranos' front lawn. After the loss they had suffered, she couldn't blame them. She'd needed a new beginning, herself. After a moment, Xenia approached the tiny figure seated on the porch steps. "Hey, Bug."

Marisol sniffed and then wiped at her face with the back of her hand. While her eyes no longer carried the raw redness they'd had in the weeks following the recovery of Sal's body and his funeral, her vibrance and boundless energy had yet to return. At the very least, Xenia observed, she no longer carried her brother's basketball everywhere she went. The tiny ladybug barrette in her hair was another promising sign. Marisol blinked up at Xenia but said nothing.

She sat beside her. "I know it's been hard, Bug. But I wanted you to know that it'll get better..." Xenia forced herself to stop, rather than recite the same platitudes she'd loathed during her own bereavement. "I hate to ask it, but I have to. Have you been seeing Sal?" She winced as the girl flinched away from the question as if she'd been stuck with a needle.

When Bug spoke, it was in a quavery little voice. "Mama says I need to stop pretendin'. Salvatore's in heaven now. But..."

Xenia smiled. "But?"

Marisol craned her neck to make sure her Mama wouldn't overhear what she said next. "I see him, sometimes," she whispered.

"Can you see him now?"

Bug stared hard at Xenia, eyes narrowed. Deliberating, no doubt, whether the teen was making fun of her or not. Decision made, she aimed a chubby finger toward the sidewalk. Directly at her brother's ghost.

While Bethany had done everything she could to assist the broken goddess's victims into the hereafter, she'd been unable to locate Salvatore before she'd... before she'd died for a second time. For reasons of his own, Sal had avoided Xenia and Bethany both, until long after the calamity at the school.

Destroying *Bēlet Kaššāpāti* hadn't returned everything he'd lost in death. Sal remained a pallid echo of his living self. His eyes were still lost in shadow, his voice stilled. But his crushing despair, his terror, and the unnerving habit of displaying the trauma that had ended his life, thankfully, had passed with the goddess that had murdered him.

He'd shown himself to Xenia the day her second cast had come off. Communication hadn't been easy; Sal was terrible at charades. Eventually, he'd conveyed to her what it was that he wanted. Without hesitation, she had agreed to play telephone one more time.

"Oh," Xenia said. "Right there? Waving? Wearing his favorite Suns shirt?"

Bug's head whipped around, eyes bigger than saucers.

"Yeah, Bug. I can see him too. He really is there."

"But…"

"Not everyone can see… spirits. Your parents can't, neither could mine. I couldn't, until the accident. It's pretty rare, what we can do. You should know, if you can see your brother, it means you'll probably see other ghosts, now and then." Xenia rubbed Marisol's back. "But you don't need to worry about that. Not many people get stuck here as ghosts. Mostly because being a ghost is no fun at all. You can't touch anything, people can't hear or see you. No eating, or even smelling your favorite food. It's super boring. So, almost everyone goes to heaven."

Marisol tilted her head in thought. "Is that what happened to your friend? She was bored being a ghost and went to heaven?"

Xenia blinked away the sudden rush of tears. "Yeah, something like that. But since you and I share this secret, I wanted you to know that I'll always be there for you. Especially if you need to talk about stuff your Mom and Dad won't understand. Here." She offered Bug a scrap of paper. "My new phone number. You can keep it safe, yes?"

Marisol gave her a very serious face as she accepted the note. She sounded out the numbers twice before she tucked it away in the front pocket of her dress.

"Now, there's something Sal wanted me to ask you." Xenia waved the ghost over.

Salvatore did a bad job of concealing his eagerness as he hurried across the grass. He dropped to one knee in front of his sister. When he held out his hand, Marisol grabbed for him, only for her fingers to pass through his. Her lip trembled as she examined her hand. "Zeenie? Why's Sal all scary lookin'?"

Sal looked away, the unshadowed portion of his face twisting in pain.

The last thing Bug needed to hear was the truth of how her brother had suffered. "Dying can be hard, especially when you're not ready for it. Staying here, when you're supposed to go to heaven, is even harder."

Sal offered her a look a gratitude.

"Is he tired?" Marisol said as worry replaced the fear in her eyes. She held up her hand, giggled when Sal poked his finger right through it.

"Bug... Marisol, Salvatore needs you to say goodbye." Xenia's heart broke just a little more as she forced the words out. "After I... well, let's just say the other thing that was keeping him here is gone, now. But he loves you so much, more than he could ever say. And because you love him back, just as much..." She balked as the girl burst into tears. "It's like this. Think of him like a balloon. You're holding on to his string because you love him. But balloons have to float away, Bug. It's time to let him go."

"NO! I miss him, Zeenie. I don't want him to go. Sal, don't go!" Marisol pummeled Xenia's arm with her tiny fists, and Xenia let her. When the girl sagged, her energy spent, Xenia pulled her into an embrace. Once Bug's tears had well and truly soaked through Xenia's shirt, she said, in a small voice, "Will Sal go to heaven? Gramma's there, and *Tío* Luis."

Xenia looked to Sal over his sister's head. Despite the sorrow creasing his face, he raised his hands in a shrug. *Some help you are*, Xenia mouthed, which got a sheepish grin in return. "Yeah. Sal will go to heaven. That's the only thing that would make him leave you. You know that, right? And remember, he came back just to say goodbye." She gave the girl a squeeze. "Not everyone gets that."

Marisol gave a mighty sniff, then pulled away. "Okay," she whispered. Then, in a stronger voice: "Okay." She nodded, faced her brother. Raised her arms. "Don't care if I can't feel it, you gotta hug me bye, Sal!" Her trembling lower lip jutted out as she flapped her hands at her brother.

Sal knelt before his sister and, with exacting care to not ruin the illusion, wrapped her up in his arms. His pale lips brushed the top of her head.

"*Te amo*, Sal," Marisol sobbed. "Tell Gramma I miss her lots."

Sal spoke, then, for the first time since the night he had been torn from his family, from the sister he doted upon. His voice was less than a whisper, no more than the memory of words spoken in an empty room, "*Te amo*, Bug."

Between one heartbeat and the next, Salvatore Serrano was gone.

"You're sure this is a good idea? Your yoga instructor?" Xenia asked.

"Aye, lass, he's no stranger to the real world. He's had a damn sight more experience with it than I have, you can be sure of that." Elspeth hauled on the steering wheel. A month after Xenia's cast had come off, Elspeth had declared Xenia to be "ready." She'd loaded the two of them into her boat of a car and aimed them north, past Eureka. "If you're to be galivanting about, getting into a row with one supernatural beastie after another, you'd best be prepared. I've done what I can, now it's time for an expert." She nodded at the building ahead.

A carved wooden sign, in English and Japanese alike, proclaimed the establishment to be the Shouga Dojo. A smaller, more modern sign beside the door added: "Aikido, adult and children's classes. Yoga for seniors."

Despite her doubts, Xenia trailed Elspeth through sliding glass doors painted to resemble Japanese-style paper doors. Inside, a young man in a white *gi* sat behind a tall reception desk. His face lit up when he spotted them. "Elspeth! Good to see you again. Sensei's waiting for you. Said you should go right through to the garden." He hooked a thumb over his shoulder.

"Thanks, love." Elspeth offered the man an airy wave and then paused by the inner door. "Shoes, lass. Sensei's quite particular about that." She demonstrated by stepping out of her clogs, which she stowed in one of the cubicles provided.

Xenia did likewise, then followed her great-aunt through the inner doors—these were authentic wood and paper—into the dojo proper. The space was shadowed, the overhead lights were off. The only illumination came from the windows at the back of the training area, and the open door at their center.

Xenia gawked shamelessly as they crossed the polished wood floor. The walls were hung with numerous works of calligraphic art, racks of wooden practice weapons, and a handful of framed photos. At the center of the longest wall, in pride of place, was a shrine. A pair of intricately inked scrolls hung to either side of a portrait photo that shared a shelf with some candles and a bowl. The Asian man in the black-and-white photo was ancient, his face little more than a mass of wrinkles. Even though she knew better, the photo's eyes seemed to follow her across the room, .

Beyond the exterior door was another training space. A square of hard-packed earth, as large as the dojo behind them, lay in the sun. Beyond that, the grounds shifted from martial training to spiritual, in the form of a well-tended garden. Stone lanterns sprang up at irregular intervals beside the path that wound by flowering shrubs and short, twisted trees. A narrow stream burbled through the center of it all, which the path crossed via a tiny, arched bridge.

A man waited for them at the center of the earthen training square. As old as, or perhaps a bit older than Elspeth, he was no taller than Xenia. The sensei might not have been a large man, but there was about him a solidity that rendered any lack of stature moot. The man's face was lined like an old leather couch, and equally weathered. If it were not for their bright spark, his eyes might have been lost for how deep set they were. Other than his eyebrows, the only hair on his head was his tidily trimmed mustache. Like the receptionist, he wore a white *gi*. Billowy black pants hung from a cord knotted about his waist, and his bare feet swished against the packed earth as he strode toward them.

"Benjamin!" Elspeth exclaimed. "Good morning."

The rosy tint flushing her great-aunt's cheeks had Xenia doing a double take. *Good for her*, she thought with more than a little satisfaction.

"This is her?" Sensei's voice was deep, and colored with more than a hint of surfer's drawl. He gave Xenia a once-over before turning his attention to Elspeth.

"Yes, just as I've told you." Elspeth made a big show of looking around for unwanted listeners. "The lass has gone and learned herself a bit of magic."

Even though she had an idea of why they'd come, it was still a shock to hear her great-aunt blurt it out like that. Xenia raised a finger. "Aunt Elspeth—"

"Oh pish, lass. Trust an old lady to know what she's about, if you please."

"Hmm." Benjamin brushed a stray mustache hair into

place with a blunt finger. "Would you mind giving us a moment, Elspeth? I'd like to have a word with her."

"Of course, of course." Elspeth favored him with a wide, if fluttery, smile before she bustled into the dojo.

Xenia made no effort to hide her grin. Aunt Elspeth was acting like a giddy schoolgirl, and Xenia planned on savoring every moment of it.

Benjamin folded his hands before the knot at his waist and stared at Xenia. "Magician?" he asked, finally.

"Yes?"

"Which sense?"

"Sorry?"

Sensei Benjamin thrust his hand forward, fingers extended. "Five senses. Touch, smell, taste, hearing, and sight." As he named each, he curled a finger. "In which way do you perceive the unseen?"

Understanding bloomed. "Oh! I see it. I can see magic, everywhere. All around." *Wait, there are people who can taste magic? How would that even work?* "How do you do it? Perceive the unseen, I mean."

Sensei nodded. "Observe." He assumed a low stance, knees bent, hands curled into loose fists to either side of his waist. His only movement was the slow rise and fall of his chest and the flutter of his trousers in the breeze.

Xenia waited, but nothing, well, magical occurred. "Sorry, what should I be looking for?"

Benjamin closed his eyes. Tapped a finger to his temple. "Observe."

"Right." Xenia tried not to feel like an idiot and summoned her second sight. Once the world about her glowed with magic's otherworldly spectrum, she said, "Ready."

Benjamin remained still. Not as much as a muscle

twitched. In her second sight, however, the currents of magic by his feet began to shift. Like water drawn into a straw, the magic of the earth rose through his bare feet, ascended his legs and gathered in his abdomen. The mass of magical potential roiled and churned just below his ribs but above his navel.

"Woah." Xenia had no idea how he'd achieved that, how he'd caused the magic to respond without moving. The only way Xenia had been able to interact with magic, to craft her spells, had been to reach out and grab it. Even then, it was slippery stuff.

Benjamin didn't say a word as he thrust both hands forward, bringing the heels of his palms together as he did so. The ball of magical energy flew right at Xenia's face.

"Ack!" Xenia threw up her hands. Caught off guard, she was just able to achieve the focus required to interact with magic. She snagged the churning ball of energy before it could strike her, muttering, "What the hell, man." She decided that the safest course of action would be to disperse the magic back where it had come from. If she let it go all willy-nilly, the backlash would knock her cold.

It took her longer to unpack and settle the earth magics than it had taken Benjamin to gather them. When she was done, her breath was ragged and her hair was soaked with sweat. She mopped at her face with the back of a trembling hand.

"Good." Benjamin favored her with a single, brusque, nod. "I believe you can be taught." He strode past her to the wooden porch, where he paused to brush the dirt from his feet. He beckoned with one hand. "Come. You have a lot to learn before we can begin."

Xenia blinked. Just like that, she had a magic teacher? Really?

Slowly, she allowed herself to smile. Finally! Someone else who knew real magic! And he had agreed to teach her! She couldn't wait to discover what a real education in magic would be like. Somehow, she doubted it'd be anything remotely like the wizard schools she'd seen in movies.

Heart pounding with excitement, she followed her sensei inside for her first lesson in magic.

Afterword

Well then, this certainly was a long time coming. Longer than I had hoped.

A brief history: After the second or third extended hiatus on *All In,* sometime around 2018, I got the bright idea to create a comic book. After all, I had this conceit that I was a *visual* artist and my novel kept stalling out. Maybe this would be more up my alley? Since it was to be, specifically, a webcomic and, at the time, I was enjoying *Steven Universe,* I drew up my own take on the whole magical girl schtick. I dithered and doodled, never quite finding my groove. Somewhere along the line I realized that the teen girl I'd thrust into magical misadventure was the younger incarnation of the magician who, reluctantly, gives Eddy a hand in *All In.* I.E. Xenia Findlay.

I lost steam on the webcomic about then, and my enthusiasm shifted to yet another, never-to-be-completed, project.

The script for *Xenia* languished in my writing folder.

As *All In* approached completion, I knew that I wanted to keep going. I really wanted to write another book, and another after that, and so on. I grabbed the script I'd written for the webcomic and converted to a novel outline. Ironically, as someone who dislikes prequels, I found myself brain deep in one! Three drafts of *Magical Girl Blues 1.0* later, I sent it off to my beta readers.

The feedback wasn't great, and I agreed. The story wasn't anything like what I wanted to tell. Worse, there was little to no point to Bethany's presence in the narrative.

Back to the drawing board.

It took most of fall 2023 to rebuild. Only a few, key, elements survived into version 2.0. I was all set.

In January of 2024, my father passed away. A week later, my mother followed. Things didn't go so well after that. I felt as if I might never have the will or desire to write again. Thankfully, there came a point where I simply couldn't *not* write. The ideas and the urge continued to bubble up until I had no choice but to return to the keyboard. The chapters concerning Xenia's bereavement were a lot harder to write this time around, believe me. I emptied more than a few tissue boxes.

On to lighter topics.

I had the opportunity, before things went sideways, to go on a little sabbatical. I wound up mirroring Xenia's journey north to Humboldt County. You see, I'd created Porter Valley out of whole cloth to fit the story. I wanted to visit Eureka, California and the nearby towns, to see how close my imagination had hit.

Reader, if I do say so myself, I nailed it. Okay, there is no one locale along that stretch of Redwood highway that is a perfect match for Porter Valley. However, one can find elements all throughout Eureka, Fernbridge and Fortuna. When the last leg of the trip took me home for the holidays, I drove around my old stomping grounds, observing them after a multi-year absence. Growing up around Danville and Pleasanton had definitely influenced PV's character.

Within Uncle's tale, you may have noticed that the passage of time is denoted in sixties. While researching, I learned that in Sumer they used, among other systems, sexagesimal numbering. I settled upon "sixty upon xxx" to note the passage of years. The formatting is intentionally arty and vague.

Sexagesimal numbering is still in use today, by the way. 24 hours in a day, sixty minutes in an hour, sixty seconds in a minute... we owe the increments of our own timekeeping to the people of the Great Continent. (Okay, Mesopotamia.)

So, here we are. As for what comes next, yes. We will return to Porter Valley soon enough. Next, however, it is long past time for us to see what good ol' Eddy Fry got up to, having seized the reins of power in Las Vegas.

The best way to find out when *that* book will be released is to sign up for my email list at russellisler.com/newsletter. You'll get a couple of free e-books, deleted scenes from *Magical Girl Blues* and *All In*, out of the deal.

Russell Isler - Friday, September 13, 2024

Acknowledgments

Thank you to my parents, Richard and Helen Isler. You put up with my oddness and supported my desire to pursue a career as an artist, even if you didn't always understand my motivations. I simply could not have done any of this without both of you. You are, and always will be, missed.

Thank you to both Renata Rowland and Gaby Michaelis for your thoughts and feedback on the earliest drafts of this book. While I did end up changing almost everything, your feedback was invaluable.

Thank you to Jessica O'Toole for your laser focused analysis of both the early and revised drafts of this book.

Thank you to my editor, Kelly Cozy of Bookside Manner. I appreciate you catching all those pernicious typos!

Thanks to Paul, and Astrud, for your friendship and support, without which I wouldn't have the will to do any of this.

Thanks to my cover designer, Damonza.

Thanks to Peter Pringle for his musical rendition of the Epic of Gilgamesh, from which Uncle gained his voice.

And, lastly but not leastly, I thank *you* from the bottom of my heart, dear reader.